PRAISE FOR THE LAWLESS NOVELS

"I love Lexi Blake. Read *Ruthless* and see why."

—*New York Times* bestselling author Lee Child

"Smart, savvy, clever, and always entertaining. That's true of Riley Lawless, the hero in *Ruthless*, and likewise for his creator, Lexi Blake. Both are way ahead of the pack."

—*New York Times* bestselling author Steve Berry

"*Ruthless* is full of suspense, hot sex, and swoon-worthy characters—a must read! Lexi Blake is a master at sexy, thrilling romance!"

—*New York Times* bestselling author Jennifer Probst

"With *Ruthless*, Lexi Blake has set up shop on the intersection of suspenseful and sexy, and I never want to leave."

—*New York Times* bestselling author Laurelin Paige

"An excellent combination of corporate intrigue and family drama—with good dose of seduction."   —*RT Book Reviews*

PRAISE FOR THE PERFECT GENTLEMEN SERIES
BY SHAYLA BLACK AND LEXI BLAKE

"Hot and edgy and laced with danger, the stories in the Perfect Gentlemen series are just that—perfect."

—*New York Times* bestselling author J. Kenner

"While there are certainly incendiary sex scenes at the top of this series opener, the strength is in the underlying murder and political mystery."

—*RT Book Reviews*

Revenge

LEXI BLAKE

BERKLEY SENSATION
NEW YORK

BERKLEY
An imprint of Penguin Random House LLC
375 Hudson Street, New York, New York 10014

Copyright © 2017 by DLZ Entertainment LLC

Library of Congress Cataloging-in-Publication Data

Names: Blake, Lexi, author.
Title: Revenge / Lexi Blake.
Description: First edition. | New York : Berkley Sensation, [2017]
Identifiers: LCCN 2016059325 (print) | LCCN 2017006110 (ebook) | ISBN
9780425283592 (trade paper) | ISBN 9780698410329 (ebook)
Subjects: | GSAFD: Romantic suspense fiction.
Classification: LCC PS3602.L3456 R48 2017 (print) | LCC PS3602.L3456 (ebook)
| DDC 813/.6—dc23
LC record available at https://lccn.loc.gov/2016059325

First Edition: June 2017

Printed in the United States of America
1 3 5 7 9 10 8 6 4 2

Mirror reflection of the Texas Capital City © Roschetzky Productions / Shutterstock;
Portrait of a young man with black shirt © Juan Silva / Getty Images
Cover design by Sandra Chiu
Book design by Laura K. Corless

Acknowledgments

Thanks to everyone who helped make writing this series such an amazing thing. To my editor at Berkley, Kate Seaver, and my agent, Merrilee Heifetz, at Writers House: I'm blessed to have both your guiding hands. To my assistant, Kim Guidroz, and my amazing mentor, Liz Berry. Thanks to my beta readers, Riane Holt, Stormy Pate, and Kori Smith. As always, thanks to my family for giving me the support I need.

Chapter One

T his is a mistake."

Like he hadn't heard that before. Andrew Lawless tried to remember that Bill Hatchard was simply worried, and rightly so. Drew was worried, too. It was precisely why he'd decided on the course of action he was about to take. He turned to look out his office windows. All of Austin was laid out before him, the lights of the buildings around him coming on as the sun set over the Colorado River. He could remember the first time he'd looked out these windows ten years before. It had been the first time he felt successful and knew everything he'd worked for would finally come to fruition. He'd known that he would find the three people responsible for his parents' deaths.

If only there hadn't turned out to be a fourth . . .

"I told you I wasn't sharing the information with anyone." He glanced at the clock. Only another half hour to wait. He'd set the meeting after hours in order to keep things quiet. Perhaps he should have had the meeting at his house, but he never knew when his brothers or sister and their spouses would show up. They were getting ready to celebrate Riley and Ellie's marriage with a blowout reception, and he didn't want to tip them off until his plan was firmly in place.

He could hear Hatch moving, and knew exactly where he would

go. There was the sound of a cork popping. Naturally Hatch went for the expensive Scotch. "You're wrong about this."

"So you've said." About a million times since that terrible night when they'd discovered who the real villain was.

"Fine." Hatch's tone was short. "Explain it to me."

How could he get Hatch to understand? He turned and looked to the man who had been his mentor his entire adult life. "Mia's pregnant."

That should suffice. It made sense to Drew. Mia was pregnant, and that meant he kept his mouth shut.

Hatch frowned. "What does that have to do with anything? That was inevitable the way she goes at it with that cowboy of hers. A pregnancy makes things worse. Now she's even more vulnerable."

Hatch wasn't a sunny-side-of-life person, but then neither was Drew.

"Yes, she is, but I suspect she'll be safe enough. She's going to try her hand at fiction for a while instead of wandering the globe looking for trouble." His sister was a reporter and a ball of chaos. Rather like the woman he was about to meet. "Case and the rest of the Taggarts will look out for her."

"And the Taggarts would be invaluable in finding our target," Hatch insisted.

McKay-Taggart was the premier security and investigative company in the country. Drew knew he wouldn't have taken down Steven Castalano and Patricia Cain without them. But he couldn't hire them for this job, and Mia was the reason why. He couldn't ask family to put up walls, to risk relationships for his revenge.

"Do you know what Mia said to me when she told me she was having a baby?"

"Hopefully she said, 'Do everything in your power to ensure no one kills me or my baby because there's a psychotic bitch running around out there who wants to do just that,'" Hatch insisted. "If she didn't say that, then she missed the point."

"She told me she wished our mother was here. She told me she wished she could hold our mom's hand and ask her for advice. She cried because her mother is dead." It had ripped his heart out. He couldn't explain to her that the mother she longed for was alive and well and had killed at least five people.

The mother Mia missed had tried to kill them all.

Hatch came up beside him, holding out one of two crystal tumblers. "You don't want Mia to know that Iris is alive and posing as Francine Wells. I get that. It's no reason to cut out Taggart."

"Ian Taggart would feel the need to tell his brother." It was why he hadn't already brought the man in. "He would tell Case and inevitably Case would tell his wife, and Mia would find out. Once Mia knows, she'll start to research Iris herself."

He couldn't bring himself to call that woman *mother*. Not ever again.

"So tell her not to."

"Have you met my sister?"

Hatch knocked back his Scotch in one long swallow before turning dark eyes on Drew. "You can't allow Iris to walk around like nothing happened."

"I have no intention of doing that, but she was quite clear in her instructions to Carly. She told us to back off or she would finish what she started all those years ago." When she'd murdered their father and his apparent mistress, then locked all the doors and set the house on fire with her four children inside.

Was it any wonder he didn't want to tell Mia the truth? She needed to think about her baby. Riley and Bran needed to concentrate on the future and their partners.

He'd promised them they would be free after they'd taken down Stratton, Castalano, and Cain. He meant to honor that promise. He would handle Iris Lawless on his own.

"Do you honestly believe she'll leave them alone?"

He had to. "She has for years. Twenty, to be precise. And I believe she'll leave Mia alone for the simple fact that she married into a vengeful barbarian horde. She won't want to start a war with the Taggarts. She can't win that one."

"But you think she can beat you?"

"I don't intend to announce the fact that we're involved in a skirmish at all," he replied. "I've ensured that there are no records of that sketch in the police file. I've also investigated the police computer systems. There were no attempts to hack in before I scrubbed the file."

"But after?"

"I almost missed it," Drew admitted. "It was subtle, but someone downloaded the report the police made the night of Patricia Cain's overdose."

"She was murdered." Hatch could definitely state the obvious at times.

"I know that. You know that. The police in LA are calling it an accidental overdose."

Hatch shook his head. "Why won't they investigate?"

"Because I don't want them to. Because I wrote a large check to ensure that they don't." Oh, it wasn't anything so gauche as a bribe. It was simply the offer of a man grateful to the police for keeping his brother out of the limelight surrounding America's most famous style maker's rather scandalous death. It wasn't anything new to the Los Angeles PD. They'd been happy to ensure Bran's name had been kept out of the press and to quickly close the investigation. The tabloids had gone insane for a few days and then the reporters had moved on to different scandals.

All except one. And he intended to take care of her tonight.

Hatch swore under his breath. "I wondered about that. So if you're not going to allow her to get away with it and you're not going to use the police or your McKay-Taggart resources, I assume you're going to do this all by yourself."

"Not at all. I'm hiring an investigator, but one I can control." One he also wanted to get into bed with, but then that was all a part of his plan.

"Another agency?"

"No, an individual." There was a reason he hadn't gone over this with Hatch, but if all went well, in a few hours he would know anyway. There was zero chance of Hatch buying the story he was going to sell to his family.

"So you hired a private investigator? I hope he's also a bodyguard."

"I intend to ensure that she's discreet."

Hatch went still beside him. "She? You hired a female PI?"

"She's actually a reporter, but she's a brilliant investigator." After all, Shelby had realized something was seriously wrong with his parents' case long before Drew had. She'd requested medical records, started digging in a way that led him to believe she knew something she shouldn't. He'd stopped her at every turn, but only because he meant to control this investigation.

Shelby Gates would be allowed the keys to the kingdom, provided she was willing to sign the agreement he'd drawn up.

Then he would have her, and he would enjoy himself for as long as it lasted. Until the moment that she realized he was a manipulative asshole and walked away from him.

"Tell me it isn't that redhead from LA. The one you got a hard-on around every time she walked in the damn room." Hatch didn't wait to sigh impatiently or for confirmation. "Damn it, Andrew, I thought I taught you not to think with your dick."

Hatch had taught him many things. And then there were the lessons Drew hadn't needed. Like how to protect the things and people he held closest to his heart. From the moment he'd felt the heat of the fire against his skin, seen his parents' bodies and not been able to get to them, he'd known that he was responsible for his siblings. He'd done a piss-poor job at times, but this move was all about protecting them.

"Shelby can get into places I can't. She's also innocuous. Most people don't see past her chest and hips and all that hair to the ambitious woman inside." He intended to use that ambition against her.

"Once I teach her how to be perfectly discreet, she'll attract no attention to our family."

"So you're sending her out there like a sacrificial lamb," Hatch mused as though the idea didn't actually bother him. "She'll send you information, but if Iris comes after someone, it won't be our family."

Hatch was very much a member of the Lawless clan. The boozy, obnoxious, brilliant uncle who fucked up but was always loyal. Hatch had been loyal to Benedict, and that fealty had switched to Drew when he came of age. Once Drew had sobered Hatch up, he'd proven to still have the business acumen he'd shown when he ran his father's company. Hatch had applied it to 4L and they'd gone the distance. A few billion dollars later and they were still on top of the world.

And still had unfinished business.

"I don't intend to get the girl killed."

"But you're willing to put her in danger. You saw what happened to the last few people who even hinted at getting in Iris's way."

Yes, he'd heard what the woman had told Carly. As Bran had lain there bleeding, Carly had listened to a recitation of Francine Wells's crimes. Of course Carly hadn't realized she was actually talking to Iris Lawless, but she knew the woman who stood before her had poisoned Phillip Stratton before he could potentially tell all, killed Steven Castalano in his hospital bed the day before he was scheduled to talk to police, and sent someone in to murder Patricia Cain.

He was well aware of the risks his black widow mother posed. "Better her than my family, and she'll agree. She'll do whatever it takes."

"How can you be sure of that?"

"Because I've done a study on her." He knew all her data by heart, but he was intrigued at getting to know the real Shelby Gates. He wanted to see the woman inside the warrior goddess.

Did she fuck like she lived? Would she be a wildcat in bed, or sweet and soft after a man had given her everything he had? Would she curl up next to her lover and let him take care of her, let him adore her? Could he soften her with sex, with affection? Could he soften her so much that at the end she would consider forgiving him?

"So you think this woman is going to do your bidding because you offer her cash?" Hatch asked.

"Cash is the last thing I would offer her."

"All right. What are you offering her?"

Drew knew the way to Shelby's heart. "I'm offering her the story of a lifetime."

Hatch frowned his way. "I'm confused, Drew. First you say you're going to hide everything so Mia and the others never have to know what Iris has done. Now you're turning it into a bestseller."

"I'll give her the story. I'll even let her write it."

"But you won't let her publish it. You're going to let her put her neck on the line and then take it all away from her. Damn, Drew. That's cold. And it could work. You have her quietly find what you need. No one ever has to know you're involved at all."

"I thought about playing it that way, but I can't. I need to be able to keep an eye on her until I'm sure I have all the research, and I can't risk letting her tell this story. I'll stick close to her and, when the time is right, I'll take her notes, her research, and everything else." He didn't like how tight his tie suddenly felt. "And I'll offer her something in return. I'll get her any job in the world she could possibly want. She wants to work for the *New York Times*, I'll make it happen. She needs cash to set herself up as a freelancer, consider me her personal bankroll."

"And if all she wants is what you offered her in the first place?"

He shook his head. "She'll be reasonable in the end. She'll see that I can't allow my family secrets out in the open."

"So you're going to leave things the way they are? You're going to let everyone believe Benedict killed your mother and himself?"

"I don't know, damn it." He forced himself to calm down. Cool. Calm. That was the only way he managed to get anything done. "Like I said, the situation is rather fluid at the moment. What I need to do is figure out exactly where Iris is and what she's been doing for twenty years. My brothers and sister know our father was a victim. That might have to be enough."

"And if she's living it up somewhere? Are you going to ruin her life? You think that will solve your problem?"

"No. There's only one thing I want to do to Iris." He felt himself go infinitely cold. This was the real reason why he couldn't bring his siblings in. He knew how this would end. "I'm going to make sure she can never hurt us again. One way or another."

"All right. I'll stand by you," Hatch said, crossing the room and getting himself another drink. "How do you intend to keep an eye on Shelby?"

"I'm going to be her boyfriend."

Hatch sputtered. It was good to know his mentor could still be shocked. "What?"

"Part of the contract is that her cover for this assignment is as my girlfriend. It won't surprise anyone. Bran and Riley saw right through my reasonable annoyance to the illogical sexual reaction I have around that woman. And Mia and Carly tried to set me up with her. I'll simply explain that the last time I was in Los Angeles, I asked her out to dinner and we began seeing each other." It was a simple plan.

"I knew you were thinking with your dick."

Luckily his dick was a strategic thinker. He sat down and sipped the Scotch. It was oaky, with a hint of caramel and smoke. Would Shelby like Scotch? He sat back as Hatch went over all the ways Drew's penis would bring them down. Twenty more minutes and the game would begin.

One thing it definitely wouldn't be was boring.

"Mr. Lawless will see you now."

Shelby looked up from her phone at the stunning receptionist. The other woman wore one of those dresses that looked like a bandage wrapped around her perfect form. "Are you serious? Is he like standing in front of a bunch of windows and wearing a silver tie? Because that would be way too much."

The woman stared at her for a moment. "Excuse me?"

So not big on pop culture references. Her humor was going to be wasted here. "You know, *Fifty Shades of Grey*. That was how it all started. It was a book. It was a movie."

"I'm a Harvard-educated programmer. I do not know *Fifty Shades of Grey*." The woman's perfectly done brow curved up in disdain. "But if you'll come this way, Mr. Lawless will conduct his interview with you and I'll be able to get back to work."

Shelby followed the woman past the beautifully decorated receptionist station. She glanced down the halls of 4L Software. It was dark to her left and right, the only ambient light coming from the cityscape around them.

What was she doing here? Why had she even said yes to this asshole? Oh, Carly swore he wasn't as bad as he seemed, but Carly could be overly optimistic. She was also madly in love with Bran Lawless, and that was keeping her from seeing the family as the ravaging sharks they really were.

So why was she following Ms. Perfection down the hall? Why had she allowed Drew Lawless to send a plane for her? Why had she accepted his phone call at all?

Oh, she knew. She'd found something wrong with the police reports concerning the deaths of Benedict and Iris Lawless. Something that got her every instinct tingling.

Right up until she'd been told by a lawyer that if she kept digging, she would be served with an injunction and taken to court by the lord of the underworld.

Well, the master of 4L Software at least.

Ms. Perfection stepped through the open doorway. "She's here, sir, and she's got terrible taste in literature."

Shelby frowned. "I'm here and she's got a two-by-four stuck up her ass."

Ms. Perfection turned, her lips curling up. "Oh, I like her, sir."

And then Drew Lawless, who had indeed been standing in front of a bank of floor-to-ceiling windows brooding as he looked out over the city, turned. Nope, she'd said yes because her reproductive system had taken over. Shelby prided herself on being a smart, independent woman, but at the end of the day she was like all the rest. Completely helpless against a square jawline and broad shoulders and alpha-male charm.

That was one gorgeous man. Too bad he was also an ass.

"Jocelyn, I believe you've done your duty. Thank you," Lawless said, his voice deep. "And Harry thanks you as well."

"Harry owes me. She thought I was the receptionist. Also, she thinks you've set this up like some *Fifty Shades* reject. Good thing you took off the tie, or she would worry you're about to tie her up." Jocelyn winked Shelby's way. "He won't, you know. He's quite staid. If you decide to go for something a little wilder, give me a call."

She floated away.

What the hell had that been? Shelby watched her before turning back to Lawless. "Did she just hit on me?"

His lips curled up in the most decadent smile. "You'll have to excuse Joss. She's a brilliant programmer, but she's got absolutely no filter. And yes, she was hitting on you."

She'd definitely gone down the rabbit hole. She'd rather expected to be ushered into Lawless's office to face a panel of lawyers who would convince her never to even mention his name professionally again or they would ruin her. She hadn't expected to get hit on by a programmer and left alone with the big boss, who seemed amused by all of it.

"Why don't you take a seat so we can talk?" He gestured to the chair in front of his desk. The light in the room was low, only half lit at this time of night. There was an oddly old-fashioned lamp on the high-tech desk, casting warm light around the space between the desk and two chairs that formed the heart of the office.

It made the space look warm and inviting, intimate. As though the light itself formed a nest to lock out the rest of the room.

"I won't bite." His face softened slightly, that cut-from-granite jaw of his relaxing. "Can I get you a drink?"

She could use one. "Sure. Scotch or vodka would be great."

"A woman after my own heart. I think you'll like this," he murmured as he walked over to his bar.

He had a bar in his office and a massive TV, complete with a couch. Someone had dumped a geek's paradise living room on one side of the office. She couldn't help but be curious. "Are those video games?"

He was busy pouring amber liquid into bar glasses. "Of course. A guy has to relax. In my particular business, video games are the new golf. I do a lot of business over those games. I've also got some movies. It's an entire entertainment system."

"And the bobbleheads?" There was a row of them lined up on a bookshelf. Superhero bobbleheads.

"My brothers thought they classed up the place."

Had he blushed a little? It made her smile. "Oh, my God. You're a big old nerd under all that alpha-male scariness, aren't you?"

"I was unaware I was scary at all." His tone had gone a bit huffy. "As for being a nerd, I did make my money off of code. I still write it. If that makes me a nerd, then I suppose I am."

"Writing code doesn't make you a nerd. Owning the entire Avengers set of bobblehead dolls makes you a nerd." And oddly more approachable.

"I accept that. I suppose you're a romance fan since you mentioned *Fifty Shades*."

"I like to read. I read a lot of different things, but when I want to unwind, I like a good romance. The hotter the better." Did she have to say that? She should have made herself sound academic.

"My sister forced me to have that movie brought in for her and her girlfriends." He offered her a glass.

"I'd heard Mia's having a baby. Congratulations."

"Thank you."

She stared down at the glass in her hand. What kind of Scotch did billionaires drink? She breathed in the scent. It always reminded her of her brother. After he'd gotten his first job, he'd splurged and bought a bottle of twelve-year-old single malt. They'd toasted that first job and all the others after. They'd toasted him in anticipation of getting the interview with Patricia Cain the night before he died.

They'd been so foolish.

She let the scent wash over her as she let go of the memory. Her brother had been wonderful, and she hated the fact that anger welled when she thought about him. She wanted to remember him in joy and love.

"What just went through your mind? You got sad."

She thought about ignoring the question or lying. She could tell him any number of things. "I was thinking about my brother. He died a few years ago."

"He didn't simply die, Shelby," Drew said quietly. "Patricia Cain had him murdered. I'm sorry about that. I'm more sorry that I can't help you prove it. After Cain's death, Carly snagged the laptop she used in Florida. We didn't find anything that would connect her to your brother's death, though I don't doubt she did it."

"I'm sorry, too. He told me he was onto a big story. I believe he discovered some of the crimes she committed. But it's done now. There's no bringing Patricia Cain to justice." This was why she had to let it go. "So I'm trying to remember how much I loved him and not how angry I am that he died. One seems to honor him more fully than the other."

"Do you think so? You don't see the point of avenging victims?"

Her heart had felt so heavy right after he died, but she was beginning to remember how he lived. It was easier to think of Johnny and smile. "The dead have already found their peace. Revenge is nothing more than a selfish pursuit."

"Why would you say that?" The question sounded perfectly academic, but she could hear an undercurrent of irritation flavoring his words.

How did she make a man like Drew Lawless understand? "Because the person we're trying to avenge would want us to live. At least I know my brother would. He would want me to be happy, and I can't do that if I'm pursuing some vengeance that won't bring him back to me."

"But you were pursuing it. You were going after Patricia Cain."

"No, that was justice. You have to be able to see the difference. I was trying to reveal the truth about that woman so she couldn't do it again. Truth is definitely a worthy pursuit. It's what my brother worked all his life for."

Lawless held up his glass. "Then we drink to your brother."

She clinked glasses with him and then sipped the Scotch with a long, satisfied sigh. "That is miraculous. Do I even want to know how old that is?"

"Much older than you." He gestured back to his desk. "Shall we?"

She didn't want to go back there. The desk was so formal, but this space showed another side of the man. "I think I would be more comfortable here. Especially if you're going to threaten me."

He studied her for a moment. "Why would I threaten you?"

"Habit. It seems to be what you do." Had he forgotten how he'd slammed her with lawyers a few months back?

He reached out, his big hand sliding over hers. "We got off on the wrong foot, you and I."

She stared at him, hoping he felt her judgment. "You catfished me."

One of the methods he'd used to keep track of her investigation was to befriend her on the Internet as another man. She'd come to enjoy her conversations with him. He quickly admitted what he'd done after he figured out they were on the same side, but it still bugged her.

He winced, proving he had at least half a conscience. "I'm so sorry about that. Would it make a difference if I told you I enjoyed those talks way more than I should have?"

"I suppose I know why you did it." She liked the idea that he'd found something meaningful in those exchanges. "Should we sit?"

"Absolutely. We can sit wherever you like. Honestly, I'm more comfortable over here, too, but I thought I might impress you with the views from my desk."

His hand was enveloping hers, warmth and strength wrapping her up. He led her over to the couch and gallantly helped her sit before taking the seat next to her.

Maybe this was a mistake. This was way more intimate than sitting at a desk across from one another. It was too easy to forget that she wasn't here on a friendly outing when he was sitting beside her, relaxed and more open than she could remember seeing him. His face was softer without harsh light illuminating it.

She nodded toward his bobblehead shelf. "I'll be honest. I'm not all that impressed with the wealth, but Iron Man is someone I admire."

"That's good to know." His lips pulled up in the sweetest smile. "When I act like an outrageous douche bag, my brothers call me Tony Stark."

"You? Never." All she'd known up until now was the douche bag. The charming, sexy nerd was infinitely more dangerous.

"Oh, I'm good at it. I can be a bastard and I'm often socially awkward. I think it's because of the years spent behind a keyboard. Zeros and ones don't require me to understand all the rules of social engagement. There's a reason Riley handles a lot of the client meetings. Now that we're all out in the open, I'm going to let him or Bran be the face of the company."

Why was he being so open with her? It was a little intoxicating. This was a man known to keep his mouth shut unless he had to. Was this the Drew that Carly liked?

"Some people say you're agoraphobic." She knew the truth but wondered if he would admit to it.

He stared at her for a moment as though trying to figure out how to handle her. "Are we on the record?"

She shook her head. That was the last thing she wanted him to think. He would go back into attack mode. "I'm not doing a story on you, Mr. Lawless. I'm merely here because who turns down a private jet and the presidential suite at the Hilton? I also appreciated the invitation to Riley and Ellie's reception. I'm sure you throw a great party." She sobered a bit. "I learned my lesson. Don't mess with you or I'll get burned."

He winced. "I'm very sorry for all the legal crap I threw your way, but you have to understand that my family is everything to me."

"I wasn't trying to hurt your family."

"You were attempting to gain access to my parents' medical records."

She took another sip. Now they were getting to the heart of the matter. She would explain herself. He would require an apology and the promise to keep her nose out of his family business, and she would be free to go.

Could she let this story go? There was a deeper truth to what happened to his parents. To Benedict, she feared. It was right there waiting for her to scratch the surface and find the real truth. It had always been like this with her. Ever since she was a child, when she caught hint of a story, she had to find the truth. This could be the biggest story of her life. She'd already decided to lie low for a month or two and then start asking a few questions quietly. He couldn't watch her forever.

"I'm a crime reporter. It's an interesting crime. I'm not attempting to harm your family in any way, but sometimes there's a deeper truth that can help others."

His hand tightened around his glass. "I suppose it is interesting. I'm not sure how it can help others. No one reads those murder tales to find clarity. They read them for the thrill."

"Some do," she allowed. "And some people learn from them. There's also the fact that there are times the police get it wrong. Not often, but when a great injustice has been done, don't you think we should seek the truth?"

"Is that what you were doing with my parents? Seeking the truth?"

"Yes." Perhaps if he truly believed her, he would let up.

"Might I ask why you chose to start investigating it now? You showed no interest in it before. You were following Patricia Cain."

"You know why." She wasn't sure why he was prevaricating. Maybe she should simply say it out loud so they didn't have to pretend they were talking about something else. "Because Patricia Cain had your father killed. She was in on it along with Phillip Stratton and Steven Castalano. Were you aware that a Russian assassin was in Dallas the weekend your father was killed?"

He stood abruptly, turning away from her. He walked back toward his desk. Shelby watched as he set his drink down and picked something up. He walked back over, handing her a stack of papers and a pen. "This is a nondisclosure agreement. If we're going to talk further, I need you to sign it."

"So I can't ever publish an article on your parents?" She stood. This had been exactly what she thought it was, a power play to get her to shut up. "I'll pass, Mr. Lawless. And that looks like one massive NDA."

"It's Drew. And the NDA is in case you don't sign the rest of the contract."

"What contract?"

"The one where I hire you to be my investigator into the deaths of my parents, their official biographer, and my girlfriend."

She stared at him for a moment and wondered if this was one of those crazy-ass dreams she sometimes had. They would start out perfectly normal and then the aliens would land. "I'm going to need another drink."

Chapter Two

S helby stared down at the contract. Specifically at the part where it outlined all the rules regarding her "relationship" with Drew Lawless. She'd done plenty of undercover work before, but this was a new one.

Party B will be affectionate and respectful toward Party A in all public outings and private interactions with Party A's family and friends.

Party B will accompany Party A to any and all social functions including agreed-upon public appearances for the purposes of establishing their relationship in the press.

Party B will stay with Party A in his home when possible and give the appearance of a normal, healthy sexual relationship. Party B will not be required to have sexual intercourse with Party A to meet the terms of this contract.

In exchange for maintaining the illusion of a relationship, Party A will aid in all research and not impede in any way Party B's pursuit of knowledge concerning the deaths of Benedict and Iris Lawless. Party A will fund all research and aid in the production of an accounting of the truth behind the crimes perpetrated on the night of June 6, 1996.

She looked up at him. He'd been silent as she read the contract. Well, the salient parts. She was not to reveal to his family members what she was working on. She was not to reveal to anyone that the relationship with Drew Lawless was a contractual one. She was to keep Drew Lawless informed at all times of her progress on the case and was to allow him to accompany her when at all possible.

In exchange she would receive monetary compensation and a publisher for her book when it was complete.

"Why?" She had a million and one questions, but it was the first one she could think to ask.

"Why you? Or why the girlfriend clause?" he asked, as though they were talking about some academic subject and not a totally fake relationship where they would have fake sex.

"I suppose both." She tried to make herself sound as blasé as he did. Like she received this kind of offer three times a week. No big deal. Just turned down the Google guy last week, buddy.

"You're smart and you're already closer to the truth after a few months' research than I was after years." He leaned back, his eyes steady on her. "And you're good at undercover work."

"Why not hire that security firm to research? From what Carly tells me, they're very good." And the Lawless clan was in tight with McKay-Taggart since Mia was married to one of them.

He nodded. "Yes, and they have years of experience and technical know-how behind them. They're the best in the country and you matched them. You, all by yourself."

She hoped he couldn't see how she flushed. "Sometimes a focused individual can do more than a company. They have to look at big-picture things. I get to think about the small stuff."

"Like what?"

"Like the fact that your father made a dentist appointment the day before he supposedly murdered your mother and killed himself." She had made a study of Benedict Lawless's habits. He'd had an assistant, but tended to make his own appointments when they were personal. The dentist's appointment had been written on his calendar, the bulk of which survived the fire. It had been left in his car and booked into evidence.

"Perhaps he was simply enraged," Lawless offered logically. "He lost control of his temper and impulsively killed her."

It was obvious she was going to have to lay out her case for him. "First, Benedict Lawless had no prior record of domestic abuse. There's typically an escalation that begins with small violence and leads to the final explosion. Do you recall your father ever hitting your mother?"

He took a long breath. "Never. My father was quite gentle, but then we all have our secrets. I was a kid. I saw my parents through the eyes of a worshipful child."

"The evidence can't be denied. There were no reports of violence in your household. So if we establish that your father was neither impulsive nor violent, we have to look at the crime itself. It took planning. The gun had to be purchased. There were no records of Benedict owning a gun until a week before the murder. He purchased that gun for the sole purpose of murdering your mother and taking his own life. So why make a dentist appointment the day before, and why schedule car maintenance on the Wednesday prior to the killing? Why waste time on a vehicle he wouldn't drive again?"

"Perhaps he intended to set this up as a burglary gone wrong."

Did Drew honestly think she hadn't examined and excluded that scenario? "Then why would he have blocked all the exits and set the house on fire? You want to tell me why you're trying to poke holes in my theories? I thought we were on the same page."

"I'm merely playing devil's advocate." His voice was low, his body relaxing a bit. "And showing you precisely why I wrote that contract. I couldn't have this discussion with a McKay-Taggart employee. I would receive a report and be left out of the intellectual process."

"Somehow I think you could pay them enough to get the working relationship you want."

He chuckled, a deep, sexy sound. "You would be surprised. The big guy makes me look like a fluffy kitten. He's also my sister's brother-in-law. If I hire him to continue, he would have to put up a business wall between himself and his brother. Ian Taggart's family is everything to him. I'd rather not put him in a situation where he's forced to choose between his brother and a client. I rather think I would lose, and I don't want my siblings to know I'm continuing the search, for reasons I'll explain to you if you sign the contract."

If he was serious, maybe she should be sure he understood what she would want from him. "Okay, I kind of get that, but there are other investigators out there who wouldn't want to write a story about their findings. You seemed extremely certain you didn't want a reporter investigating. You need to understand, Mr. Lawless, that I will want that story."

"Which is precisely why I'll pay you to write it. And please call me Drew. It's going to be awkward if you continue to call me Mr. Lawless."

Because she was supposed to be his girlfriend. "Now for the other why. Why the secondary clause? Why do I need to play out the illusion that I'm your honey?"

He got a wistful smile on his face. "Because it might be fun?"

"Drew." She wasn't going to listen to his sarcasm.

"I believe this could end up being a dangerous assignment. I want to be with you most of the time. We'll have to go to Dallas. That's not a big deal since right now my sister and Bran are both living there. I want you to be able to have the full power of 4L behind your investigation. You're a freelance writer. It makes sense for you to work from the 4L offices if we're seeing each other. You would be quite comfortable with an office in my building, but everyone will have questions if I simply offer up valuable real estate to a reporter I'm not involved with. Not only will my employees try to figure out what's going on, but my family will hear about it and they'll want the truth as well."

"You think they'll buy that we're suddenly in love and living together?"

"My brothers will. They suspect I've been attracted to you for a very long time," he admitted. "And I am, but you have to know I won't force you into anything."

She wasn't worried about that. She was a little worried she was the one who would be tempted. Of course the idea of having 4L's resources behind her was beyond tempting. "I would need a few people who could know what I'm actually doing."

He nodded. "I've already selected a small group to help you. Quietly, of course, but they're excellent at their jobs. If anyone asks, having some of the finest tech specialists at your disposal is one of the perks of dating a billionaire. Some women like diamonds, you prefer hackers."

She did actually, and she had to admit something to him. "Carly thinks I have a thing for you so you might be right about them buying into our cover."

"If you decide to take this offer, I'll have someone pick up your luggage from the hotel and you'll stay with me starting tonight. In a different room, of course, but we should stay close. Tomorrow we'll introduce you around work and give you all the clearance you need. Our relationship will also enable me to protect you."

"Protect me from what? They're all dead, Drew."

His eyes went pointedly to the nondisclosure agreement.

Damn it. He was going to drive her mad. She picked up the pen and signed the NDA. "There. Now you can sue my ass for even talking about this discussion."

"I don't want to," he admitted. "I would rather we be friends."

She was so confused. She'd expected this meeting to be with the coolly logical businessman, not this slightly lonely, entirely gorgeous guy. "I thought you hated me."

"I've never hated you, Shelby."

"You do a good impression of it."

He frowned, but somehow even that managed to be sexy. "As I pointed out before, I'm not necessarily good in social situations. Can't you see this is my way of making you an ally? Then we don't have to be on opposite sides."

Why did she have to find him so fascinating? From the moment she'd learned his history, she'd been the tiniest bit obsessed with this man. In the beginning it had everything to do with his rags-to-riches story, the tale of tragedy turning into triumph. Then it was because he'd proven himself to be such an ass.

Now she was seeing a different side to the man. Was he telling her the truth? On a psychological level, she certainly believed him. Having his whole world ripped out from under him could have an effect on even the kindest soul. Who would Drew Lawless be if his parents had lived?

"All right, I'll choose to believe you're telling the truth. I still don't understand why you think it could be dangerous."

"Because I know things you don't know. Do you find it interesting that Stratton, Castalano, and Cain all died within two years of one another?"

She did, but there were certainly explanations for that. She'd read some of the medical reports. "Stratton had end-stage cancer. Castalano had a heart attack, and Patricia Cain was an overdose."

"Stratton died two nights after he sent me an e-mail requesting that I visit him in New York. I've never told anyone that. Not even my family. Only Ian Taggart knows that."

A chill went through her system. "Castalano had a heart attack the night before he was scheduled to be interviewed by the police."

"And Cain, who according to Carly had never done drugs in her life, suddenly enjoyed black tar heroin. Yes, it's all suspicious and yet no one questioned the first two. Do you recognize the name Francine Wells?"

Her heart started to race a little. Were they going there? "I believe she was your father's mistress."

Drew's face tightened. "You're good. I wasn't aware that my father had cheated until recently. Did Carly tell you?"

"Absolutely not. I would never ask her. I don't use my friends like that." She'd met Carly while researching Patricia Cain, but they'd become close friends. Carly was one of the only friends she had left. After Johnny died, she'd pulled into herself. She wasn't close to her father. He'd walked out when she was twelve and she'd seen him rarely since. Her mother had passed away five years before from cancer. She'd pulled into her shell and focused on work. She'd pointedly not asked Carly any questions about what she knew once she realized Carly intended to marry Brandon Lawless.

Drew waved a hand, dismissing her words. "She's allowed to discuss what happened with her friends. Do you think I'm that controlling?"

She wasn't sure what she thought of him anymore. "It's your reputation."

"I guess that's true. But I've rapidly learned that there are some things I can't control. My in-laws are definitely in that category. I don't even try."

"So why hide it from them? I know you've said there's some sort of danger out there, but that didn't stop you from sending your brothers in. Riley ran lead on the Castalano investigation and Bran took it on Cain."

He pointed her direction. "Yes. Exactly. And they both have the bullet wounds to prove it. I'm not allowing them to get shot again. They have spouses and they'll have children soon. I can't allow them to risk themselves."

"So you'll risk me?"

His jaw tightened and he stood. "I was hoping you wouldn't see it like that. It's why I'll stay close to you. I know you won't believe this, but I'm quite good with a gun and I was trained by the best. It's one of the reasons for our cover. I can stay close to you and no one will ask questions."

She shook her head. "I was teasing you. Risk is part of my job. I'm comfortable with it, though I would like to understand where you think this risk is coming from."

His body moved with grace as he paced. "Why did you request the autopsy report on my parents?"

This was something that had to be handled with delicacy. "It's routine. I wanted to read the reports to ensure nothing odd came up. When I'm investigating any crime, I always begin with the reports."

"What were you looking for?"

She hesitated. If she made false accusations, there was every chance she would hurt this man, and he'd been through enough. Even though he'd been an asshole, she didn't want to cause him further pain if she could spare it. "There were certain inconsistencies between one of the documents filed initially and the official report."

"There was an initial document? I'm sorry. This is the first I'm hearing about that. When I hired McKay-Taggart, I asked them to focus on the suspects, not the victims."

It was a mistake a lot of people made. She wanted to see the whole crime, to comb through every bit of evidence. How could she find what had been missed if she didn't look through everything? "I found a single copy of it while I was looking through a file box. They hadn't gotten around to scanning it. At the time of your parents' murders, the medical examiner had an intern working under him. She did an initial report. Because the bodies were so badly burned, most of her measurements were of the bones that were left behind. It was how they calculated height. They actually used dental records to identify the bodies, but the intern made a thorough study of what she had."

"All right. Did she find something that the medical examiner didn't?"

"Not exactly. Her measurements of the female victim's femur bones were off by nearly three centimeters from the official report." She wasn't sure why it had hit her. She'd only glanced at the numbers and measurements that made up the end of Iris Lawless at first. She'd had to study the reports closely before she found the inconsistency.

"I would very much like to see that report." His voice had gone deep.

"I had to leave the original behind, but I took a picture with my phone. I can certainly get you a copy. The official report is easy to get."

"I would like to see the original," he insisted. "We can go to Dallas and visit with Bran and Carly. While we're there you can take me to the file room and show me what you found. Can you be ready to leave next week?"

"Whoa. I'll be more than happy to take you into the file room and show you what I found, but do you understand what it could mean? It could be nothing but a mistake, or it could mean something more."

"My mother was taller than Francine Wells. Would the femur bone match Francine's?"

Her stomach twisted. "Maybe. I don't know. I hadn't checked."

"You should, because the truth of the matter is my mother is alive and Francine is the woman who died that night. I want you to help me prove that my mother is a murderer."

And just like that, nothing else mattered. This was the story of a lifetime and she couldn't let it pass. As for her attraction to the man in front of her, it didn't matter either. She could ignore that.

"I'll help you." She leaned over and signed her name to the contract. She knew she should have a lawyer take a look at it, but it didn't matter. She would tell this story.

And she would help the Lawless family finally find justice.

Drew closed the door to the guest suite with an emotion he could only describe as satisfaction.

She was here. She was in his home and she'd signed the contract. She hadn't even read the whole thing. Shelby Gates needed a keeper, and he was beginning to wonder why that shouldn't be him.

Yes, she would be angry with him at the end of this particular adventure, but if he showed her how good he could make her life, she might stay with him anyway.

Of course, he would need to make sure she didn't continue to shut the door between them, no matter how sweetly she'd done it.

"Good night, Drew," she'd said with a tired smile on her face. "I'm looking forward to working with you."

He'd nodded and agreed and absolutely not said what had gone through his head. *I'm looking forward to getting in your bed, to spreading your legs and finding out exactly how hot you can be.* Nope. He hadn't said that. He'd used his filter. His brothers would be proud. He'd agreed and then let her shut the door because none of his siblings were home. It was only him and Hatch, who already knew they weren't sleeping together.

Yet.

Drew walked down the stairs, certain it would be hours before he slept. He was a night owl by nature, but lately he avoided sleep. Lately when he fell asleep he dreamed about it. He'd thought the dreams would go away once he'd dealt with Stratton, Castalano, and Cain. He'd never imagined that he would find a much worse nightmare waiting for him.

He would get some work done. His team was beta testing his new firewall. It would be fun to see if he could figure out a way to break his own system. That was how he worked. He built something, made it beautiful and strong, and then tore it apart brick by brick until he'd dragged it down to the foundation and then built it again. Stronger this time, faster and harder to defeat.

Another one of the lessons from his childhood.

"She settled?" a lazy voice asked.

He stopped in the middle of the formal living room. It was the last room before his office. He'd almost made it, but apparently Hatch hadn't confined himself to his room this evening. Drew turned and found his mentor sitting on the ridiculously expensive sofa his designer had declared to be the most elegant seating ever.

"She's in the guest suite. Don't piss her off."

Hatch sat up. "Since when do I piss off lovely ladies?" He ran a hand across his hair, slicking it back. "I assume this means she signed the contract."

"She did." And he would have a short amount of time to discuss how their "relationship" was going to work. "And she's already found proof that the body we buried wasn't my mother's."

Even in the low light he could see the way Hatch paled. "It could still be a mistake."

Drew tried not to roll his eyes. "So the fact that Carly perfectly described Iris to the police sketch artist was coincidence?"

Hatch stood, his body practically vibrating with irritation. "Maybe. She admitted it was dark in the room and she'd just seen her lover shot. Carly saw that portrait Patricia kept in her office. Maybe that was where her mind went. And why would she describe Iris looking so young? The woman in that picture was at least fifteen years younger than Iris would be."

The very thought of that portrait threatened to send a shudder through him. They'd discovered a portrait of their mother the night Bran had broken into Patricia Cain's private office looking for the files that would prove the lifestyle maven had a hand in killing their parents. The portrait had been an eerie presence in the room.

A weariness stole over Drew and he wished he was still sitting with Shelby in his office. Or in the booth at the Italian hole-in-the-wall he'd taken her to afterward. She'd run down her investigative methods and how she'd started reporting. He'd pointedly not talked about his parents' case because he wanted to know about her. He knew it all already, but it was different hearing the history from her instead of reading it off a computer file. Her eyes lit up when she talked about her work. She was passionate. She was engaging.

She'd made him laugh.

He should have stayed there with her. "Carly didn't see that portrait, Hatch. Bran was the only one who went in that room. Carly stayed outside."

"I forgot about that," Hatch admitted. "But it still doesn't explain why Iris looked so damn young."

Drew called on every ounce of patience he had. This was Hatch, and he'd had a thing for Iris. Drew had figured it out a long time ago. When he'd shown up on Hatch's doorstep, the place had been a testament to how far the man had fallen. He'd gone from millions to a filthy motel he paid for by the week. Drew had found him drunk and on the path to a very early meeting with his maker. He'd also found a single photograph. It had been a picture of Iris Lawless in all her glory. She'd been wearing a cocktail dress and smiling at whoever held the camera like she was waiting to eat him up.

"Botox and good plastic surgery explain why she hasn't aged." And evil. He wouldn't put it past the woman to make a deal with the devil. *In exchange for eternal youth, I, Iris Lawless, will eat my own children.* "You know she was always vain."

"She liked to look good. She was a beautiful woman," Hatch said, his voice flat.

"I understand you cared about her." He didn't want to listen to Hatch weep over his lost love. "But you do understand she had an affair with Patricia. It likely began long before she murdered my father and Francine."

"Yeah, I get that. Don't think I'm still in love with the woman."

But Drew had to wonder. "You knew about Francine. Do you know when it started? Obviously my mother found out about it. I would assume that's why she chose Francine to take her place."

Hatch crossed to the bar. "Sometimes I think I don't know anything."

He didn't need Hatch's guilt. He needed his knowledge. "When did my father tell you about Francine?"

"Do you really want to know?"

"I have to."

"I found out when he asked me if I knew any good divorce lawyers."

That felt like a kick in the gut. "He was going to leave us?"

Hatch put down the bottle. "Never." He strode toward Drew. "Don't you think that for a second. Your father would never have left you. He wanted the best lawyer because he wanted full custody of you and your siblings."

"How long had the affair been going on?"

"About a year." Hatch sighed and seemed to resign himself to talking. "They'd been working together for a little longer than that. Francine was what I like to call a naive idiot."

"Yeah, well, so was my father."

"He viewed the world differently. Ellie reminds me a lot of him."

Because Ellie was concerned with more than money or power. She wanted to change her employees' lives, to make them better. His father had wanted to make the whole world a better place. It was precisely why he'd been killed. He'd invented a way to make the Internet more accessible back when it was in its infancy, but he'd chosen not to sell the technology. He'd wanted to make it free. After his death the board of the company his father had helped create took his stock and divided it among themselves, and then sold the company and the technology for millions of dollars.

And Drew and his three siblings had been placed in foster homes because they had no one in the world left to care for them.

Drew tried to shake off that morbid feeling he got whenever he thought about those years. "Yes, Ellie is a lot like our father with the single exception that she's got several people in her life who never let anyone take advantage of her."

"I know I failed your father. I think about it every single fucking day of my life." He headed right back to the bar. It was Hatch's happy place.

There was nothing at all happy about this conversation. "I didn't mean that. I wasn't blaming you. You couldn't have known."

"I fucking should have."

"When he asked you about the lawyer, did he tell you why he'd had the affair? I have to ask, because in my head my parents were happy. They never fought in front of us."

"Benedict would tell me that they fought, but I never believed him. Iris always seemed so gentle. Now I understand that was all an act. She was excellent at adapting herself to someone else's needs."

Drew knew the reason for that. "I believe sociopaths are good at reading people and can be quite chameleon-like. I remember her being a good mother. With the exception of not wanting to mess up her hair, she was excellent at taking care of us."

"She wanted everyone to acknowledge how perfect she was," Hatch agreed.

"What did my parents fight about?"

"Mostly she accused him of ruining her career by getting her pregnant, but you should understand that Bran and Mia were born because she was trying to hold on to him. The affair with Francine was the first time I know he cheated, but it wasn't the first time he'd talked about divorce."

The hits kept on coming. "So they talked about splitting after Riley was born?"

"I think that was a hard time for them both. We weren't working together then so I'm not entirely sure what happened, but Benedict told me that they had agreed to divorce at one point and then Iris got pregnant with Bran."

"That would be around the time the company was formed. You brought Dad on."

Hatch nodded. "Yeah, your mom was good at picking a winner. Well, at picking someone who could potentially make a lot of money.

She always talked about how rich your dad could be if he would only concentrate on what was really important."

"And when he wouldn't, she got rid of him."

"I suppose so."

"Why were you attracted to her?"

"She was beautiful." Hatch took a long slug of bourbon. "And I was jealous of your father in some ways. I don't know. I guess in some ways I wanted to be your father. He was a better man than I was."

"You didn't know about the affair with Patricia?"

A shudder went through Hatch. "God no. I honestly didn't know about it until we found that portrait, but now a lot of things make sense. At the end she was spending time with Patricia. They were talking about starting a company that ended up being Cain Corp."

"I always found it ironic that Patricia managed to take my mother . . . Iris's ideas and work them into her own company. I recognized some of the recipes from Patricia's first cookbook. There was a woman who ran the group home Riley and I were in who was a dedicated baker. I must have gained ten pounds while she was there. She loved Patricia Cain. Claimed she'd never found a recipe quite like her snickerdoodle one."

"Yeah, I wondered about that, too. Her recipe books were supposedly lost in the fire. I suspected Patty had borrowed them or something. Now we know that Iris took them with her," Hatch explained. "I always wondered how the assassin got past the alarm. Your father had a high-tech system. The police obviously thought what Iris wanted them to think so they didn't question it, but your father was habitual. He always set the alarm when everyone was in the house. It would have been on that night. Iris either turned it off herself or she gave the assassin the code."

"Shelby figured out who the assassin was." It had taken McKay-Taggart weeks to figure that out, and they had tons of CIA contacts.

"She's a smart girl." Hatch sighed. "Though not smart enough if she signed that contract. Did she even read it?"

He would never admit it, but he'd kind of held his breath when she'd had that contract in her hand. It was all laid out. What he intended to do was all there in the contract. It wouldn't be fair if it hadn't been. "No. Not all of it. I'm sure she thought she got the gist, but there's zero probability that she knows what that contract really says and what it means. She would never have signed it otherwise."

"Well, that was a smart play. Make the contract so long and drawn out that she can't possibly read the whole thing, then dangle the one thing she wants in front of her and give her very little time to choose. Tell me why you really insisted on the girlfriend clause."

"I need her to work closely with me. I need her at 4L and you know how employees gossip. Now they can gossip about my affair with Shelby and won't look past that to figure out why she's really there."

Hatch's eyes narrowed. "I've been honest with you all night long. I think you owe me a little."

"Fine. I think if I can get her into bed, she's more likely to obey me when the time comes. She'll feel closer to me, and that might be what makes the difference if Iris figures out I haven't stopped investigating."

"Or she'll be so crazy about you she'll do anything you tell her. Is that what you're saying? You want to ensure that she has to stay close to you to protect your cover, and you think that will lead her to sleep with you."

"I never said I wasn't attracted to her." He wasn't sure where Hatch was going with this line of questioning, but he didn't appreciate the way it was making him feel.

"But you still intend to use her."

His hands fisted at his sides. "Tell me you wouldn't do the same thing. I can't allow that woman to stay out there. She's safe and happy and we spent years in hell. My father died because she decided she wanted some cash."

"Oh, Drew, you misunderstand me. I'm not blaming you for wanting revenge on your mama. She started this war, and she's had far too many years of peace as it is. I'm simply worried that if something happens to Shelby, you'll never recover."

"I'll make sure nothing happens. Once I figure out where Iris is, Shelby will be out of the equation." He would send her somewhere safe and deal with the situation himself. He would invoke that nasty clause she'd missed and she would be out of his way.

"You truly think you can control that one?" For the first time in weeks, an amused grin pulled Hatch's lips up. "That might be fun to watch." Hatch nodded toward the stairs. "I think I'll go to bed. I'm going to back off and let you do what you need to. But if it comes down to it, do you really think you can?"

"Can what?"

"Kill Iris? It's the only solution I can see. I can't see you exposing her. It would hurt the family too much. So I have to assume you're going into this with plans to murder your mother."

He felt his jaw tighten. "I haven't thought that far ahead. I need to find her first."

Hatch's head shook slightly. "Now that's the second time you've lied to me tonight. Sleep well, Drew. Tomorrow's another day to plot."

He watched as Hatch walked out.

Drew had always been compared to his father, but he was suddenly afraid he was a bit like his mother, too. It was not a thought that sat well.

He strode into his office. There would be no sleep for him tonight.

Chapter Three

Shelby sat back in her chair, the scent of cinnamon hanging in the air. She'd been asked via text to join Drew in the kitchen. The polite invitation had been waiting on her phone after her shower. She'd hustled and gotten herself ready, certain that she would be ushered into some lavish, servant-heavy meal. There had been a gorgeous buffet laid out, but only two places set and absolutely no sign of staff. "Is Mr. Hatchard not joining us?"

Drew sat down across from her, his plate covered with eggs, bacon, and cinnamon rolls Shelby was almost certain hadn't come out of a can and been heated up. Someone had spent time on those beauties. "Hatch doesn't believe in mornings. We'll go to the office without him and he'll roll in some time this afternoon."

"Where is your chef?"

Drew reached out and picked up the carafe in front of him, pouring coffee into her cup. "Evelyn is taking the rest of the day off to spend with her grandchildren. We'll have lunch at the office and then we've got reservations for this evening."

"The cinnamon rolls look delicious. But seriously, you don't have to make a big show for me. I can get by on a protein bar and some coffee."

"I'm afraid we kind of make a big show of all meals in my family.

You'll find we like to sit down and eat together. I hope you'll join me for meals while you're here."

Because she was supposed to be his girlfriend. "I've been thinking about that. I suppose we're going to be seeing Carly and Bran while we're in Dallas next week."

She had one week to get comfortable around Drew. One week to figure out if she could actually sell this cover to his family.

"It would seem odd if I didn't pay them a visit. Bran knows I have a meeting with Taggart scheduled. We'll be in Dallas for two days. Dinner with Bran and Carly and Mia and Case has already been planned."

"Exactly. And you don't want to raise a bunch of questions. So I was thinking it might be smarter for me to get my own hotel room. I can lie low and they don't have to know I'm in town." She'd sat up for a good portion of the night doing two things: thinking about how much she'd wanted to kiss Drew Lawless and then freaking out about it because that was a bad idea. *Beware of billionaires with six-pack abs.* It was her new mantra. Yes, she'd signed the contract last night, but that didn't mean she couldn't reason with her new . . . boss . . . partner . . . whatever he was.

"I told Bran you're coming with me."

This was exactly what she'd worried about. "You told him? I thought I would have more time. How am I going to explain this to Carly? I think she'll wonder why one of her closest friends didn't mention she was dating her brother-in-law."

"I've already explained it. We wanted to make sure it was real before we went public. It's that simple. We met in Los Angeles. I contacted you. We went on a few dates and we've been talking a lot. You've come out to Austin because we're contemplating moving in together. This is a trial run," he said calmly, as though he hadn't up-ended her entire life. "Also, I asked Bran not to mention it to Carly because you would rather tell her yourself. It was a safe bet Bran wouldn't ask too many questions, but Carly will want to know everything. It's why we need to get our stories straight."

She focused on the words that messed with her life. "Moving in together? You told them we're thinking of moving in together?"

"How else was I supposed to explain it when all your belongings arrive here?"

"What?" She winced because the words had come out in a screech.

"I'm having your things packed up as we speak. They'll be here in a few days."

"Why the hell would you do that?" How was she going to get everything back to LA?

Drew relaxed again as though he'd already gone over this argument in his mind and knew he would win. "I wanted you to be comfortable. This is going to be a full-time job, and not a quick one. I suspect we'll have to keep up our ruse for at least six months. Potentially a year. Also, that apartment you were living in was incredibly dangerous. Did you know it was recently condemned? The movers told me about it when they explained they were charging me extra for how fast they had to move. It's scheduled to be demolished in two weeks."

"What?" She stared at him. He expected her to live with him for six months to a year? Somewhere in the back of her head she'd been thinking a week or two tops, and then she'd go back to LA and work from there. Her apartment building was shitty and she was fairly certain someone cooked meth in part of it, but it was all she could afford. And it was solidly built. There had been no hint that anyone was planning on building in her part of LA. Gentrification had not reared its upscale, hipster head yet, so that left her with one very manipulative bastard. "Tell me you did not buy my apartment building and schedule it for demolition in an attempt to leave me with nowhere to go."

He managed to look almost angelic in the soft light of morning. "I have no idea what you're talking about."

He couldn't have done it. Of course, if anyone could, it was the man in front of her. He could move mountains when he wanted something. One small building in a bad part of town would be absolutely nothing to a man like him. He could pick it up for less than his Maserati and voilà, instant move-in fake girlfriend, because it wasn't like she had a home to go back to. And she wasn't the only one. "You know, Mrs. Harper was a nice lady. She's raising her grandson. I don't care about the other two. They're asshole criminals, but she was a nice lady and she doesn't have the money to find another place."

A single brow rose over his icy blue eyes. "Are you talking about the elderly woman who just won a brand-new house in Santa Clarita from 4L Software? We like to do these pop-up contests every now and then. Strictly to engender goodwill with the public. This one came up to promote our house-of-the-future software. It controls everything in the home from climate to security systems. All from your computer. We gave away one of those, too. I believe her name *was* Harper and her address did seem familiar."

Gwendolyn Harper. Tears immediately sprang to her eyes. Gwen had been her first friend when she'd moved to LA. Gwen had been the one to hold her hand when she had to make Johnny's funeral arrangements. She'd been on a fixed income since her husband had died fifteen years before, and things had gotten tighter after she took in her grandson. She loved Gwen. "Are you serious?"

He shrugged. "It was a contest. She entered on our website. She can't actually remember entering, but I assured her it was real. She must struggle with her memory. I believe she'll discover her grandson has also won a college scholarship from us."

Manipulative, beautiful, arrogant prick. "Stand up."

His eyes widened. "Why?"

She was trying so hard not to cry. She couldn't help it. She was emotional. "Because this is the part where I hug you."

"Oh. Okay." He put his napkin down and stood, still frowning.

It didn't matter. She hugged people who did good in the world. Even if they had ulterior motives. She practically threw herself in his arms. Everyone needed affection. Even Andrew Lawless. Maybe he needed it most of all.

He stood there for a moment and then his arms slowly wound around her. Tentative at first, and then she felt him sigh and his head rested against hers. "Does this mean you forgive me for maybe, possibly buying your apartment building and having it torn down so you can't go back to it and be murdered?"

Sometimes the wrong things happened for the right reasons. "You're paying for me to move back to LA."

"Maybe you won't want to," he said quietly. "Maybe you'll find you like it here. As much as you travel, it's cheaper to fly out of Austin or Dallas. You spend a lot of time in New York. Much shorter trip."

He was so logical. She gently pulled free because if she spent much more time in those muscular arms of his, she might melt. "Thank you for helping my friend."

He nodded, the praise seeming to make him uncomfortable. "You're welcome. But you should know the other two tenants really were thrown out. They were awful."

They were and she wasn't about to argue with him about it. But she definitely had some questions. "How long have you been planning this, Drew?"

"Since the night after Patricia Cain died. I answered your question. Now you answer one of mine. Why are you so afraid of me?"

His hands ran down her arms and she was caught. Oh, she knew if she pulled away, he would let her go, but she felt trapped by the warmth and heat of his big body, by the dark stare of his eyes. "I think you could hurt me if you wanted to."

"I don't want to hurt you, Shelby."

"Then why send the lawyers? If you're telling me the truth, then you sent them even after you decided to hire me."

"I needed time to figure out what I wanted to do. I'm a cautious man. I plot and I plan and I always follow through, but sometimes I have to give myself the time and space to do so. You were moving too quickly. I had to put a stop to it or I worried my sister and brothers would find out that Iris is alive, and I'm trying hard to avoid that until it has to come out."

"They know there was a fourth conspirator." Why did it have to feel so good to be close to him? Why did the man have to smell so good? Like sandalwood and soap.

His hands moved along her arms as though he couldn't make himself stop touching her. "They do, but they know I'm working on it. They'll let it lie for a while. They're caught up in their own lives and that's how it should be."

He was willing to take on the burden for his siblings. She could understand that, even admire it. "All right. If you honestly think this is the best way, then I'll follow your lead. But I worry Carly won't buy it."

"That I'm crazy about you or that you would ever give me the time of day?" His lips had curled up in the sexiest smile. "Did you tell Carly about the lawyers?"

"Yeah, I might have mentioned it. Why are you still holding me?"

"Do you want me to stop? We need to look like we're used to touching."

If he was going to spare his siblings from pain. Damn but he knew how to put her in a corner. Her logical, rational self was telling her they could find another way to make this work. Her body was moving in close like she was magnetically attracted to him. Which she kind of was. "You honestly think this is the way to go?"

He nodded, his hands finding her hips. "I definitely think it's the way to go."

"So according to that contract I'm supposed to be affectionate toward you. Does that mean what I think it means?"

"It means you should get used to kissing me. Or being kissed by me."

"But it's all for show."

One hand came up, smoothing back her hair. "If that's what you want it to be. I'm not going to lie to you. I want this to go somewhere. I'm going to use this time to try to convince you to find some actual affection for me. I think you showed me a weakness that I can exploit."

"I did?"

"Yeah. All I have to do to get a hug is give one of your down-on-her-luck friends a superexpensive home."

He was saying all the right things. He was melting her every defense. When she'd gotten the call, she'd been curious, but not afraid. She knew how to handle an entitled asshole who took himself far too seriously. But this Drew was infinitely more dangerous. This Drew was already making her feel more than she'd felt in years. "I'll make sure you have a list. You probably could use the good karma."

"Very likely," he admitted. "Are you going to kiss me?"

Her heart started to race in her chest as she turned her eyes up to look at him. He was a lovely man. From his blue eyes to that jawline that looked as if it had been carved from marble, Drew Lawless was a walking fantasy. "I thought alpha men liked to do the kissing."

It was only for their cover. That was all. She wasn't sure why he was telling her it could be something more. They didn't work on a fundamental level. It was insane to think they could. Maybe he was lonely. Just because he was a billionaire didn't mean he didn't have issues.

"I thought I would bow to the alpha female in the room," he said. "I know you're not going to believe this, but I don't want to fuck this up. Because of the case we're investigating and because I want you to like me. I told you before I can be awkward. I don't really have much of a personal life."

Because building a billion-dollar empire hadn't left him a lot of time to date. "Not a ton of girlfriends, then?"

He stepped back, a wary smile on his face as he sat down. "No. I've dated a bit, but it was mostly friends-with-benefits situations and mostly with coworkers. I'm sorry. I'm pushing you too fast. I suppose my family will understand that we don't do public displays of affection. I can be a bit chilly."

But he didn't want to be. What if he didn't know how to reach out and ask for what he wanted?

He was exactly the kind of man who would plan and scheme to get what he wanted because he didn't trust anyone enough to simply ask. This whole stupid, crazed plan was Drew Lawless's way of asking. She still wasn't sure it was a good idea, but she found she couldn't leave him sitting there alone.

She moved in front of him before he could pull his chair back up. "Were you affectionate with your friends with benefits? Was comfort and tenderness a benefit for you?"

He went still, suspicion plain on his face. "No. A date consisted of fucking and then talking about work. I never introduced any of them to my family. I chose logical, practical women. Women who understood it was purely physical."

"Sex is more than simply physical, Drew. When you're in love with someone, you want to be around them. Physical affection is how you show the person you love that you need him or her." Maybe he needed more from her than a story. "I'm going to sit in your lap and we're going to talk. Is that all right?"

A smile that was pure masculine anticipation hit his face. "Yeah."

"Hey, this is all an academic pursuit," she said with a laugh because she knew damn well she was lying. She lowered herself down and he curled his arms around her, one on her waist and the other against her knee.

"Understood," he said a bit solemnly. "So you've been in love?"

"You haven't?" She settled in, letting her arm drift up to his shoulders. It should have been awkward but somehow they seemed to fit.

"With the logical, practical women?" Drew asked with a chuckle. "No. The funny thing is, one of those women went completely batshit crazy over one of my engineers. I didn't understand it at the time. She would get so upset, when she was such a reasonable woman. They're married with two kids now, and she still loses her shit from time to time when he pisses her off."

"Because she loves him."

"So because she loves him she cries at the oddest times? He'll send her flowers and she cries. I don't get that. And my sister. She fell for Case and when he pissed her off, she ended up roaming the globe for six months trying to forget him. One or two voice mails when she got home, and she was all over him again."

Somehow she thought there was more to the story than that. "Because she couldn't really live without him."

"I thought my father and mother were in love."

She sighed and did what came naturally. She reached up and stroked his hair. He was always the slightest bit messy, his hair the tiniest bit too long to be truly under control. "I know you did. I did, too, when I was a child."

His eyes closed, like a large cat enjoying a pet. "They didn't stay together?"

"I thought you knew everything."

His eyes opened slightly. "I would rather hear it from you."

He'd been honest with her. She couldn't pay that back by withholding and, besides, she'd dealt with it long ago. She cuddled against him, his arms tightening. How long had it been since she felt needed? Since she'd felt the twist of desire deep in her soul? "My father left when I was a kid. My brother and I got the big sit-down talk. The one about how it wasn't our fault and he would always be our dad, but he needed to find himself, blah, blah, blah. He and Mom got married too young and he couldn't possibly be a good father until he was happy with who he was. Apparently that took a twenty-year-old waitress, and from what I understand he's a pretty good father to their kids."

"So he remarried and had more kids and expected you all to get along?" Drew asked.

"I've never met them," she explained, a wistful tone to her voice. "He came to see us a couple of times after the divorce, but he moved to Florida after he married her and then we got cards for a while. He sent me a hundred bucks when I graduated."

"My mother murdered my father and tried to kill me, then shot my brother."

So competitive. "You win."

His hand moved along her leg, but there was something soothing about it. "Sorry. I wasn't trying to win. I guess I was just trying to say we have something in common. Really shitty parents."

"My mother was wonderful. It was funny but she almost seemed to bloom after he was gone. She didn't date much, but she seemed to enjoy herself. She threw herself into work and me and my brother and her girlfriends. I miss her. I miss my brother."

"I don't know what I would have done if I hadn't had Riley and Bran and Mia to think about," Drew admitted quietly. "I couldn't give up because they needed me."

"I wasn't too young when I lost her. I was an adult and she was sick for a long time. It didn't make it easier. It only meant I accepted it more quickly. Losing my brother still aches." And talking about them made her realize how much she missed having a family.

"If there was any way to prove that Patricia had him killed, I would do it. You have to know that."

"I do. And you should know that I'm going to write the absolute best story I can. I'm going to be discreet and I'm not going to make it sensationalized. People should know that your father wasn't the monster they made him out to be."

"Are you ever going to kiss me?"

He was deflecting and she knew it, but she supposed he'd opened up enough for one day. She tilted her head up and reached for his face, cupping his cheek with her hand. "To prove we can make this work? That we can fool your family?"

"Haven't figured it out yet? I want to prove we have chemistry. I want to prove that we can work together and play together and not because we've both got an itch to scratch. I'm sick of that, and I knew it the first time I saw you. I want to be the reason you need, Shelby. I want to be the only one you want. I'm willing to take the risk that you'll use me for the time we're together because I want you that badly. So kiss me because you want to. Kiss me because it's part of our cover. I don't care why as long as you kiss me."

She brushed her lips against his, her whole body seeming to come to life. His lips were soft, his hands tight. He was enveloping her and she was completely defenseless against him.

She wrapped her arms around him as the kiss deepened, and suddenly she didn't want to play it safe anymore. She'd been in her shell for so long and she wanted to come out of it, wanted to feel again. She dragged her tongue over his lower lip, and it seemed to awaken the beast in Drew.

He took over, the kiss going from sweet to carnal in an instant. His mouth opened, tongue sliding over hers and dominating with strength and a sensuality she'd never come across before. He kissed her long and hard, his hands molding to the curves of her body. Over and over again his tongue danced with hers. Never before had a kiss seemed so effortless. It was like they'd been kissing forever.

For a man who claimed he was socially awkward, he sure could kiss like a god.

It was getting out of hand, but she didn't care. Nothing mattered except getting more of him. She could feel his cock under her, hardening, lengthening, getting ready for what it was meant to do. He could ease her back against the table, pull off her jeans and panties. It would be incendiary, like a rocket going off, an explosion she couldn't contain. She could feel herself getting soft and wet and ready for him, as though her body had recognized its natural mate and wasn't taking no for an answer.

"See, I told you we have chemistry." His words rumbled along her lips.

She couldn't argue with him. The world around them seemed hazy and unreal. There was nothing except his touch and scent and the sight of his eyes looking at her like he could eat her up. She knew she should stop him, knew it was getting out of control, but she couldn't find the will. It had been so damn long since she wanted something she could actually have.

She wanted him.

Shelby let her fingers sink into his hair, drawing him back down. Breakfast could wait. She needed more of him.

"Should I grab some coffee and go?"

Shelby shrieked and would have fallen out of Drew's lap had he not tightened his arms around her.

"You should have quietly left," Drew said with a frown.

Bill Hatchard wore pajama bottoms and a robe wrapped around his lean body. He yawned and moved to the buffet. "I didn't see a sock on the kitchen door. That's how we did it back in the day. If you require privacy, hang a sock on the doorknob and I'll know to stay out of that particular room. Ah, cinnamon rolls."

They had an odd relationship. Part father-son, part odd couple. All awkward right this second. "I should finish eating and then get ready. I assume you have a space for me to work at the office?"

He pouted down at her, the expression making him look like a gorgeous boy about to lose his favorite toy. "I've already set everything up for you."

He was going to be so much trouble. She couldn't help herself. She wanted to see the man smile. She leaned over and kissed him, a mere brushing of the lips, but it had the intended effect. His mouth curled up in a self-satisfied grin, and he watched as she moved back to her seat. She settled in as Drew and Hatch began sniping at one another over codes and business plans.

It was the first time in forever she hadn't eaten breakfast alone. It was a nice feeling.

One week later, Drew sat down across from Ian Taggart and frowned. He looked out over the Dallas skyline. Taggart's office was a little like Drew's own—built to impress. Somehow all Drew could think about was Shelby and how the game was about to change.

The last week had been both perfect and perfectly frustrating. Shelby had settled in nicely, though she was still in her own room. She and Hatch were warily circling each other, but his house seemed so much more complete with Shelby there.

Their story was working beautifully on his staff. No one had questioned the fact that he would give the gorgeous redhead anything she wanted. She had her own office and a few employees who were helping her with research. They'd been carefully selected by Drew and were bound by ironclad NDAs.

He'd enjoyed the week with her. But he didn't like the fact that he was stuck in a meeting now with the man they all called Big Tag, and Shelby was hanging out in the break room.

The massive hunk of muscle handled all of 4L's physical security, and the team ran background checks for his human resources department. Taggart was former Special Forces and, according to his brother, used to work for the CIA. Drew had zero difficulty seeing the man doing wet work for a shadowy government agency most of the time. Today, however, he had a sleeping baby draped over his shoulder, his big hand balancing the tiny thing against him. He was almost certain that Taggart was about to fall asleep.

"So no news on Francine Wells?" They'd already gone over Taggart's security plans for the reception. Drew would love to have walked away after that, but he needed to see if Taggart was still working on finding Francine.

Taggart's eyes opened. "Oh, Wells. Yeah, um, according to the records we found, she died a few years ago. Completely bogus, apparently, but that shit was well done, according to Adam. I've got a report with all the paperwork. Hopefully it's in one piece. If it's got spit-up on it, Grace can print it out again."

He was never having children. Apparently they were messy. "Why don't you give me the rundown?"

"Francine Wells," Taggart said as though he needed to prompt his memory. "She left Dallas shortly after your parents were murdered, moved to New York, and was briefly on the payroll of a start-up company called StratCast."

Well, of course she was. StratCast was the company that had been built on his father's genius. "What did she do there?"

"She worked as a legal secretary, which I found odd because she was involved in coding projects at your father's company. She left after a few years and, from what we can tell, she moved to Ponte Vedra Beach in Florida."

Ah, but Drew didn't find it odd at all since his mother had been trained as a lawyer. "The move fits. It's fairly close to St. Augustine. We know from Carly that she was working with Patricia for many years. The workers at Cain Corp thought she was some old lady Patricia was using."

"Because she never actually showed her face at the office," Taggart continued. "Patricia would go away for the weekend and return with all sorts of new ideas. According to banking records, over the course of the ten years Francine spent working with Patricia, she collected almost five million dollars off the books."

That was interesting. "Who collected the money when Francine died? And how did she pull that off?"

"Money can cover up almost anything," Taggart said, sitting back. "She died, and I use that in the most figurative way possible, in a car accident. Her sister, Anna, had the body cremated quickly. She collected her sister's bank accounts, sold her house, and disappeared off the face of the earth, which was probably easy since I'm fairly certain she didn't exist. Francine was an only child."

Naturally, his mother would have been careful and the bank wouldn't have had an issue with it as long as she'd shown up with all the proper documentation. "And this was how long ago?"

"She died four years ago. As far as I can tell, she vanished shortly after she collected her own life insurance. That was another two million."

It begged a couple of questions. "Why leave when she'd been with Patricia all those years before? What was happening four years ago at Cain Corp?"

"I don't think it had anything to do with Cain Corp. You got sloppy. Open the folder." Taggart gestured to the file folder on his desk.

Drew turned the top of the file folder to his left while Taggart hummed and patted the baby. He seemed to know what he was doing because the boy immediately quieted and seemed to go back to sleep. Drew, on the other hand, sighed. It was the cover of a national magazine with the headline *America's Next Bill Gates?* and a picture of him. A photographer had caught him coming out of 4L's office. It was precisely why he now always left via the underground parking garage or the helicopter on the roof. The article had come after 4L released its latest software, and the stock had gone soaring.

"Francine Wells died exactly two weeks after this came out. I think she recognized you. Apparently having the victim that got away turn into a billionaire power player spooked the woman." The tiny thing started to wiggle. Taggart merely stood and started pacing, his long legs bouncing to some rhythm he could hear only in his head.

"Apparently." He should have been more careful. He'd had his siblings change their last names to avoid too many questions, but he'd kept the Lawless name because he couldn't stand the thought of not honoring his father. And the arrogance was there, too. He'd wanted them to see he was one Lawless they couldn't control.

Stupid. At the time he'd only been thinking about Stratton, Castalano, and Cain. They couldn't know he was onto them, and the trio had been more than happy to leave him and his siblings alone for twenty years. They thought they'd gotten away with it, so why bother coming after the kids? It would have been risky.

His mother was an entirely different predator.

Taggart eased the kid down onto one of those things parents hauled around so their kids could sleep on the go, and stood looking down at him for a moment. "Hopefully he'll sleep for a while. God knows he doesn't do it at night."

"Don't you have a daycare here or something?" He didn't entirely understand the McKay-Taggart world, though it was already creeping into his own. Mia had been talking about on-site daycare at 4L.

"Sure, but you only get this first year once. I'll blink and Seth will be a teenager, so I'm going to enjoy this time as much as I can." He moved back to his desk. "So, are you aware there were rumors that your father had an affair with Francine?"

"I was made aware of the affair," he stated blandly, as though the idea didn't turn his gut. "Hatch never mentioned it until after we discovered she was somehow involved. I suppose he didn't want to bust my illusions about Dad."

"Yeah, I suppose." Taggart sat back with a yawn that made him resemble a somewhat sleepy lion. "Funny thing, parents. They tend to turn out to be all too human, but then we understand that when we get to be adults."

"Maybe if you grow up with your parents. It's different when they're taken from you. I didn't get to fight with my father. I didn't get to do the teenage rebellion thing. For me, he'll always be the man I knew as a kid. It's hard to process."

"Is that why the police hid the sketch of Francine? How did you manage that, by the way? Adam wasn't even able to find it."

He wondered if Miles would get curious. "As you said, money can hide a multitude of sins, Mr. Taggart. I don't need my siblings to stare at the picture of my father's former mistress. I was lucky to keep most of our involvement out of the press. Rest assured, I still have a copy if it's needed."

"Good, because it's needed. I have a few theories I want to run down. I talked to a couple of people Carly directed me to, some of Patricia's inner circle. They didn't remember meeting a Francine Wells, but they did know a woman named Leah Walker who often traveled with Patricia during the time before Francine died. She fits the same profile except Patricia was trying to introduce her to wealthy men. I believe this Leah Walker is possibly a black widow and she's used several names over the years, including her original name, Francine Wells."

"All right, what does that have to do with the sketch?" He could buy that his mother had multiple aliases.

"I want to run it through facial recognition. Adam has a prototype software that can do amazing things."

"I know. I'm going to sell it for him." For a cut of his profits, but it would still make Adam Miles a very wealthy man. "But I think I'll deal with this myself from here on out."

Taggart's eyes narrowed and suddenly he didn't seem so sleepy anymore. "Really? And why would you do that?"

This was what he'd wanted to avoid, but cutting ties to McKay-Taggart would have brought up more questions. "I think we all need a break."

"That's why you pay me an enormous amount of money to deal with this for you."

"I want us to concentrate on the future for a while. Not the past."

"Is that why you made an appointment with the Dallas Police Department this afternoon?" Taggart dropped a bomb into the middle of their conversation.

Motherfucker. "I made that appointment privately. It has nothing to do with you."

Taggart shook his head and sighed, his disappointment obvious. "Well, you should be happy the chief called to ask if I would be providing security and how I wanted to deal with it. There's no such thing as privacy for you. You're one of the wealthiest men in America. Your name opens doors but it invites people to come in with you, too. Even cops gossip, and you would have been met with paparazzi if they hadn't called me."

He hadn't even thought about that. He'd assumed the police would be discreet. But of course there was always someone willing to talk, and he was an interesting subject.

"I told them they misunderstood and that you certainly wouldn't be visiting the station to talk about your parents' closed case. I then called my contact and had him bring the file here." Taggart moved on. "So are you going to explain to me why you're cutting me out and bringing in a reporter? You know, I'm the one who ran the background check on Shelby Gates when she came on the scene. I know exactly what she does and I know that you all but hit her with a restraining order a few months ago, yet today you bring her into these offices holding her hand like she's your girlfriend."

He should have known Taggart would prove observant. "She is my girlfriend."

"Oh, I buy that you're sleeping with her. She's a gorgeous woman, but she's also a do-gooder. She was looking into your parents' case, hence all your lawyers. What changed between then and now?"

He didn't like the interrogation, but tried to hold on to his patience. "Not that it's any of your business, but we started dating a few weeks ago."

"Do you think she's manipulating you in order to get a story?"

Oh, sweet Shelby wasn't the manipulative one. "Not at all. I've had her sign a nondisclosure agreement. Look, Taggart, I think Mia and my brothers need a break, so I'm going to try to be discreet going forward. I want this time with Shelby. I want to see if we can make it work."

Taggart stared at him for a moment as though he was about to call him on the lie. "So you're lonely and horny. That's what you're telling me. You're giving up the idea of finding the last conspirator in the deaths of your parents so you can get laid."

Put like that it sounded pretty stupid. If Taggart had been a normal contractor, he would have told him to mind his own damn business. Unfortunately, the asshole was family and one Drew had come to value. He couldn't put off his suspicions so easily. "Look, I just think I need to take this slow and be in control. You know what Francine told Carly."

"That if you backed off she would leave your siblings alone."

"How far would you go for one of your brothers?"

"You know I'd do anything."

It was his turn to push Taggart a little. "Even when 'anything' wasn't in the best interests of justice? I suspect you would. I have to dig deeper, but I think I can do that more discreetly with Shelby than with you. Francine will be watching you and your whole company. I'm sure she's well aware of everything I do at this point, and we're far too connected."

"And you don't think she's watching your personal life?"

"All she'll see is me with a pretty girl having a meeting with the company that runs my security and the man who happens to be my sister's brother-in-law. We'll go out to dinner tonight with my family and make plans for Riley and Ellie's reception. All normal, especially since you saved me the trap of walking into the police station. Did they send a plainclothes with the file?"

"Absolutely," Taggart assured him. "He's a lieutenant and he's got a lot of ties to this company. He brought the file in and he'll take it back out in a plain box."

"All right."

A moment of uncomfortable silence passed before Taggart spoke again, his voice low and grave. "Promise me if this gets dangerous you'll call me, Drew."

"I will. Right now I'm doing nothing more than testing a theory." He didn't intend to do anything more than research at this point.

"Yes, I have a few of those, too. But I'll back off if you want me to. I do understand what it means to protect family, but you can't do it at the cost of your own life."

"It's all going to be fine. I'm going to let Shelby do what she does and we'll go from there. After we get what we need here, we're heading to Austin and we'll be there for a few months."

"You need to watch your back. Even when you think you're private." Taggart winced as his son tuned up and proved that even baby lions could roar. "Call me if you need me. The lieutenant's waiting in the conference room."

The door to the office opened, and a tall woman with strawberry-blond hair strode in. Charlotte Taggart walked right to the baby and eased him up and into her arms. She looked her husband's way. "I'll take Seth. You take a nap."

She leaned over and kissed Taggart.

Yeah, he definitely didn't want the screaming infant, but he kind of longed for the intimacy they had. His house had been lonely since Bran moved out. They were all gone, and he was left with Hatch and a bunch of people who took care of them because Drew paid well.

A hand touched his shoulder and suddenly Shelby was there. He reached up and threaded his fingers through hers, enjoying the warmth for once. "We have a change of plans, sweetheart."

"All right," she said, a sparkle in her eye as she looked over at the baby. "I'm game. What are we doing?"

He'd already discovered that Shelby seemed to go with the flow, and that was a good thing in his world. "We're skipping the police station. The files are all here."

Her attention moved quickly back to him. "Oh, now you're talking, Lawless. Let's get going. Those files aren't going to read themselves."

He stood, not letting go of her hand. In the last week, he'd learned that she hugged a lot, liked to kiss for a long time, and all he had to do to rev her up was give her a murder to solve.

As he led her down the hall, he prayed he learned enough to keep her when it all fell apart.

Chapter Four

T hank you, Lieutenant Brighton." Shelby shook hands with the hunky cop. He was definitely prettier than the last man who had allowed her to study the evidence. A few months back she'd been shown into a dank, cramped room by a man who looked like he never smiled and who had admonished that if she ruined anything, there would be hell to pay.

"You're welcome," the lieutenant said. "I'll be in the break room if you need anything. Let me know when you're done. I assume since you were the last one to open the file that you know how to handle it."

"I'll put it all back in the same order." The file had been repacked and taped together after her last viewing, and she could plainly see that she'd been the last person to sign for it.

The lieutenant nodded and produced a small knife to cut open the taped box. "Be careful with it."

"We will," Drew said, his eyes on the box like it was a snake that might bite him.

And it was. That was Pandora's box to the Lawless family, all their secrets and sins laid bare. All the horror that had ripped them apart neatly contained in one aging cardboard box.

The door closed behind the lieutenant, and Drew switched his focus to her. "That man was flirting with you. I think he's married."

Drew was excellent at deflecting. "He was being charming. He was definitely not flirting."

"He winked at you."

"I believe that was his way of wishing me luck with this."

"You don't need luck," Drew said, his tone grumpy. "It's a box of evidence. How did your talk with Charlotte Taggart go? You walked in with her. I assume that means you spent some time with her."

She'd found Charlotte Taggart to be very illuminating. "She knows a lot about the case. Did you know that the assassin hired to kill your parents had a brother?"

He was staring at the box of evidence. "I read it in one of the reports. I don't think he's important."

"You haven't talked to him?" It seemed like an oversight.

"What could he tell me that I don't already know?"

"Do you mind if I try talking to him?" Sometimes brothers saw things other people didn't. After all these years maybe he would talk in a way he wouldn't have right after the crime.

"Sure, ring him up if you like," Drew replied. "Let's open this sucker up and get a move on."

"Why don't you let me find what we're looking for?" He didn't need to see the photos.

"I can handle it, Shelby."

She had zero doubt that he could. The question was whether he should.

"Do you trust me, Drew?" She put a hand on his chest. She'd rapidly learned the man responded to touch.

He frowned down at her, but his hand came up to cover her own. "As much as I trust anyone. More, I suppose."

"You don't have to see those pictures because your dad's not there. He was gone long before those pictures were taken, and there's nothing about looking at them that will help you in any way. Let me find the relevant reports and you can read them, but those pictures will stay with you in a way I don't want them to."

"You've seen them."

"Yes, and they've haunted me and I wasn't his child."

"I saw him on the floor, but the fire had already started. I tried to get to him, but it blasted me back." He seemed to shake off the memory. With a squeeze of her hand, he stepped back. "Go ahead. I suppose I don't need more fuel for my nightmares."

He turned away, looking out the window at the buildings around him. "Tell me why you decided to investigate this case."

It was a good first step. He was allowing her to make some decisions, and she knew that was hard for him. His childhood had been out of control, from what she could tell, and it had turned him into a man who wanted to control everything around him. "I found out my best friend in the world was getting cozy with your brother, and I take care of my friends."

"Ah," he said, his eyes still on the skyline. "So that's why you went looking. And you met Carly while you were investigating your own brother's murder."

He was the first person ever who simply called it what it was. Everyone else in her life called it Johnny's "death," as though they weren't sure what to call something that hadn't been proven. Drew didn't use any such euphemism. "Yes. I contacted her because she could answer some of my questions."

"How did you know she wouldn't be loyal to her boss? For that matter, how did you know she hadn't been in on it?"

"She seemed nice. She didn't seem like the type of person who would help plan a murder."

"You need a keeper, sweetheart," he grumbled with a shake of his head. "You need to understand that anyone can kill someone given the right circumstances. Carly would have killed my mother that night."

"In defense of Bran, yes. She certainly wouldn't kill to protect her boss's reputation." She sighed at his cynicism and turned her attention to the box in front of her, opening the top and sliding it away. There it all was, the evidence involved in a murder no one would ever prosecute because there was so little to be had.

The first things in the file were the pictures taken by the CSI agents working the crime scene. They lay faceup. She'd put them there herself, careful to replace every single item in the same order as she'd taken them out. Except she was almost certain the pictures had begun with an overall view of the ruined house. This set began with the charred remains of Benedict Lawless. He was ash and bone, his skeleton exposed. There was a gun close to his corpse, as though he'd tossed it aside after having killed his wife. His lover. Whoever Francine had been to him.

She was positive she hadn't put that picture on top of the file. It was the most gruesome of the photos. She'd shrunk back from it when she'd seen it.

Her first thought had been *how could anyone hate someone so much?*

"Did you find it?" Drew asked.

"Give me a second." She placed the photos facedown and continued to work her way through. "I have to leave everything the way I found it. You know the gun's not in here, right?"

"It's in a different lockup," he replied. "Do you think we need to see it?"

"No," she replied, suspicion creeping into her brain. "They didn't find fingerprints. The fire was so hot it damaged the gun as well. You can turn around. I've got the pictures covered."

He moved quickly, as though he hated being left out. Likely he had.

"Is that the medical examiner's report? That's a thick file. Somehow it doesn't seem like as much on the screen."

Drew was the type of man who viewed everything through the filter of a screen. It was precisely why she hadn't wanted him to look at those photos. Something about holding them in her hands made them very real, and he didn't need that. "Yes, it's quite thorough. Lots of information all adding up to the same conclusion. Both victims died of bullet wounds."

She pulled the ME report. The official one was in front, but she was interested in the secondary report, the one at the back of the file. She remembered that report so vividly because she stared at it forever. It had been clipped together by a small silver paper clip.

"I've looked through it but I don't have a lot of medical experience."

"The theory is your father set the fire, then shot your mother and himself." She flipped through the paperwork, looking for the intern's report.

"Yes, and they also believe he covered her body in gasoline and that's why there was next to nothing of her left. I read a report that this was his way of completely obliterating my mother's existence," he said, bitterness plain in his tone. "It always bugged me that they would take pains to get rid of my mother's body and not take the same care with him. Now I know why."

Yes, it had bothered her as well, but now something bothered her even more.

Shelby stared for a moment and then checked the top of the lid again. The checkout paperwork was still the same. Years of inactivity and then a single person who had looked through the file on police property. Her signature was clear as day. Shelby Gates. No one else.

Then where had that report and its little silver clip gone?

"It's not here," she said quietly. "Could you pass me the police reports and the DA's folder? Maybe I didn't put it back properly."

Her hands were shaking because it had been sealed. He reached out and put a hand over hers.

"Shelby, calm down. Everything's all right."

But it wasn't. "I was the last person to see this evidence. Look. I was the last person to sign in."

"You weren't the last person to see it, obviously." He took her hand in both of his. "Do you honestly believe my mother would sign in and then steal the documents she needed? She would never sign in. She would find a way to cover her tracks. She would bribe someone. She probably even had someone watching the DPD computer systems. Stay right here."

She heard him striding to the door and then it closing.

It was gone. Her best evidence was gone. Except it wasn't. She took a deep breath because she'd been smart. She'd taken a picture and then transferred it to her computer. It was sitting on her laptop. That bitch could try to cover it up, but Shelby had tangled with the best. She set down the files and crossed to where she'd left her bag. The big purse might not be a stunning designer bag, but it carried everything she needed, including her laptop. She pulled it out and flipped the top open. She almost never turned it off, a fact that would get her a hearty lecture from the tech guru, but it made her damn happy at the moment. She was able to locate the file where she kept all her notes on the Lawless murders.

Except there were no files. The menu was completely empty. She could see where she'd started the file, but there was nothing in there. No tab marked *police reports* or *witness accounts*. No file where she'd gathered all the media she could find.

Weeks' worth of work completely wiped out.

She closed the laptop, slamming it down.

What the hell had happened?

The door came open again and Drew strode in, followed by Lieutenant Brighton.

The police officer was frowning as he walked to the evidence box. "Mr. Lawless said there was something missing?"

She looked up at Drew. Would he even believe her? Or would he think she'd made the whole thing up in order to get close to him, to get the real information? It wouldn't be the first time someone had lied in order to get what they wanted out of him. Would he even give her a ride back to LA or would she find herself without a way to get home?

Without a home at all.

Damn it.

"There used to be a report from the intern along with the medical examiner's report. It was important."

Brighton quickly flipped through the papers. "I don't see anything like that. And I don't see the content file. There should be a page listing everything that's in this folder."

Great. There went her proof that it even existed. "I didn't see it in there. It was there the last time I examined the evidence."

Brighton's eyes came up, the first sign that he was getting wary. "All right. I made sure the evidence box was properly sealed before I came here. I'm not sure what could have happened."

"It's worse. I made a copy of the report in question." She knew she was digging a deep hole for herself, but she was a rip-the-bandage-off kind of girl. Anticipation of pain was way worse than the actual pain. Well, not really. The pain sucked and so did worrying about it, so it was far better to get to the agony and get through it. "I kept it on my computer with the rest of my investigation finds. It's all gone."

"Shit," Drew cursed. "Is it connected to Wi-Fi?"

"Not right now it isn't, but I usually connect wherever I am." The Wi-Fi in the building required a password and she hadn't asked for it. She'd only brought the computer along out of habit. She was never without the laptop. If she had time to kill she would hop on and write, either on one of the stories she had going or on the novel she was one day going to finish if she ever got the time.

"I know the password," Brighton offered.

Drew held up a hand. "I don't want it. If there was a breach, it didn't happen here. It likely happened at a public hot spot. Unless you want to tell me you don't use the Wi-Fi at the coffeehouse you take breaks at."

She hadn't even thought about it. She'd taken to having afternoon coffee at a shop down the street from the 4L office and she used the Wi-Fi there. Just yesterday she'd been on it, looking through her file. "I do."

Drew nodded. "Lieutenant, I thank you for your help, but I think we can safely say that the evidence box has been compromised. You might want to check the rest of the evidence as well. I think you have a leak in the department."

"Shit." Brighton picked up the files and turned them over, but something slipped out of his hands and onto the floor.

Drew bent over to pick it up for the officer and froze.

Shelby realized what he was looking at. The first of the photos, the one of Benedict that should have been on the bottom, was in his hand and he was staring down at it, his father's body burnt and charred and yet somehow still recognizable in a small way.

"I'll take that," she offered.

He turned it over, his expression not changing a bit. His face was shut down and there was a blankness in his eyes that disturbed the hell out of her. He stopped again, staring at the back of the photo. "Was this here the last time you saw it?"

She glanced down and was horrified to see that someone had used a marker to draw a small red heart on the back of the photo. "No. I . . . I don't think so. And it wasn't where I left it. I tried to keep the photos in the same order they were in, but that one was on top when I opened the box."

"The scene photos should have been first." A grim look crossed Brighton's face. "This should have been at the back of the pile, but then again it's obvious someone fucked with this. I'll have to open an investigation."

"And tip off the woman who's behind this?" Drew's tone was even, as though seeing his father's ruined body was an everyday occurrence. "This is a solved case, Lieutenant. I think that would be ridiculous and a waste of the department's time. Let it lie."

His mother had likely been the one to lay that photo out like an offering to whoever opened the box next. A promise. A threat of what would happen.

Had she thought it would be one of her children? Had she known and wanted the first thing they saw to be what she'd done to their father?

Brighton took the photo and placed everything back in the box. "I understand. You're probably right, but I might be interested in pursuing a quiet investigation of who could have been in this box."

"Go do what you need to do." Drew sat down and reached for her laptop. "Again, thank you for your aid and your discretion."

He flipped open the lid of her laptop and turned his attention to the screen.

No one could dismiss a person quite like Andrew Lawless. It was like they'd ceased to exist for him. Brighton took the box and left, leaving her alone with a man who wouldn't look at her.

"Do you need my password?" She wasn't sure what he was looking for. It had to be either the missing files or evidence that someone had deleted them.

"I'm already in," he replied, his voice a bland monotone. "You have to be more creative. It took me two tries to figure out it's your brother's name and his birthday. People are too sentimental. A passcode should be something randomly generated."

"Drew, I think we should talk." She needed to know what was going through that brilliant brain of his.

"I need to work and I need to be alone. You asked me to trust you. Well, I'm asking the same of you." He never once turned away from the system.

He was typing away, working in some foreign language she

couldn't understand. He'd pulled up a long stream of what looked like complete gibberish to her.

She could push the issue or she could give him a couple of minutes with the computer. A few minutes where he could be in control.

It might be the only peace she could give him for now. But what if he was going through her every file, looking for ways to pin this all on her?

She took a deep breath and let it go. If he needed to go through her files to give himself assurance that she wasn't working against him, that was all right.

"Can I get you anything?"

He frowned and looked up. "What?"

"Like a bottle of water?"

His brow furrowed as though the thought rattled him on some level. "Can you call my brother and tell him we've had a change of plans? I want to go home tonight."

Because sitting across from Bran and Carly would be torture after what he'd seen this afternoon. "Yes. I'll talk to Carly."

He turned back to the computer, but his shoulders had relaxed slightly. "And call the pilot. We'll need a car here in an hour or so."

He was treating her like his assistant or something, but it was okay. She was willing to do almost anything in order to get that stark look out of his eyes.

"I will." She started for the door.

"Shelby?"

She turned, but he was still staring at the screen. "Yes?"

"I know you're telling me the truth. Don't think I'm angry with you. I don't process things properly all the time."

Her heart softened. "It's okay. It's going to be okay, Drew."

He fell silent again, lost to the only world he felt truly comfortable in. Shelby walked out and began to arrange their trip home.

The plane leveled out and Shelby looked through the window at the night sky, the lights of DFW sparkling under her. It had been hours and Drew was still drawn into himself. In roughly forty minutes they would land, and she wasn't sure what would happen then. A limo would pick them up and they would go to their separate rooms and he would brood all night. That was the likeliest outcome.

"Bran was disappointed," she murmured as the flight attendant handed them each three fingers of Scotch.

Drew sat back and took a long sip before nodding to the flight attendant, which seemed to be her cue to exit. "I've disappointed him most of his life, so it shouldn't come as a huge surprise."

Mopey Drew. Yeah, she was getting a full dose of him. "He wanted to see you. That was all. Carly wanted me to tell you she misses you, too."

He stared out the window. He was lonely. He might never admit it, but it was easy to see he had no idea what to do without his siblings to take care of. And Hatch had stayed behind in Dallas to talk to some new investors and show them a good time. If it weren't for Drew's penchant for tearing down perfectly terrible buildings, she might be on her way back to LA and he would be completely alone.

Why couldn't the man simply ask for what he wanted? The answer came fairly easily as she sat staring at him. Drew had learned the hard way that nothing in life was free.

She set down her drink. She couldn't forget the fact that he hadn't even questioned her in front of the lieutenant. "Why did you believe me when I told you the files had been erased?"

He finally looked up, his brow furrowing in consternation. "What?"

"I'm just saying it would have been easy for you to look at the evidence and assume I was lying to you."

"Why would you lie to me?"

"Any number of reasons." She'd thought about it all afternoon.

"I know you weren't lying, Shelby. If it helps, I knew what was happening the moment you told me the report was missing." He knocked back the rest of the drink, finishing it off. "I knew she'd probably had someone watching the file and that she'd figured out what you had discovered and managed to get rid of it. I also realized when she figured out who you were, she probably had taken over your system."

She shuddered. Drew had found the malware that had infected Shelby's computer. She hadn't even realized what was happening. She'd been going on about her days, instant messaging her friends and going on social media, never realizing someone was watching her every move. Not someone. Iris Lawless.

"Still, I was worried for a few minutes that you would think I'd made the whole thing up."

"I'm a suspicious person," he admitted. "But I'm also fairly good at reading people. You're not the lying type. So don't worry about it. Tomorrow I'll go back to work and you'll start again. I'll get you a clean system and untraceable Internet, though I think it's best if you still use the system she's watching. Because we weren't hooked up to Wi-Fi while we were in the McKay-Taggart building, she can't know you tried to access the files and discovered they're gone. I erased all evidence that you were even in that part of your system. When she looks through your activity next, she won't see anything but the fact that you watch too many puppy videos and you're writing a smutty book."

"What?" Pure embarrassment flashed through her system. "You went through my book?"

His lips curved up slightly. "Only enough to know that you have no problem with dirty talk and apparently are pretty open-minded when it comes to sex. I had to check through your whole system. Tell me something. Did you actually tell Carly I'm sex on a stick?"

That bastard. "I also said you were Satan incarnate."

He shrugged. "I've been called worse."

"How could you read my e-mails? You said you didn't suspect me."

"I didn't. Reading your e-mails had nothing to do with suspecting you and everything to do with the fact that my mother knows things about you I don't and it makes me want to hurt her." He turned back to the window. "She left that photograph for one of us. She planted it there because she thought me or Riley or Bran or Mia would be the next to open that box. She practically signed it. I wanted to see something sweet. If you'd had nude pictures of yourself on that system, I would have looked at them, too. I would have done it to make myself feel better. That's the kind of person I am. You should think about that."

Yes, he was all that and so much more. The one thing he didn't seem to do was lie, and it wouldn't have taken much for him to see the e-mails since she'd marked them plainly. The message line of the one he'd referenced was *Drew Lawless Is an Asshole*. She probably would have read that one, too.

And the book had been on her screen when she handed over the laptop. She cringed at the thought of the scene she'd been on. The superhot nerd had been dirty talking her uptight reporter heroine.

Yeah, she might have a few fantasies about the man. She'd started the damn book two years before, and her hero had been a big, gorgeous, dark-haired lawyer who'd morphed over the last few months into a blond tech god. She might have her own issues to work through.

He was lonely. She was lonely. They were working on a case together. Would it be so wrong to offer each other comfort? It wasn't a grand passion like Carly and Bran had, but it could be nice all the same.

"If I had the crap kicked out of me, how would you comfort me?" Shelby asked quietly.

"What makes you think I'm capable of comforting anyone?"

"I'm an optimist at heart," she admitted. "Are you saying you're not capable of giving comfort?"

"I don't know. I guess I'm saying I'm not very good at it."

"Try. Think about it. I've gone through what you did today."

He got up and crossed to the bar. He poured himself another drink. "I don't know. I could offer to buy you something."

"I don't need anything."

"Everyone needs something," he insisted.

"What I need you can't buy."

He slumped back down in his seat. "Then I'm not sure I'm your man. Unless you want me to write you some code. I seriously doubt that would fix things."

"What would your sister do?"

"She would say something mushy and give you a hug or some . . . Do you want a hug?" He said it like it was a completely foreign idea. And not a particularly welcome one. "I'm not a big hugger."

"So you don't believe in physical affection as a way of comforting your partner."

"I guess I haven't had the kind of partner who would find that comforting."

She stood up. It was obvious that talk wasn't going to get Drew out of his dark place. He needed something way more. While he might not recognize his need, she did, and she was completely unable to stop herself from fulfilling it. She stood and moved toward him.

She held out a hand and he reached for it, realization dawning in his eyes as he pulled her down on his lap. He set his drink aside as he wrapped an arm around her waist.

"Ah, now I understand. You were asking me how I would comfort you, but you were really asking how you could comfort me," he said with a sigh. "I told you I was slow when it came to the social stuff. Let me start over. I would kiss you, Shelby. I would kiss you long and hard. I would kiss you until you forgot about everything but me."

He might not be the quickest guy when it came to figuring out what she wanted, but once he got it, he knew how to soften her up.

Shelby ran her fingers through his hair, smoothing it back. "I'm not like the other women in your life, Drew. I don't want you to write me a check or promote me to some big job. But I do want to comfort you when you're feeling bad. Yes, I did write to Carly about you. Mostly I called you names, but I also talked about how attracted I was to you. I think she saw through the third-grade name-calling. Apparently she wasn't at all surprised to find out we're dating."

"I told you." His hand flattened against her back and he started making soothing circles there. "Bran told me I should ask you out the day we met. Forgive me for reading that e-mail. I'm going to respect your privacy, I promise, but in that moment I just . . ."

"Wanted to be close to me but couldn't figure out how?"

"I needed something to distract me. Not something. I needed you. I'm sorry."

He was going to kill her. She cupped that glorious jawline of his. "Forgiven, but I do want you to respect my privacy. Except when your crazy mother decides to infiltrate my laptop."

"I'm sure she's on your phone, too."

"Damn it." She started to reach for her phone.

He held her tight. "Let her. It's why I sent you everything via courier."

It had seemed so weird and paranoid that he'd sent messengers who stayed and awaited her answer. When she'd asked him to call her so they could talk, he'd actually sent a prepaid cell phone. "You knew?"

"I didn't know for sure, but it's what I would do to a woman who'd suddenly started investigating a murder that should be closed. If I were the murderer, that is. And I suspect now that she's been watching me all along."

"Should I get a new phone?"

"I'll have a safe phone for you tomorrow, but no. You should use yours and let her listen in on you. You're crazy about me and you're not interested in reporting right now. You want to spend time with me and work on that book you're writing. Can I read it?"

She shook her head in abject horror. "No."

"But it looked so interesting. Mostly I like how you wrote the word *cock* a couple of times. And *pussy*. Your heroine seemed very interested in what the hero was packing, if you know what I mean. Have I mentioned how pretty you are when you blush?"

Yep, she could feel the heat in her cheeks. "Nope, but I seem to do it a lot around you."

"I don't want you to be shy around me. I don't want you to be intimidated by me or scared of me. I'm sick of people pandering to me. I kind of like it when you yell at me. You're pretty when you yell, too."

He was so weird, and it did something for her. She'd told him she wasn't like the other women in his life, but the reverse was true as well. The men she'd dated before Drew had all been charming and polished and good at the social game. Drew was none of those things and yet something about him called to her.

"Are you serious about seeing where we can go?"

"I am, Shelby. If you believe nothing else about me, believe that. I want you. I want to spend time with you, and I want to see if maybe you're the woman who can handle my damage. Before you say something optimistic, you should know that it's a lot of damage. You would be smart to walk away from me."

"I think I can handle it." She lifted her face up and looked into those stunning blue eyes of his. "I might have some of my own."

He lowered his mouth to hers, hovering. "I can definitely handle yours."

He kissed her, his lips moving with power over hers. He didn't hesitate this time. He seemed to let himself revel in her. His hand found its way to her knee, sliding up the skirt she wore. Heat flared through her body.

"Tell me I can touch you," he whispered against her lips.

"Drew, we're not alone." She wanted him to touch her, craved it actually. He kissed her again, his tongue dragging along her bottom lip, requesting entry. She opened for him and was immediately rewarded with the sexy slide of his tongue along hers.

He delved deep, his hand cupping her knee. "No one's going to interrupt us. Not until it's time to land or I ask for something."

"You do this often?"

He frowned. "Oh, you think . . . no. I meant I've taken many meetings. I've never made out on a plane. I know you won't believe this, but until now I wasn't much of a creative thinker when it came to sex."

So single-minded. "You're talking in the past tense. I take it now you want to be a little wilder?"

"Maybe I needed the right woman to spark my imagination. I want to fuck you here, Shelby. I want to lift your skirt up and open my slacks and have you ride the hell out of me, and I don't want you to be quiet. I don't give a damn what anyone hears as long as they don't comment on it. This is my plane and if I want to fuck the most beautiful woman in the world on it, I'm going to do just that."

He knew how to build up a girl's ego. Something deep in the back of her brain was telling her this man was far too good to be true, but she wasn't listening. "Touch me, Drew."

A triumphant look crossed his face, and his lips descended once more. Over and over he kissed her while his hands manipulated her body. He gently spread her legs so he could run a hand over her pussy. A brief caress that had her heating up and left her wanting more. He kissed her lips and jaw and throat. His hand came out of her skirt and up her body to cup her breast.

"I want to touch you everywhere. Fuck, you're so soft."

He wasn't. She could feel his erection against her, and there was nothing soft about him. Was she ready for this? Her body definitely was, but she wasn't sure about her heart.

She did have damage. She had a horrible fear of abandonment, and yet here she was about to get seriously attached to a man she shouldn't date, much less sleep with. Her rational mind knew this wouldn't work out. No matter what he said, the fact that she was going to write a book about his family would drive a wedge between them. It would be so much smarter to keep her distance, but his hands felt like heaven on her skin. He slid one hand under the fabric of her bra, and she nearly sighed at the sensation. Her nipples had peaked, and the feel of his thumb rasping over one sent a sizzle straight to her core.

Before she knew what he was doing, she found herself turned on his lap, her back to his chest. His knees spread her legs wide, and her skirt had worked itself up so she could feel cool air on her exposed thighs. His tongue dragged over the sensitive skin of her neck as he teased her breasts. Shelby could barely breathe. Never in her life had a man gotten her so hot and ready in such a short amount of time, but then maybe she'd been ready since the first time she saw him. Every moment after had been a long, slow seduction. Even when she'd been so mad at him she could spit, she'd thought about him in bed.

All the reasons she should push him away evaporated.

"I want to make you come, Shelby," he whispered before his tongue ran along the shell of her ear. He rolled her right nipple between his thumb and forefinger before giving it a tug. "I want to make you forget that there's anyone here except the two of us. We're the only people who matter, so don't hold back on me."

She couldn't think of anything but how he was holding her, how his voice had gone low and dark and deep. "I want you to."

His right hand left her breast, and suddenly her skirt was pushed almost up to her waist and she could feel his fingers slip under the band of her panties. So close. He was so close to where she needed him to be. Just a bit more.

"You want me to what?" His finger brushed over her clit but it wasn't nearly enough. It was a delicate caress when she needed strength. Craved it.

"I want you to touch me."

"I did, baby. Look, I'll do it again." The pad of his finger barely whispered over her.

Frustration welled hard and fast. "You know what I want, Drew."

"Yes, I do," he said with an infuriating chuckle. "But I want to hear you say it. I want that smart, sweet mouth to talk dirty to me. I'm not going to be a polite lover with you, Shelby. I want more. I want demanding and dirty. I want the part of you no one else gets."

He wanted a part of her she'd never acknowledged existed except on the pages of the book she wanted to write. Somehow he made it seem natural to let that Shelby out.

"Make me come, Drew. I want you to rub my clit and make me come. Make me scream for you."

His hips moved against her, his hand pressing down. She was caught between his hands and his cock, and she wasn't going anywhere until she'd had everything he'd promised her.

"That's what I want, baby." His thumb found her clit, rotating as his fingers dipped into her pussy. "You're so wet."

She couldn't remember ever being so wet and ready for a man. This reaction was only for Drew, and she knew it deep down inside. Their chemistry was like nothing she'd ever felt before, and she was more than ready to explore it. "Please, Drew."

"Yes," he whispered. "I'll give you whatever you want. I want to make you happy."

She let go of everything but the feel of his hand on her, the hard press of his cock from behind. Over and over his long, talented fingers pumped deep inside her while his thumb worked her over. She moved against him, finding the perfect rhythm. It built and built until it was a wave she could no longer contain.

The orgasm flashed through her and she gasped. So good. The pleasure rushed along her skin and she relaxed back, her body satisfied.

"Yes, baby. That's what I wanted. Now I'm going to pick you up and take you to the bedroom and I'm going to fuck you hard. You're so fucking wet for me."

"There's a bedroom?" She heard herself asking the question, but she was concentrating on the way he handled her so easily. She wasn't a tiny thing. None of that mattered to Mr. Muscles. He simply shifted her in his arms and stood up like she weighed nothing at all. Yeah, that did something for her, too.

"Of course. It's the smallest of my jets, but I sometimes nap on the way to New York or LA." His eyes gleamed with heat as he stared down at her. "But this will be the first time I've fucked a goddess in it."

She let her arms drift up, willing to do anything the man wanted.

"Mr. Lawless, I am so sorry to bother you." A feminine voice broke through the intimacy of the moment. The flight attendant was standing in the doorway to the cabin, averting her eyes.

"Excellent, then don't," Drew replied, his voice flat.

"What's wrong? Don't mind him. He has no manners at all." Shelby knew she needed to take over because there was zero way that woman had walked into the cabin without a good reason.

"It's Mr. Hatchard," she said. "He couldn't get you to answer your cell so he called the pilot, who spoke with me. There's a driver waiting in Austin to take you to the police department."

Drew set her on her feet, suddenly interested in the conversation. "Why would I need to go there?"

"Because there's been a break-in at your house. The police have the suspect in custody," the flight attendant explained.

"Excellent." Drew reached for her hand again. "I'll talk to them in the morning."

Shelby found herself being dragged toward the mysterious bedroom. Drew was like a caveman but there was something sexy about his insistence. He couldn't seem to care less that his house had been broken into. "Drew, have you thought about this? You have a launch in a few months. What if they stole your code?"

"I'll write a new code."

"Mr. Lawless, the police claim the man in custody is your brother," the attendant called out.

That stopped Drew on a dime. "My brothers have keys."

"He says his name is Noah and that Benedict Lawless was his father. I'm sure there's some mistake, but Mr. Hatchard was extremely disturbed on the phone."

Drew dropped her hand. "How far out are we?"

The attendant moved to the bar. "We land in twenty minutes and like I said, I've already arranged a car to pick you up. Can I fix you another drink, sir?"

Drew slumped down into his seat, his eyes already taking on the far-off look he had when he was brooding. "Scotch, please."

What fresh hell were they going into now? Whatever it was she was going to be by his side. "I'll take care of him. Thank you very much."

Shelby poured him a Scotch and sat down next to him. He was as distant as they'd been close only moments before.

She slipped her hand over his, letting the silence grow between them.

She was pleased when he flipped his hand over and let his fingers tangle with hers.

"Will you come with me?" Drew asked, not looking at her.

She leaned against him. "Of course."

He went back to silence, but she held on to him.

Chapter Five

D rew stared through the two-way glass at the kid sitting in the interview room, his hands cuffed in front of him. Noah Walker looked even younger than his nineteen years as he sat talking to the police detective. He was wearing a threadbare T-shirt and a jacket that wouldn't have given him much warmth. He looked like he needed a haircut, too.

"Oh my God. Is that what you looked like at that age?" Shelby stepped in beside him, her jaw dropping as she got her first look at the young man who'd attempted to break into his house.

He hadn't gotten far, according to the police. The kid had managed to jump over the fence and had been caught on camera by Drew's security company. The police had been called out and discovered the kid by the pool, half asleep in one of the lounge chairs with nothing but a backpack full of cheap protein bars, two pairs of jeans, a sweatshirt, and some extra underwear. They'd also found a whole eleven dollars and twenty-three cents and a used bus ticket from Connecticut to Austin.

"He looks nothing like me."

Shelby looked at him like he'd said the dumbest thing in the history of time. "Drew, he's a mini you." Her voice went low despite the fact that they were alone. "Is there any way your mother was pregnant when she left?"

"You mean when she murdered my father and his mistress, failed in her attempt to kill her children, and took off with a whole new identity?"

She ignored him. "The timing is right. I read through what the police have on him so far. Noah was born eight months after your father was killed. The mother's name on his birth certificate is Leah Walker. No name at all given for the father. He was born in New York. Do you know that name? Could it have been one of her aliases?"

Oh, he recognized the name. "Ian and I talked about her earlier this afternoon. According to him, Leah Walker was a friend of Patricia's. One who Patricia introduced to her wealthy friends over the years. But there was nothing about a child. Of course I didn't tell them to look for a kid and they've just started investigating her. I meant to ask Carly about her tonight. Carly worked for Patricia for years. I assume she knew most of her friends."

She turned and looked into the room. "He looks so scared."

"He's probably an excellent actor." He was a Trojan horse. That's what he was. His mother had found an actor the right age, who looked a bit like Drew, and she'd sent him down here to . . . to do what? Create chaos? To soften Drew's heart? She was an idiot if she thought he would fall for this. He saw that kid for exactly what he was—a snake in the grass waiting to bite them all.

"So you're saying your mother died a few years back?" the detective in the interrogation room was asking.

The kid nodded, looking down at his hands as though he couldn't quite believe they were still cuffed. "Yeah. It was four years ago, but we weren't close. She shipped me off to boarding school when I was seven. Not that I saw her much before that, either. I had a nanny. My mom spent a lot of time out of town."

"What did you do during the summer?" the detective asked.

The kid, who Drew realized was nineteen and not an actual kid, sat up straighter. "I stayed with friends. It's what I've been doing since I graduated from Creighton Academy. Well, I was before they all went off to college. Mom had prepaid my tuition for high school, but apparently she left all the money and the property to her sister. I didn't know she had a sister so after I finished high school last year, I was kind of shit out of luck."

"Your aunt didn't take custody of you? You would have been fifteen at the time."

He shrugged. "She didn't call me. I didn't even know Mom had died until after the funeral. The cops said they didn't find my name on her phone or anywhere in the house. It was kind of like I didn't exist. My friend's mom took me in. She became my foster mom I guess, but she died of cancer about seven months ago. I've been staying at motels when I can ever since."

"So according to what you told the cops at the scene, you recently received a letter claiming you're the brother of Andrew Lawless?"

Noah sighed as though grateful to finally be going there. "Yes. It was in my backpack. You can read it if you like. It was on a card sent to the motel I was staying at. I have no idea who knew I was staying there except a few friends. It was weird because everyone I know sends e-mail."

"I don't suppose whoever sent the card left a return address?" the police officer asked.

"It was sent from a post office in New York. I can't exactly trace it back. Snail mail sucks," Noah said, frowning.

"So you get this note and decide to contact Andrew Lawless?" the police officer prompted.

"I always wondered who my dad was. Mom said it didn't matter, that he was dead and it was better I didn't know. The card said my father was Benedict Lawless and that if I wanted to find out the truth about my life, I should find it out from my brother Drew Lawless.

That was all it said. I tried calling but he's kind of hard to get in touch with. So I had some money left and I decided to come down here. I look like him. I think it's true. I think he's my brother. Half brother, I guess."

"Oh, I doubt that," Shelby said under her breath.

"He's not my brother." Drew didn't believe it for a second. "It's utterly ridiculous. According to Hatch, my parents were barely talking at the end."

"They might not have been talking but they were doing something else," Shelby muttered, her eyes still on the kid. "Drew, he's practically your twin."

"So she found someone who looks like me." It didn't matter if this kid took a DNA test that proved it. He wasn't Drew's brother. He was some rich brat. Creighton Academy was one of the world's premier prep schools. The freaking president of the United States had gone there. So had the dude who made all of Drew's private jets. It was for the wealthy and elite. If his mother had truly given birth to this brat, she'd obviously cared more for him than the rest of them. Noah had been lounging away at prep school while Drew and the rest had been struggling to survive.

Not his brother. No fucking way.

He was, however, a cock-blocking son of a bitch who'd ruined Drew's day in more ways than one. He should be at home right now, working on round number three or four with Shelby. He'd intended to get home, get her in bed, and not let her out for a few days.

"So you decided to come down and meet your brother?" The detective sounded skeptical. "Who happens to be one of the wealthiest men in the world."

Thank God someone else was skeptical because he could practically feel Shelby's heart bleeding as the kid continued his well-planned-out sob story.

"I got a scholarship to Harvard, but I couldn't manage the rest of the tuition," Noah was saying. "I thought I could handle it, but I ended up dropping out. I've been working for a temp agency, but there's not a lot of temp coding jobs. It's the only thing I'm good at besides studying. But then I got that card. Now I get why I'm so good at it. My brother is the single most brilliant coder in the world. He's a genius. Apparently my dad was a genius, too."

A nasty huff came out of the detective's mouth. "Your father killed his wife and then turned the gun on himself. He wasn't so brilliant at life."

Maybe Drew didn't like the detective so much after all.

Noah sat back, his jaw turning stubborn. "There are people out there who don't believe that. Some people think he was murdered so the company he founded could sell his ideas."

"Conspiracy nuts," the detective shot back.

"Well, he seems to have done some homework," Shelby commented.

"Yes. He's been well prepared."

Shelby turned to him as the detective started to question Noah about how he'd gotten to Austin. "You know there are several journalists who've worked on the case over the years."

"None who found real evidence. And calling them journalists is ridiculous. They're conspiracy theorists. Like the detective said. I believe one of the working theories is that aliens took my father's real body and he's working for them now."

A vision of his father's burned body flashed through his brain, but it had nothing on that fucking heart she'd drawn on the back. Like it had been a gift from her. Like death had been his mother's purpose and accomplishment in life.

She'd left it knowing the next time anyone looked in that box, it would be one of her children. She'd left it so the first thing he or his brothers or Mia would see was their father's body. Was it her way of telling them to stay away? Or had it been her way of reaching out?

Her way of saying, *Look at this. You're just like me, Andrew. You're ruthless. You are my child. The others are too much like their father, but you . . . oh, you are mine . . .*

"Drew?"

He had to shake his head, as though he could make the bad thoughts go away. "What?"

"I asked if you wanted me to get you something to drink," Shelby repeated.

Scotch. A shit-ton of Scotch might help him relax. "No, I'm fine."

He turned his attention back to his mother's latest gift, but his mind was on Shelby. For a brief moment he'd forgotten everything but her. When he was holding her, bringing her pleasure, he hadn't been thinking about anything but Shelby. He hadn't wanted a drink or a computer. He'd only wanted her. She'd been the thing that made all the bad of the world drift away.

"So you decided to break in?" The detective sat back as though he had all night and it wouldn't bother him to stay right there. "Did you think that would endear you to your brother?"

Noah sighed. "I wanted to wait for him. Okay? I know it was stupid, but I had to see him. I don't have anywhere else to go." Tears hit the kid's eyes, but he seemed to suck it up. "I spent everything I had on the bus ticket down here and then the taxi that took me out to my brother's place. Look, I wasn't trying to get inside the house. I got tired so I fell asleep by the pool. If I was trying to break in, wouldn't I have shoved a brick through a window or something?"

"Maybe you weren't there to steal from him. You want to explain the knife in your bag?" The cop pulled out what looked like a small, ordinary steak knife. Not even a particularly good brand. It looked serrated, but not sharp. "Were you angry with Mr. Lawless?"

Shelby's hand slipped into his.

"I'm not angry with anyone, damn it. I've been staying in a crap hole," Noah shot back. "You wouldn't understand."

But Drew did. Drew knew what it meant to be so fucking scared that someone was going to attack him, he'd walked around with a butter knife because it was the only thing he could steal. He'd kept that stupid butter knife with him all the time.

Where would he have been if he hadn't found Hatch? Hadn't convinced him to clean himself up so they could find investors and get Riley, Bran, and Mia back? What if he'd truly been alone?

There was a brief knock on the door, and the detective's partner strode in. She was a competent-looking woman wearing a tailored pantsuit, her silvery hair in a professional bun. She had a file in her hand. "Mr. Lawless, I have the paperwork all ready. I just need your signature and we can charge him with criminal trespassing and stalking. If he's telling the truth and he has no money, we'll set bail and probably hold him over until trial. That should be sometime next year."

It would serve him right to stay in jail for months. Or he would drop the act and that would tell Drew something, too.

"Excellent." If his mother gave a damn about the kid, she could show up herself and bail him out. Otherwise, Noah being in jail solved a great many problems.

"Andrew?" Shelby's eyes were wide as she looked up at him. "You can't put him in jail."

"He was trespassing." It seemed perfectly logical to him.

"He was looking for you," Shelby insisted.

"Yes, after nineteen years, he suddenly decided he had a billionaire brother. That seems convenient, doesn't it? Besides, it doesn't matter. I have two brothers and he's not one of them." He held his hand out for the file, ready to sign on the dotted line.

Shelby stepped between him and the detective. "Drew, I need to speak with you alone for a moment."

He should have known she would be difficult. Maybe a few minutes alone would be helpful. He should have dropped her at the house, but he'd been weak. "Please, Detective, could we have a moment?"

"We can hold him for seventy-two hours. You have between now and then to decide what you want to do, but I think a man in your shoes should be careful." She nodded and walked back out the door.

He was alone with Shelby and a view of Noah, the detective interviewing him having left moments before. Noah was still cuffed. He sat at the table with his head in his hands.

Not that it meant anything to Drew, but the kid had been trained to draw out protective instincts. He looked like a fucking bunny caught in a trap and ready to get eaten.

And Drew didn't give a damn because he saw that rabbit for exactly what it was. The rabbit in this case *was* the trap.

"Drew, that young man is related to you," Shelby started.

"We don't know that." He wouldn't believe it until he'd had a DNA test done. Not that sharing DNA meant a damn thing. His mother had proven that beyond a shadow of a doubt. "Besides, if he is my brother, he's been tainted by my mother. Can't you see she's the one who sent him?"

"You can't know that for sure."

She was being naive. "Who do you think sent him that card? Who else would have known about his connection? He thought his name was Walker all his life. So he gets a mysterious card and suddenly he's Team Lawless? I don't buy it for a second. He's one of two things. He's a distraction or an outright weapon against me. Either way, he can go to hell and I'll buy him a first-class ticket."

That was as baldly as he could put it. She had to understand now.

"Or he's a victim like you." She turned and looked at the scene in front of them. "Drew, he's so young. He's a young you. What would you have given for someone who could save you? Who could have taken care of you?"

"I took care of everyone. I didn't need someone to take care of me."

"Yes," she agreed. "And you've done a spectacular job. You were everything they needed and now someone else needs you."

"He doesn't need me. He's here to do Iris's work. Can't you see that?"

She sighed, a frustrated sound, and he could see the wheels of her brain working. He would give it to Shelby. She wasn't the kind of person who gave up easily. "All right, have you ever heard the old saying *keep your friends close, but your enemies closer?*"

"That was said by people who didn't have the means to keep their enemies in jail." He picked up the folder, ready to sign. Shelby would forget about this incident once she got focused on the case again. She might be irritated with him for a few days, but she would come to understand that this was the best way to handle things.

She turned away, staring into the room where Noah was perfectly placed. Now there were tears in his fucking eyes. He looked pathetic, like the dog at the pound who knew he wasn't going home with some family.

Shelby sniffled.

"You know I'm doing this for you, too." He set the folder down. His signature would be easier to write on the desk.

"This isn't about me, but I'm learning something about you."

That sounded ominous. He could admit he wasn't particularly good with women. It was precisely why he hadn't had serious relationships with them.

"What did you learn about me?"

She turned and her eyes were red. She brushed tears off her face. "I learned that I shouldn't cross you. You don't give people second chances, do you? In Noah's case, you're not even giving him a first one."

"Are you saying I should give my mother a chance to send her spy in? I should give her a chance to hurt me, or more importantly, you? I meant what I said, Shelby. This is as much about protecting you as it is me. He could hurt you. He could be here to hurt you."

She moved in, her hands coming up to touch his chest, and he was an idiot because he practically sighed at the connection.

"I think you're sweet to think that way, Drew, but I need you to talk to him. I think even if he's a plant, you won't be able to live with yourself if you send your brother to jail. We need to bring him home with us and figure out what's going on."

"I'm not taking him home."

"He can stay in the pool house. You have plenty of room," she reasoned.

"Absolutely not." But he was already debating in his head. His first instinct was to shove the kid in jail and never think twice, but it might be smarter to figure him out, to study him and see what made him tick. To find out what Mommy wanted to accomplish by sending her favorite son in to do her dirty work.

And then he could have the fucker taken someplace that would teach him what deprivation really was.

It might be fun. Except he had the issue of Shelby living with him and he couldn't risk her. "I'm sorry. I would feel better if he was in jail. Now let me get this done so we can go home."

Her hands fell to her sides and she nodded, stepping back. "All right. I'm going to go out and make a few calls."

Yes, this was precisely why he didn't date women like Shelby. Now he fucking remembered. "So you're leaving? You're going to call a cab and walk away the minute I don't do what you want? Is that it?"

She frowned. "No. I'm not leaving, Drew. I'm going to call around and see if I can find a lawyer who might take your brother's case. He doesn't deserve to stay in jail because he pissed you off. You know it's the poor of this world who get the shaft."

She was forgetting a few salient points. "He went to one of the most expensive prep schools in the country."

"Yeah, well, he doesn't anymore, and just because he has a horrible mother doesn't mean I won't help him. Aren't you lucky I think that way? Or you would be shit out of luck, too, mister."

"So you're coming home with me, but I suspect we won't pick up where we left off." He knew it wasn't her fault they'd been interrupted, but he couldn't help but feel cheated.

"Are you kidding me? You want me to go home with you and have sex? After everything that's happened tonight?"

"I thought you were all about giving me comfort. Let me tell you something, Shelby. I'm very much in need of comfort right now."

She pinned him with a hot glare that should have made him uncomfortable, but looked good on her. "Don't you dare try to manipulate me, Andrew Lawless. You won't like what happens. I was being kind before, and yes, I wanted to comfort you. I wanted you period. Right now, I'm a little pissed, so no, I'm not going to sleep with you."

It was exactly what he'd thought. "So I do one thing you think is wrong and you withdraw affection."

"We're in the middle of an argument," Shelby explained with a huff. "I'm not going to stop being pissed at you because you're horny. God, you are bad at this."

"Yeah, I might have pointed that out." He stared down at the report. One signature and he wouldn't have to look at Noah Walker again. And Shelby would think he was some kind of an ass. She would think less of him, and that bothered him. Plus she had a point about keeping his enemies close. He'd wanted this? Fuck. Fuck. Fuck. "All right. If I let him stay in the pool house, you have to move your things to my bedroom. You have to sleep with me. That's the deal."

She stared at him for a moment. It was that stare that let him know he was saying something stupid, but he wasn't going to back down. If he was going against his every instinct, then he was going to get something out of it, and that was Shelby in his bed. Maybe it wasn't the way he'd imagined it, but she would be there.

She took a deep breath, as though trying to find her patience. Yeah, she did that a lot around him, too. "Drew, not everything in the world is transactional."

Well, this would be. "That's my final offer."

She closed her eyes for a moment and when she opened them, she shook her head. "All right. I'll go tell the detective we're taking him with us, and I'll sleep with you tonight. But you should understand that getting me into bed doesn't mean I'll have sex with you. That is not transactional and not negotiable."

"Fine. It's only because I want to keep watch over you. I want to make sure you don't get murdered in the middle of the night." It was a lie. A total and complete lie, but he wasn't about to back down now. He wouldn't touch her until she begged for it.

That was probably a lie, too.

She was still shaking her head as she walked out of the room.

He turned and his "brother" was staring straight ahead, though he didn't seem to be looking at any one thing. Stoic. He'd taken on a stoic look.

Drew had done it that night. When they'd all been taken to the station after the fire, he'd had to hold it together even when the rest of them cried. He'd had to be strong because Riley and Bran and Mia needed him to be.

Why was this kid being strong?

Drew turned away because it didn't matter. And that wasn't a lie. He was doing this for Shelby and Shelby alone.

He prayed he wasn't making a mistake that would cost them both.

Shelby smiled at baby Drew. It was hard to think of him as anything else. He looked so much like his brother it was uncanny. Drew was completely high if he thought Noah Walker wasn't his kin in some way. "Are you sure we shouldn't stop somewhere and get you a few things? I can have the driver take us to a store. You can't possibly have everything you need in that backpack."

Baby Drew smiled back. Noah's smile was open and wide. One way he was unlike his brother. "I'm good. I have a toothbrush and stuff. I don't need much more. I promise I won't be any trouble. I just want to get to know my family. I still can't believe I have a family."

"Yes, I'm struggling with it, too." Drew had been broody ever since she'd played the much-needed role of his conscience earlier this evening.

The driver sped along the highway, turning toward the big houses that lined Lake Travis.

Noah sat across from them, looking fidgety and uncomfortable on the bench seat of the stretch limo.

And Drew was back to drinking Scotch. Did he have a bottle everywhere? She halfway suspected if they stopped in the middle of the street, someone would be waiting with a crystal decanter.

"I'm sorry to tell you like this," Noah began. "I guess I didn't think about the fact that if I'm Benedict Lawless's son, it means he cheated on your mom. I didn't mean to hurt you that way."

"I'm well aware of what my father was capable of," Drew shot back.

"What Drew is trying to say is, he knew his father and mother's relationship was on shaky ground. It's all right. You're not the bearer of bad news."

"I certainly wasn't saying that," Drew replied sullenly.

She growled a little his way, and he went back to his Scotch. She turned to Noah. "Tomorrow we'll go out and get you a few things. I'm sure you need some clothes. How long have you been on the street?"

"He said he was staying with friends," Drew pointed out.

"He was lying." Drew thought he was so smart, but she had street smarts, something he hadn't gotten, even in foster care. "He closed his eyes every time he explained about where he'd been staying. And I think he lied about how he paid for the bus ticket."

"You're an expert in lie detection?" Drew was suddenly interested again.

It was good to know she could surprise him. "I worked with a clinical psychologist who was also an FBI agent. I ghostwrote a book for him and he taught me a few tricks. The eye thing is more an indicator than proof. The real way to figure out if someone is lying is in how you question him. You have to find the holes in his story. He's already got several when it comes to his employment history. So I have to ask how you really got that card."

"I'm not lying," Noah said, his jaw setting in a stubborn expression. "Not about the bus ticket and not about the card. I might have been embarrassed about the fact that I can't keep an apartment. I was staying with someone, but he turned out to be a pretty bad guy so I left and I haven't found anything else. The card showed up at his place. I just don't want to get him involved."

Drew's eyes lit up. "I see what you're saying. So you used a friend's address to get mail and have an address for the temp jobs."

Noah's arms went across his chest. "Yes, I used a friend's address."

"The bad guy or another one?" Drew asked.

Noah hesitated. "The bad guy."

"And you said you don't have a cell phone," Drew continued, warming to his subject. "How did prospective employers contact you? You said you coded? Who did you code for? I know pretty much everyone in the industry."

"I don't remember them all," Noah replied. "And I went into the office every day when it opened. That was how I found out if there was work for me or not."

She winced. It was so obvious. He wasn't a good liar. Another thing he had in common with Drew. Drew Lawless might be one of the world's most successful men, but he couldn't lie to save his life.

Maybe he could do it when it was all business, but he was crap about the personal stuff.

And he was an idiot when it came to relationships. If she thought for a second that he was truly using his brother's predicament to get her in bed, she would have walked away. She'd put him in a corner, and it was the only way he knew to get out.

"Sweetie, that's not how temp agencies work," she said gently. "They're never going to hire a person without a phone. Not in the tech world. I could understand that if you were working manual labor. Then you could show up and get work. The tech world requires more."

"Can you really code?" Drew asked flatly.

No hesitation there. The question put some fire in the kid's eyes. "Yes. I'm one of the best coders in New York. I might not have some fancy house, but I'll put my talent up against yours any day of the week, brother."

Drew sighed. "Who were you working for?"

She'd suspected the same thing. "Were you hacking?"

Noah looked out the window. "I thought I was doing good at the time, and it was the only way he would let me stay at his place. I didn't realize how black his hat was until later."

A black hat hacker. She wasn't terribly surprised. If Noah was talented and had no other options, there would be a place for him on the dark web. "It's okay, Noah."

"It's not okay," Drew shot back. "Do you know what black hats do?"

Did he think she was so naive? "Like you've never hacked a system you shouldn't have? Do you think I didn't make a study of you? Why did the FBI show up on your doorstep fifteen years ago? See, you think there's no evidence of that, but I can hire my own hacker."

He turned to her. "Sometimes I forget why I find you so attractive. Then you remind me."

It was good to know that her hiring a hacker got Drew hot. "I'm just saying that you shouldn't be so hypocritical."

"I'm not being hypocritical, baby." His hand slid over hers. "If he's involved with a black hat, that could come back on everyone in his world. I do know how that goes. So tell me, Noah. Did you steal cash from this guy? Because that usually doesn't go well."

Noah sat back, his arms coming down and his whole body relaxing. "No, I didn't steal money from him. I did one last job and he gave me the money to get down here. I'm sorry. I didn't want you to know I'd done something illegal. But no one is coming after me."

"Well, they never actually tell you they're coming after you," Drew pointed out. "Even if they did, how exactly would they get hold of you since you don't have a cell phone? Maybe he'll e-mail you a convenient reminder that you're on the shit list."

If he wasn't so damn hot . . . "It's fine, Noah. I just needed to figure out the truth."

Even in the low light, she could see the way he flushed. "I'm sorry."

The limo turned into the circular drive and stopped. She was happy she'd taken a tour of the grounds before they'd headed to Dallas earlier in the day. She rather thought Drew would walk away and leave the kid wondering what to do. "I'm going to show you to the pool house. I think you'll like it. It's got a kitchenette, but you're more than welcome to come and have breakfast with us in the morning."

"He is?" Drew asked as the driver opened the door.

So frustrating. "He is."

"We eat at seven," Drew said begrudgingly. "And if I find out you're some kind of spy working me for any reason, we'll have an execution, too."

Drew got out of the limo without another word.

"I don't think he likes me," Noah said with a frown.

"His bark is worse than his bite," she tried to assure him. "In the morning, things are going to look so much better. You'll see."

"I hope so." Noah stared out the open door as though wondering if he should simply stay where he was. "He's a lot more intimidating than I thought he would be."

She was sure he'd dreamed of being welcomed with open arms. She wished she could promise Drew would change overnight, but she doubted it. Besides, she still wasn't sure why Noah was here in the first place. She only knew that they wouldn't find out if they didn't take him in. And Drew's pushing him away wasn't going to help Noah open up. "Give him some time. You'll see."

Noah scrambled out, but when she moved to exit the vehicle, Drew was standing right there, waiting to help her out of the limo.

He said nothing, but followed her into the house and toward the back. Even when they got to the pool house and she showed him how to lock the door, Drew was hanging around like a gorgeous gargoyle, looming over the situation and making everyone wary that he would swoop down at any moment.

Unfortunately, she didn't know everything about the high-tech house. "Drew, do you want to show him how to use the communication system?"

The rooms of the home and the outlying buildings were connected through a speaker system. She'd been told that even the small boathouse where Drew kept the powerboat he never used had a connection to the main house.

"Not particularly," Drew replied.

"I'll be fine." Noah stood in the middle of the house, his backpack in hand.

"I'm setting the alarm, so if you try to break into the main house during the night, you should know that I've got lasers set up," Drew said, his face completely serious. "High-tech lasers. They'll cut your legs right off but cauterize the wound so you're still alive and I can torture you later. I won't even wake up."

"He's joking." She hoped he was joking.

Noah's lips had curved up the tiniest bit. "I'll make sure I don't break in."

"Or out," Drew said. "Wouldn't want to unleash the hounds on you."

"Again, he's joking. He doesn't have any pets, much less the kind that would eat you." She found herself being tugged along. "Night, Noah."

He looked so lost as he held up a hand. "Night, Shelby. And thank you. You, too, Drew."

"That's Mr. Lawless to you," Drew said as he pulled her toward the main house. "And don't forget about the lasers."

The minute she was in the house, Drew slammed the door, locked it, and immediately went to set the alarm. He pulled out his cell phone, touching a button. "Reminder for Monday. Buy lasers."

"You know you're infuriating, right?"

He shrugged. "A guy can never be too cautious. I'll meet you in bed. If you're not there in fifteen minutes, I'll come looking for you."

She made it to the room she'd slept in for the last week and got ready for bed with a sigh. She was tired, and the evening hadn't gone anything close to the way she wanted it to. There was no way she would admit it to Drew, but she'd wanted this to end in some kind of a romantic fashion, too.

Maybe it was for the best. They'd been moving far too fast, allowing chemistry to drive them when they needed to form a friendship first.

Could he form a friendship with her? Was he capable of acknowledging what he needed? Or would she always have to fight him?

Oddly, she never remembered her parents fighting at all. They'd been a quiet, calm family, and then her father had announced he didn't want to be a part of them anymore. She suspected there had been no passion between them. Her mother had been so much happier when she was alone.

Had she ever felt passion? Had she ever wanted a man so much she was willing to put up with his odd and frustrating nature? Sometimes she wondered if her mother had thought of her father at all after he'd left.

Shelby worried no matter what happened that she would think about Drew Lawless for the rest of her days. She thought about him even when she was angry with him.

She washed off her makeup and found her least sexy pajamas.

Tomorrow, apparently she was moving into the master bedroom, and she was sure he thought once she was there she would fall into his arms and he would get the sex he so obviously wanted. She had different plans. If this was going to work, they needed to take it slow, needed to get to know each other and make a thoughtful decision about whether or not they could have a relationship once the job was over.

The minute she walked in, he looked up. He was sitting in bed, his tablet in front of him. "I usually sleep on the right side. Is that okay?"

Now he got nervous? It seemed like her main role in this relationship was to smooth over the awkwardness that went hand in hand with Drew's brilliance. "It's fine, but you should understand that I'm a cover hog."

He put the tablet on the table by the bed. "All right."

So serious. She climbed into the big bed. For a man who claimed he slept with few women, his bed had been built for getting busy. Maybe with multiple partners. It was massive. She would have no problem not touching Drew all night if she chose.

He turned off the light and settled in. "I'm sorry if I disappointed you, Shelby. I was trying to protect you. And the rest of them. I have to decide how to tell my siblings about Noah."

She hadn't thought about that. Drew would be forced to choose. He could malign his father's name or bring his siblings in on the truth—that Noah was very likely their full-blooded brother. One way or another they would have to know, but she realized it was hard for Drew. He held himself apart from the very people who should support him because he was still being their rock, still trying to play the father figure even though the children were fully grown.

"I think you have a couple of days," she offered, turning toward him.

"I don't sleep a lot," he said quietly. "If you wake up and I'm not here, I'll be in my office. I tend to go to bed pretty late."

"You can stay up if you like. I'm a morning person. You don't have to change your habits for me."

"I want to stay with you," he said quietly.

She moved closer. No sex for them, but she could give him something else. It had been a long day and he probably did need some comfort. "Why don't you hold me until I go to sleep?"

She found herself wrapped up in his arms. Maybe she wouldn't need so many covers. He was kind of a furnace. She let her head find his muscled chest.

Her hot geek.

"It's going be okay, Drew."

He sighed, his body finally seeming to relax. "I don't know. I don't like having him here."

Drew didn't like change period, from what she could tell, and having a new brother was definitely change. "You'll see. It's going to be all right."

Despite what he'd said, he was asleep in minutes and Shelby was left praying she hadn't told him a lie.

Chapter Six

Drew woke up with a start because there was something wrong. Shelby had turned on the lights. Why had she turned on the lights in the middle of the night? His heart raced a bit as he looked around his big bedroom.

Then he realized it wasn't the lights she'd turned on. It was the sun. He glanced over at the clock. Almost eight in the morning.

He'd slept. All night. He'd wrapped himself around Shelby and drifted off and he hadn't even dreamed.

There was a brisk knock on his door and then it opened. He looked up, hoping it was Shelby walking back in. Maybe if he gave her sad puppy eyes, like his pseudobrother had the night before, he could get a good-morning kiss. He'd wrecked sex for a while. He totally got that, but a kiss wasn't sex. A kiss was affection, and she thought he needed that. She was probably right.

He groaned because it wasn't Shelby's sexy sweetness that charged into the room.

"What the hell are you doing?" Hatch demanded.

He was so going to get those lasers. He should put it on R & D's schedule. He and Hatch hadn't truly respected each other's privacy. Ever. In the beginning, it was because they'd shared a crappy apartment and Drew was afraid Hatch would die on him in the middle of the

night. Later, it had become about work, and nothing was more important than work. Hatch would walk in at all times of the day or night if
something came up. They had to rethink that now that Shelby was
here. She would probably freak out if Hatch stormed in at midnight
because the stock dropped on the Nikkei. "I'm trying to wake up."

"I am talking about that kid who is sitting in your kitchen waiting
to blow up like the fucking bomb he is."

"Ah, so you've met Noah." Drew should have expected Hatch
would react this way.

"I don't need to meet Noah—whoever he is—because I'm smart
enough to see him for what he is. A liar, for one. There is no way that
kid is your father's."

Drew yawned and rolled out of bed. He thought Hatch was being
naive. "Did my dad have a vasectomy I didn't know about?"

"No, but this is all a lie." Hatch paced the floor while Drew
grabbed a T-shirt out of his dresser. "Can't you see that? She sent him.
She found someone who looks like Benedict. She hired him and sent
him here to create chaos for some reason."

"I agree."

"Then why is he here and not sitting in jail?" Hatch asked. "I
called the police last night when you wouldn't answer your cell. They
told me that not only had you chosen to not file charges against him,
but that you'd taken him home with you. Do you have a plan? Are you
going to kill him?"

"I thought about using lasers, but Shelby nixed the idea. I don't
think she's keen on living in a house where we cut off the limbs of
intruders. She's weak on crime. I tried to explain that it wouldn't even
get the floors messy, but she was insistent."

Hatch ignored his sarcasm entirely. "I knew this had something to
do with that woman."

He turned on Hatch. "Her name is Shelby and you should get used
to her. She's staying here for now."

Hatch stopped, his hands on his hips. "Damn it, Drew, you cannot let her make decisions like this. You do understand that if he's some kind of spy Iris sent in, she'll realize that Shelby is a weak point for you. Or was that your plan? Are you trying to put Shelby in the line of fire so Riley and Bran and Mia aren't in it?"

It would be a logical thing to do, but the idea turned his gut. "I'm going to take care of her. I'll keep her with me most of the time. And when I can't, I'll hire a bodyguard. Actually, that's a good idea, though I doubt she'll understand, so let's keep that to ourselves. How fast do you think Taggart can send someone down here?"

"Are you listening to yourself?" Hatch's voice went low. "Drew, you know what you're about to do, right?"

"Get some breakfast and go to work?" He wasn't scheduled to be at the office today, but he seriously doubted he could convince Shelby to spend the day with him otherwise.

"I'm talking about the launch in a few months. Don't you think it's curious that all of this is happening right before you launch a product that will make us billions?"

"I think it's happening because we figured out what my mother did all those years ago. This has nothing to do with the launch. It has to do with the fact that Carly is damn good at protecting Bran. If she hadn't been so quick, Iris would have killed them both and no one would have been the wiser."

Carly was the one who'd had to deal with Iris Lawless, though she thought it was Francine Wells who was trying to murder her and Bran. That evening his mother had shown up to retrieve the information that would have proven beyond a shadow of a doubt that she was alive. Carly hadn't even known it was in her possession. Carly still didn't know that the woman who had shot Bran and nearly killed her was actually Iris Lawless.

Hatch's head shook. "Every domino that's fallen has gotten the push from her, Drew. You act like you're in control, but you're not.

No one is when Iris is around. She's pushing the buttons and she wants Noah here."

"Then shouldn't we figure out what she wants him to do?" He'd thought a lot about it on the limo ride home. Shelby was right. He needed to figure out what Noah was here to do or she would simply send in someone else Drew might not see coming. Now he had to figure out a few things. Was Noah actually his biological brother? Was Noah working with Iris? Or was he merely another pawn?

He hated being unsure. It was a foreign feeling and not a welcome one.

"At least let me get a full report on him," Hatch said, his weariness evident.

"I've already sent Taggart his name. I expect he'll have something for me later today. Believe me, if I discover he's not who he says he is, I'll call the police and throw him back in jail and there won't be anything Shelby can do." Yes, he was feeling much more optimistic this morning.

"I don't like this," Hatch said. "It's not good."

"At least meet the kid. I'm sure he's sitting at my kitchen table making puppy eyes at my . . . at Shelby." She wasn't exactly his girlfriend. More like his future girlfriend, if they could get around the fact that he'd blackmailed her into sleeping with him and he was lying to her about what he really wanted her to do for him.

"I think he's probably introducing himself around." Hatch shook his head ruefully.

"To the staff?" Drew got a bad feeling.

A long-suffering sigh huffed from Hatch's chest. "Bran might have been with me when I got the call. I managed to keep him from coming down here last night, but he was waiting on the plane for me this morning. I'm afraid that kid knows all my tricks. I told him I wasn't leaving until after noon. That should have worked. He knows I never get up before noon anyway."

Damn it. His brother was here. "So I have to deal with Bran and Carly."

Hatch winced. "And Mia and Case."

And just like that his morning went to hell.

Ten minutes later he strode into the kitchen. He could hear them all laughing and joking from down the hall. It was obvious that no one else was taking the new guy with anything close to a grain of salt. Nope. Not his family.

"I can't believe how much you look like Drew," Bran was saying. "Damn, you got the crappy genes, man. Riley and I look like our mom. So much prettier."

"Hey," Mia said. "As a member of the blond-haired contingent in this family, I protest."

"She's right," Case's deep voice said. "She's prettier than all of you combined. But Bran is right, man. Those genes run true. Who did you say your mother was?"

Trust the Taggart to at least ask some questions.

"Hey, no invasive questions, Case," Shelby said. "I'm sure Drew already has your brother working up a thorough report on him."

He needed to be more mysterious. She already knew too many of his moves. "I'll know everything there is to know about him by nightfall."

Every head turned his way.

Noah frowned. "Everything?"

"Everything." Noah should understand that he would leave no stone unturned when it came to figuring out exactly why he was here. "Right down to when you lost your virginity."

The kid went bright red.

"Andrew," Shelby said with a smile on her face that wasn't really a smile at all. "Could I speak with you a moment?"

He was getting better at this because he knew "speak" meant "yell" in this case. Oh, she wouldn't raise her voice, but she would make her point clear. "Of course."

Mia stood up. "I think whatever Shelby has to say to you needs to wait. Drew, we need to sit down and have a nice long family meeting because I'm confused about a few things."

Excellent. He would have to thank his sister for being so assertive. She might have gotten him out of a lecture on how he should treat stray dogs. "Well, the gang's all here. Let's talk. Except the puppy. He should leave."

Shelby frowned. "If Mia has questions about Noah, shouldn't he be the one to answer them? Noah should stay and I'll leave. I have a few things I need to do before I start on work anyway."

Noah was shaking his head. "I can go back to the pool house. I had a roll and some fruit already. I don't need the omelet."

"I want to know exactly what's happening," Bran said with a shake of his head.

"I want to know when you and Shelby started seeing each other," Carly interjected.

Case leaned over. "I think it's called *doing it*. That's the polite term."

"No. *Sleeping together* would be the polite term," Mia shot back. "And I don't know that it's any of our business. The sex stuff, that is. The other stuff is very much our business."

"Don't you dare play that card with me." Carly shook a finger Mia's way. "I need details and I don't need you playing all innocent. Tell me you haven't already started looking into it."

Looking into it? Mia and Shelby had a few things in common, the chief one being they were both nosy reporters who didn't give up when they thought they had a lead. "What exactly is Mia looking into?"

Mia put her hands on her hips. "I think you've been hiding things from us, Drew. And Shelby seems to be a part of that. And yes, we need to have a family meeting. Sorry, Shelby. I'm not trying to be a bitch."

"And yet you're managing it so beautifully," Drew replied, sending his youngest sibling a frown.

Was she still the youngest? Or would that be Noah?

Shelby had gone a nice shade of red. She turned to Drew. "I think I'll go take a shower or something."

Not on his life. If Noah was hanging out for the family meeting, then his fake-girlfriend was getting to stay, too. He stepped in, looming over her, and let his instincts lead him. He stared down at her, touching her cheek and allowing his thumb to stroke her. "Don't leave me alone with the barbarian horde. I want you to stay with me. I didn't even get a good-morning kiss. I got Hatch yelling at me."

She sighed, but she went on her toes, and her lips met his in a brief kiss that still seemed to sear him. "Good morning, Drew. Your family is here."

Yes, and he suddenly saw the advantages of that. Shelby was a bit of a captive. If she pulled away, she risked giving up their game. He leaned over and kissed her again. Properly this time. He kissed her like a man who was happy to see her. No lies there. He let his mouth linger, playing lightly while his hands cupped her hips. Shelby's arms drifted up around his neck and she relaxed.

Shelby's head came down, and when he thought she would push him away, she leaned in and her arms wound around his waist. "And to think I actually envied you your big family."

God, it felt good to have her wrapped around him. He hugged her back and let the moment wash over him. His family was big, but they all had someone now. Shelby was his and his alone. For the moment. "Sometimes it's a real drag, baby."

Mia opened her mouth to speak, but Case simply put a hand over her lips and whispered something in her ear. When he let her go, she looked at Shelby. "I'm sorry, Shelby. I was worried. My brother is wealthy and I'm protective, but I just realized that no amount of money could make someone as intelligent as you put up with my brother's shit."

"That's what I said," Carly replied under her breath.

"Hey, are you okay?" Bran stood up, shoving his chair back. "Hatch?"

Drew turned and saw Hatch was standing in the doorway, his face a pale mask. His eyes were right on Noah. Somehow Hatch managed to go from pale to a deep crimson in the space of a breath. He stepped forward, his stare locked on Noah.

"Don't you think I don't know exactly what you are," Hatch practically snarled. "If you even try for a second to lay a hand on any one of these kids, I'll kill you myself. Am I understood?"

Noah's eyes had gone wide and he stammered, "Yeah . . . I get it."

"I'm watching you. They might be fooled by you, but I'm not." Hatch turned and stormed out of the room.

Drew sighed. Yeah, it looked like they would be having that family meeting after all.

He took Shelby's hand and led her out of the kitchen as his family started to talk. "I have to talk to them."

She looked up at him, her face framed by all that red hair. "I have to go make sure Noah doesn't bolt."

But if the kid left, so many of his problems would be solved. He'd learned enough to not make that statement, though. "If you must."

"I must. Are you going to tell them?"

He shook his head. "Not until I have to."

"Eventually they're going to know," she insisted. "They'll be surprised when my book comes out."

He wasn't going to think about that now. He had enough things happening in his life that made him feel like the scum of the earth. He didn't need the reminder that he was playing fast and loose with his promises to her. "Do you want a pregnant partner? Because if I tell them, there's no way that Mia shrugs and lets you take the lead."

She sighed. "I suppose you're right and we don't know that Iris won't become dangerous the closer we get to finding her. She shot Bran. She wouldn't hesitate to hurt Mia or her baby if she thought it would keep her safe. All right. Do what you need to do and I'll deal with Noah. I might ask him a few questions of my own."

He reached for her hand, bringing it up to his lips. "See you later?"

"Apparently I live here now, so yes. But I'm going to need to work at some point." She winked and turned and walked back into the kitchen.

The door to the pool house opened, and Shelby realized she'd almost been too late. Noah stood there, his backpack slung over one shoulder and his eyes rimmed with red. It had been ten minutes since Drew had declared he needed to talk to his family in private, and Noah hadn't even attempted to argue that one. He'd simply nodded, awkwardly shook a couple of hands, and slunk out to the pool house.

"Before you run away, how about that omelet?" She had no intentions of allowing him to run, but she needed to ease into that.

Noah opened the door fully, allowing her in. "I could eat before I go."

She could hear his stomach growling. She walked through the pool house, which was way nicer than any place she'd ever lived in. She set the plate the cook had given her down on the table and uncovered it. "It's what you asked for. I like to call it the predator's special. Have you considered eating a couple of vegetables?"

Noah's nose turned up. "Yuck. This smells good, though."

Yep, bacon and ham and an unholy amount of cheese did tend to smell good. She watched as he started to dig in. "How long has it been since you slept in a bed?"

"A decent one? A long time, but it's okay," he said. "I found a shelter here in the city. I'll call a cab and let them take me as far as I can go. I'll walk from there."

"I thought you didn't have any cash left."

His face went nice and pink. "I had a little."

She glanced over and saw a wallet and a note on the coffee table. "Please tell me that's not Drew's."

He sighed and pulled the cash out of his pocket. It was a couple of twenties and a five. "It was the other guy's. The not-so-scary one's."

Ah, then he was smart enough not to try to lift Case Taggart's wallet. It proved he had some intelligence. "You're talking about Bran. He's your brother."

Noah nodded and pushed back his chair. "Yeah, I know. If it helps, I didn't take his credit cards and I was going to pay him back one day. That's what the note was about. Forget it. I'll walk into town."

She knew for a fact he was a Lawless because he'd gotten the gene for melodrama. The same one they all seemed to have. "Finish your breakfast, Noah. I'm not snitching. I'll hand the wallet back to his wife and convince her he dropped it. And you don't need to leave."

Noah sat back down, his shoulders slumping. "That guy looked at me like I was the devil."

She wasn't sure what had been going through Hatch's head. She only knew it wasn't truly about the boy in front of her. It couldn't possibly be. "There's a lot going on in this family right now. You're a bit of a shock to the system."

"I bet. I didn't mean to cause trouble."

"I don't think you're going to." At least she was going to make sure he wouldn't. "We need to know more about you and where you come from. I think that would put everyone at ease."

"I thought Drew was having some security guy investigate me."

"I like to ask my own questions."

"You can look through my laptop if you want. You can see the card that was sent. I kept the envelope, too." He rifled through his back-pack and hauled out what had to be his prized possession. He opened the laptop and punched in some keys before turning it her way.

She looked at the oversized screen. The laptop was bulky and heavy to carry. "Why wouldn't you pawn this and get some cash?"

He frowned as he started looking through his backpack. "It's all I have. I don't know who I would be without it. I know that sounds stupid, but my whole life is on that machine. I gave up my cell phone. I can't give my computer up, too. Here it is."

He handed over the card. The address had been typed on the very plain-looking envelope; the note inside was typed as well.

Noah, if you want to know who your father was, look up your bastard brother. He's legitimate all right, but that doesn't mean he's not a criminal. Just like dear old Dad.

"So you had no idea there was any connection between you and the Lawless family before you received this?" She glanced at the date. "One week ago. You must have immediately started planning on how to get to Austin."

"You think it's about the money, right?" Noah's voice had gone a bit cold.

"I don't know, Noah. That's why I'm asking the questions. You have to understand that this is going to be hard on the family. They have the right to ask questions. If you're going to run every time someone asks you an uncomfortable question, then I'm going to drive to an ATM and give you some cash because you don't belong here."

He sat down, his jaw tightening in the same way Drew's did when he was frustrated. "I'm sorry. I didn't think it would be this hard. Like I said, I wasn't thinking at all. I got the card, looked him up, and he really does look like me. Also some things my mom used to say made me believe that she lived in Texas when she was younger. When I was a kid she would talk about a man she left behind in Texas. Wouldn't you want to find out about your past?"

She understood that in a way none of the Lawless clan could. It was hard to be alone in the world. Her father might still be alive, but her mom and brother were gone. The people who'd known her as a child, who'd loved her and cherished her, were gone, and she was alone until she made enough history with a new family. "Just because they have your blood doesn't mean you'll fit in. I'm not saying that to discourage you. It's the way of the world. I should know. I have a father out there who hasn't seen me in years."

"Yeah, well, I had a mom who saw me as nothing but an inconvenience. The only thing she was ever interested in was my friends. She always told me which kids I should hang out with and she would come up and spend time with me if I had the right friends. I got more attention if I could fit in with the right crowd."

"Would she come up for parents' weekend?" That was a pretty good bet. The pieces were sliding together. Creighton Academy was exactly what Drew claimed it was. The prep school for the rich and famous. The rich and famous were often divorced and looking as well. It would be a ripe field for someone like Iris, who preferred to make her money the old-fashioned way. Marrying and then murdering for it.

"When she wasn't married she would come up."

New information. "So you had a stepfather?"

He took a long swallow of the juice she'd brought him. "Two I remember. One I don't. She had bad luck. Well, she tended to like old guys. Except the one I don't remember. He was fairly young, but he had a heart attack from what I understand."

"Do you remember their names?" It was an odd question to ask, but he hadn't spent a lot of time with his mother. She had to assume he didn't spend much time with his stepfathers, either.

"Sure. The first was a dude named Wes Kirkman. He was the one who had a heart attack. Um, then there was this ancient guy. Luther

Holman. He was some kind of a banker. He sent me a money clip for my eighth birthday. Who does that?"

A really out-of-touch person. "And the third?"

He shuddered a bit. "Alan Traynor. He was the grandfather of this kid I was friends with in school. I liked him a lot. Chris, that is. I didn't know his granddad. Chris had lost his parents in a plane crash years before. He was so nice. He was my best friend for a couple of years. I thought it was cool when my mom married his granddad. It kind of made us like brothers, you know?"

She got a bad feeling. People tended to die around Iris. "What happened?"

"His granddad got sick and I guess he couldn't handle it. I found him with a needle in his arm. He never did drugs, Shelby. I still don't understand why he would do that. He still had me. He still had my mom. I know she sucked at it most of the time, but she would have made sure he had what he needed."

God, she got why Drew was doing what he was doing. She did not want to be the one who blew up Noah's world. It was already decimated. Figuring out that his mother was a psychopath might be the last blow. "Sometimes people can't help themselves. The depression is too overwhelming. It wasn't about you. It was a moment of weakness, and you should remember him as the boy he was."

Not the boy your mother probably murdered.

"Do you think you could figure out why my aunt left me alone?" Noah asked. "I understand what happened with the money. Mom was always lazy about seeing lawyers. And she didn't expect to die the way she did. She wasn't exactly old. She never updated her will, but I don't understand why my aunt wouldn't even call me, wouldn't try to help me."

"Did you ever try to contact her?"

"Yeah, but I couldn't find a damn thing on her. It's how I got involved with Jase. He's the hacker I was working for. I wrote some code for him and he was supposed to try to find my aunt. He claims she moved to France. He gave me an e-mail address, but when I tracked it down, it was registered to some man in Paris who claims he has no idea who Anna Walker is. It's like she's a ghost. Everyone leaves traces these days. Everyone's on social media. But I can't find her anywhere. Why would she cover everything up? I think she might have killed my mom for her money. It's one of the reasons I wanted to talk to Drew. I want to convince him to help me. Everyone else thinks I'm paranoid."

She knew he wasn't, but she couldn't tell him. She owed Drew her loyalty. Despite the fact that she'd felt the need to take in the kid, she knew Drew was right and they needed to vet him.

"So your mom died four years ago?"

He nodded. "It was a car wreck. A bad one. There wasn't much left to bury."

Iris was good at those. "But she'd paid your tuition in full through the end of high school."

"Yes," he replied. "It's not completely uncommon. There was a trust fund set up to ensure I got through the academy. Actually, Mr. Traynor was the one who set it up. He'd planned to set up a college fund for me, too, but he passed away before he could do it."

Or he'd given the money to his wife, who hadn't set it up at all. "So after you graduated, you were left with nothing?"

"I'd saved a couple hundred dollars from the allowance the trust gave me. The sad thing is I had lived my whole life at Creighton. Everything was taken care of. Even after my mom died, someone was willing to take me for the summer. Sometimes it was friends. Once a professor let me stay with him and his wife and kids. I never worked. And then after my friend's mom died I had just enough money to get into the city. I stayed in a hellhole in the Bronx while I tried to find some work. I finally met Jase online and he offered me a thousand dollars under the table if I could figure out what was wrong with his code. He was working on an online sales system."

Jesus. And Drew thought she needed a keeper. People who were selling normal things on the web did not hire people off the street. "When did you figure out that what he was selling wasn't legal?"

Noah set his fork down, the omelet only half finished. "I guess I always knew. I mean, why come to some kid he found on Craigslist if it was legit? I didn't know what he was selling exactly until later. He used codes for the products, obviously."

"What was it?" She wasn't looking forward to having this conversation with Drew.

"Everything. Anything. Apparently when the feds took down Silk Road, there was a massive hole in the black market, and Jase was determined to fill it. I found out he was selling everything from illegal guns to heroin. But by then I didn't have anywhere else to go."

She could understand the idea of being caught someplace she didn't want to be. "Did he threaten you?"

"A couple times. Let's just say I knew way better than to call the cops." He stared at his computer. "And then I got that card and I realized I might have a way out. He'd stopped paying me by then. I was working for room and board. Not that there was a ton of board. He went out a lot. I was lucky to eat once a day. He offered me a lot of drugs, though. I was almost ready to take them when that note came in."

Because he'd been naive and desperate. He'd been a child of privilege unable to cope with the world around him because no one had prepared him. He'd been trained to go to college, to depend on his family's wealth until such time as he'd acquired his own.

He was so much like Drew.

"Do you think it's true or do you think someone's fucking with me?" Noah asked quietly.

"I think you are absolutely Benedict Lawless's son." Shelby reached out to put a hand over his. "And I think if you hang in there, you'll end up getting a real family out of this. Now you look me in the eyes and tell me something."

He stared straight at her, emotion plain in his face. He was either one of the most sincere people she'd ever met or the best actor walking the planet. "What?"

The trouble was, he was also Iris's son, one she'd raised, and she was deadly and damn good at acting.

"Are you here to cause trouble for Drew?"

He never wavered. "Absolutely not. I want to know about where I come from. That's the only reason I'm here. Well, maybe there's one more. I don't want to be homeless and alone. I want to have someone in this fucking world who gives a shit if I live or die."

She wanted to believe him. She squeezed his hand. "All right, then. You have to ignore Hatch. He's harmless, but he's protective of Drew. Once he realizes you are who you say you are, he'll calm down."

"You think I should stay?"

Since she hadn't figured out why he was here yet, absolutely. "I do. Now, how about you finish your breakfast and then you and I will go buy some decent clothes. And is there any way I can talk you out of the Bieber hair?"

His lips curled in a smile that reminded her of Drew's. "Sure."

She closed the laptop because she wouldn't touch his again until she was absolutely certain it was clean. They needed to make sure no one was watching Noah through his system.

She could start looking. She could piece together some of Iris's history through the men who had been in her life, the men she might have killed.

And when she found Iris Lawless, she would know the truth about Noah.

Chapter Seven

"Explain what the hell is going on." Bran stared at him across the table.

"I thought I just did that." Drew had hoped the family meeting was over for now. He'd explained that he and Shelby had been circling each other for a while and were trying to give a relationship a real shot. As for Noah, he'd explained what had happened the night before.

"No, you gave me some bullshit crap about how you've been sexting with Shelby. You do realize we know you. You don't sext with anyone."

He would need to keep up appearances. Perhaps it was time to have Shelby send him some racy pictures of herself. Just for cover, of course.

"What is that smile about?" Bran was staring at him like he had two horns.

Was it so surprising when he smiled? "Sorry, I was thinking about Shelby. Now, you need to get your nose out of my private life. I don't meddle in yours."

Bran's jaw dropped. "You're joking, right? That was sarcasm, I hope, because otherwise you've gone seriously delusional. You're the single nosiest big brother in the history of time."

He didn't consider it being nosy. "I'm looking out for you."

Bran leaned back against the countertop. They'd all had breakfast while they'd talked, and now Mia and Carly had gone to get ready. They were going to work on the reception plans while they were here. Case had gone to take a nap because apparently he'd been up all night and it was making him grumpy. So Drew had been left with Bran and a deep appreciation for the fact that Riley and Ellie were living in New York or he would be facing two brothers down.

"Can't I look out for you, too?"

Drew was skeptical about that. "I think you're trying to look out for Shelby more than me."

"I like Shelby. She's Carly's friend and I've gotten to know her, but I definitely know you well. I'm surprised because she doesn't seem like your type."

"I have a type?"

"Yes. You do. Convenient. Hyperintellectual. A bit cold. Shelby's none of those things. She's messy and emotional."

"And warm," Drew replied quietly. "Can't I want a little warmth in my world? Carly wasn't your type, and then you met her and she was the only woman in the world for you. God knows Riley didn't date anyone like Ellie before, and Mia exclusively dated metro douche bags until she met Case. I think we're damaged, Bran. I think every single one of us dated people we could keep at a distance until we found the one person who wouldn't allow us to. I don't know that this is going to work out with Shelby, but I want to try, and I can't do that if my siblings are constantly questioning me."

They were smart words, meant to deflect his brother, but he was surprised at how easily they'd come.

He did want her warmth. Maybe in the beginning this had been about control and curiosity, but he was rapidly coming to enjoy her company.

Bran held his hands up. "All right. I'll back off. I just want you to be happy. You have to know that, Drew. You deserve to be happy."

He wondered sometimes.

"What do you think of Noah?" He needed to change the subject.

"I guess he's proof that Dad wasn't a saint," Bran said quietly.

"I know that's hard to accept, but he was only human."

"That's no reason to stop trying to clear his name, Drew."

"What does that mean?" He was afraid he knew what it meant.

"It means I would like to know why you've stopped trying to find Francine Wells."

"I haven't stopped. I just thought it would be nice to take a breather." He knew exactly what he wanted to do now. He knew it made him a bastard, but he wasn't above manipulating his brother in order to spare Bran pain. "I'll get back on it."

Bran blanched as Drew had known he would. "No, I get that you need a break. I do. I think we could all use one. I just had it in my head that you and Hatch were hiding something from us."

"Why would we do that?" *To protect you. To spare you.*

"I don't know. And I don't understand why Hatch would react to Noah that way. He seemed a little unhinged," Bran said.

Yeah, Hatch had nearly lost his shit. Drew wanted to find Shelby, but he needed to find Hatch and talk to him first. "I think he's being overprotective. It wasn't so long ago that we had to go through you getting shot. It affected us all, and now we've got Noah to deal with."

"I have to wonder how Hatch really feels about them all being dead." Bran crossed his arms over his chest. "I know he hated Castalano and Cain and Stratton, but at one point they were his friends, along with Mom and Dad. It has to be weird that everyone's gone."

"I'm sure it is, but he has us. We're his family now, and that could very well be the reason he reacted the way he did to Noah."

"Do you think Wells sent this kid?"

His brother wasn't a dummy. "I don't know, but Shelby is going to find out. You can have Case look into it as well. From what I can tell, she's gone again. All trace of her former self has been erased."

A low growl of frustration left his brother's throat. "So now that she has all the information, and she's gotten rid of her fellow murderers, she'll disappear completely. I don't know what to do, Drew. Part of me can't forget what she told Carly."

None of Drew could forget it. "That if we left her alone, she would leave us be. And if we don't . . ."

"She'll come after us. I'm not worried about me, but if anything ever happened to Carly . . ."

He didn't need Bran to finish that sentence. "So we take a break. Shelby's going to look into Noah, and you need to concentrate on Carly and what you want to do next. We've only got a few weeks until the reception. Afterward, we'll get together as a family and figure out what we need to do after that. Have you talked to Riley about Noah?"

Bran nodded. "He wants a DNA test. I don't know that he wants to believe it. Hell, I don't know I want to believe it, but I've seen him. It's hard to deny that he's one of us."

"Sometimes appearances can be deceiving. And he's agreed to a DNA test. They took a swab at the police station and they're sending it off."

"Will they do that even if you don't press charges?"

"I'm paying for it. It's going to a private lab so we'll know sooner than we would if we used the police lab. I'm certain I can pay extra to ensure both our privacy and that the lab is quick."

"What are they going to test it against?"

"Me," Drew replied. He'd done a swab as well the night before.

Bran pulled his phone out of his pocket, glancing down at it. "He might be exactly what he says he is. Damn. This is going to take some getting used to."

"Having another brother? Yes, I suspect it will."

Bran grinned, looking younger than he did before. "No, I was talking about you having a girlfriend and that girlfriend being

Shelby." He turned the phone toward Drew. "She's already got the women on board. Apparently Carly and Mia are going with her on the Noah makeover. Carly says they won't be back until dinner."

It would be interesting to see how Noah handled the Lawless women. "Well, we'll know soon if he's tough enough to handle us."

"I guess we will." Bran sobered a bit. "Are you going to go find him?"

Drew didn't need to ask who Bran was talking about. Hatch. "Yes. I'll go and look in his favorite bars."

"You want some company?" Bran asked.

He would love some, but it would defeat the purpose. He needed to talk to Hatch privately, needed to figure out how he could calm his mentor down. "No, you stay here and talk to Riley for me. Explain what's going on."

With a sigh, Drew went to get dressed.

"I wasn't trying to be mean." Mia stepped up to stand next to Shelby as they watched Carly and Noah talking to the salesman. They were in the men's department at Neiman Marcus. Noah frowned at the slacks as though they weren't what he'd been expecting.

"I know that." It was nice to have some company, and it might help her get a better view of Noah. She could stand back and watch how he related to the people around him. "If my brother had been a billionaire genius, I would have been protective of him, too."

"I know you won't believe this, but I'm worried about you, too," Mia said quietly. "Drew can be difficult, and he's never been in a relationship with a woman like you."

"A woman like me?"

"A woman who needs him for more than work and sex and money."

That was the question. Did she? So far their entire relationship had been about work and the tiniest bit of sex. She didn't care about the money. She'd lived without it. As far as she could tell, it isolated Drew, but then his magnificent brain might do that all on its own. "I don't know what we're doing right now. It's still a new relationship."

"And yet you're living together," Mia murmured. "I'm not judging. I'm actually going to ask you if Drew manipulated you into a position where it made more sense for you to simply move in."

Oh, she knew her brother well. "He bought my apartment building and had it condemned."

Mia's laugh was a sparkly thing. "That is the Drew I know. So he lured you out here and now I assume he's having your entire apartment shipped here."

It was due in the morning. "Yes."

"You have to understand that Drew views the world through the lens of his childhood. He didn't have value except the money he brought in. First because the people who ran the group home he lived in made money off him and then because of the company he built. He can't see that people might care about him without expecting something in return."

Drew didn't seem to talk about his childhood more than necessary. He tended to focus more on what happened to his siblings than himself. "Do you know if he had any friends?"

"He and Riley were together. I think he spent all his time and energy protecting Riley and worrying about me and Bran. He grew up fast and I think he skipped some of the socialization steps. I just don't want your relationship with him to die because he's so weird."

His weirdness did things for her. "I think I can handle Drew."

Somehow she really did. She knew it had only been a week, but they'd already settled into an oddly easy relationship. It wasn't difficult to be around him. They didn't have awkward silences. When Drew was working and lost all sense of time, she simply went to work on her own. When she got lost in her writing, Drew did the same. He didn't accuse her of ignoring him or making things uncomfortable. They worked.

But they were a transaction. They'd begun that way, right down to a contract. The sex hadn't been written in, but Drew had found a way to bargain for that, too.

Drew, who had everything, didn't trust a woman to simply stay with him, to care for him. He paid the people who helped him. Always.

"Why do you think Hatch reacted so poorly to Noah?" Shelby was interested in what Mia thought. It might give her some insight into Bill Hatchard.

Something about the man didn't sit right with her, and yet she'd already seen enough to know not to bring it up to Drew. Mia was another story. They were just two girls standing around talking about mutual friends and family members.

Mia's eyes strayed to where Noah had disappeared into the dressing room. "He's protective, too. You have to understand that Drew and Hatch kind of saved each other."

That wasn't how she would describe it. "It seems more like Drew saved Hatch. Wasn't he a drunk on skid row when Drew went looking for him?"

Mia frowned. "I don't know that I'd say that."

"Bran does," Carly said as she joined them. "Bran says Hatch was a mess in the beginning. According to him, Drew had to go looking for Hatch. He'd gone through almost every dollar he made from the sale of the company."

"Yes, I often wonder why he didn't use that money to spare you from going into the foster system." It bugged Shelby.

"He was broken," Mia replied, her shoulders sagging as though the very memory could hurt her.

Unfortunately, not understanding what had happened back then could hurt them all now.

Carly started going through a display of polo shirts that Shelby couldn't see Noah wearing. "He's apologized, you know. He and Bran had it out a couple of months ago, and I think they're in a good place. Hatch was weak and he's got some alcohol issues. From what he's told me, he didn't even realize you'd gone into foster care until it happened. He found out Benedict and Iris were dead and he lost it. He didn't show up for corporate meetings or walk onto the job sober again. They sold the company and all the intellectual property about a year later, and they shoved his portion in the bank and no one heard anything from him for years."

"Drew had to track him down here in Austin. He had a place in Dallas at the time, but Hatch always considered Austin his home," Mia explained. "He had gotten married and divorced by that point in time, too."

"To a stripper?" Shelby had heard some stories.

Mia winced. "I believe she was an escort. She's the one who actually spent all that money. He married her when he was drunk and she moved into his house. She spent every dime he had and left him nothing. Hatch was living in a crappy motel room when Drew finally tracked him down. He forced Hatch to sober up."

"Still not seeing how Hatch saved Drew." She was questioning how a grown man could leave four children to foster care when he supposedly had been their father's best friend.

"4L wouldn't exist without Hatch," Mia said.

"But Drew was the one who came up with the concept." Wasn't that the important part?

Carly nodded. "He did, but no one would have taken him seriously. He was a kid and he needed capital. Hatch still had a name in the industry even years later. Without Hatch, the only thing Drew could have done was sell his own code for pennies on the dollar of what it was worth and start over. Hatch turned him into an industry leader. He also made it possible for Drew to get custody of Riley and

Bran. So don't ever expect Drew to question Hatch. He loves him and that means something to Drew."

Drew's circle was tight, but he was beyond loyal to those he considered his. Would he be the same to the woman he ended up with?

"So he's never looked into what Hatch was doing back then?"

Mia's eyes widened. "No. Why would he do that?"

Carly's jaw tightened. "I don't think he would appreciate that, but that doesn't mean you shouldn't quietly look into it."

Mia looked down at her sister-in-law. "You know we've researched that time as much as people can possibly research a crime. We know everything."

But they didn't. "We know nothing about Hatch except what he's told Drew. Did McKay-Taggart do a study on him and his actions during the time?"

Mia's jaw formed a stubborn line. "No, but we don't need to. We know that Francine Wells was the fourth conspirator. It wouldn't have been Hatch."

Something about his reaction to Noah had Shelby thinking. She couldn't let it go, but she also wasn't about to get into a fight with Mia in the middle of an expensive mall. "Of course. I was just thinking. Don't worry about it."

Noah stepped out and looked around as if scared they might have left him behind. He was wearing skinny jeans and a violently orange T-shirt.

Mia's eyes widened in horror. "He's gone rogue. I'm going to fix that. He won't ever get a date looking like that."

Mia strode over. There was no way to miss the resemblance. Mia and Noah looked like brother and sister.

"It's weird, you know," Carly began. "They're a welcoming family, but there are things I'll never understand about them, things that bonded them. You should get used to that. They're tighter than other families."

"Like me and Johnny used to be," she said wistfully. "Like you and Meri?"

Carly smiled at the sound of her sister's name. "I guess. I guess all families are different in their own ways. We bond over shared experiences because no one else in the world can know what it meant to be us. But the incident that bonded Bran and his siblings was so traumatic it could have destroyed them. Drew made sure it didn't do that. He's got a will unlike anything I've seen before, and Mia's right. He puts people on his payroll. He doesn't have friends outside his family. He doesn't trust them. I'm worried Drew is trying to buy himself a wife."

Shelby laughed. "Marriage has not come up."

Carly's eyes were so serious as she looked at Shelby. "I think it will. I think Drew looked at you and wanted you, and he's been plotting and planning on how to get you ever since. A normal man would send you roses. Drew views courtship as a war he intends to win."

She started to laugh again but stopped because Carly might be right. Though she didn't understand everything. Or was it Shelby herself who didn't understand? "It's not that serious. I don't think you need to worry."

"Two weeks ago you were cursing the man's name. You live with him now. He's managed to draw you into his world and he'll make you crave it. Not the money. He'll make you crave the family he's built, and that's not a bad thing. But I know you. You're not going to be the sweet, supportive executive's wife, and he's going to try to control you. It's his nature. I'm worried about what happens the first time you don't give in."

"I'm not a doormat and I never have been."

Carly held out a hand. "And he needs that, but he'll try to manipulate you into doing what he wants. You have to call him on it if this is going to work. Do you want this to work?"

More and more she did, but Carly was right. Drew was consolidating power. He'd dangled what she wanted most in front of her. A mystery she might be able to solve. More than that, he'd figured out that she wanted to belong somewhere, and he was offering her that, too. She might have been able to hold herself apart if she'd been working from her tiny place in LA, only flying out to do research and report back. But he hadn't allowed that to happen. He'd brought her close, isolated her within his tight-knit group. He'd even gotten her to sleep with him. Oh, she was holding out sex-wise, but it wouldn't take long.

It was classic stalking behavior, and she should run. Except he wasn't a stalker. He was a dumbass who needed to be retrained, and that needed to start soon because she did want this to work.

"You're going to look into Hatch, aren't you?" Carly asked.

"I am." She might discover everything had been exactly as the family understood, but they needed an outside force to investigate, and it appeared they hadn't allowed Case's company to do it.

"He was in love with Iris."

That was news. "Are you serious? Drew did not mention that to me."

"Like I said, Drew and Hatch are mysterious. Drew doesn't question him. I think it's because he needs one person outside his siblings he can completely count on. Can you tell me why you want to look into Hatch? I was there that night, Shelby. It wasn't Hatch who shot Bran. It was Francine Wells. You should be looking for her. The police aren't. They're useless."

No, they were being controlled by Drew Lawless, who didn't want the story to get out that his mother had gone bad. "I am looking, but if it helps, I think she has what she wants and she's not going to surface again."

Not until Shelby's book came out and she cleared Benedict's name. She had to hope that was enough to satisfy Drew. She didn't want Carly worried that Francine Wells would show up and try to kill her again.

"I know. I remember. I think it's part of the reason Bran wants to stay in Dallas. He's not protecting himself. He's afraid for me, but we can't allow that woman to win. If there's anything I can do to help you, let me know. We're all pretending it didn't happen right now because we need a break, but I think she'll come back to haunt us all. One way or another."

"I think we've got this settled." Mia walked up with a satisfied smile on her face. "He's not allowed to ever choose his own clothing again."

Noah had a massive bag in hand. "I spent most of my life wearing a uniform. I thought the orange was pretty cool."

Shelby shook her head. "That color is only for citrus fruit. Come on. Let's get this out to the car and we can grab some lunch."

Mia clapped her hands. "Thank God. I'm starving. There's an Italian place I love close by."

Noah seemed happy to trail after his sister, his hands full of shopping bags. He looked like a completely open Drew, a Drew unburdened by the weight of the world he always carried around.

Could she take a bit of that burden off his shoulders and make him smile more?

They approached the door, and Shelby had to laugh because it was obvious Noah was trying to figure out how to open the heavy door that swung inward without the use of his hands.

"You've proven you're a gentleman, Noah." She went to open the door for him. "You don't have to be perfect."

"I already want to keep him," Mia said. "I like having a younger brother to boss around."

"Don't listen to her." Carly walked through the door. "She bosses everyone around. It's her thing."

Shelby followed along, her mind already working on what she needed to do. It was exciting to have so many leads. Dangerous, yes, but she couldn't help it.

Thanks to her handy new 4L credit card, she had a source coming into town. Pavel Volchenko, the assassin's brother, was going to be in Austin in two days. It might be a horrible mistake and the man could know nothing and was just getting a trip to the US out of it, but it seemed like a place to start.

Drew had even told her he was fine with her talking to him. She might not have mentioned that the talk would be in person, but then this was her investigation. She would share what she learned with Drew and he would have to be satisfied with that.

Mia and Carly started toward the car while Noah turned to Shelby. The sun was shining and it was a stunning Austin day.

"I can't thank you enough, Shelby," Noah said. "I know I'd still be in jail without you."

Carly looked down the road. The parking lot wasn't terribly busy. There was a big black SUV sitting in front of one of the entrances. Shelby started across the street to join Mia and Carly, Noah following behind.

"I seriously doubt that," she lied.

"Do you think Drew will be more comfortable when the DNA test comes back?" Noah asked. "I've heard that can take a long time."

Not when Drew Lawless was requesting it. "I think it will be faster than you think. Just let everyone get to know you."

The sound of tires rolling made Shelby bring her head up. The SUV was moving. Fast.

"Mia's husband seems cool," Noah was saying. "Scary, but cool. Did you know he used to be a Navy SEAL?"

Noah was paying no attention to anything but his conversation. That SUV sped up and Shelby had little time to react. Before she could take another breath, the big vehicle was bearing down on them. Specifically on Noah, who was slightly behind her.

Shelby heard someone scream out, but she reached for Noah, whose eyes went wide. He dropped the bags and stumbled as Shelby pulled him away from the SUV. Her foot hit the curb and she went flying backward. She held on to Noah's hand as hard as she could because that SUV wasn't backing down. She could have sworn the damn thing swerved to hit them. Noah hit his knees as she pulled him to the small green space separating the road from the parking lot. He slammed into her, pain jarring through Shelby's body.

The SUV sped away without stopping.

Noah's new clothes were all over the place.

"What the hell was that?" Mia ran over, kneeling beside Noah and trying to help him up and off Shelby.

"I think he was trying to hit me." Noah got to his feet and held out a hand.

"Or it was an asshole on his cell phone. Damn distracted drivers." Carly started to gather the bags again. "I didn't get a plate number."

Mia shook her head. "It was some jerk. We're lucky Shelby is so quick on her feet. Come on, sweetie. I think everything's okay."

She started to look Noah over, but Shelby couldn't help but wonder. Her mind went back to that moment when Hatch had stormed into the kitchen, staring at Noah like he was a snake about to bite them all.

If you even try for a second to lay a hand on any one of these kids, I'll kill you myself.

What would Hatch consider a threat? Noah's very existence? What he represented?

She would like to know where Bill Hatchard was.

Chapter Eight

I'm fine, Drew," Shelby said. Hours later, the house had finally calmed down. Noah was settled in the pool house and the family had all gone to bed.

Drew frowned her way. "Have you noticed the scrape on your shoulder? You're not fine. You should have seen a doctor. I'm going to call and see if I can get the security cameras. There have to be some around that parking lot."

"I already put in the request with security," she replied in a calm tone because it looked like she would have to soothe the savage geek tonight.

Drew was restless, his irritation evident in the way he paced. Drew was normally still, like a predator waiting for a nice fat rabbit to show up. Not tonight. He was a tiger in a cage.

Likely because he'd spent the day trying without any luck to find his mentor.

She was interested in that SUV, too. Though it seemed like Noah had shaken it off and Mia and Carly had moved on to helping plan the reception, Shelby couldn't quite stop thinking about the incident.

She hadn't been able to tell if it was a man or a woman driving. The SUV had swerved out of the proper lane and into the oncoming one. If she hadn't pulled Noah away, he could have been hit and killed.

"I know what you're thinking," Drew said as he closed the bedroom door.

"What am I thinking?" They were finally alone. It had been interesting to sit beside him during dinner. Seeing him with his family had been a revelation. They all looked to him. Every one of them.

Mia had asked his advice about buying a condo in Dallas. She wanted him to look at the contract before they signed on the dotted line, but she also wanted his advice on whether they should go ahead and get a house.

Bran wanted to talk about work and managing some difficult project. Carly needed advice on her start-up company.

Even Riley had called.

Drew was the head of the family, but from what she could tell, he took nothing for himself. He was there for everyone in his family, but he forgot that he could need support, too. When she'd gotten back and asked Bran if Drew had found Hatch, he'd merely smiled and told her not to worry. Drew would find him.

Shelby knew beyond a shadow of a doubt that his brothers and sisters adored him, but Drew needed to realize that they had families now.

And Drew had someone he could count on, too.

Drew paced the floor. He was still wearing his slacks and shirt from earlier in the day, though he'd taken off his loafers. The sight of his socked feet struck her as intimate. "You think it's Hatch."

She'd changed into jeans and a tank top, but she was ready to get comfortable. A long, hot shower was exactly what she needed.

Maybe she shouldn't take it alone. Maybe it was what they both needed.

"I think it could have been a lot of things." She definitely wasn't having an argument with him when she had no proof. The security team had promised to check the tapes and send her anything they could find in the morning. Even then she probably wouldn't discuss it with Drew. He had enough on his mind. "Besides, I don't think Hatch drives an SUV. He has a Porsche, right?"

Drew nodded. "Yes. It's a midlife crisis on four wheels. And I swear, Shelby, he's not capable of this. Hatch might be worried about Noah, but he wouldn't physically hurt him. He's at some cheap-ass motel with a bottle and a prostitute who I pray to god knows to use a condom."

"He needs some time," Shelby pointed out. "Things are happening quickly and he needs time to adjust. He found out a woman he thought was dead isn't, and now she had an extra kiddo. Some people would say it's a reasonable reaction to a shocking life twist."

Drew frowned. "I should go back out. I checked his usual haunts, but I haven't started on the dive bars yet."

He had a meeting at eight in the morning. She knew because he'd spent every second he wasn't out looking for Hatch on the phone talking about the board meeting. If he was out all night looking for Hatch, he wouldn't get any sleep. Stress would heap upon stress, and no one would even know because Drew wasn't human to them. He was Superman and Captain America all rolled up into one. Never faltering. Never, ever failing.

Never needing.

"Or you could stay here and get some rest."

He scrubbed a hand through his hair, his weariness apparent. "Even if I stay, I have to work. I have a meeting in the morning."

Which she was sure he'd already prepped for. "You're ready for the meeting. Come to bed."

His eyes strayed to the bed, longing plain in them. He might not know how to ask for it, but it was clear what he wanted.

He wanted a little peace, some pleasure. A few moments that belonged to him.

She was the only one who could give him that.

"I don't think so. I've been thinking, Shelby. It wasn't fair of me to force you to sleep with me." He flushed a little, but he looked straight at her. "I thought if I could get you into bed, you would end up sleeping with me. I mean not sleeping . . . fucking. I thought you would end up fucking me."

He was cute when he was flustered. The very fact that he was apologizing meant something to Shelby. He wasn't a man who apologized. He manipulated.

"I agreed to move in with you."

"Because I kind of put you in a corner and forced you to," he pointed out.

He'd also given a whole new life to a woman who'd needed it. She'd talked to her friend earlier and she was beyond happy in her new home.

"Would you have left Noah in jail if I'd refused your bargain?"

He sighed. "If you'd walked away entirely, then probably, yes. I would have been perturbed and he would have been a logical target. If you had simply stood your ground, I would have backed off."

"I knew that, Drew."

"Then why . . . were you trying to teach me a lesson?"

She stood up. It was time to make a few things plain to him. "I let you manipulate me into this room because deep down I wanted to sleep with you. I signed that contract because I wanted to get to know you. Now that I know you better, I think I would like to move forward, but I can't do that if you never concentrate on what you need for yourself. What do you need more tonight? Do you need more work or do you need to spend the night in bed with me? Think about it while I take a shower. It was a long day and if you decide on work, understand I'm going to masturbate, and if that offends you, too bad. I'll be out in a little while."

Shelby turned and walked into the monstrosity of decadence that made up his bathroom. It was far bigger than her apartment had been and probably cost more than her entire building.

She turned on the water to hot. The shower itself was practically a room.

What would he choose? Would he no longer enjoy the game because she'd taken control of it? Would she scare him off? It was better to know now than to get her heart broken later. Carly was right. She couldn't change who she was, and maybe her assertive nature wasn't what Drew would be attracted to.

She turned and had her answer. Drew was standing in the bathroom, his eyes on her.

"Tell me this isn't some play to get me to do something you want," he said.

Really? "It isn't, but you're kind of the king of that move. Do you want to accuse me of that?"

"I want you to be better than me. I want to be able to trust you even if I don't deserve it at all. Even if you can't trust me. How fair is that? If I had any honor at all I would walk away from you right now and spare you the pain."

So much drama. She pulled her top over her head and tossed it aside. "I don't see you walking away, Lawless."

His eyes went straight to her chest. "I told you I would do that if I had any honor. I don't."

She slid out of her pants so she was standing in front of him wearing nothing but her bra and panties. They weren't particularly sexy, but she couldn't tell it from the way he was looking at her.

"Tell me why you picked me."

"I have to do that when your breasts are on display?" His voice was husky as steam began to fill the room. "Have you looked at yourself? You are absolutely the sexiest woman I've ever set eyes on. Take off the bra. I want to see all of you."

She wanted to see him, too, but beyond that she needed to lead him to a place where they could be totally honest with each other. "So you just wanted to sleep with me and I happened to have a set of skills you could use?"

His lips curled up in the sexiest smirk. "Baby, if all I wanted to do was sleep with you, I would have come at you in the beginning. I do have some charm when I want to call it up. I don't want to use charm with you. I want you to like me for the nasty bastard I am. I want you to know me and still not be able to walk away."

That was exactly what she wanted to hear. "So this isn't some kind of one-night stand? Are you planning on continuing the relationship even after we've finished the work we're doing together?"

"I will want you after all this is through. I'm not some wishy-washy prick who's going to change his mind, but I think you will. I think when you figure out who I am and what I'm capable of, you'll walk away."

She was made of sterner stuff than that. She let her hands drift back to unhook her bra. "Well, if I'm going to run soon, I should at least enjoy you while I have you."

His eyes darkened. "If that's the way it's going to be, then I'll take it. I'll take anything you give me. God, you're beautiful. Let me touch you."

She slipped her undies off, her body heating up at the thought of finally giving in to him. Though it was more about giving in to herself, her own needs. She'd spent the years since her brother's death in a holding pattern, mourning everything she'd lost. It was time to live again. She'd lost one family, but if Drew was being honest with her, she could find another one here with him.

It was what she'd thought about all night long.

"I told you what I was going to do, Drew. I want a shower. I want to wash off the day and I want to feel good. If you want the same thing, come and join me." She stepped into the shower, hot water hitting her skin.

It wasn't more than half a minute before she felt something else. Big hands cupped her shoulders.

"I want to be with you," he whispered against her ear, his body pressing against hers. "I want to be the one who makes you feel good. Let me do that for you. For however long it lasts, I'll be your man. I'll take care of you."

She was sure he would, and in more ways than sexually. "Will you let me take care of you, too?"

His hands slid down her arms and she could feel warm, naked skin against her own. "Oh, I will definitely let you take care of me, baby."

She turned because this was important. "I mean it, Drew. You push yourself too hard. If we're actually going to try this, I want to be able to take care of you."

He stared down at her, his hands coming up to smooth back her hair. "I need you. Just like this. I want this between us."

"I want it, too."

He wouldn't understand how she could take care of him until she'd shown him. And for now, she didn't want to think about anything except how good his hands felt and how much muscle he hid under his shirts and slacks.

She'd been one hundred percent correct. He was a Greek god under all those clothes. She took a moment to take him in. Broad shoulders, a magnificent chest, and abs that belonged on a superhero. She let her hand drift up. So smooth and warm and alive. His hand quickly covered hers, holding it to him.

"How long has it been for you?" Drew asked.

"A while, but don't think I'm a blushing virgin. I enjoy sex and I've had a couple of long-term partners."

"I ask because it's been a while for me. Almost a year."

This man hadn't had sex in a year? "Seriously?"

"I got sick of it being a bodily function. I want it to mean something, but until I met you I didn't find anyone who moved me. I think watching my siblings pair up and move on affected me. Do you think it's a herd-mentality thing? There has to be a psychological reason for it."

If she allowed him to, he would discuss the biological reasons for love. She wasn't about to let the professor side of Drew take over. "I think it doesn't matter as long as it makes you happy."

He was staring down at her breasts, and then his big hands came out to cup them. He sighed as he stroked her, his thumbs running over her nipples, getting them hard and aching. "This makes me happy. Oddly enough, sleeping with you made me happy. I even like fighting with you. No one fights with me."

Because he was the ultimate authority in his world. He called the shots and made the rules. Some people would think that sounded amazing, but she rather thought it made Drew lonely. He had to question everyone's motives.

"I'll fight with you and then we can make up," she teased him.

He towered over her, his eyes so serious as he looked down. His hands came up, tilting her chin and gently forcing her to look into his eyes. "Promise me. Promise me that when we fight, we'll talk it out and make up. Promise me you won't walk out and decide I'm a lost cause. Promise you'll listen to me before you toss me out."

She wasn't sure why he was practically begging her for forgiveness when he'd done nothing wrong. Her whole soul softened and she gave him what he wanted. "I promise, Drew."

"I'll hold you to that," he vowed before his lips descended.

He took her mouth with dominant power, his hands caressing down her back to her hips. He molded their bodies together, nothing between them now. This felt good and right, and Shelby didn't bother to play demure. She let her hands roam over the warm strength of his skin. His back was strong and supple, and she loved the way his ass felt in her hands. He was so masculine and for a while, he was all hers.

His tongue surged in, moving against her own. Pure heat sizzled through her and she could feel her body getting ready.

His mouth stroked against hers before he moved down, kissing her jaw and neck. She let her hands run through his hair. She liked it like this, wild and out of control. Just like she wanted him. Suddenly he lifted her up and settled her on the bench that would normally be used to place shampoo and conditioner. It was oversized, like everything in Drew's house, and she fit neatly on it, her legs dangling. It fixed her at the right height for Drew to make a place for himself between her legs, lean over and suck a nipple into his mouth.

A shiver went through her body as she felt the bare edge of his teeth at her breast. The tiniest pain sizzled through her and tugged deep inside. Arousal made her moan. His tongue whirled around her nipple as he held her. Her back bowed, offering him everything he could possibly want. Shelby leaned back giving Drew access to her breasts, her body, anything. He teased one nipple with his lips and teeth and tongue while he rolled the other between his thumb and forefinger.

Without conscious thought, she wound her legs around his hips. She wanted him closer. As close as they could be.

"Please, Drew."

"Anything you want."

"Make love to me. Make love to me now. Don't make me wait."

He straightened up, his eyes intent on her. "Yes."

It was all she wanted to hear from him.

Drew's head was spinning. It had been from the second Shelby made her announcement that she would be masturbating if he wouldn't give her the real thing. The minute she'd turned and walked away like she didn't care what he chose, he knew he was in serious trouble. Like a lifetime's worth of trouble.

Except he likely didn't have a lifetime with her.

And he was totally wrong. It hadn't begun with Shelby's announcement. It had started when he learned from Case, who'd heard from Mia, that Shelby was nearly murdered by a runaway SUV. Oh, they'd called it an accident, but he wasn't so sure about that. It was so coincidental. Too coincidental that just as his mother resurfaces he learns about a surprise baby brother and his girlfriend almost gets killed.

"Don't leave, Drew." Shelby's soft voice brushed over him. "Whatever you're thinking about, forget it for now. Stay here with me."

"I was thinking about the fact that you nearly died and you didn't bother to call me." His hands moved on her breasts, palming her. It didn't matter that he had a flare of anger running through his system. He couldn't stop touching her.

His anger dissolved in the face of his need.

"I was going to tell you, but we were fine and I didn't want to worry you," she said even as her body moved restlessly against his.

At least he wasn't alone in his need. "You can't leave me out like that."

"I promise I won't. Please, Drew. Stop thinking and feel. This is our place, our time. We can go back to everything later, but when we close the door to that room, I want you here with me."

She'd looked at him with hot eyes and asked him to make love to her. He wasn't a man who made love. He fucked. So why did he find himself nodding and agreeing?

Because this meant more to him.

He wanted more than a quick fuck from her. He wanted to be in her bed, to be the only man who brought her pleasure, who took care of her. He wanted to be the man she looked to when she was in trouble, the first person she called.

He sucked her nipple again, unwilling to rush things. For once in his life, he wanted to take it slow, to lavish her with his affection. He let his hand slide down toward the juncture of her thighs.

His fingers found her pussy and he nearly groaned at what he found there. Shelby was soft and soaking wet. So fucking wet. She responded so beautifully to him. And naturally she was right. He needed to stop thinking about anything but her. Anything but how good she made him feel.

"Drew, please. You're killing me."

Sweet words to his ears, but he wasn't ready to be done with her yet. His cock was hard as granite, but he needed her to come first. He wasn't sure how long he would last. It had been a long time and, if he was right, she was going to be tight and hot around his dick. He might get inside her and completely lose control. He needed to make sure she enjoyed herself.

Pleasure was the key to keeping her.

"You stay still," he ordered.

"I need you, Drew."

"And you'll get me, but first I'm going to have everything I want out of you. I want to watch you come. I want to feel you come all over my hand and then I'll do it again with my cock. You wanted to distract me from my problems? Well, this is the way to do it."

A slight smile curved her lips. "Didn't fool you, did I?"

"I don't want you to fool me," he admitted. "I want you to want me."

He kissed her again, moving from those glorious breasts of hers back to that mouth that made him hot as hell. He loved how she talked to him. She challenged him in a way no one ever did anymore.

He let his thumb find her clitoris while he slid two fingers between her labia. So plump and wet. Perfect. Even those two fingers were a tight fit. She was going to strangle his cock.

He was fairly certain he couldn't think anymore because all the blood in his body rushed to his dick.

Hot water beat on his back, the sensation heightening his desire. His whole body ached for her. He'd never wanted anything the way he wanted to be inside this woman.

Her head fell back as he began to fuck her with his fingers. He pressed down on her clit as he stroked her deep inside. Her legs were wound around him, holding him tight. Her body went perfectly taut, every line gracefully bowed as she came. He loved the way she gasped, her eyes widening. Her hips thrust up against his hand, rubbing hard, as though she couldn't stand to stay still.

Now he didn't have to, either. He could do as he liked with her. She was soft and sweet, her whole body languid.

Drew had come prepared. Before he'd joined her in the bathroom, he'd grabbed a condom. He'd placed it on the shelf. Now he picked it up, moving away from Shelby so he could prepare himself.

He stopped and caught his breath. She was so wanton and hot with her legs spread and body relaxed.

She'd had what she needed, but she was pouting his way because she still wanted him. She stared at him while he tore open the condom.

"You know you're quite lovely yourself, Lawless."

It meant something coming from her. Actually, now that he thought about it, he'd never had any woman tell him he was lovely. Hot, yes. Sexy at times. Never lovely. He stroked his cock and hoped he wasn't preening in front of her. He was pretty sure he was.

"Yeah, that's lovely, too," she said with a smile. "Now, why don't you bring it over here?"

He rolled the condom on and stepped close to her again. He loved the warm press of her flesh against his, how she opened up to him and circled around him. He didn't have to tease her, and she wasn't pretending she needed coaxing. It was one of the intoxicating things about being near Shelby. She didn't pretend anything. She said what she wanted and made zero apologies for her desires.

"Do you have any idea how fascinating you are to me?" He let his hips move, his cock rubbing against her core. So close to where he wanted to be.

She reached up, wrapping her arms around his neck and giving herself over to him. Now she couldn't balance against the wall. She was wholly dependent on him, and that was exactly what he wanted. "I have no idea why you would say that, but back at you."

He kissed her. God, he loved her mouth. He loved her lips and the way she flowered open for him, how her tongue came out to duel with his. His cock found her pussy and he started to push his way inside.

He'd been right. So hot and tight. She was a vise around his dick. So good. Nothing ever felt as good as working his way inside Shelby Gates. He thrust in and pulled back out, gaining ground each time. He groaned as she dug her nails into the flesh of his back, but welcomed the sensation. He wanted her here in the moment with him. He wanted her to leave a mark so when he was sitting in that shitty meeting tomorrow and everyone was looking at him, he would feel the little pang her nails left and remember that this was what was waiting for him when he finished.

He pressed her back against the shower wall and forced her to take all of him.

Her nails dug into him, her breath gasping into his shoulder. "Drew, it feels so, so . . ."

So good. So right. So beyond anything else. "You're perfect. So fucking perfect. Do you have any idea how long I've waited for you?"

Forever. It felt like freaking forever.

He pressed up, grinding himself against her. She was his. He'd never felt as sure of anything. And he was hers.

He fucked her hard, emotion riding him.

She tightened around him, holding him and screaming his name as she came. She clamped down, sending him right over the edge.

Drew let loose. He gave up all semblance of control as he fucked her over and over again. He held her up because she'd gone languid in his arms. His whole body stiffened as he let go. Pleasure raced through him, blurring his vision. Nothing else existed except how good she felt, how close they were.

He held her tight as he came down from the high of orgasm. This was normally when he would step back and disconnect. Except he didn't want to. He wrapped his arms around her and held her close. He didn't need space and he wasn't about to go back to his routine. She'd said it. This was their time.

"I think I should clean you up," he whispered, his mouth playing against hers.

She sighed, a happy sound. "So you can get me dirty again? Or so you can go back to work?"

He lifted her up. He knew exactly how he was going to spend the evening. "I'm not going anywhere. You're getting so dirty tonight."

She let her head fall back, the water cascading off her perfect body.

Satisfaction washed over him. He knew there were things he needed to do, but suddenly nothing was more important than getting her in bed, making love to her again, and sleeping with her. Bonding with her.

He turned her to the warm water and started to learn every single inch of her.

Chapter Nine

Drew came awake and wondered how the hell he'd managed to live so long without Shelby. It had been two days since the night he'd first made love to her, and he was an addict. When had nighttime become so damn attractive? Night was when everyone else slept and he got back to work. Night was a lonely but needed time.

Night was sexy time. Night was forget-the-rest-of-the-world time and lock the doors. Night was perfect.

Sleep was good. Had he said once that he didn't need sleep? He'd been an idiot.

Sleep made him a much more reasonable human being. Not even the fact that those security tapes from the mall had managed to show them absolutely nothing, except that Noah was clumsy and Shelby was fast on her feet, could change things. The camera had been too far away to easily catch the license plate. They would have to see if they could enhance it to get the plate number.

Not even that could ruin his good mood.

Shelby turned, her body stretching. She reached for him, sliding in and wrapping her body around his. "Morning."

Yeah, morning was pretty awesome, too. He loved how much she looked like a sleepy, adorable kitten cuddling next to him. "Morning, sunshine."

He was going to turn into one of those weirdos who smiled all the time for no good reason, who went to brunch and saw movies that didn't involve robots or car crashes.

Guilt twisted in his gut as he realized he was smiling and Hatch was still missing. Motherfucker.

"Stop," she murmured. "You're worrying again. No worrying allowed in here."

It was Shelby's main rule. When they were in this bedroom, he wasn't Andrew Lawless, head of the family, CEO of 4L, and master of the long brood. Her words, not his. When they were in here, she wasn't Shelby Gates, reporter extraordinaire and all-around nosy busybody. His words, not hers. When the bedroom door closed at night, they were Drew and Shelby, and no one else mattered.

In the last few days, she'd ruthlessly shoved out his siblings who showed up at all hours of the night needing things. She'd closed the door on Bran, who wanted a tutorial on how to work the gaming system, hung up on Riley, who'd called to talk about the reception at eleven o'clock at night, and told Mia she needed to talk to her husband and a financial planner about setting up a trust fund for her baby.

He'd explained to Shelby that he'd kind of trained them to come to him after hours, since he tended to be so busy during the day, but she'd explained that was going to change, too. She'd snarkily introduced him to the word *delegate* and proceeded to invade his business life as well.

No longer was he allowed to work fourteen hours without a break. Not while Shelby was in the building. She would have his assistant schedule meetings that turned into long lunches or walks where he held her hand and showed her around the campus. His employees all thought he'd lost his damn mind.

His siblings had been sure he would cast Shelby out. He'd even heard Mia tearfully begging Shelby not to push him, that Drew might explode. Shelby had laughed.

It was nice having someone who wasn't afraid of him.

"What's my schedule like today?" He knew what it was supposed to be like. Jam-packed. He had a meeting with the R & D crew that would take up most of the morning. He was scheduled to sit down with a group of beta testers for the new security systems, and he had an afternoon of meetings with his vice presidents that would make him want to tear his own hair out.

But it would be okay, because he would catch a glimpse of Shelby as she walked through the building. He was fairly certain there were already whole teams of his coders who were madly in love with her. A goddess walking among the geeks.

God knew his youngest brother was ready to fall at her feet.

She sighed and let her head rest on his chest. "I did nothing to your schedule today. I have too much to do myself to distract you. You're on your own."

He didn't like the sound of that. "I'll find someone to terrorize, then."

"Drew, you have to be nice to the boys," she insisted. "They already think you're some kind of fire-breathing dragon who will turn on them in an instant."

"I'm perfectly polite."

"You fired Matty Kowalski for no reason," she pointed out. "And you made him cry."

"I had a great reason. He annoyed me." Then the crying had annoyed him even further. The one drawback to having Shelby around was her lack of understanding that annoyance was a perfectly fine reason to fire someone. She was all about tolerance and understanding and patience even when it came to whiny assholes whose mothers were still hovering in the background.

She propped herself up on one elbow and stared down at him. "You've had five complaints against you that HR has had to settle."

"None of those were for sexual harassment. Not a one."

"No, they were because you're a jerk sometimes. You cannot fire someone because they like the wrong house on *Game of Thrones.*"

She didn't understand his world. "I was perfectly reasonable. He doesn't understand the Seven Kingdoms at all. No Lannister belongs on the Iron Throne. Not even Tyrion."

She laughed and he suddenly found himself staring up at her as she straddled him. The sheet fell away and he totally understood why all his geeks fell at her feet. "You know, I find you quite charming when you're being a total nerd."

He let his hands find her hips, and his whole body went on alert. Morning sex. One of his favorite things, followed only by nighttime sex, and afternoon sex, and sex on the couch while watching TV. "Baby, let me tell you about all my favorite episodes of *Doctor Who.*"

He just had to tilt his hips a bit more and he would be able to slide against her pussy, get his dick nice and warm and ready to start the day.

Her laugh rang through the room. She was completely unselfconscious about her nudity. She sat back, her breasts on display. "Oh, I'm definitely in for a fun morning, then."

He flipped her, growling a little. Sometimes she forgot that while she might make the rules about locking the bedroom door, he was still the boss of this. He might be willing to let her run roughshod over his schedule, but he was going to show her who was in charge. "You are in for such a fun morning. I think I'll start by making a feast out of you. I need something to tide me over until I make you my lunch. How about it? You want the Big Bad Wolf to eat that pussy of yours for lunch? I'll lock the doors to my office and spread you on my desk and make a meal out of you."

Her eyes had gone hot. "Yes, I think I would like that, but we'd need to be quieter than usual. People might hear me."

He rubbed himself against her. "I don't care who hears you. If they say anything, I'll fire them."

She groaned, but her arms came up around his neck. "You can't fire them, Drew."

She was far too attached to his employees. "I can. I do it so well. I'm going to play with you now, and then I'll spend all morning thinking about playing with you at lunch. I'll have Henry order something from that French place you like."

He was about to kiss her when she frowned. "I can't have lunch today. I'm not going to be in the building actually." She winced as she glanced at the clock. "Damn. I didn't realize it was so late. I have to go, but I will see you tonight. Ellie and Riley get in at five, right?" She pushed at him lightly and then slid away. "I might have to meet you at the restaurant. Could you have Henry forward that address to me?"

He rolled over. "What do you mean you're not going to be at the office?"

She strode across the room, her perfect ass swaying as she moved. "I've got things to do. Remember? You brought me here for a reason. I've got a man coming in today I need to interview. He's only in town for a few hours. I'll tell you all about it tonight, but I have to hurry if I'm going to make it."

The bathroom door opened and closed, and he heard the sound of the shower coming on. Drew took a deep breath. Sometimes it was easy to forget what she was working on.

Who was she interviewing today?

There was a knock on the door and then his brother's voice. "Hey, Drew, I know you're getting your sex on and the bedroom is now apparently a sacred place and stuff, but I was wondering why you sent the jet to Moscow? It's scheduled to land in a couple of hours, but then it's heading back this afternoon. Should I send the other one to New York to pick up Riley and Ellie?"

Moscow? He rolled off the bed, tugging the sheet with him and wrapping it around his waist. He practically slammed open the door.

Bran's eyes widened. "Dude, you could go get dressed."

"I did not send a plane to Moscow. I want to know who did it, why they did it . . . forget that. Get me a name so I can fire the mother-fucker." He wasn't letting Shelby talk him out of this one. Someone was joyriding in his jet. Some dumbass had thought they could slip one past the boss because he was getting regular sex? Maybe one of his coders had sent the plane to pick up his prepaid Russian bride. He'd already had a talk with the group about that. He'd banned them from any and all websites that promised them wives who would get here, screw the sad fuckers until they got a green card, and then waltz away with the first jock they saw. It caused an endless amount of trouble and he wasn't doing it anymore.

Unfortunately, HR had killed his Friday hooker plans. Apparently they didn't care about biological imperatives, and there was a law or something. He'd even offered to bring in some dudes because he had female coders, too. He was an equal opportunity employer. He simply wanted them to focus on their jobs and not their junk.

Now he was going to make a singular example of someone.

The day was looking up.

"Uh, it was you," Bran said. He frowned suddenly. "You don't think Hatch took it, do you?"

"Hatch would take it to Bangkok or someplace suitably decadent. Why the fuck would he go to Moscow? And he wouldn't need to forge my . . ." He stopped, the answer coming to him in an instant. "Bran, I'm going to need you to take over my morning meetings with R & D."

Bran nodded. "No problem, but I'm supposed to be showing Noah around Austin. You okay with him coming to work with me?"

Drew wasn't certain why Noah needed to be shown around. He

wanted to give the kid a bus pass and a skateboard, and he should be fine. He could go and hang out on Sixth Street and try to find someone who would sell him beer. It's what all the young vagrants were doing these days. "You have to watch him. He can't leave your side. Do you understand what I'm saying?"

"You're worried he's going to steal our secrets?"

"Don't joke around. I'm not kidding, Bran. I know he looks harmless, but that DNA test hasn't come through, and even if it does, I still won't trust him entirely. Make sure he doesn't take his own system in or sit down at one for any amount of time. As a matter of fact, I'll have a security guard escort him around." That was a better plan.

Bran sighed. "I have no idea how Shelby puts up with you. I will handle Noah. I won't let him rob us blind, but I'm also not going to scare him. I'll keep him with me all day. So you want to explain what's going on with the plane to Moscow?"

"My beautiful girlfriend is chasing a story, and I think we have her to thank for Riley getting stuffed on the small jet. Somehow he'll survive. I'll see you tonight." He started to close the door.

Bran held it open. "Hey, you're walking away from a big meeting and not telling me why. Shelby's a reporter. She's done this for a while. I know she probably shouldn't have used the jet the way she did, but she's smart. She doesn't need you to hold her hand."

He frowned his brother's way. "If Carly was meeting with some weird man you'd never met, who might or might not be a criminal, would you shrug and go back to your job? I'm going with her, and she and I are going to have a long talk about the way this relationship works."

Bran stared at him for a moment. "Holy shit, you're in love with her. I thought this was some weird reaction to the rest of us getting married, but you're actually serious about Shelby."

"I moved her in with me. Yes, I'm serious. I don't know that I would call it love, but it's definitely *like*, and we work well together when she's not meeting with criminals behind my back or telling me who I can or can't fire."

Bran threw his hands up with a frustrated huff. "You're telling me. I would have fired Matty, too. No Lannister belongs on the Iron Throne."

At least someone understood reason. "We'll have to find something he's doing wrong. See if he's watching porn on his work computer. I've got to deal with Shelby."

"Drew?" Bran asked.

"What?"

"I'm happy for you." Bran turned and walked away, humming as he went.

Drew shut the door. Somehow Bran's approval meant something to him. It shouldn't, but knowing Bran liked Shelby, approved of their relationship, did something odd to his chest.

And it had felt good to shove his responsibilities for the day off on Bran. Bran would take care of it. He was a man now. When had Bran moved from a responsibility to a partner? Riley, too. His brothers were grown and they were good. They'd figured out a way to move past their own damage.

Could he do the same?

He pushed the question aside. He had something he needed to do. He dropped the sheet because this was a conversation better had while naked.

He strode into the bathroom, steam hitting him. His woman liked it hot. He watched her for a moment, her back to him as she soaped her chest. His reasonable anger warred with lust. Did they have to war? Wasn't this one of those cases where he could do both?

He stepped in behind her. "Baby, would you like to explain why my corporate jet is on its way back from Moscow?"

She stopped, though she didn't move away as he pressed his front to her rear, his cock rubbing against the small of her back. "Well, you did tell me to do whatever I needed. I needed to send the jet to Moscow to pick up my witness. Would you rather I had gone to Moscow myself?"

"I think I advised you to call him up." He let his hands drift up to her breasts. "I assume we're talking about Yuri Volchenko's brother."

She'd mentioned that Charlotte Taggart had found the man.

She turned and her hands came up, caressing his neck and shoulders as though trying to soothe him. "Yes. His brother is still alive and I have some questions for him. He wouldn't talk on the phone or over the computer. He'll only talk in person, and I thought the fastest way to deal with him was by sending a jet so he can't change his mind. I'm meeting him at noon. We'll talk. I'll give him some cash and then he's heading back home. You told me I could spend what I need."

He wasn't pissed about the amount of money she'd spent, but there was something he was upset about. "Yuri's brother is also a member of the *Bratva*."

"I know. It's why he's going to be such an interesting witness," she agreed with a smile. "As long as I have him here, I'm going to ask him a couple of questions I've always wondered about. I have a whole list. Like what guns does he prefer to use? Does the organization provide those, or is he responsible for that on his own? It's the kind of thing that will help me in my fictional world."

Her fictional world? He'd kind of thought it was filled with safe things like sex and daisies and stuff. He needed to shut this shit down now. "McKay-Taggart already tried to talk to this guy. He gave them nothing. He's using you to milk me for cash. Have the plane refuel and turn around."

"He wouldn't talk to McKay-Taggart because he's a member of the Gorev syndicate and Charlotte Taggart has ties to their rival, the Denisovitch syndicate. I've got no ties to anyone. Just heaping mounds of your cash. I can get the information we need."

"What kind of information could he possibly have?" He didn't want to let her go.

She went up on her toes and brushed her lips against his. "I won't know until I ask. I promise I will give you a full report when I'm done."

"You won't need to."

She grabbed a towel and stepped out, wrapping it around her body. "You're not interested? Drew, I think he might be able to tell us a few things. I've asked around. He was close to his brother."

Drew turned the handle of the shower from hot to cold. He wasn't getting any love and affection this morning. "You won't have to tell me because I'm going to be there. Bran is handling my meetings. I'm going with you."

He stepped under the now chilly water. Yes, this was what he needed. His lovely morning had turned into an interview with what would likely be some chain-smoking criminal who reeked of vodka.

A look of pure horror crossed her face. "Drew, I don't think that's a good idea."

He shrugged. "I don't think any of it's a good idea, but that doesn't seem to matter. I'll be ready in ten minutes."

She turned, irritation obvious in the way she stomped off. If she hadn't wanted him to find out, she should have used her own private jet.

He was smart enough to not say that out loud.

Drew let the cold water wash over him. It wasn't fair to be annoyed that she was doing the very job he'd hired her to do. He knew that. But every step she took brought them closer to the day when she would find out what he'd done.

Or he could honor the spirit of the contract and let her write the damn book. She didn't need to know he'd given himself a hard out. She wouldn't read that contract again. It would be nothing more than a cute way he'd gotten close to her. It didn't have to be the thing that broke them up.

She would have her book and he would survive the press. The

never-ending press that would savage his family. The media would smell a great story and his status would fuel the fire. He could handle it. He could roll his eyes and move on, but what would happen to Mia's child? He remembered vividly when the kids at his school found out about his past. The best that would happen was a nauseating sympathy. The worst . . . he'd seen some parents who wouldn't let their kids around his brothers because the family was trash. They'd painted him with the same violent brush that had tarnished his father.

Now it would be a national story, fanned by his success. The story had died down, but a book by Shelby would go global, and all his family secrets would be laid out for the world to pick apart and use as entertainment. *Billionaire Software Guru's Mother Tries to Kill Him.* The headlines would write themselves.

Perhaps he could handle it, but Mia wasn't the only one who would soon have a kid. He knew Ellie and Riley were already talking about it. Bran and Carly would be next. A whole new generation who would have to deal with the scandal.

What would his father want? His name restored or his grandchildren protected? Did it even matter since his father was dead and everything rested on Drew's shoulders?

Yeah, mornings sucked.

Shelby sat down across from the Russian and pulled out her notepad. "Do you mind if I make notes?"

He'd been clear that he wouldn't accept any kind of recording. He didn't trust phones or computers. He would only speak to her in person and only if she sent a jet. He seemed to enjoy flying first class.

Pavel, who must have been almost sixty but looked rather older, pulled a cigarette out of his pocket. "If you do not mind if I be smoking. They do not allow on plane."

"Sorry, buddy, but this is a nonsmoking establishment," Drew said with a smirk.

He was going to be so much fun. There was a reason she hadn't mentioned today's meeting to him. "You own this building, Drew. He can smoke and then he's heading back to Russia."

They were meeting at a private airfield, in 4L's personal hangar. She'd made sure everything was nice and friendly. A luncheon had been placed on a well-set table in the corner of the hangar. She'd attempted to make sure Volchenko felt like a welcome guest.

Drew kept looking at him like he was going to murder someone at any moment.

She sighed and passed Pavel a coffee mug to use for the ashes. She wasn't thrilled about the smoke, either, but one did what one had to do to get the story. Lord knew she was putting up with Drew's broody ass. "Please, feel free."

"Yes, to give us all cancer," Drew muttered under his breath.

Pavel waved him off. "You Americans. I don't understand you at all. Do you think to live forever?"

"Not the way he eats, he doesn't," Shelby said under her breath. "So you're Pavel Volchenko and your brother was a man named Yuri Volchenko."

He lit the cigarette, taking a long drag before sitting back. "This is correct. I have several brothers. Yuri was worst. He is horrible person, but good brother. He go into mob to help his family."

"Is that why you went in?" She had to admit, she found the whole scenario fascinating. This was a man who had an entirely different experience in his life than anyone she knew. Even if he didn't have information she might be able to use, she would still be interested in talking to him.

He shrugged. "Some people go into army. I choose this path, though not the same as Yuri. He had different talents than I."

"You mean he was good at killing people," Drew said with a frown.

If it bothered Pavel, he didn't show it. In fact, a hearty smile crossed his face. "He was so good at it. Such talent. When he was working, no one survived. He take the job. He does it professionally. Some assassins, they feel the need to be . . . how do you say? Peacocks. Yes, peacocks showing their feathers. You know what I say?"

"Murder them fast?" Drew snarked.

She sent him her sternest look. "Will you stop?"

Again Pavel plowed through. "I say killing is profession like any other. You get to work, do job, and don't be hole of ass. You know what it take to keep blood to minimum? This is mark of professional."

"Did Yuri ever talk about the job to you?" She was thankful Drew sat back in his chair. He seemed to settle in, so she continued. "From what I understand, you remained close to him. You worked for the same syndicate, right?"

He waved a hand, taking a long drag off his cigarette. "Bah, Yuri moved around. He liked to work for several. Yuri was all about paycheck, but I wanted to move up in world. I become a *vor* for Gorev almost forty years ago."

"A *vor*?" Drew asked, his natural curiosity coming into play.

She'd done her homework on the *Bratva*. "It means thief. He was a made man in the syndicate."

"Pretty girl is smart, too," Yuri said, winking her way. "She is correct. I become *brigadier* years later. That mean I have my own men within the family. It also mean I don't discuss business with shits like Denisovitch. He can eat my balls. If you speak with that fuck, I will come back and deal with you."

Drew's face went red, but Shelby had already prepared for this eventuality. Apparently being one of the world's most sought-after CEOs hadn't prepped Drew for small Mafia skirmishes.

She put a hand on his chest and looked at the mobster. "You don't have to worry about that. I don't have any ties to Dusan Denisovitch. The closest Drew comes is his sister is married to a man who's a half brother to a man who's married to his cousin who never gets back to Russia. We're practically strangers, and neither one of us has any loyalty at all to the Denisovitch syndicate."

Pavel seemed to settle back. "You're sure?"

"America isn't like Russia," she assured him. "We don't keep our ties to the old world. Is this why you wouldn't talk to McKay-Taggart when they questioned you?"

"Charlotte Taggart is daughter of enemy," Pavel replied. "I will not be telling her anything. But if you have no ties and are willing to pay, I talk to you. What does Yuri care? He is dead. All he has left is his reputation, and that has been maligned."

Now they were getting somewhere. "How has your brother's reputation been maligned?"

"My brother would never have made mess of job. All his years of work and he never fail." Pavel's expression turned grave. "Yuri was dedicated to job and took money seriously. He is paid based on how risky job is."

"Risky?" Drew asked. "I would think all murders would come with some risk. Prison comes to mind."

"Prison is always chance we take," Pavel allowed. "But certain jobs, there is more risk. A rival brother in Russia, one who is known to police, he will not be missed. Police will turn other way because they consider a matter for the *Bratva*. This is cheap job. Depending on who it is, some assassins would do this job for fun. A government employee who is not cooperating with something boss needs, this is more. People notice and police must investigate, so he charge more."

"So an American businessman would be expensive?" Shelby asked, knowing the answer.

"He would have charged a hundred thousand for American," Pavel said, flicking his ashes into the mug. "Americans very expensive. American dies and everyone is in uproar."

"Excellent. We know nothing more than what we already did," Drew said with a long sigh. "Can we be done now?"

"Are you listening to him? According to everything we know, the assassin who killed your parents was paid two hundred thousand dollars. Yuri charged a hundred grand a piece." For someone who was so damn smart, he wasn't following the conversation well. "Two people, Drew. He got paid for two people who would have caused him no end of trouble had his plan not worked. Had anything gone wrong, the heat would have been incredibly high, hence the cost of two hundred thousand dollars. For two people."

Drew frowned, the weight of what she was saying finally seeming to sink in. "For two people, but there were six of us in the house that night. He must have only gotten paid for the ones he managed to actually take out."

"My brother never fail once, and he always require money up front," Pavel said solemnly. "Too many people decide not to pay if you do not get money in the beginning. And one rule my brother has? He never, never kill children. He watches our mother lose our sister. He never kill a child. Some say he make this rule because of his carefulness, because killing child can attract much attention, but I know truth. My brother would never have taken a job where children were involved. He would have gotten in, killed his targets, and left children peacefully sleeping."

Drew had flushed slightly. "So there's honor among murderers?"

This was precisely why she hadn't wanted him involved. He couldn't look at this rationally. It was why she shouldn't have tried to investigate her own brother's death. She was too close to it. Logic and reason had to come into play, but all Drew could hear was someone speaking kindly of the man who'd pulled the trigger on his father.

Pavel simply shrugged. "Even killer has line he will not to be crossing. My brother does not do this for fun."

Drew was quiet for a moment. "If he wasn't hired to kill the children, then why were the doors barred? Why set the fire at all?"

Again he shook his head. "My brother, he was afraid of fire. When we were young, we were in apartment building that caught fire. It is how we lost sister. She burned to death and Yuri said he could never forget how she screamed. He would never have set fire. He was simple man. He used poison when job required finesse, a bomb when it required certain level of shock, and gun all other times."

Drew stared directly at the man. "And I should believe you, why?"

"Why would I lie? My brother is killer, but does have some honor."

She wanted so badly to reach out and hold Drew's hand because the answer was right there, but he'd drawn in on himself. She needed to get everything she could out of this interview. "Did he ever talk about this particular job? How did the clients find him?"

"He has contacts in many parts of world," Pavel explained. "Oftentimes he is contacted through syndicate by private persons . . . how would you say . . . the people who look into problems. Not police."

"Private investigators?"

He nodded. "Yes, this is word. Sometimes he is contacted by investigators, sometimes it is lawyers. You think assassin is bad. Lawyer is worse, I say," Pavel theorized. "But I believe in this part of America he spoke with investigator. A man."

"Does a man have a name?" Drew asked, his voice tight.

If Pavel was worried about Drew's tone, he didn't show it. "Most do. I believe this one was called Williams. I do not remember first name, but he live in Dallas with cowboys. He would make arrangements for payments. Always through private banks. Nothing traceable. He have connections to syndicate. Even syndicate needs outside eyes to come in from time to time. It is better this way. Too many emotions among the families. And outside contacts would deal with police for us. In return they send clients and would be given a fee for bringing in work."

"Is there any way to find out who contacted your brother?" She would be interested to know who the go-between was.

"Everything would have been taken care of remotely, and he would have received instructions from handler here in Texas. This man Williams would have set up payments and everything would be private." Pavel poured a bit of the vodka she'd had set on the table. "He would do job, but never meet client. If he did, he would have to kill client and this is bad for repeat business, if you know what I mean."

"I didn't wake up from the gunshot," Drew said quietly. "I would have thought the shot would wake me up. There would have been two and my room was right above where my father's body was found."

Pavel looked halfway sympathetic. "He would have used suppressor . . . what you call . . . silencer. Due to nature of crime, he would have taken suppressor with him and left the gun behind. It was to look like murder and then suicide. This is to keep police in the dark. Was it heat from fire that woke you? Or smoke detectors?"

"They didn't go off." Drew was staring at some place in the distance, as though he was right back in that house and not seeing what was happening in the here and now. "Someone disabled them that day. It wasn't the heat that woke me. It was the crackling sound. Like a log in a fire on a cold night. And then I realized I was inside the fireplace."

Drew looked like he was going to be sick, but he took a deep breath and then let it out slowly. "I think I'm going to call the office, make sure everything is going all right. If you need anything, I'll be right outside."

He stood and walked off.

Her heart ached for him.

"I have looked into this," Pavel said. "They could have gotten someone who would have killed children, but why? The people who pay my brother already had a way to take company, yes?"

He wasn't an unintelligent criminal. "Yes, there was a clause in the contract. If Benedict was found to have perpetrated any kind of felony, his stock defaulted to the other investors."

"Ah, this is why murder must come first." He nodded and sat back. "I wondered. More simple to shoot them both. So that begs question: Why set fire? It raised questions where none needed to be raised."

"I agree."

"Only person who would do this is person who hates. My brother kill quickly. But burning the house with the children inside, that would take a dark heart. From what I read, this person locked everything. They gave the children no way out. They would have burned to death. This is horrible way to go. He is one who saved them all, no?"

She fought to blink back tears because she couldn't help but think about how terrified Drew must have been, how alone he would have felt. His parents were dead on the floor. At least he would have believed that. He'd been fourteen years old and the world had come down on his shoulders.

Had it just happened again? He knew his mother was evil, but somehow discovering that she'd done what a hired assassin wouldn't do was so much worse.

"Yes, he saved them."

"He should to be careful," Pavel said quietly. "He has much to lose and if this person is still alive, he will be wanting to cover tracks. Sometimes these things, they are better left alone. Sometimes it is best to let God sort these things out, no?"

"I don't think he can let that happen. Would you?" She couldn't see a world in which Drew simply lived out his life without pursuing some kind of revenge on his mother. He might not be capable of it. She had to hope he would allow her exposing the truth to the world to be that vengeance. She didn't like the thought of him going toe-to-

toe with a woman who had hated her life so much, she'd been willing to burn it down along with her children.

His lips curled up in a devilish grin. "I would not let such crime go unanswered. I enjoy violence. Though if I had billion dollars, perhaps I enjoy other things. You have more questions, you said."

Suddenly they didn't seem so important. "I think this should do. If you can think of anything else, I would appreciate it."

"You are good girl. You call me if you want to ask questions about life. For the fictions, though. Everything I say to you is not truth." He winked pointedly. "If I tell you all about how I take down the worst criminal in Moscow using nothing but a pencil and a rubber, this would be mere fiction. But I did this brilliantly. You see the pencil was extremely sharp and I used the rubber to make a bow. It was extra large, of course. My aim is true and I hit the carotid artery from twenty feet away. Then no more bad guys. Well, except for me, of course."

He continued on, but she was thinking about Drew. And Iris.

She had burned her house down and tried to kill her own children. She'd wanted to start over and leave nothing behind.

Would she try again?

Drew stepped back in and sat down beside her as Pavel continued on. She reached for his hand. He tangled their fingers together, but didn't look at her. Sitting so close, he'd never seemed further away.

Chapter Ten

Drew held Shelby's hand as she eased into the limo. He closed the door behind her before looking to his driver. "How bad is traffic? Can you get me to the office fairly quickly?"

Bennett was in his late fifties, a professional rapidly approaching the end of his career. He'd told Drew he planned to retire in the next two years. One more change Drew would have to deal with. "It could be thirty or forty minutes to downtown, but getting home will be just as long."

He sighed and opened the door again. "Traffic is bad through downtown. I need to get back to the office. I'll have Bennett take you home and I'll call a cab."

She frowned his way. "No."

"Shelby, it will take more than an hour to drop me off at the office and take you home. I can spare you a good portion of time."

"Then it's good that I wasn't going home. I'm going to the office with you. I want to transcribe some of my notes and then I'll go with you straight to the restaurant."

He could argue, but she would see through him. He simply nodded Bennett's way. "To the office, please."

He climbed in beside her. Luckily the window between the back and the front of the limo was down. Maybe it was time to refocus on his work. He'd neglected it in favor of spending enormous amounts of time in bed with Shelby.

Yes, it was time to look to his work. The launch was coming up and he wasn't going to fail. This was where his father had gone wrong. His father had paid too much attention to his mistress and not enough to what was going on around him. Perhaps if he had focused on his work and his family, he wouldn't have gotten himself killed. Perhaps he would have noticed that his wife was a raging psychopath who should never have been allowed to breed. Perhaps he would have realized the danger he was in.

Perhaps he wouldn't have left Drew holding the bag.

"Babe? Can we talk about it?" Shelby's quiet voice broke through his inner rage.

He was so fucking angry with his father. With Hatch. With his mother. With all of them. They'd fucked up everything and he'd been left to deal with it.

"I need to make some calls. Check in with Bran." He was pleased his voice was so even. "I might be able to make the last afternoon meeting."

He pulled out his cell, but she slid her hand over his. "I don't think you're in any place to go into a meeting, Drew. We could stop somewhere and get a drink and talk this through. Or we could go home and relax before we meet everyone."

"I told you, I need to get to work, so unless you're offering to blow me right here in the limo, I suggest you get your own work done." There went his even tone. He sounded arctic, but then this was probably closer to who he actually was than the idiot lover he'd been playing for the last two weeks. She should get used to it. This was who he really was.

Cold. Calculating. Controlling.

He was silent as she leaned over.

"I'm sorry you had to hear that, Bennett. We're going to need some alone time," she said before pressing the button to close the window between them.

"Not a problem, ma'am," Bennett managed before the window shut him out.

And left Drew alone with a woman who might walk away tonight. He thought he would have more time with her, but he wasn't sure he could control the roiling anger in his gut. He should never have gotten in this damn car. He should have walked away because he knew this would happen. He would explode and show her how much of an ass he could be, and she would realize how much better she could do. He would be alone again, and that was probably the way it should be. He had nothing but cash to give her and she didn't value that.

"Drew, talk to me."

"I don't want to talk, and I'm sick of you interfering in my life and my schedule. I told you what to do if you want my attention." Better to show her how awful he could be. He looked back down at his phone. That should shut her up.

He was about to press the button to connect him to Bran, when he felt her move. She twisted on the seat next to him, unbuckling her seat belt and flipping her body over so she was lying on the bench, her head in his lap.

"Why do you always try to make me feel like a prostitute when you're upset?" Her green eyes stared up at him.

Damn, but she was pretty. "Why do you have to keep pushing me when I've made it plain I don't want to talk?"

"All right, you don't want to talk. Let me hold you."

"Why? What would that do?"

"It would help me feel close to you."

"I don't want you close to me. Get up."

She shook her head. "If I thought for a second you didn't want me close to you because you didn't want me, I would. Drew, what she did to you was beyond horrible."

Why couldn't she understand him? "I don't want to talk about it."

She sat up, putting a hand on his chest. "Okay, then let me hold you. Hell, I'll do that thing you asked about if you tell me you need me and don't turn it into something trashy. I'm okay with giving you what you need, but you have to accept it for the gift it is and not some kind of transaction. If you need sex right now to take your mind off what you learned today, I'm your girl, but I'm not your punching bag."

Frustration welled inside him. "Are you? And how do you know you're the only one? Girl, that is. You don't want me to treat this as a transaction, but isn't that exactly what it is?"

"I suppose everything is, but the question is, what do I get out of it?"

He should have known this would happen. It was too good to be true. "I don't know. I wish you would fucking tell me because I don't know. I guess you get the book. I guess you get to push your career forward and I get to fuck you."

"I get your sparkling personality," she replied. "I came for the story but I stayed for the sarcasm. You can say all the nasty words you like, but I see through you. I know you need me. You need me to push you to take time off and to enjoy your life, and I'm starting to think that you can't enjoy your life without me."

He didn't like how vulnerable she was making him feel. "You think a lot of yourself, don't you?"

"I didn't. Not for a long time, and then I met this insanely brilliant beast who has no idea how to deal with a woman who cares about him. You're trainable, though. You've done so well, but this is a speed bump we're going to have to get through. So one blow job and then you'll listen to what I have to say?"

Despite the anger inside him, his dick hardened at the very thought. "I thought you weren't going to prostitute yourself."

She gave him a smile. "I'm not. It's the only way you know how to accept comfort right now, and you need it so badly, Drew. So yes, I'll give this to you, but you should understand that if you say one bad thing about me afterward, if you aren't appreciative, you might not have anything left for the next girl."

He gave up the fight. He reached out and hauled her up and into his lap. Somehow she always managed to find a way through his every defense. "I don't want another girl. I don't want fucking anyone but you."

She cupped his face, looking him deep in the eyes. "I know because I feel the same way, Drew. So stop pushing me away. Tell me."

He shook his head. "I already told you. I don't want to talk, but I can't do what I should do, either. You should get out of this mess."

"I'm not going anywhere."

Then she'd made her choice. "I can't be gentle right now."

"I don't need gentle. I need you."

He let his hand find her hair, fingers tangling in all that soft red glory. "I hope you don't regret those words, baby. Because I need a lot from you right now. I want to forget. I want to fucking forget that my mother did what an assassin wouldn't. She locked us in. She set the fire."

"And you brought them all out and you took care of them and you were a man, Drew." There were tears in her eyes as she stroked his skin. "She did her best and you saved them all."

But he hadn't. He hadn't saved his father. He'd been a fool for years, thinking his parents were some pure thing that evil had cut down.

He'd only found one pure thing in the whole world, and she was sitting in his lap and offering him everything.

And he was going to take it. He forced his mouth down on hers, her arms coming up and around him. The woman had no sense at all, but he wasn't going to complain. Need wiped out all his rage. He needed her. If he could please her, keep her close, maybe all of this would be survivable.

He let his tongue play against hers, devouring her like a starving man. How could she do this to him? He'd had her twice the night before and yet his whole body ached with need. She was the only thing that could make him forget. He'd been foolish to think he could work when what he needed was to make her scream.

"Lie down on the seat."

She looked up at him. "What?"

"Don't argue with me. Lie down." He needed to be in control. The last several hours he'd been so out of control. This was the one place he could rule.

She turned and lay down, her feet toward him. He eased the heels off her, tossing them to the floor. Such soft skin. He let his hands drift from her ankles up to her calves. Her skirt was modest, but those bare legs got to him. Soft and warm. Like the rest of her. That was what she was to him—all the softness and warmth he'd missed out on for years.

"Spread your legs," he ordered.

Her eyes had already gone hot and she spread herself for him. "I thought I was the one who was going to be on my knees."

"I like you on your back," he growled as his hand moved up to her inner thigh. "I want to lose myself for a little while. I want to surround myself with your taste and touch and the way you smell when your pussy gets greedy. Do you have any idea how much I love the way you respond to me?"

"It's never happened with anyone else, Drew. I like sex, but it's so different with you. All you have to do is walk into a room and I want you."

For now.

He let his hand drift up, rubbing against the cotton underwear she wore. It was already damp. He slipped under the hem to stroke the petals of her sex. "Do you want me to taste you, Shelby? Do you want me to put my mouth on you and let my tongue explore every inch of your pussy?"

She nodded. "Yes. I want that. I want you to put your mouth on me."

His finger slipped over her clitoris, that plump bud already prominent. "Can I suck you here?"

"God, yes," she replied quickly. "Please."

Yes, he needed this. Hearing Shelby beg for him, seeing her making a place for him, giving herself up to him—that's what would burn away the shame he'd felt. He shoved her skirt up with rough hands and leaned over, putting his face right against her, inhaling the intoxicating scent of her need. "I love how you smell."

Her body moved restlessly. He sat back up and dragged her underwear down. He had to move a bit, but he managed to get them off her legs and tossed them aside. She wouldn't need them again. He liked the thought of her walking around for the rest of the day without any underwear. All he would have to do was push up her skirt and he could take what was his.

"I also love how you look. You're so beautiful." In every way. He was staring at her pussy. It was the single most perfect pussy he'd ever seen. Plump and wet and perfect and all for him.

He'd been accused of being selfish before, but it wasn't true. He hadn't known true selfishness until this moment. Everything he'd done had been to protect or avenge his family. He hadn't spent his college years partying and having fun and learning who he was. He'd spent them working eighteen-hour days to lift them all up. 4L wasn't his. It was theirs. The houses and cars weren't really his. They belonged to his family.

Shelby was his. Only his. This relationship was just the two of them. "I lied when I said I didn't like you interfering with my schedule."

He leaned down, grateful for the roominess of the limo. Her back arched, offering her body up. "I know that. I'm sure you're an excellent liar when it comes to business, but I see through you, Lawless."

No one else did. He let his mouth hover over her, breathing her in. "I want you to fuck with my schedule because that means you want to see me."

"It means I care about you," Shelby agreed. "It means I want you to spend more time with me and enjoy your life more."

"I've enjoyed my life so much more since you came into it." He kissed her clit. Just a peck.

She groaned, a frustrated sound. "I feel the same way, though right now I'm ready to smack you. Please, Drew."

He chuckled. "But this is pleasing Drew. You screw with my schedule to show me how much you care. I tease you. I make you crazy and then give you what you want. I think it's a fair trade-off."

"It doesn't feel like it right now. How can you do this to me? Five minutes ago I wasn't thinking about sex and now I'm pretty sure I'm going to die if you don't hurry up and put your mouth on me."

He gave her a teasing lick. "Like this?"

Her breathy moan was all the response he needed.

He settled in, licking and sucking at her like she was the ripest of all fruit. Sweet and tangy and so uniquely Shelby. He delved deep, his tongue spearing up.

Over and over he licked and sucked and made sure not to miss a single inch of her precious flesh. He laved her with affection, with devotion. Her hands came up, stroking through his hair as she pressed her pelvis against him. She whispered his name like it was some kind of prayer.

He parted her labia and ran his tongue over her again, licking up to her clitoris. He pressed one finger up inside her. No matter how many times he fucked her, she was always so tight. So perfect.

He pressed a second finger in and then sucked her clit between his lips.

No thin privacy wall was going to stop the driver from hearing the way she screamed out.

He pressed her down as her body bucked.

Finally she relaxed, shuddering as he lapped up her arousal. It was his. It belonged to him the way she did. Every orgasm was his.

He kissed her clit one last time and pushed himself up and off her, his hands going to his belt. His dick was hard and throbbing. So ready for her.

She shook her head. "Not on your life."

He'd never known that four little words could devastate.

Deep breath. He hadn't expected that. He forced himself to sit back. Act like it was no big deal. Why didn't she want him?

"You are so lucky I keep an extra set of undies in my desk," she said, her tone breathless as she pushed her skirt down and sat up.

"I suppose you're always prepared." He wasn't going to look at her. He stared out the window. The limo was stuck in traffic. Excellent. Now he had half an hour where his brain was going to go over and over what he'd done wrong.

"I have to be. I'm working in this building where the boss is a total horny hottie and he seems to like me a lot." She sounded as though nothing had gone wrong at all. Just another day.

"I suppose so."

She switched to the bench opposite him. "You know you're the touchiest man in the world. Everyone thinks your ego is the size of Jupiter, but I know differently. One of these days, you're going to trust me, Lawless. You told me what you wanted. I want it, too."

She sank down to her knees, her hands on his thighs.

His dick was right back at full mast. "I thought you were done."

Her pretty green eyes rolled. "I know. Like I said, one of these days, you're going to trust me. Until then, I will put up with your touchy ego."

She ran her hands up his thighs and to the buckle on his belt.

He only had a touchy ego when it came to her. He didn't give a flying fuck about anyone else. If one of his previous lovers had told him to stop, he would have rolled off her and gone back to work. No harm. No foul. Not everyone was always in the mood. He wasn't the guy who demanded repayment.

But the idea of Shelby not wanting him was devastating.

"It's only for you," he said quietly.

The smile that crossed her face lit up his whole fucking world. "I know. That's why I put up with it. Well, maybe there are some other reasons. Like one I can think of."

She eased his zipper down and smoothed back the sides of his slacks. Her hand skimmed over his cock and he felt himself jump at the touch. Her pink-tipped fingernails slipped under the waistband of his boxers, drawing them down and freeing his dick.

He had to take a deep breath because that felt so damn good. She took him in hand, stroking him gently.

"You know you're beautiful, Drew." Her eyes were on his cock as she stroked her thumb over the head.

From anyone else, he would roll his eyes and look for what the person wanted from him. From Shelby, the words made him blush. "I'm glad you think so, though I do think we should get your eyesight checked."

"Nope. You're very pretty," she insisted. "You're also extremely good with your tongue. I'll have to learn from you. I love the way you eat me up. I want to make sure you feel the same. I want you to love the way I suck your cock."

He couldn't imagine doing anything else. He loved the way she ate toast. It was stupid but he noticed everything about her. He let his hands slip into her hair, twisting it lightly. Yeah, he knew she liked that, too. Shelby enjoyed when he took control in certain situations. "Lick me."

She let him guide her down, her tongue darting out and running lightly over the head of his cock. He bit back a hiss of pure pleasure as she flattened her tongue and found the *V* at the back of his cock head. She rubbed the sensitive flesh, teasing it until he was sure his eyes would cross.

"Take more." He watched her, watched as her lips opened and his cock began to disappear.

Her tongue whirled, the sensation sparking through him like lightning.

"More."

She took him slowly, inch by inch. Her tongue worked him over, rolling around and around the stalk of his cock. All the way down and then back up to the head only to start all over again.

He leaned back, watching her as she worked him over. The woman needed no coaching. She was a natural when it came to pleasing a man, and he had zero problems with that. He was happy that every other man she'd cared about had been a fucking idiot to let her go. This woman was magnificent, and he didn't want to be one more in a line of men who let her down. He wanted to be the one she could count on.

He wanted to be so selfish about her.

He tilted his hips up as she worked her way down again. Every inch of his cock was in her mouth, and her hand reached down and cupped his balls.

"Damn, but that's perfect. Your mouth is perfect. Fuck, baby, you're perfect for me."

She sucked her way up his cock and then her face turned toward him with a smile. "I think so. We work well together, Lawless. So the next time I tell you to get off me, don't think I'm rejecting you. Think I'm doing something superhot because I'm your girl and that's what I do."

His girl. His. "I'll try, but I'm not great at this. You need to know that I've been thrown for a loop and it's all you. You, Shelby. You're unlike anyone I've ever known and I'm all in. Do you want to know what I'm thinking right now?"

"You're scheming."

"I am. I'm trying to figure out how to keep you close to me even when I screw up and do things you won't like." *Even when you find out I'm lying to you.*

He would change the rest of his world if it meant he could keep her. He simply couldn't barter the next generation, because that might include their own kids. He couldn't lead another generation into a scandal that wouldn't stop. He couldn't.

She sucked him hard, going from head to base and back again. Her hand cupped his balls, rolling them in a way that made him gasp for breath. His hands clenched around her hair, holding her hard against him. *Deep breath. Don't come. Not yet.*

She ran her tongue over him, and then her head came up. Her head moved down, her hands cupping his balls.

He couldn't hold back when she rolled him up and her throat worked down around him. His cock hit something so fucking soft, and he couldn't hold back a second longer.

"I'm going to come." His fingers tightened in her hair.

She didn't fight him at all. Her hands clamped down and she moved her head, sucking roughly. He let go and let her take over. Her lips moved down his cock, owning him and everything he had to give to her. He watched as she sucked him. Her hands rolled him, tugging hard on his balls because those belonged to her, too. Everything he was belonged to her.

His hands dug into the leather of the seats, and he called out her name as he came.

He pressed up as she took everything he had to give her. He pressed up hard against her mouth and yet she still sucked him. His hands held her head lightly, allowing her to move away. She didn't. Her throat worked hard, taking every ounce as she pressed against him.

His whole body relaxed, pure pleasure making its way through his veins. He leaned back, every muscle softening. It was more than his body. His whole fucking soul relaxed as she looked up at him, a smile on her face. Like she'd accomplished something amazing.

"I'm crazy about you, Shelby." She shouldn't think anything less. She was the single most amazing person he'd ever met.

She wiped her hands across her perfectly plump lips. "Back at you, Lawless. And you taste like fucking sunshine. Did you know that?"

God, he was in love with her.

The traffic moved on slowly, but he was pretty damn sure he never would.

Chapter Eleven

The limo stopped in front of the 4L building but she hesitated. For several reasons. Mostly because her panties were stuffed into her purse since they weren't wearable at this point.

God, Drew was going to kill her. She'd never had a man who could make her do the things he did. She'd thrown off all norms, all societal niceties. They didn't matter because Drew Lawless was such a brooding hottie that her panties melted off and her body spread wide the minute she knew he needed her.

Yep, her feminist friends were going to disavow her. They would put her name on a list of women who succumbed to the needs of their female parts.

He knew how to make her female parts sing.

The door opened and Drew winked her way. He slid out of the limo and immediately turned and held out a hand.

There was her gentlemanly lover.

"Does this mean you're feeling better?" She scooted out of the limo. She needed to wear pants more often. It was infinitely easier to get in and out of limos in pants. Of course, Drew would simply get them off her, and then she would find out how hard it was to get dressed in a limo.

He pulled her close. When they began their relationship, she'd worried he would be a bit cold in public, protecting his image above all. Not Drew. He didn't care who saw them. The building was 4L's campus, and pretty much everyone walking around was one of his employees or clients. It didn't seem to matter to Drew. He leaned over and kissed her. "Infinitely better."

She was the one who blushed.

She let her hands drift to his waist. "I'm glad. And I'm so sorry you had to hear that, but I was happy you were with me."

That was the key to Drew. He would take almost anything if he thought he was helping. Taking responsibility was the core of Drew's personality. She'd been wrong to try to leave him out this morning. He needed to be needed.

One day she would be able to tell this man how much she cared about him and he would believe her. All it required was time and a little patience.

"No more Russian mobsters," he said, leaning over to kiss her again. This time he laid a sweet peck on her nose. His tenderness fed her soul. She loved how passionately he made love to her, but she craved his softness. He gave it to no one but his family.

"No promises, but I do swear I'll tell you the next time I make an appointment that could be considered dangerous." She slid her hand into his.

He nodded toward Bennett, who had a knowing smile on his face. "See you at five thirty. We'll need to go home before we go to the restaurant. Are you picking up my brother and his wife?"

"Yes, sir. I'll make sure to refresh the car before heading to the airport."

"Thank you." He tangled his fingers with hers and started toward the front doors.

Refresh? She felt herself go a wild pink. "Oh, God, he thinks he needs to clean the limo because we had sex in it. He knows we had sex in the back."

"Baby, most of Austin knows it. You're enthusiastic and Bennett is an intelligent man."

Pure embarrassment flooded through her. "I didn't even think about that."

He held the door open for her. "Why would you need to? It doesn't matter what anyone else thought. It's not like we're living in the Victorian age. Hey, Michaelson? I just had sex in the back of a limo. Do you think less of me?"

A young man with headphones around his neck smiled Drew's way. "Nope. Makes me want to be you, boss."

She lightly slapped his arm. "Andrew Lawless, you need a serious lesson in tact."

She shook her head as the doors opened.

Case Taggart was standing there. His eyes flared as he caught sight of them. "Thank God. I've been trying to get hold of you for the last half hour."

"I was busy and I turned off my phone," Drew replied.

"We had a meeting that couldn't be interrupted," she said quickly before Drew could explain that there was no way he was answering his phone while getting a blow job.

"There's been an accident. Noah was hurt. We have to get to the hospital." Case started walking toward the parking lot. "I've got a car here. Everyone else is already at the hospital."

"What happened?" Shelby asked, hurrying to keep up with the taller men.

"Noah and Bran were walking across the street to get some lunch, and out of nowhere some SUV hit Noah."

A chill went through her. "A black SUV?"

Case's jaw was tight as he nodded. "Yes. I've been going over the footage from the security cameras in the area. I've got a partial plate. It's a rental. I'll call around and see what I can figure out after I drop you two off at the hospital."

"How bad is it?" Drew asked, his tone perfectly even.

She knew that when he seemed unemotional, it was all an act.

"He hit his head on the concrete. He wasn't conscious by the time the ambulance came. I haven't gotten an update. Bran went with him to the hospital."

Drew pulled his phone out, staring down at it while he walked. "Damn it, Case. I'm sorry. Is Bran all right?"

"He's shaken up, but he didn't get hit," Case explained. "From what some of the witnesses said, it was like the SUV was trying to hit Noah."

They walked into the parking garage, going from sunlight to gloom in a second.

Case nodded to where he'd parked the Audi that Mia used when she was in Austin. There was a clicking sound as he opened the locks. "I've already talked to the police. They're treating it like a hit-and-run. They think the driver was probably distracted and then panicked and fled the scene. I'm not so sure."

Drew opened the back passenger side door, ushering Shelby inside before he slid into the seat next to Case. He was silent for a moment as Case backed the car up and started out.

"It's not Hatch."

Shelby leaned forward, touching his shoulder. She understood why he couldn't think about this being Hatch, but there were reasons Hatch might want to get rid of Noah. She also had to consider that this was Iris or someone she'd hired. Not that she could say anything about that in front of Case. "We'll find him."

"It's not Hatch," Drew replied, a chill in his tone. "He wouldn't do that. He's got no reason to do it."

Case looked back at her, his face grim.

Shelby let her body rest against the seat, hooking the belt. She hoped the hospital had good Wi-Fi because she had a few leads to follow. She had to unravel the mystery before someone died.

Two hours later, she stared down at her computer. She'd narrowed down the list of private investigators who might have hired Yuri to two. Luckily one of them was still in business. Williams Investigations was run by a forty-year-old man named Kevin Williams, but she'd found records that it had once been run by the man's father, a Maurice Williams who had died a few years back after a long illness. His son had taken over and contracted his services to several large companies in the DFW area.

According to his social media, he also spent a good deal of time in Russia. There were pictures of him with his St. Petersburg–born bride and their children smiling and waving from various landmarks.

Yeah, she liked that connection.

The question was whether his father had done any work for the original company. She needed a way to tie Williams Investigations to Benedict Lawless's company.

Drew sat down beside her, a disposable cup in his hand. "Any luck?"

She kept her voice down because they weren't alone in the waiting room. "A bit. I'll forward you anything I find. How about on your end?"

His jawline tightened. "No. Not yet."

He was still looking for Hatch, but it appeared he didn't want to be found.

Or he'd rented a black SUV and was trying to take care of a problem.

The thing she couldn't quite wrap her head around was why Noah would be a problem at all. If Hatch was truly worried that Noah would hurt Drew, shouldn't he have stayed behind and watched over him like he'd said he would? Why pursue it in this fashion?

Unless he was trying desperately to hide something.

Bran walked into the waiting room, his eyes tired. Carly jumped up and practically ran to her husband. Mia and Case were holding hands as they approached.

Drew stood but didn't reach for her. "What's the news?"

"He's got a concussion, but they're positive he's going to be okay," Bran explained. "He doesn't remember a thing after we walked out of the building. He remembers us talking about tacos and then he woke up here."

"Is that normal?" Carly asked.

"According to the doctors it is," Bran replied. "They're going to keep him overnight, but they think he'll be fine to go home in the morning. I didn't even see it coming."

Case put an arm around his wife. "I think we can safely say this is the second attempt on Noah's life. It was a black SUV then, too, wasn't it?"

Mia nodded. "Yes, and we were all too worried about Shelby and Noah at the mall to get a plate number."

"I wasn't there so I can't be absolutely sure, but it was definitely a dark-colored SUV that came out of nowhere this time," Bran replied. "Do you think it was waiting for us?"

"The question is how would he or she know where Noah was going to be?" Shelby felt a need to point out the obvious.

"We changed our plans at the last minute." Bran ran a hand through his hair, brushing it back. "Noah and I shouldn't have been at the office until after lunch. I was going to show him around Austin for most of the day."

Drew turned his phone around. "Our homeless, pathetic brother might not have a phone, but he does have his computer. Has anyone checked his social media?"

"I got him a phone two days ago." Mia looked to Carly. "We felt bad because what if he's stuck somewhere and needs a ride?"

"I have his phone." Bran reached into his pocket, pulling it out. "He asked me to hold on to it for him." Bran snorted. "He alerted social media that he was in the 4L building. And there's the selfie. And the announcement that he was going to get tacos."

"Does he even have his accounts locked down?" Drew asked.

Bran passed him the phone. "He doesn't even have a passcode on the phone."

Drew snatched up the phone. "I'm going through it, then."

"Shouldn't we be worried about his privacy?" Carly asked.

Shelby wasn't having that argument. "I think privacy is the least of his concerns. It's not anything Drew won't do already. The minute he's in front of a computer again, he'll hack Noah's accounts and try to figure out what's going on. This simply saves him twenty minutes or so of decoding Noah's passwords."

Drew snorted. "Twenty minutes? I can do it in five. How can he say he's worked for a black hat and then not bother to lock any of his systems down?"

"I think we should ask him," Bran said, putting a hand out to stop Drew. "Come on. Let's give the kid a chance. I got the results from the lab today."

Drew went still. "And?"

"He's our brother." Bran pulled an envelope out of his back pocket, handing it to Drew. "No question about it. He's your brother and that means he's mine. He's awake. Let's go talk to him and try to figure this out."

Drew handed Bran back the phone, opening the envelope and reading the report. He sighed heavily before passing it to Mia. "All right. One of us is going to need to stay with him tonight. Or should I hire a guard at this point?"

"I'll stay," Case volunteered. "And I'll bring someone in if we need to. We've got a whole team of well-trained bodyguards in Dallas."

"I'll stay, too," Shelby offered.

Drew frowned. "Absolutely not. I'm going to talk to my brother. Be ready to leave when I come back."

He turned and he and Bran walked out.

"The king has spoken," Carly said. "Long live the king."

The king wasn't going to last for too long if he didn't get out of his snippy mood. Shelby looked to Case. "I need you to find Hatch. I don't care what Drew says. I'll hire you myself if I have to."

Mia tucked the envelope away in her bag. "Why would Hatch try to hurt Noah? I get that he doesn't believe Noah, but Hatch has never been violent."

Case looked to Shelby. "I'll do it. It's time for someone to figure out what the hell is going on. I don't buy any of this. I don't like it. Did you know that Noah's mother lived close to Patricia Cain?"

Mia's eyes widened. "You didn't tell me you were looking into Noah."

"That's because Drew said he would do it," Case explained. "But Drew isn't a private investigator and he's got way too much on his plate right now. He's hiding something, and I'm sick of waiting for him to let the rest of us in on the joke. So yes, I've been quietly investigating Noah."

"It's not a joke." The minute the words were out of her mouth, she wanted to call them back. "Look, Drew's under a lot of pressure right now. No one's trying to hide anything. Drew is worried about Hatch and he's got Riley and Ellie's reception coming up and his whole family is in transition. Give him some space. If he acts like a king, it's because you guys have treated him like one for a long time."

"I've learned to follow my instincts, and I don't like what they're telling me right now. It's too coincidental that suddenly a brother shows up just as we've taken down our enemies but discovered there was a fourth conspirator. Hatch goes missing." Case held up a hand to stop Mia's impending argument. "I know you love the old guy, but I didn't grow up worshipping at Drew's and Hatch's feet. I can view all of this unemotionally, and something's wrong. Noah knows something or he's here to do something."

"What could he do?" Mia asked, frowning her husband's way.

"Do you think it's possible that he's Francine Wells's child? I know that's not the name on his birth certificate, but it would make sense for her to change it," Carly said quietly. "She likely changed it a couple of times. We know she was having an affair with Benedict, so Noah's DNA would prove a familial connection."

Guilt twisted through Shelby, but she owed Drew. "I think we should all calm down."

Carly stared at her. "You can say that because you know whatever it is Drew's hiding."

"Carly," she began.

She shook her dark hair. "No. You're not the one who nearly lost her husband to that bitch. You don't get to tell me to chill out and not worry about her. I know you're investigating and I remember exactly what she told me. She told me if we kept looking for her, she would come back and finish the job."

Mia's hand slipped into Case's. "I know you're scared, Carly. I know you still think about that night a lot, but we can't let her get away with it."

Carly threw her hands up. "Why not? The cops don't seem to care. They dodge my calls. They're not looking for her at all, and as far as I can tell, there's not even an APB out on her."

Because Drew had manipulated the system. "I'll look into it for you."

Carly sighed and shook her head. "You're already looking into it. I get that the two of you are together, but I also know you're up to something, and I can't tell you how much that hurts. I thought we were friends."

Her heart twisted. Carly was her closest friend, and she'd been hurting while Shelby was chasing a story.

It was more than a story though, wasn't it? It was everything to these people. She'd been viewing all of this as a book she could write, something that had happened a long time ago so there would be distance, but it wasn't true. That woman was still Mia's mother, would be her child's grandmother. She was still harming her children, including her youngest. Noah thought she was dead.

How would he feel when he read Shelby's book? When his childhood was spilled out on the pages for all to see?

She'd started this as a reporter, but suddenly this was her family. These people were precious to her, and she had to question whether or not it was worth it. Writing her book wouldn't bring Benedict back, but exposing Iris could hurt his children. It could hurt her relationship with Drew. How would he look at her when she was the one who put the scandal back out there, when she was on tour, reaping the benefits of his family history?

Drew was more important than any book. She would gather all the facts she could because she thought Carly was wrong. No matter what Iris had told her, she would come after them all.

She might be doing it right now.

"Can you check and make sure nothing odd happened this afternoon at 4L, Case? You can check all the security protocols, right?" Shelby couldn't understand what hurting Noah would have bought Iris except perhaps a distraction.

Case took a deep breath. "I can, but from what I understand it was fairly chaotic. Everyone came outside to figure out what was going on. I've looked at a couple of the security camera shots and there was quite a crowd. What are you thinking?"

"I don't know." She had no idea what Iris would get out of creating chaos in front of the building, but it seemed like too much to be a coincidence. She wouldn't have gotten the same effect had she managed to hit Noah in front of the mall.

Was she trying to kill her son? Or manipulate him again? To what end?

She had to figure out what Iris could gain.

"I'll send you everything I have on Noah," Case offered. "But for tonight, I think I'm going to take my wife home and let her rest. I'll come back in a while and let Bran go home. Carly, can you drive Shelby and Drew home, or should I send a car back?"

"Of course." But there was no enthusiasm in her friend's voice.

Mia and Case walked away hand in hand and she was left with her best friend. Carly had always been there for her, and now Shelby felt so far away from her. Carly stepped back and returned to the waiting room seat she'd been in for the last couple of hours.

Drew was wrong. They needed to know, and now. How would they feel when they figured out he'd done everything under their noses? That he'd known all along and hadn't told them even when they'd felt something was wrong?

Still, she couldn't be the one to tell them. She couldn't break his trust that way, but there had to be some comfort she could give Carly. She slumped down in the seat next to her, the silence between them heavy.

"Do you still think about it?" That night Bran almost died seemed to haunt her friend.

Carly sighed. "Of course I do. It was almost the worst day of my life. I think about it and I still hear her telling me that she would finish the job if I didn't do what she wanted."

She turned toward Carly. "You have to be able to see that she's a liar. I think she'll try to finish the job no matter what you do."

Carly's hands twisted in her lap. "Why? What could she get out of it?"

"I don't know, but I feel like she's playing a particularly long game and we don't know the rules yet. I understand that you're scared, but you have to know Drew will do anything he can to protect you."

"How about you?" Carly turned, her wide eyes taking in Shelby. "Do you think he'll protect you?"

"I'm pretty tough." It was good to know Carly still cared enough about her to be worried. "This isn't the first story I've investigated that had some danger to it. I'm going to be careful and cover my tracks. I've come to care about this family very much."

"I can see that. It's why I'm so worried about you."

"What's there to worry about? You know I'm pretty good at self-defense."

Carly shook her head. "I'm not talking about you being physically hurt, though I think that woman is capable of anything. I'm talking about Drew. I'm talking about the fact that while Drew is one of the best men I know when it comes to taking care of his family, he can be ruthless with everyone else."

"I think I've gotten to know him pretty well. I do know he has a ruthless side. And a manipulative-bastard side." She'd gotten to be an expert on the many moods of Andrew Lawless. "But underneath it all he's looking for a woman he can trust. I care about him."

"Yes, I knew it the minute I found out you were sleeping with him. I have to say I kind of hoped that it was all one of Drew's weird plans to throw everyone off the scent of what he was really doing, but you two are together, aren't you?"

"The relationship is real."

No matter how it had started, it was definitely real now. She couldn't hold back her feelings for him. She was crazy about that man. Every insane inch of him. He was closed off right now because he'd had a rough day, but tonight when she climbed into bed next to him, she would hold him and show him it was going to be okay.

"I know your feelings are real," Carly said, sympathy plain in her eyes. "But what about Drew? Drew will do anything to protect his family. Why are you investigating this and not McKay-Taggart?"

She couldn't exactly explain that one. "I think Drew trusts me and he might also see this as a way to bond us together. He's surprisingly awkward when it comes to intimate relationships."

"Drew doesn't have relationships that I've heard of. He's told Bran that he has no intention of marrying or having kids."

That was kind of a kick to the gut, but then they weren't exactly at a stage where they would discuss marriage and kids.

"I can see you haven't talked about it." Carly's hand came over hers, squeezing softly.

She gave her friend a bright smile. This wasn't something she was going to worry about now. "We just got together. I assure you, we're not talking marriage and kids."

"But you're living with him. You don't have any place to go if you break up. Moving in with Drew is risky, especially at the start of a relationship."

"He didn't give me much of a choice. Like I said, I've been introduced to Drew's manipulative side. He maneuvered me into a corner, but it's worked out. If we'd gone at this like normal people, it would have failed. Drew isn't normal. He needs to feel close to the people he cares about. When he cares, he's passionate. He's incredibly loyal and protective. Those are good traits. They go along with his weird ones."

"Yes, he's incredibly protective," Carly agreed. "So why, if he's so in love with you, is he allowing you to work this investigation? I love Drew, but he is capable of many things. If he thought putting a target on you would take one off his siblings, he would do it."

She didn't understand. "He trusts me. He knows I'm smart and capable."

"And you are, but I don't know that you're seeing the truth about Drew. I want this to be real. But I think if Drew was in love with you, he would do anything he could to keep you out of harm's way. I just want you to think about it. I can't stand the thought of you getting hurt because Drew was worried about the rest of us."

That wasn't what he was doing. Not at all and Carly didn't understand it. She couldn't understand it because she didn't have the whole story. He was protecting them from the knowledge that Iris was alive.

Or Shelby was a complete fool.

It was one of the two.

Her cell chirped and she looked down. She'd left a message with Williams Investigations hoping to get an appointment. She hadn't expected them to get back to her so quickly, but now it was a welcome excuse to get out of this painful conversation. "I have to take this."

Carly was wrong. She had to be. She would see that this was a different relationship for Drew. She was his partner, not some kind of distraction. And he'd given her some safety. He'd given her a contract. For Drew, that was his way of protecting her, of making her feel safe.

She pushed aside the worry. She trusted Drew. Hell, she was fairly certain she was falling in love with the man.

She answered the phone and got back to her investigation. That was what she needed to focus on now.

"My wife is worried," Bran said as they stepped out of the waiting room and moved down the hall toward Noah's room.

He was sure everyone was worried at this point. "I'm sorry about that. I can up our security if you think that will make her feel more at ease. Right now, though, it seems like Noah's past is catching up with him. I don't think this person is going to come after Carly. If I did, I would have both you and her at a safe house."

He was worried he needed to shove Shelby in one, and she wasn't going to like that. How had he started this with the utter certainty that he could handle it? He should have known he wouldn't last long. In the beginning, he'd been the asshole who thought he could use her for both her investigative skills and the fact that she would be a good shield. Now he was scrambling because the idea that she could be harmed in any way made him crazy.

"I don't think a bodyguard is going to make Carly feel better," Bran replied. "She needs to know that someone is still searching for Francine. From what Case has told me, no one's working on it."

"The police are certain she's left the area," Drew pointed out. "She's quite good at hiding. She's done it for twenty years or so."

"Since when did we let something like that stop us? I understand the police can't spend all their time trying to hunt down one woman, but I want to know who's working on it from McKay-Taggart."

"I'll have Ian give me a report as soon as possible, but I think we're going to have to shift some focus for a while until we figure out who's trying to turn baby brother into roadkill." He needed to shift the focus of this conversation. Noah was a pain in his ass, but right now he was a good diversion.

"This conversation isn't done, but I will shelve it while we deal with Noah." Bran stopped in front of Noah's door. "He needs to know that you give a crap whether he lives or dies. He thinks you hate him."

"I don't know him." Or anything about him, and that had to change. He'd allowed himself to be distracted with sex and work. He had a cursory report and Shelby was combing through Noah's e-mails and his files, looking for anything that might tip them off that he was working for their mother. It was a slow process.

"Spend some time with him. Honestly, he reminds me a little of you before."

"Before what?"

Bran stared at him. "Before the fire."

Before the fire. Before death and tragedy and horror and loss had changed him. "Try to remember that just because he looks innocent doesn't mean he's got nothing to hide. That fourteen-year-old kid you're comparing him to used to hack government sites to prove he could."

Bran nodded as he pushed the door open. "Yes, that's exactly what I meant. Hey, Noah, how's the head holding up? You know you actually left a mark in the concrete."

Noah looked tired, his shoulders slumped and circles under his eyes. Still, he managed a small smile. "I have a hard head. Hi, Drew. Thanks for coming. I'm going to find a way to pay you back for the medical bills. Sorry about that."

"Who said I was paying your medical bills?"

Bran huffed. "He's joking."

Well, no one had mentioned it to him, but he felt a little bad. Noah already looked like shit. "Sorry. Sarcasm is my primary language. Noah, we need to talk."

His mouth was in a sullen line, but his shoulders came up. "All right. You want me out of the house, don't you? I get it. I'm causing trouble."

Drew turned to Bran. "Am I that pessimistic? And how does he get his mouth to do that? It's like the sad opposite of a smile. I didn't know lips could turn down that harshly."

Bran's eyes rolled. "Brother, you are practically mopey most of the time. And you look a whole lot like that. Check a mirror sometime. Noah, no one's throwing you out. You're our brother. Get used to the big brother's sarcasm. Give him hell back."

Noah leaned against the pillows, his exhaustion obvious. "I don't want to cause trouble."

"He's nothing like me because I loved causing trouble." He hated the fact that he was starting to feel for the kid, especially when he still wasn't sure he knew the whole truth.

"See, more sarcasm," Bran pointed out. He moved to stand beside Noah's bed. "We do need to talk, though. Can you think of anyone who would want to hurt you?"

Noah was silent, his head shaking in the negative.

"What about your friend Jase?" He wasn't sure what the kid was thinking. If someone tried to kill him, Drew would look to the criminals in his life.

Noah groaned, a deeply frustrated sound. "Why would he? I didn't steal anything from him. I did the work he asked me to do. When he's needed updates, I did them."

"I thought you no longer spoke to this asshole." He'd been clear on that. What the hell else had Noah left out of his story?

A fine flush hit his skin. "He hit me up online a couple of days ago. It was easier to simply do what he wanted than to fight him. He's a serious hacker and he's got connections. It was a couple of lines of code. He's struggling with his POS. I fixed it and everything is fine now. He's got no reason to hurt me. He knows I'm not going to turn him in and I'm not a threat."

POS. Point of sale. In this case, though, it could mean *piece of shit* because that's what this Jase guy was. He remembered what it was like being vulnerable. It was Hatch who had saved him from this kind of problem when he was young and starting out. Hatch had been there to tell him he was being a dumbass. He'd been there so Drew didn't get taken advantage of. Sure, he'd done it half drunk at all times, but Drew had known he could count on Hatch to make sure he wasn't indebted to assholes.

"Is his number on your phone?" Drew asked.

Noah flushed. "It's a new phone, but he managed to figure out what my number was."

Bran chuckled. "That's what happens when you give girls your number on social media."

What? "Tell me you didn't. It's bad enough you announce your every move on the Internet. You give out your phone number, too?"

"She was hot," Noah protested. "You don't understand. She was like the hottest girl at the prep school a mile away from Creighton. When I posted that I might be your brother and I was heading to Austin, she wrote to me. She never paid any attention to me before. I think she's interested now."

He needed a keeper. "Yes, since you posted a ridiculously personal piece of information on Facebook about your freaking paternity. There is such a thing as privacy, you know."

Noah shrugged as though the idea had never once occurred to him. "Why? If I hadn't talked about it, Brittany wouldn't have reached out to see if we could meet up sometime."

"She's willing to date you because you're suddenly the brother of a billionaire." He was definitely missing the point.

"I'm totally okay with that," Noah admitted. "She's got double D boobs."

Ah, youth. Damn millennials didn't think anything was real until they'd posted it on the Internet. He reached his hand out to Bran. "Give me his phone. When did the asshole call?"

Noah frowned as Bran handed Drew the phone. "Yesterday morning around ten. I got it done. I told him it was the last time. He agreed."

"Did he?" Drew doubted that.

"Well, not really, but he didn't argue with me."

"Why should he? He's not going to waste his breath when he knows damn well he can yell at you and you'll fold on him. Watch and learn, brother. This is how you handle a bully." Drew pressed the button to dial the correct number.

Noah sat up, his mouth dropping open. "What are you doing?"

Bran smiled. "He's being your asshole big brother. Get used to it. Remember how I told you Drew giving a crap about you would have a trade-off? Here it comes. He'll be superprotective, but he'll be a total dick about it."

He wasn't a dick. He was having a perfectly normal reaction to someone taking advantage of his youngest brother.

There was a beep and then a masculine voice came on the line. "'Sup, Noah? You know I told you not to call me. I'll call you if I need you. This isn't a two-fucking-way street, you asshole."

Oh, he was going to have so much fun with this. "Hello, Jase. You don't know me but my name is Andrew Lawless."

"What the hell?"

"Yes, what the hell. That's what you'll say the first time the feds invade your house and take everything you own, and then you get buried so deep in the penitentiary system that you finally understand why we call it our penal code. That is what's going to happen if you call my brother again. So here are your choices, you little shit. You can leave my brother alone, forget his name. He never helped you. You've never even met him. If you do that, maybe I'll forget that you exist. If you ever call my brother again, I will not only ensure your swift downfall with multiple government agencies so far up your asshole you'll forget what it felt like to be whole, but in addition to that nasty fate, I'll send in a team of former Special Forces soldiers who haven't killed anyone lately. They're cranky, and torturing your pathetic self would make them feel better. And after they've had a turn at you, I'll get my own freak on. Do you think I reached the top of my field based on smarts alone? Oh no, my friend. I got where I'm at because I'm the worst human being on the face of the earth. I tear apart my enemies, and you are going to be my enemy if you continue to pull my brother into your schemes. Do you want to be my enemy, Jase? Do you want me to put every dollar and connection I have up against you?"

There was a wonderful pause on the line that reminded Drew that it took a while to pee one's pants. "No. I don't think you have to do that. I don't need Noah's help anymore."

"And do you feel the need to hurt him?"

"Absolutely not, sir," he said quickly. "I'm good where I am. Noah's a good dude. I wish him all the best."

"Do you understand that if I find out you're lying to me, or if you get off this line and an hour or two from now have a couple of beers and decide you're braver than you should be, what I do to you will make most serial killers look merciful, and I'll get away with it. I'll skin you and make a rug out of you and put it in my office. Do you want to be the thing I walk on in my office?"

"No, sir. Like I said, Noah and me are all good."

"Excellent. Good-bye, Jase. I will be watching you."

He hung up the phone.

Noah's eyes were wide as Drew handed him back his cell. "Dude, that was awesome."

"I told you." Bran put a hand on the kid's shoulder. "He's fuck-all crazy, but he's a damn fine brother."

Noah was quiet for a moment. "He definitely isn't what I expected."

"Good, then we've established that I'm not a total asshole. So tell me who you think is doing this to you. And don't lie and shake your head like you did a minute ago. You have a name in mind, but you're afraid to say it to me." He couldn't let Noah stay in his corner. They needed to have this out.

"Fine, I think it's your friend." The sullen boy was back.

God, he hoped he didn't look like that when he got pissy. "It wasn't Hatch."

"Then where is he?" Noah asked, some fire back in his posture. "He lives with you, but he's been gone since I showed up. He told me flat out that he hates me."

"No, he said he didn't trust you," Drew corrected.

"Hatch is a good guy," Bran said. "I don't think you know the whole story. There's a woman out there who helped to kill our parents and she's resurfaced lately. She nearly killed me a couple of months ago."

"So you think Hatch believes this woman is the reason I'm here." Noah couldn't quite meet Bran's eyes. "You think I'm working for her or something."

He was the touchiest thing. "No, we didn't say that. But Hatch can be paranoid."

Noah's head swung around, obviously happy to grasp on to that statement. "And paranoid people do crazy things like try to mow down an enemy. You know he's been arrested a couple of times."

He should have known Noah would look into Hatch. "Yes, but so has Bran. You don't think he's trying to hurt you."

Noah ignored him entirely. "Hatch has been arrested for drunk and disorderly and for assault. Twice. He's a violent man."

"He's an idiot when he's drunk," Drew corrected. He took a deep breath because patience was required here. Noah didn't know Hatch the way he did. "Look, I'm going to find him and we're all going to sit down and talk and figure this out. I promise you he's not the one trying to hurt you. I also promise you that I'm going to find out who is and take care of it."

Noah seemed to deflate. "All right. If you say he's cool, I guess I have to believe it."

"I'm going to prove it to you. Bran is going to hang out with you for a while, and then we'll all take turns so you're not alone tonight. In the morning, we'll take you home."

Noah's lips curled up slightly. "I would like that."

"Good." He wasn't sure how far he trusted Noah, but the kid was family, and that meant something to Drew.

There was another reason. Shelby's voice urging him to be more open, to let the kid in because it was the right thing to do. When had her voice become his conscience? Damn it all, when the hell had he developed a conscience? It was annoying, but he couldn't ignore it. He wanted to do the things that would please her, make her comfortable being his wife.

His stomach dropped because he was absolutely thinking about marrying Shelby. If he married her before she found out what a shit he was, would she honor their vows? Would it buy him some time to show her he could change?

Of course if he changed his stance on marriage, he would have to consider the rest of it, too. Shelby would want children. He'd never truly wanted them because children were fragile. He didn't want to fail his own children. But perhaps if they had a wonderful mother, they would be okay.

"Is he all right?" Noah's question broke through Drew's introspection.

"That's his deep-thought face," Bran replied. "Someone's in trouble."

Yes, someone was definitely in trouble. Drew was pretty sure it was him.

Chapter Twelve

Shelby stepped into the offices of Williams Investigations and couldn't quite shake off the feeling that someone was watching her. She wasn't sure why she felt that way, just an instinct, but the last several days she'd felt odd.

She stopped at the door and turned, looking around and trying to find the source of her anxiety. Nothing. The building was a two story in a lower-class neighborhood on the outskirts of downtown. There was nothing around her but a Mexican restaurant, a bail bond office, and across the street was a thrift store. No one was staring at her.

Of course it could be all about Drew. This feeling she had could be displaced anxiety. It had been five days since Noah nearly died, and Drew seemed to have distanced. Oh, he wasn't distant in bed. He was quite enthusiastic there. He made love to her every single night and most mornings, but it was obvious he was thinking about something. He was anxious, but when she asked what was wrong, he simply told her not to worry.

He hadn't even asked where she was going this morning. He knew she was leaving Austin for the day, but he hadn't questioned further than that. He usually wanted a full schedule if she wasn't going to work at the office, but this morning he'd kissed her and told her he'd see her at home this evening.

Maybe it was because she hadn't come to Dallas alone. She told herself it was because most of the family was heading to Dallas for a few hours to shop and help Ellie pick up her gown for the reception. It was a normal everyday outing for a family with a private jet.

He had no idea she was breaking from the pack and taking a meeting with the daughter-in-law of the man who had brokered the deal to kill Drew's father. After how hard he'd taken the last meeting, she'd wanted to spare him this one.

Also, she couldn't get Carly's words out of her head.

Perhaps Drew was getting bored with her. Maybe he didn't have a long attention span and her investigation was taking a while. Had he thought she would be done quickly and he could send her on her way?

Her cell trilled. She looked down, hoping it was Drew. No such luck. Case's number came up on the screen. She slid her finger across the screen to accept the call. "Hi, Case."

"Hey, how's it going?" In the background she could hear the sounds of people talking and someone asking if anyone wanted champagne. "Are you absolutely sure you don't need backup? Because I could have a bodyguard out here to watch after the women in a heartbeat."

"Hey, what am I?" Riley's voice came over the line.

So Case wasn't enjoying a day of shopping. Still, she didn't need him hovering over her. "I'm fine. It's a quick errand. I'll be back in plenty of time to make the plane."

"All right," he said, his reluctance clear in his tone. "I called for a reason. I tracked down the SUV."

Finally they were getting somewhere. "That's amazing. You were able to track down who rented it?"

"Yes, but it's still shitty news. It was rented two days before the first attack and they used a corporate card. Two businessmen from Seattle took possession of the vehicle at the DFW airport branch of the rental agency."

She could guess the end of this story. "Where was it stolen from?"

"From the parking garage of their hotel. They didn't even realize it was gone for days because they were attending a conference inside the hotel. It was only when they had to go meet a client that they realized the car was gone."

Another potential dead end. "Please tell me the hotel has security."

"That's where it gets fun," Case began. "It does, but there was a technical glitch that afternoon, and the cameras turned off during the time the car was picked up. The valet says he can't remember who picked up that particular car because he ran through about a hundred that day, but he had proper tickets for every single vehicle."

"So someone stole the valet ticket, got the car, and we still have nothing," she said with a sigh. "How long are the businessmen in town? Can I talk to them when I get back? Maybe they remember who took the ticket."

"Already done," Case replied. "They think they lost the valet ticket their first night here in Dallas."

"Let me guess, they got drunk, hooked up with some women, and woke up the next day hungover and without a car, but the idiots didn't realize until days later that the car was gone." So they were at another dead end. "Let's see if the hotel has security footage of the bar that night. Maybe we can pick up something."

"I'm on it. You be careful, and seriously, if you want backup, Riley can watch the girls. He loves this Manolo Choo stuff."

There was another masculine denial from the other end of the line.

"Thanks for the update, Case." She hung up. So they were absolutely nowhere. She couldn't even be sure it had been whatever women the businessmen had hooked up with, since someone could have easily slipped the valet ticket out of a jacket pocket while the men were drinking in the bar.

Some investigator she was turning out to be. Noah was afraid to leave his room. He seemed a bit afraid to be in the main house at all. He'd avoided coming to family meals since he'd gotten home from the hospital. He spent all his time holed up in the pool house. He'd been friendly enough, but there was something about him that felt secretive.

Just as she'd managed to get Drew on Noah's side, she might have to pull some shady stuff to figure out what was going on with the kid. He'd gotten a new computer, gifted to him by 4L Software a few days before. She needed to get a look at his new system. Drew was still combing through the old one. Shelby hadn't found anything, but perhaps the expert could.

If Noah was hiding something, he was smart enough to have erased it before showing up on Drew's doorstep. It was time to get hold of something he hadn't had time to protect.

Shelby pushed through the doors to the office inside. A low hum of conversation greeted her, though there was no one sitting at the reception desk. The space was nicely kept, but nothing fancy. It looked like nothing more than four or five desks with some private offices in the back.

"Hello, you must be Ms. Gates," a friendly voice said.

She shoved aside her worries and focused on the woman in front of her. Katja Williams was a lovely blonde who looked far younger than her forty-plus years. She also didn't look like a woman who'd had four kids. Her figure was as slim as it had been back in her modeling days in St. Petersburg before she'd met Kevin Williams and settled down. Shelby had studied up on the family before this appointment, though all the data she'd found didn't answer the one question she was curious about. Did they still have the same ties? Was she walking into a hostile situation?

"Ms. Williams, I thank you for meeting me. I appreciate that you're willing to talk to me on such short notice." She held her hand out.

Katja shook with her own perfectly manicured one. "Of course. I have to say I was curious when you called me. You're an investigative reporter?"

"Yes. I specialize in crime reporting."

"I pulled the files you asked about, but I didn't see that there was anything interesting in them. It's all notes on the cases and billing information. Though, I have to admit, when it came to my father-in-law, rest his soul, it could mean anything. My husband is practically a saint, but that man was the devil."

She followed Katja back through the small office. It looked like they had three investigators working at desks and two private offices for the owners. "Some people say that about my boss, too."

She didn't mention her boss was also her boyfriend. Was he her boyfriend? That seemed like such a juvenile term to describe Drew. Lover. He was her lover.

"Oh, unless your boss was a horrible tool for the Russian mob, my father-in-law likely wins that battle." Katja closed the door behind Shelby.

"Wow, I was wondering how I was going to broach that subject." She'd been planning on tiptoeing around it. "I take it your husband isn't on the payroll?"

She laughed. "My Kevin would never work for them. He saw how much trouble it caused his father, though I am thankful because it brought Kevin to Russia and allowed me to meet him. Luckily, times change and we didn't feel much pressure to continue the relationship. The mob is much more interested in hackers these days than in investigators. I told my husband that if he marries me, there will be absolutely no ties to the *Bratva*. I came here to build a real business with him. When you are tied to the brothers, your business is not your own. My father-in-law made more money than we do, but our work is honest."

"I'm particularly interested in some of the work your father-in-law did for a company owned by a man named Benedict Lawless."

She picked up a folder that had been sitting on the edge of her desk. "Please have a seat. I researched some of the names you asked me to look up. Benedict Lawless was nowhere to be found in the old records."

She should have known. It wasn't like there would be a file marked *assassinations*. "So there's no mention of the company, either?"

"Not at all. I'm in the middle of trying to digitize all the records so I have them available," Katja explained. "Could you tell me a little more of what you're looking for?"

"I spoke to the brother of a man named Yuri Volchenko a few days back."

Katja sighed and sat back in her chair. "I worried that name would come up. The minute you mentioned Benedict Lawless, I had a feeling."

"You've heard of the case?"

"Of course," she replied. "I didn't live here when the crime was committed, but there was certainly talk about it. When you called and mentioned you were looking for anything on Benedict Lawless, I couldn't help but be curious. I did not find any of the names you asked me to look for. No Castalano, Stratton, or Cain. If my father-in-law did business with them, it was off the books."

Another dead end. "Well, I knew it was a long shot."

Katja held out a hand. "It still might be. I said my father-in-law didn't do business with them, but there is some information I found. Let me start at the beginning. You know that Volchenko was an assassin the Gorev syndicate used from time to time. He also did freelance work. My father-in-law would help him with this. He would help transfer the money to offshore accounts, taking a small sum for himself, of course. When I couldn't find the particular names you were looking for, I decided to look at files that were opened or closed six weeks before or after the murder. This would be when payments would show up."

Shelby sat up, adrenaline starting to flow again. "You found the payments to Volchenko?"

She shook her head. "No. He was too careful. But I could find evidence of something else. Naturally my father-in-law would be paid for his aid, even if it was a nominal amount. I found four deposits into the company accounts during the time he would have been paid. They were marked *miscellaneous investigative necessities.* If anyone looked at his tax records, it would show these monies were paid by clients for expenses like getting reports or camera equipment. These in particular, though, do not have receipts attached to them, and they're all the same amount. Five hundred dollars. Four of them within a week of the date you referred to. They add up to two thousand dollars."

"One percent of what Volchenko charged for a risky assassination." The money trail was interesting. "Do you have the files that were associated with the miscellaneous expenses?"

"I pulled them, but they're seemingly random. Two are cases about missing persons. One was an insurance case. And the other was a man who wanted to make sure his lover wasn't cheating on him. I don't know that the cases actually have anything at all to do with the clients who would have paid him. My father-in-law would not have wanted anyone to be able to trace that money back to the clients or to connect it to Volchenko."

"I understand." At least she had confirmation that she was in the right place.

"Here are the files from the four cases the money was attached to. I'm going to allow you to look at them because there's nothing particularly scandalous about them, but I would appreciate your discretion."

"Of course. Do you mind if I take notes?"

She slid the files over. "Not at all."

She reached out and took the folders from Katja, fanning them out so she could read the names. The room seemed to drop ten degrees, a chill covering her skin. It didn't really have anything to do with the temperature. No. It had to do with the folders in her hand.

Collins. Varney Insurance. First Auto Insurance.

Hatchard.

"Your father-in-law worked for Bill Hatchard?" She pushed the other folders aside. She had the one she needed.

Katja leaned forward. "Yes, he did several jobs for someone by that name. He was a businessman of some sort."

Her heart pounded in her chest as she looked at the file. "So he was a long-term client?"

"Mostly he was looking for background checks, but in that case, he had an investigator follow his lover. I'm not sure. It's written in a sort of shorthand. The investigator tracked the woman who is known only as 'I' to a house in the Dallas suburbs. He describes her arguing with another man but no one is named, and even the address was marked through. There were supposed to be pictures attached, but it appears they were sent along with the film to the client. That happens sometimes when the client is paranoid about privacy. I believe the woman was married and he didn't want her husband to know. The majority of the file was sent back to Hatchard, and then he never used the company again."

She looked down at the date. The file had been sent to Bill Hatchard the day after the murders. No wonder he hadn't needed another case. He'd gone into a hole shortly after the last one was done.

She opened the file in front of her. The one that might kill Drew's soul. He would never forgive her for bringing this to him, for taking his last father figure away from him.

She looked down at the proof of Hatch's lies, and tears began to fall.

Two hours later, Shelby sank into a seat at a small café and wished it was a bar. She needed a drink or five.

What the hell was she going to tell Drew?

She glanced down at her phone. She had an hour and a half to get to the airport. She could have met up with the family. They were probably making plans for having dinner later in Austin.

How was she going to get through that? She had no choice. She looked down at her coffee mug and promised herself that she would plaster a smile on her face and get through dinner. The bad news could wait until after.

Tonight she would blow up Drew's world and pray they survived the aftermath. It was the best she could do for him.

"Do you mind if I sit with you?"

Shelby looked up and a woman stood by her table. She was petite and slender, her hair wrapped in a scarf and her eyes hidden behind sunglasses. It was a weird request since there were only two other patrons in the café and plenty of tables left. "I'm sorry, but I would rather be alone."

"I imagine, but this might be the only chance I get to talk to you," she said quietly. "My son keeps a close eye on you. I wonder why he does that."

The room seemed to go cold. "Iris?"

She settled into the seat across from Shelby, putting her cup in front of her. She eased the sunglasses off, and her eyes immediately reminded Shelby of Riley's and Bran's. Emerald green.

"I haven't gone by that name in a long time," she said quietly. "Please don't call the police. I'll have to run and I need a couple of minutes of your time. We're in public. I would never do anything to hurt you. I'm here because I'm afraid for your safety."

Sure she was. "Yes, I'm a bit afraid for my safety right now, given how many people you've murdered."

Her eyes slid away, her mouth firming. "Well, I should have suspected he would tell you many stories about me. I will admit to hurting some people along the way, but everything I've done I did to survive."

"Including shooting Bran a couple of months back?"

Her eyes came back up, shock plain on her face. "I didn't shoot Bran. I would never harm him. I did pay someone to take out Patricia, but I had my reasons."

"That's not what Bran's wife says."

"She was mistaken. I hate what I did to Patricia, but she threatened to do the one thing I couldn't allow."

"What's that?"

"Tell Andrew I'm alive. Somehow, she still managed it, didn't she?" Tears glistened in the woman's eyes, like perfect diamonds that clung to her, refusing to drop.

"Carly saw you that night. She was there when you turned a gun on your son." Would the police even arrest her? Could she tackle the bitch and wait around only to be the one arrested, while Iris showed her probably well-faked ID and then disappeared at the end of the conversation?

According to all records the police had, the woman in front of her was dead, and the California police were no longer searching for her thanks to Drew. He'd wanted to deal with this himself, and it left Shelby with few options.

"I don't know why she would say that, but it isn't true," Iris said evenly. "All of that said, I still have to protect myself. I need you to understand that if you call anyone or try to stop me, I'm not alone here. I don't want to hurt you, but this is about more than just me."

"Spoken like a truly innocent woman."

"My innocence will be proven shortly, but until then I need you to look into this story. I know Drew hired you to gloss things over, but you're smart and you can get to the truth."

"And what's the truth?"

She took a long breath. "I didn't want to leave my children. I might have had issues with Ben, but I loved him once. I couldn't have guessed that his cheating on me would be the thing to save my life. I would have been the one to die that night if Andrew had been more careful."

Another chill went through Shelby. "What?"

"You heard me. I wasn't the one who planned this out. It was Andrew. It was my own son and now he has Noah."

It took everything Shelby had not to roll her eyes. "I know that you hired an assassin named Volchenko."

Iris shook her head. "This is all Drew's way of covering his tracks. Can't you see that? Now that he's finally gotten what he's wanted all these years, he's trying to clean up the family name. He hates scandal. He can't stand it and he wants all the scrutiny off him because he knows if you scratch the surface too hard, they'll discover his crimes."

Shelby couldn't imagine the audacity of the woman. "You honestly believe I'm going to buy any of this?"

"I understand how difficult it is to realize someone you love is capable of such evil. I don't say any of this to hurt you, but you should know that he's playing games with you."

"I think you're the one playing games. You can't convince me that Drew is behind this. I'm not sure what you think it accomplishes."

Iris looked behind her before turning back. "He doesn't trust you. He's got someone following you. I'm sure he's taking pictures of us right now."

Shelby glanced around. "Is it the dude who's playing online games or the chick who's flirting with the guy behind the counter?"

"He's not in the café. He's out in the parking lot. At first I thought perhaps you had a bodyguard, but he never got close to you. This is Drew's way of keeping track of you. You won't be allowed to go off Drew's script. He'll send you where he wants you to go. Has he insisted you do all your work at his office?"

"I work at 4L or at the house. Wait, I did some work at a Starbucks. Do you think he secretly owns all the Starbucks?" Drew's sarcasm was rubbing off on her.

"It wouldn't matter because the minute you plugged back into his network, he would have a copy of everything on your system."

"How interesting that you would say that. I found some spyware on my system that I think came from you."

One perfect brow rose on Iris's face. "You found it? Or Andrew did? He's manipulating you to reach his conclusion and to not trust anyone outside the family. He's built that family like it's a cult and he's their priest. He makes all the rules. He's cut you off from your resources. Anyone who could fight him is suddenly a member of the family, and they have something to lose. Stop thinking with your heart and look at it with your reporter's mind. Ellie Stratton ended up married to Riley because she had no choice. If she wanted to stay out of jail, she needed Andrew and his family money. The only way he would give it to her was if she married Riley."

"She loves Riley."

A bitter huff came from Iris's mouth. "I'm sure she does. The Lawless men are good at getting women to do what they want. Carly Fisher was the only person who could tell Patricia's side of the story, and now she's got the Lawless name, too."

"Your children married because they were in love."

Iris ignored her. "And then there's you. You weren't going to give up. You were going to continue on, and you might have figured out what really happened, but he brought you in, too. He ensured you couldn't change the narrative. He set you on a path to find this mysterious assassin. I'm sure he discovered I survived that night and he started planning his revenge."

"It's not revenge. He was and is looking for justice."

"If that's what he's doing, why hasn't he brought the police in? I would think he would go to the press to denounce me."

Shelby had heard enough. She reached for her cell phone. It was time to bring the police in if for no other reason than the fact that she felt uncomfortable talking to this woman.

The large man sitting at the table behind Iris stood up, his eyes finding Shelby's.

"Please don't make this ugly," Iris requested. "I'll be gone before you can do anything and if you try to hurt me, Warren will have to step in. He takes his job as a bodyguard seriously."

Shelby believed her. She'd caught a glint of metal when Warren's jacket opened slightly. She eased her hand back, placing them both flat where Warren could see them.

The big man sat down again though now he didn't pretend he wasn't watching them.

So she was stuck here until Iris let her go. If Iris let her go.

"What do you want from me?"

She hesitated for a moment. "I want to know if Drew is planning on hurting Noah."

"The child you were carrying when you . . ." She almost said, *When you killed his father and tried to take out all his siblings*, but she was sitting here with a crazy person and the crazy person apparently had hired guns, so maybe irritating her wasn't the way to go. "Left."

"Yes, I'm talking about Noah. He believes I died, but once I realized that Andrew was onto me, I knew I had to protect Noah from his brother. Noah has none of Andrew's selfishness and naked ambition. I don't know how he came to find out the relationship between them, but it's dangerous for him there. Can't you see that?"

She could see a lot of things. Her head was spinning with a hundred different possibilities, but she had to figure out what Iris wanted out of this conversation. She had no doubt that this was a mind game and if she got emotional, Iris would win.

"I know someone in a black SUV has tried to run him down twice already." Shelby watched carefully. The lies would be in the way she held herself, in forcing Iris to put herself in a corner and seeing how she tried to get out.

Her eyes came up, horror flaring. "I knew it. I knew he wouldn't let my Noah live."

She was good. Shelby would give her that, but then she had to be an excellent actress. It was all part of her line of work.

"Drew had nothing to do with it. In fact, he was with me during the second attempt and that time almost harmed Bran as well. Drew would never hurt Bran."

Iris managed a sniffle. "Wouldn't he? You don't know him like you think you do. He's a predator. And he would never do the job himself. He's good at keeping his hands clean."

"What would he get out of hurting Noah?"

"Revenge on me for getting away. He's so angry because he thought it would work. He didn't understand the contracts Ben had signed with the company. He thought all that stock would come to him."

"I think I would love to hear what happened that night from your perspective." This was the corner she could put Iris in.

Iris gripped her coffee cup like it was a lifeline. "It wasn't what you think it was. Ben had gotten distant. I was involved with an old family friend. I didn't realize what he was doing. You have to understand that Drew was never truly a child. He was born so brilliant that he never fit in with his peers. He preferred the company of adults. When he was a teen, he spent most of his time with his father or his father's friends. He said he was learning the business, but Drew always thought he was smarter than anyone else."

Well, that was still true most of the time. "Who were you having an affair with?"

Please don't say Hatch. Please don't say Hatch. Please don't say Hatch.

"Bill Hatchard. We'd been friends for a long time. I thought our friendship had simply moved to something more. I was such a fool. I was lonely and I knew Ben was seeing someone at work, and Bill was so kind to me. I didn't realize what he was doing."

"Are you trying to tell me that you believe Bill and Drew worked together to kill your husband?"

"All I know is I was there that night," Iris continued. "Bill asked me to meet him at my house. We were going to Ben to ask for a divorce. It was everything I'd hoped for, but when I got there, the house was dark and quiet. I heard Ben talking to someone. I came in from the garage. They were in the living room. I started to walk in and that's when I saw Andrew. I guess from the back Francine looked a lot like me. We had the same build for the most part, the same general coloring. She had her back turned. Andrew shot Ben first. That was when I ran. I didn't even get in my car. I was afraid he would hear me."

She told the story well. There was a perfect tremor to her voice.

"You didn't want to save your other children? You watched your son kill your husband, his own father. Why would you think he wouldn't take out his siblings?"

Iris wiped away a tear. "I'm not proud that I ran. That single moment has haunted me every day since. I panicked and by the time I realized what had really happened, it was over."

"It didn't occur to you to show up at the police station and turn in your son?"

"I knew what Drew would do," she insisted. "He would pin it all on me. I realized Bill was in on it and I ran away. I found out I was pregnant with Noah and realized I still had something to live for."

"Why not kill his siblings? If he wanted the company all for himself, why would he leave anyone alive? He'd set it up for the fire. Why not follow through and claim to be the one and only survivor?"

Iris sat back, her shoulders squaring. "He realized I wasn't the woman he'd killed. When he figured that out, he had to change his plans. He needed his siblings to keep me in check. He sent me a note stating that if I didn't stay away, he would kill them off one by one."

"How did he know where to send a note to you?"

She didn't hesitate, her story obviously well thought out. "Bill. I reached out to him a week after it happened, but he was devastated by what Drew had done. He wouldn't see me. He thought he would be implicated. He thought no one would believe that a teenager had managed the crime. By then the others had figured out what they could do and they told Hatch to keep his mouth shut. That's when I knew he had never loved me. Not really. He wasn't willing to risk himself. I'd sought refuge with Patty by that time. I didn't have anywhere else to go. She was willing to take me in and give me some work to do. Why not? She had all of my important assets at her disposal. My son didn't understand the contract. Andrew thought it would come to him, but because of the way he'd planned it, the others were able to use the morality clause to seize Ben's stock. They sold it out from under us, and I was left with nothing but scraps and Noah. I knew if I ever came forward, Drew would stop at nothing to see me dead."

The woman had a vivid imagination. "I would like to see your proof."

"And I would like you to tell my story, but I don't know that I trust you yet," Iris stated quietly. "Come with me. I still have a place in Florida. I'll charter a plane for us and we can be there tonight. I'll tell you everything."

It would be a hell of a story, but unfortunately her ambition was dimmed by the probability that she would get murdered. The woman in front of her was lying. There was so much wrong about her story.

If Drew had shot his father from the staircase, then why had Francine stood with her back to it, waited for Drew to step into Benedict's place, and then allowed him to neatly shoot her through the head?

How did Iris sneak in and out of the garage, since both doors were already blocked at the time? A neighbor reported hearing a single shout, and then ten minutes later the entire house was in flames. Everything had been set up ahead of time.

And then there was the coincidence of the assassin being in town.

If she took Iris up on her offer, she would be walking into a trap, and then she would be used against Drew in whatever plan Iris had set in motion.

"I'm not going anywhere," Shelby explained. "I need to see some proof before I'm willing to talk to you."

Iris nodded, reaching into the Chanel bag at her side. "All right. I'll give you something. I've watched my son over the years. I always knew he would come after me eventually. I knew he would go after my friends as well."

"You mean the ones who took the company away from him?"

"Yes, and now they're all dead. I feel bad about what happened with Patty, but she was going to sell me out to Andrew to save herself. I had to stop it. I wanted to live out my days in peace, watching over my children as best as I could."

A chill went through Shelby as she realized what she was dealing with. It was one thing to put a label on this woman and another to sit in front of her and watch her cry with absolutely no emotion behind her eyes at all. The tears were perfunctory, the well-learned habit of a woman whose whole life had been about gaming the system. She knew what to say and how to say it. There were so many people who would look at her and believe her. They would put her against Drew, who had the reputation of being a ruthless ass, and gravitate to her soft voice without ever seeing the calculation behind it.

This was a sociopath. She didn't love her children. They'd been tools for her to use to get what she did love.

Iris passed a folder Shelby's way. "Read this. It's about your brother. Did you know that Andrew was in town the same day your brother was? Did you know he was seen close to your brother's rental car?"

Shelby's whole body tightened. "Why on earth would Drew kill my brother?"

"Because he was going to break the story wide open. Because Patty told him that day. Because he met with me and I gave him the story of a lifetime. Look inside. Andrew might have been able to get rid of the records of your brother's notes of our conversation, but I took pictures."

She opened the folder, and her heart seemed to twist in her body. There was a picture of Drew walking into a gas station, walking right past Johnny's rental car.

And then there was her brother, his smiling face looking out from between the two women he was sitting with. Patricia Cain looked regal on one side, and Iris Lawless was sitting on the other. He had his ever-present notebook in his hands. The one that had burned up in the car accident.

How long had Iris been setting Drew up?

She had some serious questions for him, but she knew one thing. Drew wouldn't have hurt her brother. He didn't have a reason to.

"I know he says he'll let you tell the story, but he won't," Iris said quietly, as though she pitied Shelby. "He's an attractive man, but he's rotten to the core."

"If I don't get to the plane, they're going to wonder what happened to me." She held Iris's eyes for a moment. "They'll look for me, and this place has security cameras. They'll see that I was with you."

"If you tell Andrew about this, he'll find a way to twist it. If he thinks for a second that you'll side with me . . . well, I'm afraid of what he'll do to you. He's taken much from your family."

For the first time, real fear spiked through her system. Fear and rage. This was the woman who'd ordered her brother's death. Not Patricia Cain. She'd ordered it because she'd likely figured out that Johnny was smarter than she'd given him credit for.

Had he asked too many questions? Or simply the wrong ones, the ones that would put a killer in a corner and expose her? Had she tried to run this story by him only to have Johnny point out all the fallacies?

Somehow she'd figured out Johnny wasn't going to play her game, and she'd ensured he couldn't play at all.

The urge to leap across the table and wrap her hands around the woman's throat was nearly overwhelming. She could squeeze until Iris turned blue and got what she deserved. She could put an end to all this pain.

The door jingled. "Hey, you! I thought I saw you when we went through the drive-through. Mia needed French fries. Are you ready?

I'll ride back with you and you can tell me all about your mystery stop. Who's your friend?"

Carly was standing in the doorway, a cup in her hand. Carly, who would recognize Iris if she turned around. Carly, who was so close to Iris's gun-toting escort. He'd stood up behind her, threat plain in his stance.

Shelby stood as fast as she could, nearly spilling her now cold drink. She had to get Carly out of here and away from the threat.

She moved quickly, grabbing Carly's arms and hauling her out. "She's a witness for a story I'm writing. A confidential one. It's better you don't meet her."

"That's exciting," Carly replied with a smile. "All I did today was buy a bunch of shoes. Wait. That was exciting, too. You will not believe the wedges I found. They're perfect."

She let Carly chatter on about the shopping they'd done. Shelby unlocked the car doors and slipped behind the wheel, her eyes going to the café again.

They were gone like they'd never been there at all.

Shelby tried to stop her hands from shaking as she pointed the car toward the airport.

Chapter Thirteen

Drew stared down at his phone, his blood pressure ticking slowly up. There it was. Proof that Shelby was . . . he wasn't even sure what to believe at this point. What was she doing? He only knew that Shelby had been going shopping with his sisters and she'd completely violated his trust.

She'd met with his mother. The photo proved it beyond all doubt. She'd fucking taken his plane, snuck away from his family, and met with his greatest enemy.

If he hadn't put a guard on her, he wouldn't even know. She would walk back in smiling, her arms laden with packages, and she would lie to him.

Or she wouldn't come back at all. She would walk away because the story was more important than anything to her.

He shifted his focus, putting his phone down and moving to his laptop. The report would be easier to read there.

The McKay-Taggart agent accounted for Shelby's time from the moment she'd gotten off the plane to the moment she'd gotten back on. Drew had almost let it go, almost told the guard he didn't need to shadow Shelby today because she was going to be with Case and Riley. He'd made the decision at the last minute because he'd looked over at Noah and thought *what the hell*. A little more muscle couldn't hurt since someone was after his family.

Now he realized she'd planned this all along.

He read over the report, trying to stay calm. She would be walking through those doors any minute, and he couldn't have it out with her until they were alone.

Where she would probably try to distract him with sex. After all, he'd proven to be so easy to manipulate. He shouldn't blame her. They'd both gone into this relationship wanting something from the other.

She'd broken off from the group immediately and went straight to meet with someone at Williams Investigations. Naturally she hadn't mentioned that to him. She'd spent several hours there and then rushed to meet his mother in a café outside the private airport. The agent hadn't gotten close enough to hear anything, but Shelby had sat with his mother for nearly half an hour and left only when Carly had interrupted the meeting.

What had Carly interrupted?

There was a knock on the door.

How was he supposed to hold it together? He didn't want to see anyone or deal with anyone. Maybe never again. After the way Shelby had ripped his heart out of his body, he might become a hermit.

"I'll be out in a minute, Noah." Perhaps Shelby could take Noah right back to his mama. They could all live happily with Iris.

"Is he still here? I should have known you wouldn't be able to turn him away," a familiar voice said.

Drew breathed a long sigh of relief. "Hatch. Thank God. Where the hell have you been? Do you know what I've gone through looking for you?"

His mentor walked in, his eyes rimmed with red. Hatch was wearing the same thing he'd been wearing the last time Drew had seen him. He was wrinkled and looked beyond tired. "I'm sorry, Drew."

"Where the hell have you been?"

Hatch's shoulders slumped. "After what happened with Noah, I went on a bender. I didn't want you to find me, so I got a bunch of cash and found a couple of friends who wouldn't talk."

"You mean hookers."

Hatch shrugged. "A man's got needs. You know I still prefer to pay."

Hatch refused to date. As long as Drew had known him, he'd never seen Hatch spend time with a woman who wasn't a friend or a professional. He'd taught Drew that sexual needs could be met without the burden of an emotional connection.

Until Shelby. Until he'd figured out how good sex could be when he was emotionally engaged.

He shoved that thought aside. "So you hung out with a hooker until your cash ran out? I've been worried sick."

"I know you have been, and you can't know what that means to me. You have no idea what having this family has meant to me." Hatch took a deep breath before continuing. "When I ran out of cash, I hitched a ride and ended up in Houston. I didn't fare well there. I might have gotten into a fight over a bar bill I couldn't pay and ended up in jail. So everything's fairly normal. I got out this morning and decided to come home and apologize."

At least one thing had gone right. Hatch hadn't gotten himself killed, as Drew had feared. He'd been worried about it for days. "You want to explain why this hit you so hard?"

Hatch's hands were shaking as he found his way to the chair in front of Drew's desk. He clutched the back and shook his head. "I don't know. Seeing Noah got to me. It was like seeing Ben walk in and look at me. It was a real kick in the gut. I thought I'd left it behind me. I felt like we were almost done, like we could finally put it behind us. I think coming on the heels of finding out Iris had fooled us all made me go a little crazy. Tell me something, Drew. Did the test come in?"

"Yes, Noah's definitely my brother. No question about it." He needed Hatch to understand that Noah was staying. Noah was a Lawless and, until he proved that Noah was playing him, he couldn't dump the kid on the street. "You had to know he was somehow related to me. I don't like to admit it, but we look similar."

Hatch slumped down into the seat. "I knew it the minute I saw him. I suppose that's why I had the bad reaction. I didn't realize your mother and father were still intimate when he died. I was fairly certain they weren't."

Drew didn't want to deal with this. It made him nauseous. The past needed to stay in the past. He had too much future crap to deal with. "I get why you were surprised, but we need to think beyond the past. We've got bigger problems. Shelby met with Iris earlier today."

Hatch's eyes widened. "Are you kidding me? She's here in Austin?"

"Shelby went to Dallas for the day. They met in a café outside the airport. I've got pictures of them getting cozy." It made him sick.

Hatch was silent for a moment. "Maybe you should give Shelby the benefit of the doubt. You care about this woman. Give her a chance to explain what happened."

"Explain? What the hell could she possibly say? Give me another explanation, Hatch. I would love to hear a reason I can live with." It was something Hatch was good at. He could poke holes in any theory Drew came up with. It was how their relationship worked. Hatch was the person he bounced ideas off of.

Except lately that person had been Shelby. She might not know code, but she actually had quite a head for business, and she'd definitely become his conscience.

She'd lied to him. It was right there, a sick, roiling feeling. He couldn't take a deep breath and figure out how to best use this to his advantage. He needed to sit down and plan the battle to come. Maybe it would be best to keep Shelby close. He could continue to watch her, figure out where his mother was staying, what her end game was. He could turn all of this around on her.

Anger flared through him. White-hot rage. It felt so much better than the horrible, nasty emptiness that had threatened to overwhelm him.

"You're sure she set this meeting up?" Hatch asked.

"How else would Iris have found her?"

"You have no idea what she's capable of. Iris is excellent at getting the proper pieces into place without those pieces even knowing they're being moved. This is exactly the kind of game she would play."

"I know she's evil and I know Shelby should know better." Why hadn't she called him? Why hadn't she told him what she was doing that day?

"Yeah, well, that's one word to describe your mother. She's also incredibly intelligent. If she wanted to meet with Shelby, she would make it happen. You already think she was spying on Shelby's computer. Why not have someone following her?"

He'd already considered and discarded that scenario. "I've had a bodyguard trailing after her since the first incident with Noah. There's one working here in Austin, and I had another follow her in Dallas. These are men trained by Ian Taggart. If they'd seen someone tailing her, it would be in the report. He didn't see anything out of the ordinary until she walked into that café. My mother followed her in within ten minutes and sat down to talk to her. Shelby didn't try to run. She didn't call the police. She didn't call me. She sat there and talked to her like they were old friends. Now she's about to walk through that door, and I have no idea what to do about the situation."

"You should give it time. Don't blow up on her. Talk to her and find out what Iris wanted. I think some of this might lead back to Noah. I know you don't want to hear this, but it's too coincidental that Noah's been alive all this time, but he suddenly gets a note pointing the way to his brother. That was Iris. She did that. We have to figure out why he's here."

"I've had several investigators working on his background and they've found nothing to contradict his story. He actually seems like a nice kid." But then Shelby had seemed perfect to him, too. Shelby had seemed like the kind of woman who would see past his weirdness and his awkwardness, the type of woman who could love him.

She'd seemed like the type of woman he could love.

How was he sitting here? He wanted to go out there and fucking find her and have it all out right here and now. The waiting was going to kill him, but he swore he would do it. He would let her walk in and work her wiles on him. Patience would win this game. Let her think he really was the idiot. Let her believe her plan was working, that he was so invested in her he couldn't see straight.

But how would he lie next to her at night knowing she was using him?

"He might be a nice kid, but he also might be Iris's Trojan horse. Have you thought about that?" Hatch asked.

Was Noah working with Shelby? Had they been working together all along, or had Shelby simply seen an opportunity and taken it?

"Of course I've thought about the fact that Noah isn't what he says he is. I told you I've checked into his past. I've scoured the computer he showed up here with and found nothing. If he's hiding something on it, then he's damn good. If Noah is working with Iris, why is she trying to kill him?"

"Trying to kill him?"

He quickly brought Hatch up to date on what had been happening with Noah. "The good news is if you were in jail, you couldn't have tried to kill Noah."

"Getting my ass hauled into jail is the best alibi ever," Hatch agreed with a frown.

How much longer would it be before Shelby walked in the door? "What does she get out of meeting with Shelby?"

Hatch stared at him for a moment, his gaze more serious than Drew could ever remember. "You never thought it was me, did you? You didn't think I was the one who tried to hurt Noah?"

"Of course not." He stood up. Sitting was killing him. He needed to move. He was restless. He hated the feeling.

Hatch shook his head. "Why the unwavering faith in me, son? Do you remember what I was like in the beginning?"

He'd been difficult and surly. He'd told Drew to fuck off, that he wasn't the man to help him out. He wasn't good for anyone. Drew could still remember the look in Hatch's eyes when he'd told him to get the hell out of his room. Sometimes Drew thought Hatch had been waiting to die. "I remember everything, but I also remember you couldn't kick me out. You were the reason I had somewhere to sleep that first night."

He'd gotten on a bus for Austin the day of his eighteenth birthday. The ticket drained most of his cash and he remembered how hard it had been to say good-bye to Riley. He hadn't been sure when he would be able to see his brother next. Any of them. It had been a terrible gamble and if it hadn't worked, he would have found himself in a strange city with no one who would help him out. Far from home. Far from his family.

He'd found Hatch in a crappy motel he paid for by the week. He'd been halfway through a fifth of whiskey and he hadn't been happy that Drew wasn't a hooker named Barbie.

"I was too drunk to kick you out, Drew. I couldn't physically manage it."

"You were always rough around the edges, but we made it through."

"Do you know why I really let you stay?"

Drew paced, glancing out the window to see if he could catch a glimpse of the car coming up the road. "I was persistent."

"I did it out of guilt."

He'd known that, too. Sometimes when Hatch had been too drunk to know he was doing it, he'd talked about Drew's dad. He'd begged his father for forgiveness. "I told you already I forgive you for not coming forward after Dad died."

"It was more than simply leaving you behind. There was far more to it," Hatch said. "I prayed this would all be over after we dealt with Patty. Iris being alive was my single worst nightmare. I never wanted to hurt you, Drew. At first all I could see was my own misery, but after a while I realized I could make your life better. I could do something to make up for what happened back then."

The limo came into view. There she was.

Calm. He had to be calm. It didn't matter how his stupid heart felt. He didn't need his heart. He needed his brain, and his brain told him that it was far more important to maintain his place in her bed. It was how he would figure out what his mother was doing. He would smile and kiss her and listen to her lies. He would pretend everything was fine.

"Drew, are you listening to me? We need to talk. There's something I have to tell you, something that could change everything. I hoped you would never have to know, but it's time."

He kind of heard Hatch, but he needed to see Shelby. He needed to look at her and see her through new eyes. Now that he knew the truth, perhaps she wouldn't look as good to him. Her attractiveness had always been wrapped up in her innocence. She'd seen the world in a way he didn't quite understand. She'd gone through pain and heartache and still had an openness that called to him.

All lies. More manipulation.

"I have to deal with this." All his good intentions flew away the minute he saw her. She was getting out of the limo, laughing at something Carly had said. Mia got out of the car behind her. His sister's face was grim.

What had Mia seen? Did she know something?

Noah was smiling as he opened the gate and offered to help carry the massive amount of packages the women had brought back with them.

"Holy shit!" Bran was coming down the stairs. He smiled as he caught sight of Hatch. "Hatch, it's so good to see you alive. I was sure you'd finally gone to that great strip club in the sky."

"No, just jail," Hatch replied quickly as he stepped close to Drew. "You keep your cool. Take her somewhere private and ask her what's happening. That woman is good at manipulating people. This isn't Shelby's fault. If she was talking to that woman, it's because she thought it would help."

"What's going on?" Bran stood at the bottom of the stairs. "Who's *that woman?*"

The door came open and Carly walked in, followed by Ellie and Riley. Bran went to his wife, slipping his hand into hers and tilting her face up for a kiss.

"I bought fewer shoes than Riley," Ellie was saying.

"When you find a pair of dress shoes that comfortable, you buy a couple of pairs," Riley replied. He stopped when he realized who was in the room. "Hatch!"

Riley greeted Hatch as Mia and Case strode in, and then there she was.

Shelby, with her red hair and soft skin. Shelby, who'd taken over his entire life only to shove him back in the dark with her betrayal.

She looked over and her eyes widened when she saw Hatch there. He could have sworn she took a step back, as though she realized how much trouble she was in.

She had excellent instincts because he couldn't do what Hatch asked him to. He couldn't be reasonable.

He strode over to her, reaching out to grasp her arm. He leaned over, whispering in her ear. "I know what you did. Did you honestly believe you would get away with it? Did you think I would allow you to play me?"

She gasped, her eyes coming up. "What are you talking about?"

Good. He had her attention. He leaned over so he could whisper in her ear. Even through his rage, the simple act of being close to her had an effect on his body. "Walk into my office and we'll talk about this, but if you say a damn thing in front of my family, you should understand I'll destroy you. There will be no discussion or bargaining. You're going to tell me the truth, and I'm going to explain to you how things will be from now on. Do I make myself clear?"

Now that she was here, his plans changed. He'd thought he could shove her out, but he couldn't. Even knowing exactly what she'd done to him, he couldn't stand the thought of her not being close. The idea of never being in bed with her again made him want to rage.

Just because she'd betrayed him didn't mean he had to give her up. It simply meant the rules of their game were about to change and he would dictate them all.

She looked up at him, those big eyes wide with fear. "You've made yourself clear."

"Hey, Shelby, are you okay?" Noah set down the bags he was holding. His gaze went to the place where Drew was gripping her arm.

He eased off because this would be something else he kept from his family. He was about to enter into a relationship that had nothing to do with love and everything to do with the fact that somehow he needed her. She would stay with him, and he would watch her for the rest of her life. He would never trust her again.

But by God he would have her.

"Shelby and I have something to talk about in private." He sounded perfectly reasonable. He didn't at all sound like a man who was about to blow up his world.

"Yes, I definitely think we should talk." Her lips had firmed, the fear fleeing her eyes to be replaced with pure stubborn will.

He meant to break that will. "We'll talk in my office."

"I want to know what he's doing here." Noah had gotten a look at Hatch.

Hatch's hands came up. "I'm sorry for how I behaved before. I was out of hand."

"Sure you were." Noah set the packages down. "Did you decide it would be easier to take me out yourself? Since nearly running me over didn't work."

He did not need this. "Noah, I told you it wasn't Hatch. He's been in jail. I'll get you the confirmation of it, but it's not him. He's an asshole, but he's not a killer."

"Noah, I wouldn't hurt you. Like I said, I had a bad reaction, and one day I'll explain it," Hatch said. "I did a lot of thinking while I sat in that cell. I have a lot to make up for, but hurting you isn't something I would ever do."

Noah seemed to relax a bit.

"Shelby and I will be back in a while, after we talk." Drew was ready to get this out of the way. His stomach was in knots.

Mia stepped in front of him. "No. I think we all need to talk, and it won't be private, Drew. I'm sick of the lies and I want answers."

"What are you talking about?" The whole room went quiet. Everyone was looking at him, and there was a stillness to the air that made the room feel heavy with anticipation.

Case shook his head. "You should have told everyone. You should have known she would figure it out."

"Figure what out?" Riley set down his bags and stared at Drew. "What have you done?"

Naturally everyone looked at him. What the hell had happened? He looked down at Shelby. "What did you tell her?"

"What did I tell her? Absolutely nothing, though you should remember I told you I thought this was a bad idea," Shelby shot back.

Mia reached into her bag, pulling out a familiar envelope. "Shelby didn't tell me anything, though it doesn't surprise me that you would bring her in on your plotting. All I needed was this. I knew there was something about this letter that bugged me."

"That's my DNA test." Noah looked between Mia and Hatch, who he seemed to shrink back from. "Are you saying it was wrong? I'm not your half brother?"

"I'm saying Drew lied and he knew all along. You're not my half brother, Noah," Mia announced.

Shit. He'd been lazy, sloppy. He should have known Mia would never let things lie. "I can explain."

Noah stepped back. "I'm not a Lawless?"

Mia reached out to take his hand. "Noah, you're not my half brother. This test proves that we're full-blooded siblings. It also proves that my mother didn't die in the fire."

There were gasps and shocked looks, and Drew knew what it meant to be the villain.

Drew took a deep drink of Scotch and wished he were anywhere but here.

Not anywhere. He wished it was yesterday and he was in bed with Shelby. He wished he was reaching for her and drawing her into his arms. He wished he had no idea what was going to happen next.

Unfortunately, he was in the here and now, and it pretty much sucked.

The family had moved into the living room. It seemed they wanted to get comfortable for this particular trial.

Drew had zero doubt he was about to be found guilty.

"I don't understand." Noah had chosen a seat close to Shelby, as though she might protect him from whatever Hatch would do next. "Your mother died before I was born. There must be something wrong with the test. Maybe they left off the word *half* in the report."

Convincing Noah would be so simple. He could nod and agree with him, and Noah would go right back into his happy, ignorant world. Unfortunately, it wasn't Noah who was questioning him, and Mia would have done every bit of her homework before she even thought to confront Drew. He could now see his biggest mistake had been not picking up the results privately.

Shelby had done this to him. She'd made him soft, lazy.

Why wouldn't she look his way?

He'd expected her to appeal to his more primitive instincts. He'd expected her to plead with him, to try to stay close. From the moment they'd decided to retire to the living room, she'd moved away from him. Now she and Noah were huddled together like the last survivors on a life raft, trying not to fall into the sea of sharks.

"It doesn't work that way, Noah," Mia began. "If we were half siblings, you would share twenty-five percent of your DNA in common with us. You would show up in the testing as having a familial connection, but it would be more like a cousin. That would be all they could tell without parental DNA. This test states plainly that you and Drew are full siblings, and there's only one way that could happen."

Riley's head was shaking, his hand clinging to Ellie's as they sat together on the couch, sharing it with Bran and Carly. "I don't understand how any of this happened. What does it mean?"

"It could mean a lot of things." Ellie rubbed Riley's back with her free hand, obviously desperate to give her husband comfort. "Did your mother ever donate eggs to a fertility clinic?"

No one was going to comfort Drew. Maybe not ever again. "She didn't donate eggs, Ellie. The truth is right there. Noah is my full sibling, therefore he is the biological child of Benedict and Iris Lawless. Noah was born eight months after our father died."

"But that's impossible," Carly said.

"It's not impossible if the woman who died in that house with your father was actually Francine Wells," Shelby explained. "The body they found is roughly an inch shorter than your mother was, according to the forensics. They overlooked it because it was an open-and-shut case. Or they overlooked it because the medical examiner was paid to."

Bran had gone a pasty shade of white. "But if it wasn't our mother who was killed, then . . ."

"Yes, Bran," Drew said. "The look on your face right this second is exactly why I didn't tell you. I thought I could figure this out and you wouldn't have to know that our loving mother took over the identity of Francine Wells, and she walked away from all of us. She had Noah and lived with Patricia Cain for the last twenty years."

"Are you talking about Patty? My mom's friend Patty?" Noah asked.

"Yes, I'm talking about Patricia Cain, who along with Steven Castalano, Phillip Stratton, and Iris Lawless conspired to murder my father and take his company." It made him sick even saying it. Like it was finally real because the rest of them knew.

Now it all hit him at once. He was the child of a murderer.

How much of his mother lived inside him?

"Then she was . . . ," Carly began.

"She was the one who shot Bran." Now that it was out, they all had to face the harsh light of day. "She was the one who nearly killed you both. As far as I can tell, she's killed a lot of people."

"No." Noah stood up. "This is all a lie. My mother was not a murderer. She wasn't a great mom, but she tried."

Shelby reached for Noah's hand. "I'm sorry, but he's not lying. Your mother is the one who's lied to you."

He pulled away, his head shaking. "No. This isn't true. You're all trying to trick me for some reason."

It was obvious it would take far more for Noah to believe. Luckily Drew had some small amount of proof. He strode to the bookshelf. There was a box he kept there. He'd kept it ever since the day he'd found Hatch and discovered the single picture in Hatch's wallet. At the time he'd been thinking about stealing any money Hatch had in an attempt to get back to Dallas, but he'd found the picture and somehow it had given him strength.

It was the only remaining picture of his mother. She was smiling at the camera, her hair around her shoulders. He'd loved that small

Polaroid because it was proof she existed. Everything else had been destroyed in the fire.

Now it was proof of her lies.

"This is my mother." He strode to Noah, showing him the photo. "Does she look familiar to you?"

Noah stared at the picture like it was a grenade about to go off. "That can't be right. She can't be . . . she would have told me. Also, she died years ago. My mother is dead."

"She faked her death because she realized I'd come into some power." How much did he have to lay out for the kid? "Four years ago, I screwed up and some pictures of me were leaked to the press. She realized that I had the power and money to potentially come after the people she'd conspired with. Two weeks later your mother had her car accident. She knew I would figure it out eventually because she knew I would go after the people she worked with, and they would turn on her if I let the fire burn hot enough."

"She wouldn't have left me with nothing." Noah sounded hollow.

They were all damaged now. He should get used to it. "Well, she's a murderous sociopath who probably killed off all your stepfathers for their cash, so it's not really a shock she's also a shitty mother."

"Drew!" Shelby stared at him like he'd grown two heads.

She'd lost the right to adjust his behavior, but still he found himself sighing. "I'm sorry, Noah. I didn't mean to tell you like this. Honestly, I didn't mean for you to find out at all."

"Yes, that's clear," Bran said, a hard edge to his tone. "It's clear that you intended to lie to us forever."

He tried to hold on to his temper. "Tell me how you knowing would have made your life better. Tell me how taking this burden on myself was a fucking selfish act. I didn't want you to have to look at our childhood and wonder if anything at all had been real. They were all we had, and finding out Dad had an affair and he wasn't perfect damn near killed me. That information is nothing compared to the revelation that a woman I adored turned out to be a fucking monster."

"I think I'm going to be sick." Noah turned and walked out.

Shelby stood.

"Give him some time." He didn't want Shelby running after Noah for several reasons, not the least being he wasn't sure she wouldn't keep running.

"He's had a shock," Shelby argued.

"Yes, and I know damn well how it feels. I wanted to be alone, too. I needed it."

"But you didn't stay alone," Mia pointed out. "You didn't keep this to yourself. You told Hatch, didn't you? You didn't tell the rest of us, but you told him."

"I don't think any of you should blame Drew. He was doing what he always does. He was trying to protect this family." Hatch sat back in his seat.

"And Shelby," Carly said quietly. "Hatch wasn't the only one Drew told. She knew. I have to wonder why he did that."

"He needed help investigating," Shelby replied, her cheeks flushing.

He hadn't thought about the position keeping his secret put Shelby in. Carly was her closest friend. Had he just taken her best friend from her?

"He's got an entire investigative firm at his fingertips." Case put a hand on Mia's shoulder.

"Yes, and if you'd known, would you have told Mia?" He wasn't the bad guy here.

Case sighed. "Probably, but you could have used someone other than me. You could have been specific about who the agent was allowed to talk to even in-house."

"I didn't trust that it wouldn't still get out. I used Shelby because she was willing to stay close to Austin and allow me to help her." Until today.

Riley looked up at him, his eyes weary. "I get why you did it, brother. You were trying to protect us. It's what you've done all your life, what you taught me to do, but Drew, I don't think you can protect us from this. She's out there and now Noah's here. I can't imagine she's going to let things lie."

At least someone halfway understood him. "I've been trying to figure out what she's planning. I know she's not going to leave us be, but I didn't want anyone to panic. I wanted to try to handle the situation as quietly as I could. Now I suppose I'll tell you everything I know, which isn't a whole lot."

"She won't leave you alone," Shelby said, her voice dull. "She came after me today. I was checking out some leads in Dallas this afternoon, and she found me in a café outside the airport."

"She did what?" Case asked, his voice rising. "I knew you should have had backup."

Drew stared at her for a moment. He hadn't expected her to admit it. He'd expected her to cover it all up.

"I got done early with my errand and I stopped at the café where you found me. I had some time to kill before the flight." Shelby's voice was a monotone. "I wanted to think for a while and she walked in. She sat down and she told me her side of the story, which was complete and utter bullshit, but I didn't argue with her because she'd also brought a guy with a gun with her."

"What? There was nothing in the report about a guy with a gun." She'd been alone with his mother and someone had a gun?

"Report?" Shelby's voice went low.

"I knew there was someone tailing her," Case said, snapping his fingers. "I thought I saw Bear's truck hanging around. See, you hired McKay-Taggart to follow Shelby around and no one told me. You could have done the same thing with the investigation. You didn't have to drag your girlfriend into this."

"I'm not his girlfriend." Shelby stood up, every line of her body a testament to how pissed off she was.

"Shelby, we should talk about this alone." Maybe he'd been hasty.

"How long have you had someone spying on me?"

"In my office." He wasn't about to have it out with her here in front of his family. It might also give him a few seconds to figure out a way out of this.

She could still be playing him.

Shelby stood her ground. "I'm not going in your office, Drew. I only have a few questions and then we can be done. So tell me how long you've had someone spying on me."

"I haven't had anyone spying on you. I had a bodyguard watching you and protecting you." He'd been worried about her, worried he was placing her in danger.

"Ah, so the bodyguard didn't write reports on what I was doing. Think about it before you lie to me, Drew. What was the drama when I got home about? What did you mean you knew what I'd done?"

"I don't want to do this in front of an audience, Shelby."

"Too bad, because we have one."

Hatch stood up. "Come on, guys. I think we should give them some privacy."

"So Drew can lie to me again?" Shelby looked to Carly. "Don't leave me. Please."

The pain in her voice damn near killed him.

Carly stood up. "I am a member of this family, but I'm your friend, too."

"Shelby's family," Bran argued. "Drew's serious about her. She's living with him."

Shelby shook her head. "It was all part of the deal we made. I signed a contract to be his girlfriend so you wouldn't ask too many questions about why I was here. In exchange, I investigated your mother, tried to tie her concretely to the crime, and I got to write a book about the entire thing."

The room went quiet.

"But you were sleeping with him," Ellie said. "Was that part of your contract?"

"Hey, don't even make that inference," Drew warned.

Riley stood up, facing him. "Don't you talk to my wife like that."

"I didn't mean it that way." Ellie looked up at Shelby. "I was worried Drew had done something he shouldn't. He can be pretty single-minded. He can forget about things like morality and human kindness. I was worried he'd forced you into a sexual relationship."

"Is that what you think of me?" God, how bad was it?

Shelby ignored him, turning to Ellie, her whole face flush. "No, that wasn't part of the contract. That was me being foolish. I wanted to write that story in the beginning. It was scandalous and juicy and I wanted it. And then sometime today I realized I was never going to go through with it because I loved all of you and it would hurt you. But then I wasn't going to be allowed to write that book, was I, Drew?"

"I wasn't going to stop you from writing it. I told you that." He couldn't say the rest of it. When had he become such a coward?

Mia stepped up and took Shelby's hands in her own. "He would have let you write it, but it would never have seen the light of day. Did you actually read the contract? Because I know my brother. He never intended to allow any of this out. He never meant for us to know a damn thing. He would have gotten the information he needed from you and then taken all your notes and wrapped you up in a nondisclosure agreement, and he would have dealt with our mother on his own. You would have been collateral damage."

Shelby sniffled. "No, I didn't read the contract as thoroughly as I should have. Like I said, I wanted the story, but I wanted him, too. I wanted all of it. I wanted a family, and I was going to see if it could work. I'm sorry if I upset you all."

Carly practically jumped out of her seat, rushing to envelop Shelby in a hug. "I'm so sorry this happened. I knew this wasn't going to end well."

Bran stood up, coming to Drew's side. "Carly, you don't know Drew the way I do. This isn't what you think."

At least one of his brothers was on his side. "Everything I've done has been to protect the people I care about."

Including Shelby, who had him in knots now. Was she twisting this to get what she wanted? Or had he misinterpreted the situation?

"Shelby, my brother is a complete dumbass," Bran continued.

So much for being on his side.

"He really is," Riley agreed. "He might seem like a ruthless prick in all of this, but there's no way he sleeps with you without having feelings for you. He moved you in here. Somewhere in that brilliantly deranged brain of his, he was planning a future with you."

She took a deep breath and brushed back her hair. "There's no future here. He doesn't trust me."

"Of course I trust you, but you have to admit that this looks bad." Damn it. They kept trying to turn him into the bad guy. He had the right to question why she would sit with his mother and not make a move to call him or the police. She hadn't called him at all. She'd waited until she'd gotten home. He had no idea if she'd intended to tell him what had happened.

"I guess I do need to talk to Drew alone," Shelby said. "I appreciate the support and I'm happy that I'm not going to lose a friend, but I have some things to say to him that I would feel better about if we were in private."

One by one they filed out, the women offering Shelby their support while the men simply gave Drew shakes of their heads.

And then he was finally alone with her.

"Tell me what you meant when I walked in the door." She stood apart from him, her shoulders squared as if for battle.

He took a step toward her. It was past time to step this back a little. He needed to show her he could be reasonable. "I was angry, and I can see now that I might have overreacted when I got that report."

She put a hand up, holding him off. "The report from the spy you've had on me without my knowledge."

She had to read that in the worst possible light. "I did it after the first attempt on Noah. I didn't know at the time if it was you or Noah this person was after. I was worried and I wanted to ensure your safety."

"If you'd asked me to take a bodyguard with me, I would have," Shelby replied evenly.

"How was I supposed to know that? None of the other women in the family have been reasonable about it." Except Mia, who had been forced to tote a guard around with her for six months while she worked and she and Case were apart. And Ellie, who'd only ditched her guard to save someone's life. He was fairly certain if Bran asked Carly, she would take one on to make him feel better.

"I've agreed to everything you've asked for, Andrew. I've been the idiot who accepted everything you gave me and never asked why. There was no reason for you to not talk to me about it. Well, no reason except one. So that means that you didn't want me to know someone was watching me. Have you been waiting for me to screw up? Did you need an excuse?"

"An excuse for what? And no. I wasn't waiting for you to screw up. I told you why I did it."

"And I told you I don't believe you. Not for a second. We promised to be honest with each other. I need you to be honest with yourself, too. You don't trust me. You've been waiting for me to prove to you that I'm like all the rest."

He felt his fists clench at his sides. "Damn it, I'm not some woman-hating asshole."

"I didn't say you were, but you've never let yourself get close to a woman. And you never intend to. You told Carly you weren't ever getting married."

Finally, maybe they were getting somewhere. He'd fucked up. It was easy to see. He should have done what everyone had told him to, but she made him crazy. If he could give her something, perhaps they could turn this argument around. "I did say that, but honestly that was before I saw how it works for my brothers. I've already started to rethink my stance. Riley and Bran are happy. They can make it work. Maybe I can, too. We do quite well together."

Her head shook sadly. "Oh, we're compatible in bed, but we don't work anywhere else."

"That's not true."

"Tell me what you meant earlier today. You told me if I said a word, you would destroy me."

Her calm presence was starting to grate on him. He was a mess and she was cool and collected.

"I was upset."

"No, you were being honest," Shelby corrected. "You would have destroyed me and you wouldn't have thought twice about it. You were ready to do it without even hearing my side of things."

He moved to the sofa. "I'm willing to admit I might have rushed into this without thinking. Sit down with me and let's discuss what happened this afternoon."

She didn't make a move toward him. "It's too late now. The sad thing is people have been trying to tell me for a long time. If I'd believed them, we might have come out of this as friends. That's my fault. I knew I shouldn't have gone to bed with you."

"Naturally now it's all my fault. I do understand sarcasm when I hear it. I wasn't the one who didn't bother to call the police when a psychotic killer sat down across the table from me. You didn't call me, either. Were you going to bother to tell me? Or was this going to be a part of your story?"

Finally some emotion started to show on her face. "When should I have called, Drew? When she threatened me with her guard? The one she knew she had. I couldn't pit my guard against hers because I didn't know about mine. Or should I have called when Carly showed up? Carly would have recognized her. And what exactly would I have told the police? All of her identification would be under another name. Iris Lawless is dead until I prove otherwise. What would the police have been able to do except decide I'm crazy? I didn't call you because I was surrounded by your family and I decided it was better to tell you in person."

He hadn't thought about the ramifications of her calling. His rage and fear were dying down, and he was beginning to realize he'd handled this all wrong. "Let's stop blaming each other and have a drink and talk. I'm willing to admit that I was hasty. I can see where you were put in a bad position. Can you see where I was scared?"

"You weren't scared, Drew. You were angry. You took one look at that picture, and what did you see? Did you see me in trouble? Did you see the possibility of me getting hurt?"

"No, I saw you betraying me." He couldn't lie about that. It had been the first thing he'd seen. He hadn't even questioned it. He hadn't read the report or thought to call her. He'd known she was in the act of hurting him.

"I know you did. You don't trust me, and there's absolutely nothing we can do without trust."

"What would have happened if you'd seen that photo and our positions were reversed? You would have questions, too. I'm not crazy for thinking this way."

Her shoulders slumped, and the anger that had taken her over seemed to deflate. "No, it's part of who you are, but I thought I was special. It's the mistake women make most. We think that we're the ones who can change a man, who can heal him." She walked to where she'd left her briefcase and pulled out a folder. "As to our positions being reversed, this is what your mother gave me today. After she explained that you were the one who killed your father. She made a decent argument for that. Well, for anyone who doesn't know the case as intimately as I do. But this was her real play to get me to shift sides. I have no idea why she would want that, but it's another piece of the puzzle. She gave this to me, and all I could think about was getting back to you. What kind of sister am I? I see evidence that someone I know might have killed my brother. I'm given a reasonable and rational motive for why he would do it, and never once do I question the man because he's my lover. I think my brother would be disappointed in me. You're a better sibling than I am. You would never let a lover come between you and your family."

What the hell was she talking about? He took the folder out of her hand and opened it up. There was a picture of him at a gas station. He was walking in front of a car. He didn't even recognize the place. "What is this supposed to mean? Why do you have pictures of me?"

"The car you're walking in front of is my brother's." She pointed to the picture. "It's an hour before the brakes failed and my brother died."

His blood seemed to go cold. "Shelby, I never met your brother. Never once in my life."

She held up a hand. "I know that. Like I said, my first thought after she explained to me that you'd had my brother murdered was, how do I tell you she's been following you all this time? What else does she have on you? She's been waiting to use this. I didn't even think for a second that you could have done anything like this. So you should look through that. At least now you know she might hit you this way."

He'd been close to Shelby's brother before he died? He turned the page. There was a picture of Patricia and his mother on either side of a smiling, attractive young man who looked a lot like his sister. Johnny Gates. Shelby's brother, the last of her family.

"I don't know why I'm walking in front of his car, but I assure you—"

She cut him off. "I know you didn't kill my brother. Worry about your mom, not me. I'm going to transfer all my files to you and I'll leave all my notes behind."

"Behind? What are you talking about?"

"I'm going home. You've made it plain that I will get nothing out of this. I won't get my book. I won't get a loving boyfriend. I'm done." She frowned. "But there is something I have to tell you first."

He didn't need to hear anything else. "You don't have a home. You don't have anywhere to go. You'll stay here."

"I am going to leave, Drew. You can't stop me. I'm not some possession you can keep or dispense with at will."

"You're in danger. She knows exactly who you are." Panic started to threaten. If she walked out on him, he might never get her back.

"The minute I leave this house, I'm no longer of any interest to her."

"That's not true. She knows you're my weakness."

"Oh, Drew, you don't have any weaknesses," Shelby said with a sigh.

"I'm not going to let you leave." He knew he sounded like a stubborn child, but he couldn't help himself. He'd fucked up and he wasn't sure how to fix it.

"I understand that you're used to getting what you want, and maybe you've decided you want me again since you figured out I didn't betray you, but I'm done. You can't force me to stay here with you. So the best thing you can do right now is calm down and listen to me. I would rather do this with some kindness because I know it's going to be hard on you, but you need to read the information I found at the investigator's."

How could she be so calm? "I don't give a damn about the investigator. I know I fucked up, but that doesn't mean you get to walk away. You promised me you wouldn't do that. You told me if you had a problem, you would stay and fight it out with me. Well, here we are and you're already running away."

Her skin flushed, obvious anger surging. "I made that deal with you when I believed you were honest with me. You had me sign a contract you knew you would never honor."

He had to keep her talking, had to stop her from walking out his door. "The contract plainly states that I would purchase the manuscript from you for an agreed-upon price. I never once stated that I would allow you to publish it. I'll still honor that. How much do want for it? A million? Two? I don't know why we're arguing about this when you said yourself you'd already decided not to publish it anyway."

Her eyes widened as she stared at him. "Are you serious?"

"Damn straight, I'm serious. I get that you're pissed I wanted to watch you. I can't help it. More people have betrayed me than ever gave a damn about me."

"Yes, you're damaged. It's not my responsibility to fix you. Call a therapist and when you've fixed yourself and you're not such a massive ass, maybe you can give me a call." There was fire in her eyes again and she stalked her way to him, getting into his space. "We were supposed to be partners, but you used me. I was nothing but a shield for the people you really do care about."

He had to be honest with her. "Maybe in the beginning, but that changed. You have no idea how much I've worried about you. Shelby, baby, we don't have to fight. I was wrong. I should have trusted you. I'm not good at that, but you've taught me so much. You can teach me this, too."

"I don't think anyone can teach you this, and after I tell you what I've done, you might not want me here at all. Drew, I've been investigating Hatch. I asked Case to help me."

Anger flared through his system again. "I told you not to do that. Why are you wasting time on this?"

"Hatch was the fourth. It was his money," she said, her voice flat. "It's all in the report. He handed over fifty thousand dollars to Williams. He was the last payment. Volchenko carried out the job the next week."

Drew stopped, his stomach bottoming out. She was mistaken. It was obvious someone wanted her to believe Hatch was the fourth and she'd listened. He needed to calm everything down. "Can we have a drink and start this over?"

"Drew, did you hear what I said?"

He slumped down on the sofa, unable to stand up a second longer. "I'm processing it. I told you I'm not good at stuff like this, but I know I don't want you to go."

"Drew, this isn't about you and me. This is about Hatch now."

He shook his head. "Why would Hatch do it? I don't want to argue with you. I don't want to talk about this. I want to talk about us. I don't want you to leave."

Her voice went soft. "I know, but I need to."

"You can stay here. I'll leave the bedroom. I'll sleep on the couch if it makes you feel better."

"Poor Drew, always looking for the next transaction." She dropped to her knees in front of him, putting one hand on his cheek. "You can't write me a check or bargain your way out of this. And you have to read that file. I'm so sorry to be the one to do this to you."

He had to make her see reason. "It's a lie. It's something she's fabricated. She wants to break us all apart because we're more vulnerable that way. Baby, I'm sorry. I'm so sorry for how I reacted. You're right. I was waiting for you to betray me, too. I swear I won't do it again. I was wrong and I'll make it up to you. I don't want to lose you."

She stood, but not before he caught the hint of tears in her eyes. "I'm sorry. I knew you weren't ready. You might never be ready, but I can't be in a relationship where you spend your time manipulating me so you feel safe. It's never safe. Anything can happen."

He felt numb, all the previous emotion draining out of him because she was leaving and there was nothing he could offer her to make her stay. He had nothing she wanted. All he had was money and power, and they were both useless now.

He stared down at the folder she'd placed on the table. He didn't have to open it to know it was a lie. Hatch had been the only person he could count on for so long. Hatch had been devastated by his dad's death. Hatch had been so devastated he'd thrown himself into the bottom of a bottle for years and years.

Grief or guilt?

"Please read it, Drew. I need you to see the truth." She started up the stairs.

"You're wrong." He understood Hatch suddenly. Anytime the world got to be a bit much, Hatch started drinking. Drew wanted to himself. He could walk away from that fucking folder and from Shelby, with her accusatory eyes, and not give a shit about anyone or anything but his next drink.

"I'm not wrong about Hatch," she said, her voice so filled with sorrow.

"I meant about never losing a woman. I lost her. The her I thought she was. I thought she loved me because I was her son. It's stupid but it hurts to know I never had that. Never."

He picked up the folder and retreated to his office, closing the door and shutting the rest of the world out.

Chapter Fourteen

Shelby watched as Drew closed the door, and her whole heart clenched.

He shouldn't be alone. He shouldn't have to look through that particular truth by himself, and yet what was she supposed to do?

"Hey, are you all right?"

She realized she'd been standing on the stairs for way longer than she should. Mia stepped down, followed by Carly and Ellie.

"I'm fine," she managed. "I was going to get a drink."

There was some wine in the fridge. She could use a glass.

She was going to miss him so much.

"Good, I could use one, too." Carly was right beside her. "Now that the men are gone, we can try to figure out what the hell we're going to do."

"Yes, thank God. No one can think around all that testosterone." Mia strode ahead. "And wine makes everything better. Not that I can have it, but I can watch you guys while we figure out how to fix things."

"I can't believe she's alive," Ellie said. "Mia, you have the most brilliant and devious mind I've ever encountered. The way you manipulated those men to get them out of the house was pure genius."

"You have to know what they're afraid of," Mia replied, walking into the kitchen. "Someone else's relationship imploding is Case's worst nightmare. He hates talking about his own relationship, much less someone else's."

"I thought they would show more solidarity with Drew." Ellie opened the fridge door and grabbed a bottle of white wine.

"Nope, they're not foolish." Carly strode to the cabinet that held the wineglasses. "They know how this ends. Now what the hell are we going to do about Psycho Mom? Sorry, Mia."

Mia waved her off. "You will get no arguments from me. That's my bio mom. She's definitely psycho. My real moms are totally awesome, despite the crunchy granolaness they raised me in."

How had they gone from angry mob to happy housewives? She couldn't do it. She needed to be alone. "I think I'm going to go."

Carly handed the glasses to Ellie, who started to pour. "Oh, no. You're the reason we sent the men off on their own. Shelby, please sit down. I know you're hurting, and that's why you need to be surrounded by people who understand what you're going through. Ellie and I both went through a bunch of crap with our guys, and Mia . . . well, Mia's actually one of them."

"Hey." Mia sat up and frowned. "I married a Taggart. I've got all you covered. Even Shelby, who I have to say has the worst of my brothers. But that doesn't mean you get to walk because the going got tough."

Was she fucking kidding? "Got tough? He brought me here on false pretenses and used me."

Mia nodded. "I know. It's absolutely the most trouble he's ever gone to over a woman. It's like he's already declared his love for you."

Shelby huffed. "Yeah, I'm feeling the love. Look, you guys are the ones who told me I was crazy to even start up with Drew. Awesome. You were right. Congratulations. I was an idiot."

Carly threw her arms around her. "There's nothing happy here. I'm so sorry. I know I said all of those things, but Mia set me straight. I was wrong about Drew."

"No, you weren't. You were absolutely right." Shelby stepped back, completely unsure of what was really going on. "He used me. I thought I could change him. I was stupid. Now, if you want to know what happened with your mother, it's in the report I gave to Drew."

Mia took a glass of water from Ellie. "I want to know what happened this afternoon, and you are absolutely necessary to the talk we're going to have about what to do with my psychotic mother, but first I have to make Drew's case for him because he's not going to be capable of making it for himself. How mean was he?"

"He wasn't truly mean. He was just Drew. He was pissed off and sure that I'd done something I shouldn't have."

"He got emotional. That's not something he does easily," Mia explained. "How often have you guys seen Drew lose control of his emotions?"

Ellie shook her head. "Not once. Even when we were in the middle of all that crap with StratCast, he never got truly angry."

"I've never seen him mad. Intimidating, yes, but the man doesn't get mad," Carly agreed. "Drew's cold, not hot."

He'd been hotter than hell several times during their relationship. Hot in bed. So hot she'd been sure that he would singe her. He'd been hot today, too. His anger had been palpable. "Well, I finally might have pushed the right button."

"Yes, it's the Shelby button, and he's never, ever had that button pushed before," Mia said. "He's always been able to be alone. He's not like Riley, who had a long train of girlfriends."

"Why did I get the manwhore?" Ellie set a glass in front of Shelby.

"Hey, Bran had a long line of strippers," Carly pointed out. "So I think I got the short end of that stick. I think what Mia's trying to say is that Drew might have had women in his life, but he's never, ever introduced one to his family."

"Never," Mia affirmed.

"I explained why he did that." It didn't matter that it had felt real to her. "He didn't want you to ask too many questions. He wanted our relationship to be a cover for what I was really doing."

"Drew would never introduce you to us if he didn't plan to keep you, to make you part of the family," Mia explained. "I've thought this through. I know I was worried in the beginning, but I think he's really fallen for you."

Ellie set her glass down. "Drew's actually kind of old-fashioned when it comes to stuff like that. It's why we were all shocked when he said you'd moved in."

Carly huffed a little. "Well, Bran told me he wasn't shocked. Apparently I don't see as much as I think I do. Bran says Drew fell hard when he met you. Said he's never seen Drew as into a woman as he was into you. He also wasn't surprised he screwed it all up."

"None of us was surprised by that," Ellie agreed. "Drew is brilliant and I adore him, but he's awkward as hell when it comes to interpersonal relationships. I think it's because he spends all his time around people who worship him like a tech god."

"No, I think it happened far earlier than that." Mia moved her chair closer to the table. "Drew was always weird. He learned not to care what people think of him. He definitely learned how to guard himself. He doesn't have friends outside his family. He doesn't care about people outside this house, but when he does, it's forever. He's loyal to the core. I think that's why you threw him for a loop. He realized he wanted more from you than his normal work-friends-with-benefits. He's been so much happier the last few weeks than I've ever seen him."

"All he had to do was ask me out. I would have said yes." She'd been fascinated by him from the moment he'd walked into the room.

Mia leaned over. "I don't think he trusts himself to date like a regular person. Drew plots and plans. He views the world as a war he has to win. I think he believed that his family might lure you into his web. It's the kind of thing Drew would do. He would move you into a position where you would sink into the role, where he could ease you into the relationship he wanted. He would move you into his bedroom, into his office, introduce you to his employees."

All things he'd done.

"But Mia, the first time he thought I'd done something wrong, he was ready to destroy me." He'd said it himself. She'd seen the look in his eyes. He'd been so angry with her.

Mia put a hand over hers. "I know, and I'm sure that hurt like hell. I know exactly what you're going through because it happened to me. Case was in a bad place at the beginning of our relationship. He'd lost his brother and then, when we found Theo again, I was the reason he got away."

"Case blamed you?"

"Yes, and rightly so. I did it to save Case, but he didn't see things my way. He was so mad at me that he said some things I couldn't handle. I walked away. I was willing to let the love of my life go because he'd said some nasty things to me. I left and didn't see or talk to him for six months. I can't imagine it now because we don't fight that way anymore. We're only together because Case wouldn't let it go. I would have. I would have let my pride and my fear keep us apart forever. Someone has to bend. It sucks and maybe that's the hardest thing to realize in a relationship. It's easier now because we found our way through the first hard time. Now we sit and talk, and sometimes his Taggart temper flares and I threaten to murder him, and then I take his hand and we get through it. I don't think Drew knows how to get through this."

She didn't know how to get through it, either. And the worst was yet to come. "I think after he reads the report I gave him, he'll have more things to worry about than me."

"You found something bad on Hatch." Tears pierced Ellie's eyes. "Oh, God, I've always worried about it."

"Shit." Carly reached for the wine bottle and poured herself a glass. "I don't know if I want to know."

"Is he gone? Did he go with the guys?" She hadn't been thinking at all. She'd been so wrapped up in how she and Drew were ending that she hadn't thought about the fact that Hatch was here. He wasn't hiding anymore. She didn't trust him the way everyone else did. She hadn't spent time with him. All she knew was he was the fourth conspirator.

How far would he go to cover that up?

Ellie was sniffling. "I don't think so. I saw him heading outside toward the back."

"He was going to talk to Noah." Mia was pulling out her phone. "I'll let the guys know not to stay out too late. Shelby, I need you to tell us everything."

She stood up. "He's with Noah?"

Mia stood with her. "I'm sure it's fine. He wanted to apologize."

Noah. Why had someone been after Noah? He had to know something he shouldn't. Shelby took off, rushing toward the back door that would take her to the pool house.

"Shelby!"

She could hear the others rushing after her, but she couldn't stop. She had to find Noah.

The door to the back opened and Hatch stepped in.

Shelby nearly fell backward. She tumbled back, but Ellie was behind her, her arms catching her.

Hatch stopped, his eyes widening. "Hey, are you all right? Is Drew still here? I need to talk to him."

"Where's Noah?"

"I'm here." Noah stepped inside. "Hatch is cooler than Drew. He says I can have a beer since someone's trying to kill me. But no Scotch."

Hatch nodded. "I think after two murder attempts, the kid needs a beer." He glanced around. "Noah, go on to the kitchen. Pop open one for me, too. I'll be there in a minute."

Carly reached a hand out to Noah. "Come on. I'll show you where it is. You can join me in my drinking binge. I think it's how this family deals with stress."

"I'll go with you." Ellie followed after.

Mia stared at Hatch. "What did you do? Shelby found something that disturbed her."

His eyes closed and a shudder went through his body. When he opened them again, he seemed to have aged; the light that was usually in his eyes dimmed. "So you know?"

Shelby nodded. "I went to Williams Investigations."

Mia reached out to Hatch. "Please tell me what's going on."

Hatch's arms came out and hauled Mia in for a hug. He held her like she was fragile, his face so sad as he smoothed back her hair. "I love you like you were my own, baby girl. Do you know that?"

"Of course." Mia hugged him tight. "Of course I know that."

He kissed her forehead gently. "Remember that always. I have to go talk to Drew." His eyes moved Shelby's way. "I'm so sorry. You'll never know how sorry I am."

He disengaged and began to walk toward Drew's office.

Mia turned, her face pale. "Oh, God, what happened?"

She watched as Hatch disappeared down the hall, and wished she'd never investigated this case at all.

Mia's cell trilled. Her hand was shaking as she swiped her finger across the screen. "Hey, babe, can I call you . . . what? Are you serious?" She looked up at Shelby. "We have to turn on the TV. Apparently my mother is giving an interview."

Shit. Iris was making her next move.

Drew stared down at the folder, telling himself over and over again that it wasn't true. He was perfectly willing to accept that Shelby thought it was true. She wouldn't bring him a bunch of lies. She thought this was true and she was afraid for all of them. That's why she'd acted the way she had. Between this news and his mother showing up, she was justifiably scared, and that had affected her behavior.

This was some kind of trick by his mother. She was trying to sow chaos. She wanted them as broken as possible for whatever her next move was.

She'd been planning it for years. The picture she'd given to Shelby proved that his mother's game play was superlative. He took a deep breath. He needed to figure out how to keep Shelby close. She couldn't leave. If she did, he wouldn't get her back. She would move on with her life and forget about him.

It was of the utmost importance that he keep her close. He would sit her down and explain that it didn't make sense for her to leave when she didn't have a home to go to. It made much more sense for her to stay here while she decided what to do. She was welcome to stay as long as it took.

There was a knock on the door.

Thank God. Maybe she'd come to her senses.

He opened the door and then sighed. Hatch stood there, one hand on the doorframe. Drew stepped back to let him in. "I was hoping you were Shelby."

Hatch stared at him for a moment before entering. "I thought I told you to let her lead the way. You should have gotten the story from her before you ever said a word."

"I know." He should have done a lot of things differently with Shelby.

He hoped he still had a shot at convincing her about the dangers of being on her own. Maybe he could talk to Carly and she could convince Shelby.

"You going to let her go?" Hatch asked.

"I'm trying to figure out how to stop her without actually tying her down somewhere. I know that works in the Taggart world, but in the real world, it might get me arrested." He sighed and slumped down into his chair. "I don't know what to do. I can't let her go. Despite what she might think, my mother knows who Shelby is, and there's no way she leaves her out of this. She's planning something."

"Iris was always good at planning," Hatch said quietly. "I need to talk to you, Drew."

"About this?" He gestured to the folder with a dismissive wave of his hand. "Shelby gave it to me. It's all bullshit, of course. Apparently Mommy Dearest has been watching me. At least she's been tracking my movements. She took pictures of me in Florida a couple of years back. I was there checking a lead on Patricia Cain the same day Shelby's brother died. Naturally I walked right by his car and someone has a picture of it. I think whatever she's planning she's been planning for four years, ever since she decided to die a second time. She figured out how powerful I was becoming, and she's going to try to take me down. The question is how. And what role is Noah going to play? I'm not saying he's a bad kid, but I don't believe in coincidences when it comes to my mother."

"It was me."

Drew halfway heard him saying something, but he continued on. "What if Iris is the person who's targeting him? If she thought killing Noah would buy her something, she would do it in a heartbeat."

"Drew, are you listening to me?"

"It would have been easy enough for her to steal the keys to that car and use it herself. Unless she hired someone. Apparently she's got some muscle with her."

Hatch's palm slapped against the table. "Goddamn it, we have to talk about what Shelby found."

He was worried about that? "Did Shelby confront you? I have to admit, the stuff she brought back from Dallas is pretty damning. I have to find a way to convince her that this is all just another part of Iris's plan."

"Maybe it is, but the money trail Shelby found isn't. Well, it was, but not how you think it was. It was my money, Drew. It was my fifty thousand dollars. I gave that money to Maurice Williams. He turned around and gave it to the assassin."

The words coming out of Hatch's mouth didn't make sense. Drew tried to figure them out, but couldn't come up with the reason for them. "Why would you do that?"

Hatch leaned forward, seemingly eager to make his case. "Your mother convinced me this was how we ensured she got what she deserved in the divorce."

"Why would my mom come to you for money?"

There was a moment of heavy silence before Hatch spoke again. "Because I was her lover. I've lied to you for twenty years, the same way I lied to your father, but I'll be damned if my lies cost you the way it did him."

Drew shook his head because he wasn't hearing things right.

Hatch continued. "I remember the night you found that picture. I'd carried it around for years. I could lose everything with the exception of that picture. It was the only thing I cared about because I thought it was real between us. But she was gone and you were . . . you came along, and for the first time in years I figured out that I could do something to make up for what I'd done wrong. And then you found that picture and asked me why I had it."

He remembered that night well. "You told me you loved her. You told me you loved my dad like a brother, but that my mom caught your heart because she was so beautiful. You told me you missed her, and you told me you were only friends because you would never have hurt my dad that way."

"I couldn't tell you the truth. I couldn't look at you and tell you how fucked up we'd all been back then. I was a piece of shit, and then you walked in and you were sure of yourself. You were a kid who'd had the shit kicked out of him, and you were already a better man than I was. You were so strong."

"I was not. I was scared."

"You never once looked scared," Hatch said. "You were the single most self-possessed man I'd ever met. When you walked in, you reminded me so much of your father I thought his ghost had come back to haunt me. You were like Ben. You knew what you were capable of, and you would let no one at all tell you what you could or couldn't do. You were a fucking force of nature. You still are, but I think you've found your match."

His gut was in knots again. "I don't understand why you would give an assassin fifty thousand dollars."

He felt dumb, like he wasn't capable of grasping the situation placed in front of him. Like it was in a foreign language he never wanted to learn.

"I didn't. I gave it to a private investigator Iris convinced me to hire. She said your father was hurting her. She showed me the bruises. She told me she needed proof so that she could get her fair share of the company in the divorce. She was a lawyer. I believed her, but eventually I got suspicious."

Drew forced his nausea down. "Suspicious of what?"

"She was spending a lot of time with Patricia. I would catch her coming out of Patty's office while you kids were in school."

"Yes, she was apparently screwing Patty while she screwed you." His childhood had been a fucking soap opera of moving body parts.

"I hired a PI to try to figure out if she was cheating on me. He wasn't on the job long, and then it happened. I thought she was dead. It wasn't until Phillip Stratton showed up to thank me that I realized what had happened."

"She set you up so you couldn't talk about it. She placed your hand in the cookie jar. She managed to get her quarter of the payment in without having to cough up a dime, and she put you in a corner. You couldn't go to the police because you would be implicated. So you let us go into foster care and you went on your merry way."

"I wasn't merry, Drew. I was devastated. I hated myself. I still hate myself. I might hate myself even more because I love you kids so much."

He didn't want to look at Hatch. The very sight of him made him sick. Still, he forced himself to face the man head-on. "Yes, you loved us so much you left us behind after you had a hand in killing our parents. I don't understand. If she'd lived, she would have been able to take her portion of the company. Why wouldn't she have done that?"

"I think anger got the best of her. Or she wanted out more than she wanted the money. She likely blackmailed the others over the years."

Nothing was making sense to him today. "Then why kill them now? From what Carly told me, she's had a hand in every single death."

"Because they could have told her secret," Hatch replied. "Even if she's caught at this point, she's the only one who can talk. I'll be implicated because it was my cash. Her hands are clean on that side. All I've got on her is some pictures the PI took that I placed in a safe deposit box years ago along with a letter to you and my will. I know it won't mean anything to you now, but everything I have is yours. You're the son I never had. I love you, Drew. I love every single one of you, and I'm so proud that I could be a part of this family."

Anger bubbled over and he couldn't help the words that spat from his mouth. "This wouldn't have happened if you hadn't decided to fuck my mother."

Hatch sat back, visibly startled. "It wouldn't have. Not this way. I think she would have found another way to make it happen, though. When Iris wants something, she doesn't stop until she gets it. I know I was foolish, but I thought I loved her. You have to understand that now. Now that you've had Shelby in your life, you have to know that you would do anything to keep her."

Drew stood up, pointing all that righteous anger at the man who'd been his partner for years. "Don't you even mention her name in the same breath as that woman. Shelby is worth ten of my mothers. Shelby would never abandon her children or slaughter her husband. You're not fucking fit to be in the same house that she's in, that any of them are in. Get the fuck out."

"Drew, I know how angry you must be, but this is what Iris wants," Hatch began. "You don't have to look at me or speak to me, but you have to allow me to stay around so I can help."

He was about to explain to Hatch what he would and wouldn't do, when the door opened and his sister was standing there, tears rolling down her cheeks.

"Mia?"

"Drew, you have to come out." Her blond hair was up in a perky ponytail that belied the slump of her shoulders, the red of her eyes.

He moved to her, his stomach threatening to roll again. How much could he take in one day? "What is it?"

"Mom's on TV. She's talking to a reporter and she claims she knows who killed Dad."

He braced himself because he was fairly certain he knew the answer. "Who?"

"It's you, Drew. She says it was you."

Well, at least he finally knew what she was planning to do.

Chapter Fifteen

Shelby couldn't take her eyes off the TV. Iris was there looking perfectly forlorn as the interview was winding down. "I didn't expect this today. I knew she wanted to blame Drew, but this is so soon."

"She already had it in place," Drew said under his breath, his eyes staring straight at the wide-screen fixed to the wall of the living room. Since the moment he'd stalked out of his office, he hadn't said a word, merely stared at the woman on the screen. Even as he spoke now, the words were a hard, chilly monotone. "She probably taped this yesterday or the day before. She knew this was coming out."

"Then why come after me today?" She hated how still Drew was, how his eyes seemed flat and unfocused even as he watched. Iris was telling the same sob story she'd given Shelby. She explained how scared she'd been of her son, how he'd been single-minded even from a young age, how she'd always known her child was capable of hurting someone, but she hadn't realized he could kill until that terrible night.

"Did she offer to take you with her? To get you away from me?"

Shelby nodded. "She told me she would keep me safe and that then she would go after Noah."

"Optics. She was thinking about the optics." Drew's head tilted as though he was considering the woman on the screen from all sides. Like she was some kind of animal he was studying.

"Optics?"

"If you had been with her tonight, it would look like you were taking her side," Hatch said. Unlike Drew, his emotions were written all over his face. He pulled a cell phone out of his pocket. "I'm going to need you to get legal and publicity together. Now. And I need the name of the best defense attorney in Austin. I need him on retainer tonight, like in the next twenty minutes, and send security guards. We'll need to beef up for the press."

"Defense attorney?" Shelby turned away from the interview. The TV had a picture of Noah in his old school uniform, and Iris wept openly, begging Drew not to kill her baby. "Why would you need a defense attorney? Her whole story is bullshit."

"The fact that she's alive and making accusations will bring the police to our doorstep," Mia said. "I would bet a couple of detectives from DPD are already on their way down. They'll want to interview Drew."

The door opened and the men rushed in. Riley and Bran and Case all strode to their respective wives, taking them in their arms.

Mia looked up at her husband. "Did you find anything out?"

"DPD is already here, but we have to deal with the feds, too," Case explained. "They're sending in an agent to talk to Drew and Hatch and the rest of you. They want to question Riley and Bran about what they recall. I think they believe Mia was too young."

"Well, I certainly was old enough to remember that it was my brother who picked me up and carried me out of a burning building," Mia replied fiercely.

"That's my point," Shelby said. "I don't see how this can work. The evidence is going to be against her."

Riley had his phone in hand, too. "She doesn't have to get Drew actually thrown in jail to hurt him. All she has to do is start some rumors, and 4L stock will suffer."

"The press is already here." Case hugged his wife close. "We managed to get through because there are only a couple of local news vans right now, but in thirty minutes or so, the nationals will be here and then all bets are off."

At least they were back from the street and there was a nice-sized gate around the complex. It would afford Drew some privacy while his nightmare played out.

"You think she's doing this so your stock will tank?" Shelby asked, her mind playing through the possibilities.

"I assume she'll come to me at some point and offer to stop talking to the press if I give her enough cash," Drew said, turning the TV off. "I'm sure she'll get an offer to write a book, probably somewhere in the ten-million-dollar range, and I'll have to top it to get her to stop. In the meantime, she'll ruin our every public moment. She'll make my life miserable by being everywhere."

"You can't pay her off. If you do, she'll only come back for more." It would never end. The family would be stuck in a cycle, always waiting for Iris to reemerge. She could haunt them for years.

"The police aren't going to be able to charge me with anything," Drew said, his voice still bland. "There's no evidence, but simply being brought in for questioning is going to cause trouble. Where's Noah?"

"He watched the beginning and then he ran out." Ellie glanced toward the door. "He was upset. If he was faking that he didn't know she was alive, he's an excellent actor. I think he's in the pool house."

"I'm going down to talk to the press," Hatch said, his jaw tightening. "I'm going to clear everything up right now. I'll get all of you out of this and bring it down to me and Iris."

"You will do nothing of the kind." Drew's head came up, his eyes flashing with anger. "You've done enough. I won't have you blowing this up any further. Get out of this house and don't you come back again. The next time I see you, I'll kill you."

"What's going on?" Riley asked.

"You want to tell them, Hatch? Or should I?" Drew asked. "You want to explain to them how you fucked our mother, called Dad your best friend, and then lovingly stabbed him in the back?"

"I thought the money would be used for the divorce," Hatch said, his voice a tortured whisper.

"The divorce?" Bran asked.

Drew slapped a hand on his brother's shoulder. "Oh, you didn't know that Hatch here intended to marry Mom. Unfortunately, instead of marrying her, he gave her the money she needed to have us murdered."

"Drew, this is not the way to tell them." Shelby had known he would have a real problem with this, but she'd never once seen him so unhinged.

"How should I tell them, Shelby? Should I let you write a book about this, too? I should have let you write the first one, since nothing I did or tried or was willing to sacrifice spared them a single second of pain. All this time wasted on revenge plans, when the real person I should have avenged myself on was the very one I went to begging for help."

"Drew, I get that something's happened with Hatch," Mia started, "but he's still the man who did help us when we needed it."

"Hatch was having an affair with Mom?" Bran asked. "But he told us he didn't do that."

Hatch had gone pale. "I know, son. I'm so sorry."

Drew pointed a finger Hatch's way. "Don't you call him son. He's not your son."

"I love him like a son," Hatch replied. "Drew, let me go down there. I'll take it all on myself. None of you has to go through this."

"Don't you dare. You don't get to fuck this up." Drew began to stride toward Hatch, his body moving in predatory lines.

Shelby had to do something. She stepped up and put herself between Drew and Hatch. "Let's all go sit and talk about this like an actual family."

"You said you didn't want to be in this family," Drew shot back. "I think that means you don't get a whole lot of say in how we do business. So if I want to throw down with the asshole who ruined my life, I will."

"I never said that. I said I couldn't be with a man who lied to me," she corrected.

He turned away from Hatch, all that predatory focus settling on her in an instant. He moved toward her, gripping her elbow and starting for the kitchen.

Was he planning on tossing her out? She hurried to keep up with him. "This isn't the way to deal with the problem. You can't fight with Hatch right now. I know he's disappointed you, but if he's willing to talk to the press or the police, you have to think about it. He could save you a lot of pain."

Drew stopped, dropping her arm and turning to look at her. He'd gotten them far enough from the crowd in the living room that they likely couldn't hear. Still, his voice went low. "I want a week."

He was not doing this to her again. "This is not a bargain."

He towered over her, his face set in tight lines, like he was barely holding on. "Everything is a bargain, baby. You want me to sit down and deal with my family issues like a man who isn't about to murder someone? I want a full week of you staying with me."

She kind of wanted to murder someone, too. Him. "Are you serious? You're doing this here and now?"

"Here and now. I'll do what you want me to do if you promise me you'll stay here with me for one more week and you won't kick me out of our bed." He snapped his fingers. "And you'll stay in our bed. You do that and I'll sit down and try not to physically throw Hatch down the driveway."

"You have to talk to him." Surely he could see that reason. She'd watched Hatch, seen the pain in his eyes, and she believed him. She also knew Drew had to work through this. "You have to figure out what he really knows about Iris and how all of this is going to play into her plans. You know she's got something in mind, right? Maybe it's the blackmail scheme, but maybe it's something else."

"I'll behave if you take my deal."

"And if I walk out right now?"

"Then nothing else matters and you won't care what I do."

He wanted to use this tragedy to get her back into bed? How crass was he? How . . . did he have any other way to communicate with her? Anything else he trusted? She looked up at him and realized in some ways he was still a lost boy. Yes, he'd built something amazing and he'd pulled himself out of the depths of where he'd been left, but he wanted something more. Something he wasn't capable of asking for. Something he tried to bully and bargain for.

The one thing that could never be purchased or coerced.

"Oh, Drew, staying with you for a week won't change my mind." She reached up to stroke his cheek. There was only one thing that could change her mind. She wanted him to love her, but she wasn't sure Drew was capable.

"I'm willing to risk that. You'll just stay in the same room and the same bed you've been in this whole time. I don't see how it can hurt anything." He stared at her, but there was a blank look on his face, as though he'd already accepted that she would reject him.

He was willing to risk her leaving. He was plotting and planning and trying to get what he really wanted. Her. She didn't doubt that, but she couldn't stay with a man who didn't trust her, who might never love her. But she could have a few more nights. One week of extra memories to stock up on before she left them all.

She sighed. "All right, Drew, but it doesn't mean I'll sleep with you."

She would and she knew it, but she couldn't make that part of the bargain. Their sexual relationship couldn't be some deal between them. She had to keep one thing real.

His hands came up, finding her shoulders, and she felt a shudder of relief go through him. "Okay. Now, I'll talk to him. It doesn't matter. He doesn't matter. He's a means to an end. I don't need him for anything but some information. You should come with me. You're good at telling when someone's lying. I could use that. I'm quite bad at it."

She was good at seeing through deception, which was precisely why she knew Drew was lying about Hatch. His heart was breaking, but he wouldn't let anyone see it. He wouldn't let anyone in.

She heard the bell ring, and Drew cursed.

"Do you think it's the reporters?" How had they gotten past security?

Case walked in, a grim look on his face. "Drew, it's the police. They want to take you downtown. They have some questions."

Drew leaned forward and kissed her forehead. "Don't wait up for me. We'll talk in the morning. And you'll see. I need a week to make it better for you. It can work. You just have to decide what you want and I'll give it to you and we'll be fine."

He turned and she followed him, her heart shuddering in her chest. It was surreal. There were police officers standing in the room and they were waiting for Drew. The press had seen them coming up to the house. They'd probably filmed it and it would be all over the news.

"Officers," Drew said in an even tone. He held a hand out like nothing was wrong. "How can I help you?"

So civil. So courteous. Like nothing was going on, when she knew somewhere inside he was screaming.

The uniformed officer shook his hand. "Mr. Lawless, Mr. Hatchard, I'm real sorry about this, but given the accusations made earlier tonight, there are some FBI agents who would like to talk to you both. Now, I said we could do it all civil-like and speak to you here, but I've found feds like to show their butts at every given opportunity."

"They want to get as much press as they can," Hatch complained.

Likely, they wanted to look like they were taking this seriously and not ignoring the pleas of a woman in possible need of protection. She'd stated over and over again that the reason she hadn't come forward was her fear of Drew's power.

"The police can't look like they're taking sides," Shelby said dully.

"Do you need to cuff me?" Drew asked as though commenting about the weather.

The officer shook his head. "Not at all. You're not under arrest. Just some questions."

"Yes," Drew agreed. "I suspect there will be a lot of them."

Riley ran down the stairs. He'd obviously dressed quickly, changing from his earlier casual wear to a suit and tie. The tie was slightly askew, but he looked like the lawyer he was.

"I'm acting as my brother and Mr. Hatchard's attorney," he said to the officers. "I'd like to be allowed to drive them in. I would prefer the press didn't get pictures of my clients in the back of a police car."

The officer frowned. "The feds will come down hard on us if we don't bring these two in. I suspect before this is over, they'll want to talk to all of you, but they're interested in getting statements from Mr. Lawless and Mr. Hatchard tonight."

"Your partner is more than welcome to join us in the limo if he would like, or you can," Riley continued. "Or we can follow you. I assure you there's no flight risk. Mr. Lawless wants to get this settled as soon as possible."

"Follow us. We'll get you through the press." The officer turned and started for the door.

"Case, keep things locked up here," Drew said.

And then he walked out and Shelby was left behind.

Mia walked up and slipped an arm through hers, and then Carly and Ellie were surrounding them.

She'd been left behind, but at least she wasn't alone.

There was nothing quite like a police station interrogation room to make a man feel dirty. Drew wanted a shower after six hours of talking to the feds, who wanted to go over every moment of that night twenty years before in minute detail about twenty times. He knew what they were doing. They asked him questions about the minutiae, trying to trip him up, to catch him in a lie. They did it over and over again, hoping exhaustion would cause him to screw up and give up.

He explained to them over and over again that his mother was a liar, but a lot of the damage was already done. He wasn't sure what his stock price would do in the morning, but it probably wasn't good.

Riley stepped up, smoothing out his shirt. "Do I even want to know what you're thinking?"

"I'm wondering who's going to buy software from the dude who supposedly killed his father and sent his pregnant mother on the run for years. You seem to forget that I'm the villain of this piece."

"And you seem to forget that this is America, and no one will give a shit as long as the software works. It's the best, most cutting-edge piece of technology on the market, and no one is going to shy away from it because you're the target of a smear campaign. She's underestimating the American public. She thinks she can go on TV and cry and all the men will practically fall at her feet because she's still beautiful, but she's forgotten about one thing."

He couldn't think of what it was. His mother seemed to plan perfectly. "What's that?"

"The women of this world," Riley replied with a surety Drew couldn't feel. "The mothers who would never have left their children in foster care even if they were in fear for their lives. Honestly, she's forgetting the dads, too. There are going to be fathers out there who will have little sympathy for her because she didn't stand up to her fourteen-year-old son and protect her other children. This is one place where she's weak. She doesn't have any empathy or understanding for other people. She can't think they'll see this in a different way than she wants them to. Drew, this is going to be all right. We're going to win this because not a single one of us will back away from you."

Maybe they should. Maybe it would be better if he let Bran run the company with Riley advising him. He could sell off his stock to his brothers and Mia so they would maintain their voting shares and control. He could become a hermit somewhere. He'd always thought he'd make a good hermit. He could buy some land in Montana and become the mean old man he was destined to be. Maybe if he did that, the press would stay away from his family.

And Shelby.

"You all right?" Riley asked, sitting back as the limo rolled down the highway.

"Of course." He was feeling better now that he didn't have to look at Hatch. He'd had to share a car with him on the way to the police station, and they'd been forced to sit together until they'd been split up for separate interrogations. "The new lawyer seems good."

"He better be for what he's charging us," Riley replied. "I'm sorry I left you with him, but I wanted to hear what Hatch had to say. I needed to make sure he wasn't martyring himself. I convinced him not to admit to anything more than giving Iris the fifty thousand she requested for the divorce."

"If that's what it was for." He still had some questions.

"Drew, why would he lie now? Do you honestly believe he would have paid fifty thousand dollars to see our father assassinated, and then blow through every bit of cash he got from the company? You have to look at his actions after that night. They're not the actions of a man who was happy with his crime."

"I suppose he felt guilty. Or he was pissed because he didn't get everything he wanted." He knew he was being a stubborn ass, but he couldn't think anything good of Hatch right now.

Had Hatch conspired with their mother to make a true clean break of things? Had good old "Uncle" Hatch not wanted the burden of four children in his new life with the woman of his dreams?

Riley sighed, the sound weary. "I know you've been thrown for a loop, but you can't believe that Hatch was pissed because we didn't die. We have to figure out how to deal with him and get through this."

"He can go to hell for all I care." He would offer to buy Hatch out in the morning. Through lawyers, of course, since he never intended to see the man again if he didn't have to. He would send him a notification of his termination in the morning, too.

"Drew, you should have seen him tonight. He defended you every chance he got. I believe him. I think he did lie about the affair with our mother, but everything else was the truth."

"He claimed to have loved Dad." That had been a blatant lie.

"People do funny things when they're in love," Riley replied. "I think Hatch was blinded by love for our mother, and she used him like she used Dad. Like she ended up using Patricia. It's kind of her MO. You should understand. After all, you're the guy who's blackmailing the woman you love into bed."

He felt his whole body flush. He hadn't meant for that to be public information. "That was a private conversation."

"Then you shouldn't have bought a house with an open-concept kitchen and excellent acoustics. I could easily hear you from the living room. I'm sure everyone else did, too. All I'm saying is you're acting like an idiot about Shelby right now, and Hatch did the same a long time ago."

"He tried this argument on me already. I told him what I'm about to tell you. Don't you ever mention Shelby's name in the same sentence as our mother's. It's totally different. Shelby is kind and strong and our mother is a criminal." It should be obvious to anyone that Shelby wasn't in the same league as his mother. They weren't even playing the same game.

A smile tugged at Riley's lips. "Do you have any idea how happy I am to hear you say that?"

"Why would you be happy?"

"Because I was worried you would start painting every woman with the same brush as our mother. You can quickly shut yourself off when you want to. I thought you would cut Shelby out the minute we found out about Mom. That was what I thought was going on with the two of you earlier."

For the first time tonight, he felt how long a day it had been. He'd been hopped up on adrenaline for hours, and now he was finally coming down and the world seemed like such a darker place than it had been twenty-four hours before. "But I've known about Iris for a long time, and it never stopped me from trying to get Shelby. She's nothing like our mother, but she's also nothing like me, and I have to think about what I'm doing with her. I care about Shelby. I care about her more than I realized, and this thing with our mother isn't going to be easy on any of us."

"Shelby's tough and she's loyal as the day is long."

"Tell me about it. She saw evidence that I murdered her brother and never once did she question that I'd actually done it." He was still in awe of that. The trust she'd shown in him. He'd only ever had that from his family and . . . he wasn't going there. "I get one picture from a bodyguard and blame her for all the ills of the world. And she was right about Hatch. I yelled at her and she was right."

"I think she can handle some yelling. She might even do some of her own, but you have to stop trying to buy her. She's not something you can purchase. And you can't throw Hatch out."

"I already did. It's why he's not in this limo with us. He knew better than to try to come back to my home."

Riley's fingers drummed against the armrest, a sure sign he was getting irritated. "It's his home, too, and he's not in the limo because I sent him on ahead of us so the press could see him going home. It's not as good as the two of you presenting a united front, but I figured it would have to do for tonight. Tomorrow, I expect you to walk into the 4L building with Hatch and me and Bran and Mia. We're going to walk in together, and you're going to give the press a statement about how close we are and how you've forgiven the sins of the past. I've already been working it up for you."

Drew sat up straight. Maybe he wasn't done with the adrenaline high tonight. "He's in the same house with Shelby and our family? With your wife?"

He didn't miss the way Riley's eyes rolled. "Ellie stayed up late to make sure he got in okay. I'm sure we're going to walk in to some people waiting up for us, too."

"Do you understand what he did?" Perhaps Riley didn't get the scope of the crime. "You can't expect me to continue to work with him."

"I understand that he screwed up. I also understand that Dad was having an affair, too. They were human. They were dumb and screwed up, and Hatch loves us. He's kept this secret for years because he loves us."

"He kept the secret because I would have killed him."

"Drew, you were a rail-thin teenager when he met you. You weren't a physical threat to him. And he's sacrificed for us. I know you're angry, but you're more angry at yourself because there's no one in the world who's harder on Drew Lawless than you."

"I'm angry that he lied to me, and don't psychoanalyze me," Drew practically snarled. "I'm willing to talk about how to keep our stock from free-falling until such a time as I can eviscerate every single one of our mother's claims, but I will not have anything to do with that man outside of business. I'm the one who brought him in. I'm the fucking idiot who gave him a percentage of our company, and now I have to deal with it."

"Thus, my point is made." Riley sat back with a sigh. "God, it's a circus and it's three in the morning. What's it going to look like at noon?"

It would look like a bloodbath, and that was exactly what his mother wanted. How would this affect Shelby? There was nothing he could do about the rest of them. They were his blood, and this would taint them one way or another, but Shelby could get out. Shelby could walk away.

Would his mother leave her be? Or would Shelby be alone out in the world without any protection and a massive target on her back?

He'd screwed her in every way possible. If she stayed with him, she'd get smeared in the tabloids for being close to him. If he let her walk away, she could get hurt physically.

He turned away even though he knew the photographers and reporters couldn't see through the tinted windows.

He hated press. He hated anyone looking into his life. It should be his and his alone, but they would tear it apart now and judge him for everything he'd ever done or said.

It was a good revenge.

"Why do you think she hates us?" Riley asked as the car made it through the throng at the gates.

The lights died down as the limo moved up the drive toward the house.

"I don't know." He wished he had the answer because it pounded through his head. "I don't know that she hates us at all. I don't know that she's capable of feeling much." Drew watched the trees go by. He'd bought this place because it seemed like its own little kingdom, apart and away from the world below.

He was going to be so lonely if she left him. Every kingdom needed a queen.

"What are we going to do about Noah?" Riley asked.

That was a good question. "I have no idea. I should shove him out and back into Mommy Dearest's arms. She wants him so much, she can have him." Then he thought about what Shelby would think, how Shelby would think. She would tell him Noah was his brother. She would point out the fact that if Iris had been willing to sacrifice them, she would hurt Noah if she needed to. "But I can't do that. He's our brother. If he wants to go join her . . . I can't believe I'm going to say this . . . I'm going to try to talk him out of it."

"I don't think it would be a good idea to send him to her. I think she would use it to her advantage, but I also don't think we can ask him to come out against her. He's just figured out his mother is a psychopath."

"So have we."

"We're older and we're used to having each other to hold on to," Riley reasoned. "He's got to get used to not being alone. Have you thought about the fact that he might be working with her?"

"Of course. I think it's likely that he is." In one way or another. Noah might not even know what he was doing, but Drew was fairly certain Iris was using him.

"I'm worried about it. What are you going to do if he is?"

He was right back to tired. "I don't know. Probably whatever Shelby tells me to do. God, when did I get to be this guy?"

Riley's chuckle reverberated through the car. "You mean the guy who's madly in love with a woman?"

"I started out thinking of nothing but revenge, and now all I can do is worry about whether or not I'm going to lose Shelby. I would even forgive that little shit for not understanding how awful his mother is if it meant Shelby would forgive me. And I have to wonder if that kind of thinking is going to bring us all down."

Riley leaned over. "No, it's not going to bring us all down. If you love this woman, you can't let her go. We're going to get through this."

The limo pulled up to the house.

Drew wasn't so sure. He wasn't sure of anything except the fact that Iris was coming, and he needed to figure out exactly what she wanted.

The door opened and Drew stepped out, forcing his legs to move. He felt like a zombie, walking along but not really seeing anything, alive but not feeling.

He knew Riley was behind him, but he didn't care. He wanted to be alone.

He wanted to be with her.

He would go and find her and take her hand. He would lead her back to the bedroom and pull her into his arms and forget about everything else for the rest of the night. He would beg if he had to. He would try to convince her that if they only had a week left, they should spend it wrapped up in each other because neither would ever find another lover like this.

He would find the words to turn this around.

He walked toward the back. It was more private. The front entrance could probably be seen with a telephoto lens, but the back of the house was completely closed off. Too many trees. Too much Hill Country to deal with.

The pool area was illuminated in a deep blue, the lights casting shadows all around. It was enough light to see that he and Riley weren't out here alone. Noah sat on one of the lounge chairs, his stare turned to the water. There was a slump to his shoulders that let Drew know he wasn't the only one who was miserable tonight.

"I think I'm going to go talk to him," Riley said.

"No, go on. Let them know I'm home and everyone can go to sleep. This is my job."

Riley nodded and moved toward the door, leaving him alone with Noah. His youngest brother.

Was he also the brother who was betraying them all? Either way, Drew had to deal with him.

Drew sat down on the lounger next to him. "I've always found it peaceful out here. It's why I like to leave the lights on. Sometimes I come out here late at night and I stare at the water and it helps me think."

Noah kept his eyes on the pool. "I don't want to think."

"Yeah, it can help me do that, too." A silence sat between them. He wasn't good at this. He never had to drag anything out of Riley. Riley liked to talk. He was practically Oprah when it came to talking about his feelings. Bran would have just required a beer and some manly silence. He wasn't sure what the hell to do with Noah. "You okay?"

Stupid question.

"Sure." Noah didn't look up. "It's all cool."

Yep, this was where it would be nice to be with Bran. Hand him a beer, put on a baseball game, and they would be good.

Of course, Bran had nearly killed a few people and was now in treatment for anger issues. So maybe that hadn't worked so great.

"It's not cool. It's awful to figure out that the person you looked up to is . . . I was about to say *only human,* and that does work when it comes to Dad. When I first found out he'd been having an affair, I got angry with him. I was only fourteen when he died. In my mind, he was frozen forever as the perfect parent, and everything would have been fine in my life if he hadn't died. I think that happens to a lot of kids who lose their parents. You forget about how he forced you to eat peas and only remember how he never failed to make time for you."

"He never told you he was working and to go play by yourself? Because I got that a lot from my . . . from her."

"No." It was good to think about his father with some fondness. "He would stop everything if one of us came into the room. Dad worked hard, but he would put it aside to play touch football with us or to have a tea party with Mia. We were all expected to come to those, by the way. There were boas and gloves and everything. Dad would say if our masculinity couldn't handle a couple of tiaras to please our little sister, then we didn't deserve to call ourselves men at all."

For the first time, Noah looked up, his lips curling faintly. "You played tea party with Mia?"

"Sure. She was my sister." His father had been the one to teach him that family mattered. "He would have loved you, Noah."

"How could she have lied to me like that?" Noah asked, his voice a tortured growl. "She called me earlier. I don't even know how she got my phone number."

That hadn't taken long. He was sure it was one more play in her game plan. "What did she have to say?"

Noah was silent.

Noah didn't know the case the way the rest of them did. He might have listened to her interview and been confused. It was odd how much that thought hurt. He shouldn't give a shit. "Noah, if you're worried I'm going to hurt you, then let me set you up at a hotel or someplace where you'll feel safe. I don't think you should go back to her."

Noah's head swiveled, his eyes coming up to take Drew in. "I don't know what to think. She says you're the one trying to hurt me, but you could have done that so much easier than hiring someone to hit me with a car. And I don't know why you would need me gone. All you had to do was tell me to go away and I would have."

"I'm sure she would say I did it for the press."

"But you hate the press. You always curse when you mention them and then you spit a little."

Not a pleasant thought. "I'll try to control that. No, I don't particularly like the press. They can bend a story any way they like, and they often don't care about the truth. I'm the least likely person to think I can manipulate the press." He certainly hadn't done a good job of it with Shelby, though somehow he couldn't put her in the same category with the bottom-feeders currently circling his property. Shelby wouldn't report on anything without confirmation, and she wouldn't sensationalize. She was like Mia, always looking for a story that could help people, not a way to turn someone's pain into cash.

"I don't understand any of this," Noah said, turning back to the water. "I don't know what to do."

"Think it over tonight. I promise not to murder you in your sleep."

Noah snorted. "You have a terrible sense of humor."

Wasn't the first time he'd heard those words. "So I've been told. Know that if you decide to stay, you're welcome. But I have to ask a few questions. Did you tell anyone about Shelby heading into Dallas today? I've been trying to figure out how she would have found out Shelby was going to be there."

Even in the low light, he could see the way Noah flushed. "Sorry. I was texting back and forth with a friend. And I mentioned on my page that everyone was heading into Dallas, but I was staying here. I suppose she was the one who sent me here."

"Probably."

Noah's legs came up, knees bending so he could wrap his arms around them. "Did you find anything on my system? I'll give you the new one. And my phone since it looks like she's already invaded there."

"Good. I think that will make us all feel better."

Noah was silent for a moment. "I don't think you should be mad at Shelby."

"I'm not. Not anymore." Before Shelby, he would have taken the kid's computer without asking, and there wouldn't have been anyone to stop him. He would have found out what he wanted to and that would have been that. Shelby had done that to him. Shelby made him . . .

He needed to fucking stop that. God, what the hell was he doing? He was blaming Shelby and turning it around in his head. He constantly thought about how she made him crazy, but she didn't do that. He did it to himself. She was the one who calmed him, when he allowed her to do so. She was the one who tried to make him a better person, because if they were ever going to have any kind of a shot at this, he had to be better than he'd been before.

He'd done everything she'd accused him of and more. He'd blamed her, pushed her, turned everything they were into a transaction because he didn't trust her. She was the freaking reason he was sitting out here with Noah when all he wanted was to pull in on himself and shut out the rest of the world.

But to be with her, he had to be worthy, and to be worthy, he had to give a shit about people he didn't want to.

The trouble was, it was getting easier and easier to care about Noah. It was easier to see how he fit with the rest of them. How he'd been lost the same way they had. They had more in common than they didn't.

Noah sat back, relaxing for the first time. "I would rather stay here for now. I don't know what to think, but I know she lied to me."

"She lied to all of us."

Noah turned, looking at him again. "I know you think I had it easy."

"I'm turning around on that."

"Good, because I didn't. I'm so fucking envious of Riley and Bran and Mia."

"Don't be. It was hard. You have no idea what foster care was like. It was never-ending quicksand, and just as we figured out how to navigate it, the surface changed and we went under again. It was terrible."

"I get that, but I would have gone through it all because I would have had the one thing I didn't get while I was growing up. I'm jealous of them because through it all, they had you. They got you. They knew. No matter how bad it got, they knew."

"Knew what?"

"That you would come for them. That you would save them."

His heart actually ached. Yeah, that was Shelby's fault, too, but he didn't curse her for it. Now he could see how much strength it gave him. Perhaps this war wouldn't be won with revenge. Perhaps it would be won with something else. Drew dropped to one knee in front of his youngest brother. "Noah, understand this. You're my brother and I will do everything I can to save you. Do you understand me?"

Noah had tears in his eyes as he nodded. It was easy to see he wanted to believe but simply couldn't yet. Drew could understand that. He had to pray that the hope he'd tried to give Noah tonight, that the family he could offer his brother, was enough to break any familial connection Noah felt to their mother.

He patted his brother on the back. "Try to get some sleep. Tomorrow's another rough day, but we'll get through."

He stood up and realized they weren't alone.

Shelby stood by the pool house wearing a tank top, pajama bottoms, and no shoes. Her hair was pulled up in a messy bun and she'd taken off her makeup. He'd never seen her looking more beautiful.

She walked over to them, her bare feet padding against the concrete. "Are you okay, Noah? If you want, the rest of the family is sitting up and talking. I think Mia's making some hot chocolate."

Noah's lips turned up. "Okay. That might be nice."

So she'd come out here to get Noah. He expected her to turn and walk away when Noah scampered inside.

Maybe he would sit by the pool for a while and enjoy the silence while he tried to figure out what to do about her.

Her hand slipped into his, her fingers tangling theirs together. "I think you should come to bed with me. You've had a long day, Mr. Lawless."

He hesitated. He'd been so stupid earlier, and he couldn't go through with it. He couldn't force her into bed with him. "Shelby, I'm sorry about the thing from before. I'm sorry I tried to blackmail you into sleeping with me. I was afraid of losing you, and I'm not good at the relationship stuff."

"Not from what I saw out here tonight." She moved close to him, so close their bodies brushed together. "From where I was standing, you did pretty good. So come to bed with me. I don't know what's going to happen between us. I still think I should leave, but I know I can't right now, and I don't want to pretend that I don't want you."

"I want you more than my next breath." He needed her. Somewhere along the way she'd become necessary to his life, to his happiness.

"Then come to bed and we'll figure it out tomorrow."

This time when she began to lead him toward the house, he followed.

Chapter Sixteen

Shelby led him past the living room where the whole family was gathered, but she didn't stop. Maybe it was selfish of her, but she wasn't sure how much time they had left, and she wanted him to herself.

He followed after her, not even trying to stop and talk to his brothers. When they reached the bedroom, he closed and locked the door behind them.

"I'm sorry, Shelby."

He was sorry for trying to blackmail her? Or sorry that this couldn't work? Either way, she understood. Drew didn't understand any relationship that he didn't control, and she couldn't be one more person he controlled. "I know. I am, too. Are you all right? Were the feds okay with you?"

"They were nosy bastards, but they asked questions I could easily answer. I don't think they'll be here in the morning to arrest me." He slipped out of his jacket and stepped into the closet to hang it up. "I'm surprised you didn't leave."

She hadn't even thought about it. She'd thought about the fact that she was needed. She'd immediately gone to work, putting together all the evidence she'd managed to gather, showing it to Mia and strategizing how to use it against Iris. "I can help you. I thought I should try."

He walked back out of the closet wearing nothing but his slacks, his cut chest on display. "I don't know if that's a good idea."

Of course he didn't. What else had she expected? In Drew's mind she'd betrayed him by going after Hatch. Somewhere deep down he would always blame her for it. He wouldn't be able to help himself. "Of course. I sent a copy of everything I have to Mia. I'll let her handle it from here on out. You can certainly trust her."

He stopped, his eyes narrowing. "I trust you. This has nothing to do with trust, Shelby."

Sure he did.

He stepped up, towering over her, but he was gentle this time when he'd been so tense this afternoon. "I understand if you want to leave, but do it because you want to protect yourself. Not because you think I don't trust you. I realize I've been putting a lot of my baggage right on top of you. I also get that I should have sat you down and asked you what happened with Iris this afternoon instead of behaving like an asshole. I'm struggling because I've never felt like this about a woman. I know by my age most men have had a couple of serious relationships and gotten married, but I was practically born with a family to raise. I didn't get to be a selfish prick about anything. I had to do what I needed to do to save my brothers and sister, and then I did what I had to do to raise us all up so no one could hurt us again. I've never had moments when I could think of only myself."

She practically purred when his hand found the side of her throat and stroked down to her shoulders. Without even thinking about it, her hands moved up, cupping the sides of his waist. She'd missed this, missed feeling so connected to him. "You have to think of them. And now you have Noah."

His hands moved over her shoulders, fingers sliding under the straps of her tank. "I wanted to ignore him, but I heard you talking in my head. You're the reason I want to be better. You make me want to be more than I am." He stared down at her. "I know I was hard on you this afternoon, but please don't put more meaning behind everything I say. I'm not smart enough to not say what I mean."

"You're the smartest man I know."

"I'm not when it comes to you. I wish I could get on my knees and beg you to stay with me, but I think I have to tell you to leave in the morning. I want you to hide until this is done."

The world went watery. She clutched him. "I thought you wanted me to stay with you for a week."

"I was being truly selfish. I want you. I want you with me always, but if you stay beside me, your career is over. You do undercover journalism. If you're with me, your face will be everywhere, so tomorrow I'm not simply going to ask you to choose. I'm going to have you dragged out of here if you don't choose correctly. I'm only going to hurt you, and I can't stand the thought of it." He leaned over and his lips brushed against hers. "But give me one more night."

One more night in his arms. Earlier in the day she'd been ready to walk out, and now her heart ached at the thought.

"Touch me." If this was the end, she wanted his hands on her. Maybe that made her weak, but she didn't care. She needed his touch, his affection. She wouldn't find anything like it for the rest of her life.

He reached down and dragged the tank top up and over her head. Her nipples peaked, the cool air hitting them, but it was more about the fact that she was bared to his eyes. "You are the most beautiful woman in the world."

When he looked at her like that, she felt beautiful. They might not fit in the real world, but when they closed the door and it was simply the two of them, their bodies nestled together like they'd been made that way.

She was going to miss him so much. Miss this. She let her hands drift up, and they stood there for a moment, stroking each other's bodies as though trying to memorize the feeling.

Her body was already warm, already preparing itself for the inevitable. No one made her feel like this. Perhaps that was the problem. Drew made her feel too much, want too much when she knew the world wasn't kind enough to allow it. Happiness came in short bursts that were almost always followed by sorrow.

His hands moved to her breasts again, cupping them. His thumbs flicked over her nipples. "Take off the rest of your clothes. I want to memorize the way you look. You're so fucking gorgeous. Take them off for me."

She shoved the pj pants over her hips, dragging her undies with them so she was completely naked for Drew. She was sure with someone else she would feel vulnerable, but there was a sense of power that came over her when big bad Drew Lawless, the king of all he surveyed, couldn't quite stop his jaw from dropping every time he saw her naked.

"I like the way you look at me, like you could eat me up. Just the way your eyes move over my body, it feels like you're touching me."

He stood back, his eyes taking her in. "Remember that when we're apart. Remember that every second I don't see you, I want to be touching you. I'll think about it all the time. I'll never stop."

She wouldn't think about that now. She moved toward him, enjoying the feel of her body. Somehow when she was with him, she was so aware of her own skin, of how each muscle moved, her body becoming a fluid thing under his gaze. She found her grace, and it made it easy to do things that seemed so awkward before.

He unbuckled his belt and kicked his slacks away. His muscled body came into view, and he looked like he was ready for anything. His cock was long and hard, reaching almost to his navel. "I want your mouth on me, but I need to taste you, too. Come here."

He strode to the bed, laying his big body down on the mattress. He held out his hand.

He wanted her on top, laid out against his chest, his mouth trapped between her legs while she had access to that gorgeous cock of his. His big hands grabbed her thighs, spreading them wide. She was caught by him, and there was no place else she would rather be. She could feel the heat of his mouth hovering over her flesh, making her warm and soft and ready for everything he could give her.

His hips thrust up, offering her his cock.

She balanced against the bed as she licked his cock, her tongue moving over him. This was what she needed. She needed to feel the way his body reacted to her touch. Even as she sucked the head of his cock behind her lips, she felt the first seductive touch of his lips to her core.

"You taste so good. I won't ever forget the way you taste." The words were growled against her, the sensation making her shudder. His hands came up, cupping the cheeks of her ass. His tongue moved all around her pussy, licking and sucking her like she was the sweetest peach he'd ever tasted.

His cock was a thing of beauty. Thick and long. She gripped the stalk in one hand and squeezed, loving how his whole body went tight under hers. A pearly drop of cream covered the slit of his cock. She dragged her tongue over it and he moaned against her pussy, his hands clamping down. He speared up into her, his mouth covering her while his tongue fucked deep inside. She couldn't contain the groan of pleasure and let the sound reverberate against his cock.

Give and take. Pure connection. Pure pleasure. Shelby let go. Tomorrow would sort itself out. She sucked at the head of his cock, her tongue whirling around and lapping up the cream that pulsed there. She settled in, finding that perfect place between the feel of his tongue and the taste of his cock. She worked him over and over, opening herself more each time, taking him deeper.

He suckled her clitoris, bringing her to the edge again and again. She felt the wave start low in her body and knew she couldn't hold out. He was too good. She sucked him hard, taking him almost to the back of her throat and letting loose with her own pleasure. She moaned around him and felt his body stiffen. As the wave crested over her body, she tasted him on her tongue. His body bucked as he came in her mouth.

She sucked him down, enjoying the way he softened in her mouth as his body relaxed.

He flipped her off him and he was up and over her before she could take her next breath.

"If I only have one more night, don't think you'll get any sleep." He dropped his mouth to her, and she could taste her own arousal.

Shelby let go completely. One more night.

Drew covered her with his body, unwilling to spend a second away from her. He'd meant what he said. He had one last night and he intended to spend it inside her. Every second. He leaned over and kissed her, his tongue delving deep. His dick was already stirring again. No one could get him hard as fast as Shelby could. All he had to do was think about her and he would get aroused.

What the hell was he going to do without her?

Her tongue played against his, and her body was soft under him. He loved the way her nipples rubbed against his chest and how wet her pussy was as she pushed her pelvis up. Her legs moved, wrapping around him. This was where he'd needed to be all day, surrounded by her scent and touch and skin. She softened all around him, her body welcoming him home.

She was his home, and he had to let her go.

He would send her to Dallas and she would be safe. She wouldn't have to see the ugly side of his world. He wouldn't let his mother use her and tarnish her name and reputation. If he won this war, if he could make it safe for her again, he could claim his prize.

His prize? She was his fucking salvation.

He let himself revel in her, kissing her again and then letting his lips find her neck. He loved every curve and plane of her body. God, he loved her.

He breathed her in and promised himself he would never forget how it felt to be so close to her.

He could still feel her mouth pulling at his cock, drawing on him like she couldn't stand the thought of letting him go. Her tongue had been soft and hot on his dick, and now he was getting hard again. He pumped himself against her, his cock easily sliding through the juice of her arousal. She gasped.

Her clitoris was so sensitive. He brushed against her again, rewarded by her breathy moan.

He moved down her body. He laid kisses across her skin, over her collarbone and her chest, making his way down to those breasts he'd grown to love.

He licked at her nipple before diving in and sucking her deep. Her body stiffened under his, her nails biting into his back. He would love that tomorrow. He would love how his muscles ached from how hard she clawed at him. His Shelby didn't play around. She wanted her pleasure, and he was the man who could give it to her.

He switched to her other nipple. She loved to have them sucked on. She was sensitive, her breasts attuned to his touch. Her body shuddered every time he licked her, his normally proper girl turning into a sweet sex kitten when he pulled her clothes off.

That was his real accomplishment. Some people would say it was creating a multibillion-dollar company, but he knew the truth. It was all about turning brilliant Shelby Gates into a shivering sexy thing, begging for his touch.

Being the man who could bring that out in her—that was what made him feel powerful.

"Please." Her body bucked under his as he bit down on her nipple.

He dipped his tongue into the valley of her breasts, tracing the line between them. Everywhere he touched was soft and sweet.

His dick was hard again. Hard and aching. He needed her. He'd never needed anyone the way he needed her.

His hips moved again, rolling over her. His cock was wet with her juice. All he would have to do was thrust up, and he could join them together.

"Please, Drew." The words were sweet and sultry.

He kissed his way down her chest, and licked her belly button before kissing his way even lower.

He couldn't get enough of how good she tasted, of her spicy scent. That peach was juicy and ripe, and he needed another bite. He sucked at her, loving how she squirmed under him, but he held her legs down. He offered her no respite from the gentle lash of his tongue. He spread her wide and laved her with affection all over again.

Her hands came out, tangling in his hair as she started to ride his tongue. She didn't hold back on him. Her enthusiasm fed his own. He sucked on her clit and felt the moment her body tightened and released, heard her cries of pleasure.

That was a sound he would never forget.

He reared up. He would take her now. He reached out and grabbed a condom. He rolled it on, ready to fuck her hard, and then he looked at her.

The breath flew out of him because she was so fucking gorgeous. Everything about this woman called to him, from her beautiful body to her strong soul. It struck him hard that he was never going to love another woman. Shelby was it. She was the only woman in the world for him.

She looked up at him, her hands reaching. "What's wrong?"

Nothing. Everything. "Do you know what I thought the first time I saw you?"

"Since you were irritated with me, I'm sure it wasn't pretty."

She'd been his opponent in the beginning. She'd been a ghost he'd chased across the Internet as she'd delved into his past. At the time he'd been playing his revenge games with Patricia Cain, and Shelby had threatened his plans. He'd cursed her name.

And then he'd seen her.

"I thought you were the most gorgeous hacker I'd ever laid eyes on, and I would have given you all the information you wanted to get you into bed with me." She'd been screwing up his plans at the time, but all he'd known was he wanted her.

He couldn't have known how important she would become.

She tugged at his shoulders. "I'm here now, Drew. You should know I don't want to be anywhere else."

He covered her with his body, his cock finding its way home. He'd been so desperate to fuck her, but now he simply wanted to make it last. To make love to her and to do it forever. They wouldn't have to leave this room. They could stop time and spend the rest of their lives connected to each other.

He moved slowly, letting himself mark every simple movement, every sensation. "You were wearing a green dress, and I couldn't take my eyes off you."

She wrapped her legs around him. "You could have fooled me. I thought you couldn't stand me. I was in awe of you, and I thought you barely noticed I was alive."

"You're all I've been able to think about since the moment I saw you." He thrust in and dragged back out. She was so tight around him. She'd been made for him. "I started plotting and planning on how I would get you where I wanted you."

Right here. Underneath him. Around him.

She tilted her hips up, taking him deeper.

He rocked against her. He wouldn't be able to keep it up forever. No matter how much he wanted to. She felt too perfect. He could already feel a shiver beginning at the base of his spine. He didn't want her to leave. Not ever.

But he would force her to. He would do what he had to do to ensure her happiness and safety.

Because he loved her.

Chapter Seventeen

Shelby came awake slowly, enjoying the warmth of the bed and the delicious ache in her limbs. The previous night had been damn near perfect.

She reached out for him, her hand sliding along the sheets. They needed to talk this morning.

She didn't want to leave him. She didn't want to leave this family. She knew it would be better if she did, but her heart ached at the thought of not waking up next to him.

She opened her eyes and realized he wasn't in bed with her.

The clock beside the bed told her she'd slept in. With a groan she started to get up. Had he already left for work? Why hadn't he woken her? She looked around the room.

He was standing at the window, his back to her. He was certainly dressed for work. He wore black slacks and a button-down. Though she couldn't see it, she knew he wasn't wearing a tie. He never did. He was the casual billionaire, more comfortable behind a computer than in front of investors.

"Hey, it's late. Are you not going into work? I thought Riley had sold you on the whole everything's-normal plan." She clutched the sheet around her as she slid to the edge of the bed. While he was at work, she would hide out here, maybe talk to Noah and convince him to let her have a go at figuring out who'd sent him that original card.

"I wanted to let you sleep in." His voice was low.

"Come back to bed." She didn't like the tight set of his shoulders or the fact that he hadn't turned around yet. "Forget about plans and plots for the day. Let's stay here."

One more day.

He turned and the grim set of his lips told her everything she needed to know. "The helicopter's ready when you are. I don't want the press to catch you leaving the house. The helicopter will take you to the airport where the plane is ready for you. Case is going with you. He'll hand you off to the bodyguard in Dallas. He'll shadow you when you're not at the McKay-Taggart building, and he's got a room set up at my place in Dallas. If you like it, I'll sign the deed over to you. Otherwise, you should start thinking about where you want to live."

Her heart clenched at the cold words. "I want to talk about this. There might be another solution."

He shook his head. "I've already settled everything. You'll have an office to work out of at McKay-Taggart. I've ensured you have everything you could need, and you'll have access to all files concerning the case. I've also torn up our original contract. You'll be free to take the book to any publisher you like."

How could he talk to her in that chilly voice about calling her agent about a book she wasn't sure she even wanted to write anymore? "I told you I wasn't going to write the book."

"I think you should. You have to think about your own best interests now."

Because she wasn't going to have him to look after her anymore? She needed to pull this back a bit. "Drew, I know you said you wanted one last night before you let me go. Don't you think that's a little dramatic?"

"I think I told you what I wanted and I'm following through," he replied, his eyes steady on her.

"And if I want to stay?" Now that she was looking down the barrel of the gun he was about to fire, she knew all the logical reasons they couldn't work didn't matter. They should give it a shot.

He turned away again. "You won't be allowed to stay. I would greatly prefer not to have to drag you out, but I will if I have to. I made myself plain last night. This can't work right now. You're a distraction I don't need."

Somehow those words cut deep. She'd thought he was doing this to protect her. All her insecurities began to bubble up. "So you expect me to go and sit in your approved-of home and wait for you?"

His head shook briefly. "Not at all. I expect you to move on with your life. You can do better than me. This was a brief affair, Shelby."

"You're going to tell me that what happened between us last night was nothing more than a bodily need?"

He turned around. "Of course not. But it will be from here on out. I don't know that I want to feel this way, Shelby. It hurts and I . . . I'm helpless against you, so this is the only way to handle the situation. I stayed up all night trying to figure out a way we could work this out, but it just won't. I'll be honest—when I really look at the situation, I don't know that I want it to work. It makes me too vulnerable."

"Too vulnerable?"

"Yes," he replied, his voice perfectly academic as though he was talking about some piece of code that wasn't functioning properly and needed to be rewritten. "It's been a lovely few weeks, but I realized yesterday that the pain isn't worth the pleasure. You're a weakness and I can't have any. Do you understand?"

A weakness? She thought she'd been his strength. "Drew, if this is some whacked out plan to protect me, I don't need protecting."

"I do. This isn't about you. This is about me and this family. I can't protect this family if I'm constantly worried about you. If I'm obsessed with you, I'm not serving them."

"It's not one or the other. And I thought I was becoming part of this family."

"You thought wrong." His face was a perfect blank and she wondered if this was how he fired employees. "You were a very pleasant means to an end and yes, I think it's best for you to go as well. I'm not getting married and I'm almost certain to get bored with you at some point. Keeping you with me right now would ensure that you couldn't do your job later on. I don't want to do that to you. I don't want to leave you without a means to support yourself. Unless . . . unless that was your plan. We could come to some sort of contract if that's amenable to you. What is your career worth? This time around I would insist on writing sex into the contract though. I find myself deeply distracted by your body. I would want a guarantee."

Maybe he was saying all of this to manipulate her, but it worked. Her whole body went cold.

He couldn't care about her much if he could let her go like this. If he could look at her like she was some kind of prostitute after everything they'd been through together. The world wasn't some dumb movie where an act of sacrifice could free them all. The trouble was if he'd asked her to stay and not turned it into some disgusting transaction, she would have. She would have given up her career and everything she'd worked for on nothing more than the promise that maybe he would change his mind about marrying her someday.

She wasn't this girl. She couldn't allow herself to be this girl. She wasn't the idiot who gave up everything in hopes that some man might someday say he loved her.

Even if she loved him with all her heart.

"I think you should let me get dressed."

He hesitated. "Shelby, I'm truly sorry. I didn't mean for things to turn out this way."

But he'd said what he wanted to say. If he didn't leave, he would see her cry, and she didn't want that. "It's fine. Like you said, this was a brief affair. I wasn't looking to get married. I'll be ready to go in thirty minutes."

She held the sheet close to her. Last night she'd been so comfortable being naked around him, but this morning she was back to reality. He meant what he'd said. He'd wanted one last night of sex and then he was done.

For whatever reason, he was pushing her away and he'd proven he would burn her if she didn't comply.

He stared at her and for a moment she thought he might say something else, but then he stood and nodded. "All right. I'll give you some time to yourself. I'm sorry, Shelby. If I'd known . . . well, I would have spared you."

The door closed and she dissolved into tears.

Thirty minutes later, Shelby stepped outside the bedroom, dressed and made up and packed. Her armor was fully in place, and there would be no more tears. She'd cried them all out in the shower, careful to stay quiet. The last thing she needed was for Drew to know how much he'd hurt her. She still had her pride. It was all she had.

She rolled her suitcase down the hall and toward her first caretaker. Case was standing there with his wife. There was a frown on his face as she walked up.

"Are you sure this is what you want?" Case asked. "Because you don't have to leave. Drew doesn't make all the rules. No matter what he thinks."

The pretty blonde was makeup-free this morning. Despite the fact that she couldn't have gotten much sleep, Mia was still vibrant and beautiful. "You can stay as long as you want. Drew can't kick you out."

Oh, but he could and he had. He wasn't here to witness her goodbyes. She gave Mia what she hoped was a convincing smile. "It's fine. We talked about it last night and realized we don't work as a couple."

"He's being ridiculous," Mia argued. "He thinks he's protecting you, but he needs you."

Drew Lawless didn't need anyone. She was fairly certain of that. "It's fine. I think it's best this way."

"It's not better for him," Carly said, walking into the room. "And I don't think it's better for you, either. You've been happier the last few days than I've ever seen you, and Drew's different, too. He's more settled and open."

"I think he loves you," Mia agreed.

He'd never said the words and his actions spoke volumes. She had to go by his actions. "That's sweet of you to say, but we've decided to be friends. And for a while we're not going to have much contact at all. We started this thing on a lark and it's time to end it. We don't need the relationship as cover anymore."

Why was she having to explain this to them? Every second she had to stand there and act like the world wasn't falling apart was pure torture.

"You didn't sleep with him for cover." Carly put a hand on her shoulder. "I know you. If you slept with him, it was because you loved him."

She would never admit that to anyone. "Come and see me in Dallas. I'm staying there while I figure out my next move."

Carly looked unsure, but nodded. "All right. I'll see you soon. Be careful."

"No worries." She had to keep it together. "Apparently I've got some hot bodyguard waiting for me when I get there. It should be fun."

It was almost like Drew had given her a new life so he didn't have to feel guilty about taking the old one from her. New city. New apartment. New man to live with.

It didn't matter. All that mattered now was figuring out what she wanted to do with the rest of her life. It was time to find herself again. The Shelby she'd been without Drew. Strong and confident.

Alone and lonely. Like she'd been missing part of herself and it had fallen into place.

Intelligent and independent.

That Shelby. That Shelby would simply move on and find another man or be fine with no man at all. She could buy a vibrator, and that vibe wouldn't rip her heart out.

She gave Carly a wink and turned back to Case. "I hear there's a helicopter waiting for me."

Mr. Lawless only sent the best for his castoffs.

"If you're sure, I'll go fire it up. I'll take your bag. The helipad's where the tennis court used to be. I'll be ready in a couple of minutes." Case took her bag and started walking to the back of the house.

She turned and gave Carly a hug, wondering how long she had with her friend. Carly was a Lawless now, and eventually they would drift apart because she would find herself spending more and more time with Mia and Ellie. They were a tight-knit clan, and family won out every time. In a couple of months, maybe a year, Shelby would find herself talking to Carly less and less, and they would move on, too.

Nothing was permanent. She should have remembered that in the first place.

She gave Mia a hug and Ellie appeared, rushing out to say goodbye to her.

This could have been her family, too.

She had to stop thinking that way. She forced herself to smile and hug and make promises about lunches and dinner dates that likely wouldn't happen. When she got to Dallas, she was going to bury herself in work.

She made her way to the back of the house, happy to have missed

Drew. When she began to open the door that led outside, she heard a deep voice.

"Don't leave him. Please."

She turned, and Hatch was standing there in the same clothes he'd worn the night before and looking way worse for the wear.

How dangerous was he? He didn't look dangerous. He looked sad and tired. He looked like every year of his life hung heavily on his shoulders.

"I should think you would want me gone."

Hatch shook his head. "Nah, you were doing your job. I always knew Drew might find out. I was in love with her. At least I thought I was. When I saw Noah and realized . . . well, I knew he wasn't mine. I guess I got caught in her web, too. Over and over again. The fact that my mistake meant the end of Ben, well, I've dealt with that. It was easier when I thought she was dead, too."

She couldn't help herself. She had to ask the question. "When did you know they'd used your money?"

"Phillip came to see me the next day. Showed me the proof. Told me if I didn't keep my mouth shut, he would send it to the police and make sure I was the only one who went down. At the time I was in mourning. I didn't even think about the kids. I let them go. Please don't do the same thing to Drew today."

She'd held her tongue with Drew's siblings. She didn't want to cause more problems in this family, but something about the way Hatch was challenging her made it impossible to stay quiet a moment longer. She wasn't the bad guy here. "It's not even similar, Mr. Hatchard. I'm not leaving Drew. He's kicking me out. He says it's for my own good, but I offered to stay with him."

"He's sacrificing himself for you. It's all he knows how to do. Shelby, he's lived with the responsibility of his family for so long he doesn't understand what it means to lean on someone, to be selfish. He thinks that if he loves you, he has to let you go."

"I told him he didn't." She wasn't sure what Hatch wanted her to do. "Drew's always honest with me. If he wants me to leave, it's because he does."

"He's not good at being honest with himself, and he doesn't want you to leave. He's dying inside and he's going to die some more every day you're gone. He finally found the one woman who could handle him. You can do this, Shelby. You can stand up to him. He's fought for everyone. He needs one person to . . ."

"That's enough, Hatch." Drew's cold voice broke Hatch's impassioned plea.

She turned and Drew was standing in the hallway, his arms over his chest. He stared at Hatch with hard eyes.

"You don't have to do this, Drew," Hatch said softly. "You don't have to let her go."

Drew glanced down at his watch. "We have to be at the office in thirty minutes for a photo op. I suggest you stop worrying about my love life and get cleaned up so we can worry about our company. The stock is down two percent this morning, and it will drop again once my face shows up on *People* magazine next week."

"Damn it." Hatch's head hung as he started back toward the living room. "I'll get legal on them."

"Don't bother. They won't be the only ones." Drew turned back to her. "I'm sorry. I didn't mean for him to disturb you."

He was so beautiful. How did he manage to be both entirely manly and beautiful at the same time? She had to force herself to speak. "Drew, what would you say if I told you I want to stay here?"

His lips curled up slightly. "I would say you're a sweet girl, but I can't allow it. I care about you. I want us to be friends somewhere down the line, but I have to choose my family. This is for the best."

She was on the outside, the girl looking in at the happy family, never a part of one. Not again.

He held out a hand.

No more kisses. No more plastering his body against hers like he couldn't stand the thought of there being an inch of space between them. Just a friendly handshake to end the most intense relationship of her life.

She turned away without another look. She couldn't touch him again.

The sound of the helicopter thudded through the air as Case turned on the rotors.

She started for the door.

A hand wrapped around her arm, pulling her back. Drew stood looking down at her, a frown on his face.

"I meant what I said," he shouted over the whine of the chopper. "I owe you. Keep the bodyguard close until we're absolutely certain Iris won't come after you. I don't need to worry about your safety when I should be concentrating on what's happening here."

Well, of course. She certainly wouldn't want to keep him up at night. And yet she would do it because she would give him no cause to blame her. "Good-bye, Drew."

His hand didn't let go. "Promise me if you need me, you'll call."

"I'll call," she lied. She was never going to call him again.

His hand let go and she was free.

She strode to the helicopter, buckling herself in. As it took off, she looked down, and Drew was standing there with his hands in his pockets, looking very much the lost little boy he'd been once.

Shelby watched him until he faded into the distance.

She was gone. Drew felt the absence like a hole in his fucking heart. Shelby was gone and she wasn't going to call him. She was gone and there would be nothing he could do to get her back.

It was all for the best.

He stared out the limo windows as they rolled down the highway.

"You should go after her," Hatch said.

Yeah, he was in the car with Hatch because Riley was running the game right now. He had to stop that, but he couldn't work up the will. He should take over, but all he could think about was the fact that she was on a plane to Dallas. His plane. He'd called the night before when he couldn't sleep and had it stocked with her favorite wine and tea so she could have a choice. He'd forced some poor guy to go out and find cave-aged Gruyère because she loved it with crackers.

"Why would I go after her? I sent her away." He wasn't going to engage in this with Hatch. He didn't get to play dad anymore. Hatch had killed his real father.

Or his idiocy had made it possible for his father to die. It didn't matter in the end.

"He made the right choice," Riley said. His stalwart brother. Riley was always with him. "Shelby could get hurt if she stayed here."

"Ellie could get hurt, but I don't see you sending her away," Hatch pointed out.

"That boat sailed long ago. Everyone knows how connected Strat-Cast and 4L are, so Ellie keeping her distance would hurt us all. Ellie's tough. She won't back down from this fight. Not even if I asked her to." Riley had been cool under pressure. He hadn't blinked as they'd gone through the mob of reporters. "Very few people know about the connection between Drew and Shelby. She's a reporter who does undercover work from time to time. She needs her anonymity."

Thank God for Riley. He was the only one who understood. The rest of his family looked at him like he'd kicked a puppy.

Couldn't any of them see how much this was killing him?

"She wouldn't have that if she'd stayed with you," Hatch pointed out. "If she'd been with you for more than a few months, it would have been noted. It would have been reported on, and her undercover days would have been over. The same way they are for Mia. Shelby knew that. She would have found other work to do."

"She shouldn't have to." But she'd asked him to let her stay. She still could write her books. "No one should be put under this kind of scrutiny."

"You've got your father's brain but none of his spirit," Hatch complained. "Ben might have made mistakes, but he wouldn't have let this happen. He wouldn't have kicked out a woman who loved him."

He felt his blood pressure tick up. "My father loved a psychopath and when he decided to leave her, he got his girlfriend murdered along with himself. Don't compare me to my father."

Hatch's expression softened. "Drew, you can't stay mad at him forever. I'm sorry for saying what I said. He had a brilliant mind, too, and it often left him wondering how to fit in with the people around him. The normal people. He could understand the most difficult of concepts, but I don't think he understood what it meant to be loved. He accepted Iris because she told him she loved him. He stayed with her because it was easier than leaving. He didn't get what love was until you kids came along."

He didn't want to have this conversation. "Why don't we discuss Mother's morning talk show circuit? From what I could tell, she managed to do at least two major network morning shows today."

Hatch continued like Drew hadn't spoken at all. "You know what dutiful love is, but I don't think you have any idea what it means to let someone love you."

Loving him might be her downfall and he couldn't live with that. "She can love me from afar. So Riley, what do you think about the morning shows? How much are they going to hurt us? And when can I dump Hatch?"

Because he really wanted to dump Hatch.

A long sigh came from Riley as he sat back. "You're not dumping Hatch. I've explained this about a million times. Bran is already at the office. He's going to have a carefully crafted statement ready for you to deliver to the press and our employees. Hatch will be by your side. I heard from the feds early this morning. They want to talk again, but they're willing to do it at the house. That's a good sign. I think they're getting that Iris's story is full of shit."

More interviews. No Shelby. She wouldn't be sitting next to him, holding his hand.

"I'll do what you tell me to do." Riley and Bran knew this kind of stuff better than he did.

Would he have admitted that before Shelby? Would he have let them do their jobs and shine?

He'd started all of this to get revenge on the people who'd stolen his childhood, their childhoods. How had they found their futures by trying to avenge the past? Mia had found Case before they'd even started, but none of this would have been possible without him. Riley had fallen for Ellie, and Bran had stumbled Carly's way. Now they were all grown and taking care of themselves, and soon they would have families.

He was alone. He'd found his perfect mate, but she was gone. He'd sent her away and she wouldn't forgive him.

"I'll do whatever you want me to as well," Hatch said. "Including telling the press that I did it all. I don't see how you can't understand it would solve everything."

Drew rolled his eyes. "It would solve nothing. Iris would get away with it."

"Then I'll admit we were lovers and that she and I did this together," Hatch offered. "I can take her down with me."

"Or you can make everything worse," Riley said. "Will you let this play itself out? You've told the feds the truth. Now we let them handle it. I know it's a decades-old case, but they can figure this out now that we're talking about it."

"Let's be patient. Iris looked desperate this morning, and our stock is only down two percent." He wasn't willing to let her dictate the terms of battle. They needed to take a step back and figure out what she wanted. He could take his time now that Shelby was going to be safe. "Speaking of safe, have we canceled the reception plans?"

He hated to do it. He knew it would hurt Ellie, but they couldn't go through with it. It would hurt her more when her long-awaited wedding reception was ruined by no one showing up.

Riley snorted a bit. "Yeah, I'm not going to do that. Do you have any idea how much it would cost to cancel at this point? The hotel alone would be a fortune, and then there would be the problem of my wife murdering me. She's worked her pretty ass off to ensure this is her dream reception. If you remember, our first wedding kind of sucked since it happened at a courthouse and was all about keeping her out of jail."

He remembered it all too well. "I'm sorry. Please let Ellie know I'll make it up to her at some point."

"There's no need. We're going through with it," Riley replied breezily. "We've got about five hundred people coming. I'm not canceling."

Riley wasn't thinking clearly. "There won't be five hundred people. I'm sure most of them will cancel. They won't want to have anything to do with me. Did you see the headlines? They're asking if I'm a monster."

Drew had seen the Internet news headlines. The story would be all over the tabloids by next week. Just in time to screw with Riley and Ellie's reception. But then he was sure his mother had calculated all of that into her plans.

"You're joking, right?" Riley stared at him.

"I wouldn't joke about this." He rarely joked about anything. It was Shelby who could make him laugh at how pretentious he could be. "I don't want her hurt when no one shows up. How many respectable people would show up at a party thrown by a man accused of murder?"

Hatch groaned and his head fell back against the seat. "He knows nothing of the world."

Riley had a smile on his face. "They'll all show up. The people who told us they couldn't come will all show up now. This is Texas, not England circa nineteen hundred. Scandal sells. The fact that the press will be there will bring them out in droves. They're all upping their game, hoping to be photographed by one of the magazines. We're not canceling. We're happily inviting the press in, and we're going to show the world how close-knit we are, how we stand behind you. We're going to show them that we're a family and she can't break us."

But they were a family missing a member, and maybe they always would be, because no matter what he said to anyone, he didn't know that he could touch another woman. He belonged to Shelby. She was the only one who could ever really know him.

"I don't think this is a good idea. I think we should concentrate all our efforts on poking holes in her story. This shit with the press isn't going to help us. I don't do well in interviews. You say so yourself. I come off as hard and awkward and overly intellectual."

"Not around Shelby you don't." Hatch wouldn't let it go.

"Shelby is gone." He didn't want to be here. He wanted to be back at home throwing himself into work, trying to forget. "We should hammer Iris in the press. Make her look bad."

"No, we're going to concentrate on making you look good," Riley said patiently. "This is my time to take care of you, brother. I know and understand the press better than you. I know how to manipulate a jury, and make no mistake our jury is the American people. Iris made a terrible mistake. You're looking at the headlines, but you need to go and read the comment threads on the articles."

"People are asking questions." Hatch yawned behind his hand. Drew had noticed he seemed to have eschewed his morning Bloody Mary in favor of actual, nonalcoholic coffee. He held the travel mug in his hand. "The press wants a sexy story, and your long-lost mother accusing you of murdering your father is sexy as hell. But the actual people reading the story have questions. They want to know why she would leave her precious children with the monster who killed her husband."

"I told you that would happen." Riley straightened his tie as they made the turn off the freeway. "Now we launch a campaign of our own. We're going to win hearts and minds. By the way, you'll be donating a million dollars' worth of computer equipment and software to fund a new inner-city STEM project. Science, technology, engineering and math programs for underfunded schools."

"I know what STEM is. When did I decide to do that?" He sat back. The better question was when the hell had his brother turned the tables on him? When had he become such a confident, competent man?

"Last night. Let me tell you, my wife can put together a charity project in no time at all. You'll announce the project in a few days with Ellie by your side. She and I will be doing an interview with CNN where we're going to discuss not only what happened that night, but also the part her father played in it."

His hands clenched, tightening on the armrest. "She can't do that. It could hurt StratCast stock."

"It won't," Riley replied. "And she's insistent. I am, too. We decided something last night. We've kept this secret because we wanted revenge. The best revenge we can have now is telling the truth, and that means letting the world know who you are, Drew. It means standing beside you and letting them all know that we're alive because you wouldn't give up. We're healthy and whole and successful because when our parents failed us, you stood up and took over. I call you brother, but you were the best father I could possibly have had. Any of us. So you sit back. It's our time to take care of you. And when this is done, you go get your girl because you deserve her."

The car slid to a stop in front of the 4L building. Drew could see reporters were here, too. He could sort of see. The world had gone a bit blurry. What was up with that? Something was definitely wrong with his eyes.

"Are you ready?" Riley asked. "I need you to let me do most of the talking, but you have to stand beside Hatch. I don't want any signs of discord between the major shareholders."

Hatch was silent.

Maybe it was time to understand that Riley had become someone Drew could count on. He could let go and let Riley take care of this. Bran could take care of the day-to-day operations because he'd become a great man, too.

Drew took a deep breath. "Yeah, I'm ready."

It was time to take his brother's lead for once. He followed Riley out of the car, ready to face his fate.

Chapter Eighteen

S helby stared at the computer screen in front of her. Fuckwits. One week in and the Internet was still obsessed with the Lawless family and their feud. She watched as one of the online news agencies rolled out its version of how the murders could have played out. They were using 3-D cartoons, but there was no way to miss how accurate they'd gotten Drew's character.

Her stomach turned as 3-D Drew shot his father.

It was all bullshit and it still didn't address key facts. Why would Drew have shot an innocent woman? For the shot to work, he would have to have looked Francine in the face and pulled the trigger. He would have known it wasn't his mother. He then would have turned and immediately shot his father through the head.

Easy peasy for an assassin. Not so much for a fourteen-year-old kid who'd never held a firearm before.

And yet some people were buying it.

Shelby shut her laptop and sighed, turning to look out the window at the view of Dallas. The McKay-Taggart building was in the heart of downtown, so she was surrounded by skyscrapers.

She missed the view of the river back in Austin.

She missed him.

At night she watched the news, hungry for even a hint of him. The rest of the Lawless family had been hard at work. Ellie and Riley had given an interview that ran the night before, and Mia and Bran had sat down with a reporter to talk about how much they loved their brother and what they remembered from that night.

She'd sat with her bodyguard and watched each one.

Remy Guidry was a big, gorgeous Cajun charmer who she would have been all over not a few months before. The Shelby before Drew would have been in heaven, but now she could only appreciate the man on an aesthetic level while her soul longed for someone else.

Unfortunately, it didn't seem to go both ways.

She'd heard absolutely nothing from Drew. She'd sent him a text and a few e-mails, but heard nothing back from him.

It was over, but she felt completely stuck.

There was a knock on her door. She glanced at the clock on her desk. It was almost lunchtime. Remy was early, but he always showed up and asked her what he could bring her for lunch or if she wanted to go out. She never wanted to go out. She ate at her desk while she poured through file after file and read every single interview Iris gave. Drew's mom was living it up right here in Dallas, allowing the paparazzi to photograph her at every turn.

Meanwhile, Shelby was putting together a list of her crimes.

"I'm not hungry, Remy," she said, opening her laptop again. The quicker she compiled all her data, the faster she could send it off and move on with her life. She had to make sure Iris Lawless was behind bars at the end of this, or it would have all been for nothing.

"Not Remy," a feminine voice said. "Sorry to disturb you. I'm trying to get everything off my plate before we head down to Austin for the big party. I've got the files you asked for."

Charlotte Taggart walked in like she owned the place. Which she totally did. The tall, gorgeous woman with strawberry-blond hair was holding a set of files in her hands. She was dressed in a chic business suit that did nothing to mask her femininity.

She would look stunning in whatever designer gown she wore to the reception tonight. The emerald-green Prada cocktail dress that Drew had bought for Shelby was hanging in the closet. She should send it back and save him the ridiculous price tag, but she hadn't worked up the will yet.

Shelby was actually surprised they were still going through with the reception. "I would have thought Drew would cancel."

Charlotte set the files in front of her. "Apparently he's been listening to Riley and Bran. They don't want to hide. They think getting their own story to the public is far better than waiting Iris out."

She agreed, but she never thought Drew would. "I don't understand. Drew was against dragging anyone else into this, but now he's letting Riley go on TV every day. Mia did an interview. I'm surprised he would let them do it."

Charlotte shrugged. "Oh, I don't think he had a choice."

That wasn't at all how Drew worked. "Drew makes all the choices. He won't have it any other way."

Charlotte sat down in the chair across from her desk. Serious blue eyes studied Shelby. "You're joking, right?"

"Why would you think that?" Maybe she shouldn't have started this conversation. She was still so hungry for any news of him, and didn't that make her pathetic? "Sorry. I was surprised because the Drew I knew ruled 4L with an iron fist."

He ruled everything. King Drew.

"Oh, that was absolutely the Drew Lawless I met in the beginning, but something changed a few weeks ago and now he's a real live boy. It's been kind of fun to watch. And then you showed up here and now it's sad. I thought you would be the one to take down that man."

Yes, she wished she'd never started this conversation, because Charlotte seemed to be getting settled in for a nice long, uncomfortable chat. Shelby was not going to engage. Charlotte could be every bit as sarcastic as her husband. Shelby reached out for the files. "Not me. It was fun while it lasted, but Drew and I are not a good match. Does this include the security reports from the last few months?"

Charlotte nodded, but didn't move to get up. "Yes, the 4L team sent them over. Is there a particular reason why you're interested in someone hacking into nonproprietary systems? There were a couple of flags on some lower-level systems in the building, but it's not terribly surprising. Someone's always testing systems like 4L. It could be anyone from hackers trying to prove they can get through Drew's firewall to competitors who want to show that he's vulnerable."

Shelby opened the file, looking through the data. Charlotte was right and it was probably a long shot, but she wanted to see if anything stuck out. "I'll go through this tonight. Did they find anything interesting?"

"Not really. Most of the attempts were at getting banking records from the online purchasing system or data from people who registered their software. The only outlier was the fact that the admin desk got hacked. I thought that was a little weird. They're the only ones who got through, but the security there isn't as tight because there's nothing proprietary and the admins are allowed to work offsite in their own hub."

"What did they take?"

"Someone downloaded the entire vendor contact list." Charlotte frowned. "All they would get was a list of companies and people who work for 4L, but the phone numbers are almost all public record. I don't understand except that maybe it was an exercise. My sister assures me that sometimes hackers try to practice on big-name targets."

"When did it happen?"

"It was one of the earlier hacks. It happened about four months back."

So it happened before Noah had been informed of his parentage. She wasn't sure it had anything to do with what was happening now, but at least she had a list of what the hacker thought was so important.

Like caterers and a temp agency. Drew's personal law firm was listed, as was his housekeeper's number. So woo-hoo. They could get their houses cleaned like Drew's. "Thanks so much for getting this for me."

"We got no flack from 4L. Apparently if Shelby Gates asks for something, they've been told to give it up and fast. That doesn't sound like the Drew I met before, either. He used to be supersecretive. Even after he hired us, he would hem and haw about giving us information we needed."

She happened to know there was no special reason Drew would be happy to give them the info. "He considers me an employee. That's all. He wants me to write this book as quickly as I possibly can, so he's giving us the information we need. That's all that's happening."

Charlotte groaned. "Wow, you are no fun at all. I thought you were smarter, way more ballsy than you turned out to be. I lost so much betting on you."

"Excuse me?"

Charlotte waved off her chilly tone. "It's a hobby here. We bet on everything. I met you and knew that you would be the one to take down Drew Lawless. It didn't hurt that Mia told me the whole story."

It was good to know she was the subject of gossip. "Well, I guess you were wrong."

"I wasn't. You did take him down. You left him lying there, though, and that seems cruel. When you take down a man like that, he's your responsibility, and you walked away and left him bleeding."

What the hell was she talking about? "I'm sure he's bleeding. Drew is such easy prey. Look, it's none of your business."

Charlotte nodded as though encouraging her. "See, there you are."

Charlotte wanted to see her inner bitch? Oh, she could give her that. "Yes, here I am. If having this office and working in this building means I have to put up with you taking me apart for your own entertainment, then I can certainly leave."

"And you're done again." Charlotte stood up and straightened her jacket with a long sigh. "I apologize. You are more than welcome here. Please let me know if there's anything else we can do for you. Drew is important to us, and he wants you comfortable here."

She said it all with a smile on her face, but it was easy to see she'd disappointed Charlotte Taggart, and that meant something here. Charlotte was the alpha female at McKay-Taggart. If Charlotte didn't accept her, no one would.

Not that it mattered. She wasn't here to make friends.

"You know, I don't appreciate whatever it is you're trying to do. I get that you're in the Drew camp, but have you thought about the fact that maybe you don't have the whole story? That you're judging me without knowing me at all?"

Charlotte turned but instead of anger on her face, there was pure relief. "That's what I'm trying to say. I can't know the whole story unless you tell me, and you're all of a sudden twelve kinds of silent, and it is not looking good on you, girl." She moved back to her previous chair. "Okay, hit me. What did he do? And then I'll tell you how you fucked up, because this was really all on you. I don't need to hear the story to know that."

"Seriously? You want to put this all on me? Wow, you are not who I thought you were, either." She could give as good as she got. And you know, anger kind of felt good. It definitely felt better than the horrible numbness that had marked the last week. Since that moment when she'd realized Drew was truly sending her away, she'd shoved all the pain deep and wrapped herself in a steady diet of work and sleep and trying to distance herself from the fact that she loved a man who couldn't love her back. So getting pissed at Charlotte Taggart, who had her shit together and had a loving if sarcastic husband and three gorgeous kids and a business with a sterling reputation, felt good. "Mia talks about how you're all girl power, but that's bullshit."

Charlotte grinned. "Oh, no. I'm all about girl power. Keep going. Tell me how I'm wrong."

Somewhere in the back of her head she realized this was some kind of a trap, but again it felt good to rip into someone. She'd been so careful since she left Drew behind. All her anger had been tamped down and squeezed into a too-tight space, and it felt like it was going to explode now. "You want to judge me? Fuck you. You have no idea what I've been through, what I'm going through."

"Nope. I don't know because you won't talk to anyone. It's been frustrating. Tell me, have you talked to your friends? Your family?"

The question cut through her because for a few moments, she'd thought she would be able to answer this question differently. "I don't have any family. My only family is dead, and my closest friend is a member of Drew's family so I'm not going to burden her. Now, it's none of your business, but I didn't want to leave. Drew told me to get out. I was the idiot who fell in love with him."

"And you asked to stay."

Was she listening at all? "Yes, that's what I said. I asked him to let me stay, but he's a control freak and no one changes his mind about anything. He spent the night with me and shoved me on a helicopter the next morning because Drew doesn't change."

"Except you kind of changed him," Charlotte argued.

"No, I didn't."

Charlotte shook her head. "He never introduced any woman to his family before he met you. That was a change."

"He needed me to do his dirty work." She was under no illusions as to Drew's motivations for beginning their relationship.

"Did he? Really? Those were some thin arguments. I think he convinced himself he had to have some reason other than his own desire to bring you into his world. He's bad at being selfish or thinking about himself at all, so he basically manipulated his own brain into a relationship he thought he shouldn't have. I found that fascinating."

"His actions speak louder than your psychoanalysis. He asked me to leave and told me he hoped I found someone I could be happy with in the future." That had been a kick in the gut, mostly because she'd known what it really meant. It meant he intended to move on and didn't want her to think he would be pining away for her.

Charlotte sat back, staring at her. "Did he drag you to the helicopter? Because I would be surprised if Case would let that happen. Case kind of lives to let the people Drew tries to strong-arm know they have a choice. I think it's his way of rebelling against all dictatorial older brothers."

"I wasn't going to make him drag me out though he did threaten to do it." Her anger was deflating, a horrible sorrow taking its place. This was why she'd stayed numb. She'd known the sorrow was right there under the surface. "I don't know what you want from me, Mrs. Taggart. I don't want to be entertainment for the office."

Charlotte leaned forward, her face softening. "I want you to stop calling me Mrs. Taggart to start with. And the entertainment thing is because most of us are all married and settled in and we don't have any more drama. It's not a cruel thing. They're interested in you because they care about Drew and because they're starting to care about you. Mia talks about you a lot."

Mia was nice. She still didn't see what Charlotte's point was. "It doesn't matter. I'm not going to be here for long. I'm going to finish my research and try to figure out where to go from here. I'm thinking I might try Seattle."

"Why didn't you stay and fight?" Charlotte asked quietly.

"There was nothing to fight for." Drew had made that clear.

"I don't think you understand what I'm asking, Shelby. I wasn't asking if you thought Drew's love was worth fighting for. I was asking if you thought yours was. I meant what I said before. Maybe I should have said it more kindly, but I've lived with Señor Sarcasm for way too long. This is your responsibility. You walked away."

"Because he told me to."

"Fuck him. He's a man and he's not smart when it comes to things like this. You say you judged him by his actions, but what are those actions? Not the last day. You have to look across the whole relationship. Did he dictate everything to you? Never listen when you had something to say? Did he put his foot down constantly?"

Aside from lying to her about the contract, he'd actually given in on most of the things she'd asked him to do. He would put a price on his acceptance, but it was never a price she wouldn't want to pay. Sleeping in the same bed with him. Staying with him.

Transactions made Drew feel safe, like he had something to bargain with because he couldn't believe she would simply stay with him for no real reason. Drew had seen the world through the harshest filter and he needed control.

So why had he given in when it came to Noah? She knew Noah had scared the crap out of him, and logically it would have been better to keep Noah at arm's length. Until they figured out what Iris's plan was, Noah was a wild card. Drew hated wild cards.

But she'd asked and he'd given in.

"No," Shelby admitted. "He did pretty much anything I asked of him. He gave me a bunch of rules and I broke them."

"And he sent you away for that?"

"He got extremely mad when I continued looking into Hatch. He said some nasty things, but I don't know. I worried that after being the one who found the dirt on Hatch, he might not be able to forgive me." But that last night had felt like so much more than sex. It had felt like forever. She could still remember how he'd stared into her eyes, his hands tight on her body as he'd driven inside. They'd been connected. Deeply. Wholly.

She hadn't ever felt as close to another human being as she had to Drew.

"He told me he would destroy me." And ten minutes later he was bargaining with her.

Charlotte nodded. "Wow, he really did it. How do you like that Audi? You know it's in your name, right? He's moving the condo into your name, too. His version of destruction is rough."

He was soothing his conscience.

Or he was doing what Drew did. He was adjusting the transaction. He was trying to show his remorse, his affection, his hope. He was the kind of man who might try to show her how he felt by giving her things, by trying to ensure her comfort.

"He told me to go." She couldn't look past that.

"That doesn't mean you have to. That just means he's a dumbass, and a self-sacrificing dumbass at that. It's all he knows."

Because sacrifice was all he'd done for years. What had Hatch started to ask her before Drew had interrupted? He'd been defending Drew.

He's fought for everyone. He needs one person to . . .

Fight for him? Fight with him?

She'd walked out because she'd accepted that he would want her to leave, believed it deep in her heart. No amount of logic could change the fact that everyone had left. Her father had left and started a new family. Her own family was all gone now, and somewhere deep down she was still a little girl whose daddy hadn't wanted her so she was always waiting to be walked out on.

She'd told herself it had been for the best, that her mother had been happier without him. But Shelby hadn't. And she wouldn't be happier without Drew. Maybe this was a question of fighting for more than one person. Maybe it was a question of fighting for herself.

"He changed for you," Charlotte said quietly. "A man like that will only change for one person. Well, maybe for his children, too, but the responsibility is always on you. A man like Drew can do great things, but he needs someone willing to stand with him, beside him, and sometimes against him. You do it all with love, and you do it because you're building something with him. You do it because you are important, possibly the most important piece of him."

Because she was his conscience. She forced him to examine the world in a way he hadn't before.

"I'm the right woman for him. I always have been."

Charlotte smiled, and this time it was brilliant. "Yes. Yes, you are."

"He's afraid he'll hurt me." She should have told him to fuck himself and then sat down and talked it out with him. Drew needed firm boundaries, but he also needed to know that when he screwed up, she wouldn't leave.

"He will. He'll hurt you and you'll hurt him. It's what people in love do, but you grow and learn and forgive and move on," Charlotte said. "He's thinking in terms of good times, but marriages aren't simply about the good times. The bad times define who we are far more than anything else. What kind of partner do you want to be? Do you want to be the one who's only around for the joy?"

She wanted to be the one he could lean on. How could she be that if she wasn't with him? If she let things come between them. She'd given him a halfhearted plea to let her stay. She hadn't shown him that she was strong enough to handle his world. Every single time she'd stood up to him, she'd won. Why had she lain down when it was most important?

Because she didn't believe. Because she was letting the past drag her down.

It was dragging Drew down because Charlotte was right about that, too.

Drew had no idea how to have a real relationship. He thought he was in control, but he was about to find out that a relationship with her wouldn't always go his way.

"Charlotte, I'm going to need a ride to Austin tonight."

It looked like that dress was going to get some use. And her man was about to find out that when she took him down, he stayed down.

Drew stared at himself in the mirror and wondered if there was any way at all he could get out of tonight's party. He'd dreaded the thought of it before he'd had Shelby, and then he kind of looked forward to it because she would be with him and she would enjoy the opulence. Without her, it all seemed useless. A full week in the new post-Iris lifestyle, and he was ready to head into his hermit hole and never come out. He'd talked more to the press in the last few days than he had in all his years as CEO of 4L. He'd had to force a smile, and he was bad at it. When he'd watched himself the night before, he'd looked like an idiot, and an uncomfortable idiot at that. Now he looked like an idiot in a tux.

He took a deep breath and forced himself to reach for the jacket. Tonight would be like all the other nights. He would force himself to move, force himself to talk. He wasn't real. He was nothing but a robot moving through his days. The only person he wanted to talk to was the only one he couldn't.

According to all the reports, she was working hard. Remy sent him a daily report on her activities. She went to and from work at the McKay-Taggart building. She stopped for the occasional latte, but her bodyguard reported that she rarely talked to anyone. Even him.

There was a knock on his door, and one of the people he didn't want to see walked in. Hatch was wearing a tux, too. He was still living in the house, but they rarely spoke when they didn't have to.

"What do you need?" Drew asked.

"So many damn things, but I don't think I'm going to get them." The last few weeks seemed to have aged Hatch. There was a weariness about him that never seemed to go away. "I need a damn drink, but then I have to start the sad-sack story all over again, and I don't want to be the asshole who has a collection of one-day-sober chips."

Drew stared at him for a moment. "What?"

He'd ignored Hatch as much as he could. Riley could force him to live with the bastard, but he couldn't make him talk to him. Riley couldn't make him love Hatch again.

He'd lost Shelby and Hatch all in one day. How much more would he lose before this was over?

"I'm in AA. Riley took me to my first meeting the day after the world exploded. I figure I can kill myself over this again or I can try." Hatch ran a hand through his hair. "Sobriety sucks, but I'm not going to let you down again, Drew. I know you think you don't need me, but you do. I'm not going to leave until I'm certain you'll be all right."

The idea of Hatch standing in front of a group and confessing his sins made Drew's heart twist a little. "I'm all right now."

Hatch closed the door behind him with a long sigh. "No, you're not, and that's another reason I'm not leaving. The FBI agents are downstairs. I tried to explain that it would have to wait."

The feds wouldn't care that he had a reception to go to. "Is Riley here?"

"We're the only two left. Everyone else either went on to the hotel or is picking up our friends from Dallas. I should call the lawyers in. Give me an hour or so and I can have them here. I'll call Riley, too. He won't like the timing of this one bit."

Oh, but Drew was sure it had all been timed perfectly. Iris certainly would know what was going on tonight. "Where's Noah?"

Hatch had his phone out. "He went on ahead with Ellie and Riley. He said he was going to see if he could help. Mia and Case went to the airport to meet his brother, and they're going to the hotel from there."

Big Tag and his wife were coming in for the reception. It was a big night for the entire family, and Drew wasn't about to ruin it all by dragging Riley back into his hell. Riley deserved a night to celebrate his marriage. "I can talk to them alone. I've got an hour and a half before someone will notice I'm not there. Tonight is about celebrating Riley and Ellie's marriage. I won't turn it into another circus."

He started out of the room, Hatch hard on his heels.

"I think this is a bad idea."

"I have plenty of those." Like thinking he might be able to live without her. "I won't say anything dumb. If it seems like it's getting too serious, I'll stop everything and we can call the lawyers in, but we'll do it quietly."

He wasn't a complete idiot. He knew what he should and shouldn't say. At least when it came to this. He walked into the room, his hand held out. "Gentlemen. What can I do for you today?"

The special agents stood in the middle of his living room wearing their typical dark suits and dour expressions. The lead agent shook Drew's hand and nodded Hatch's way. "I'm sorry to bother you, Mr. Lawless, but it seems we have a problem."

Special Agent Johnson handed him a set of papers.

It took Drew very little time to figure out what it was. An order of protection. "So I have to stay five hundred feet away from my mother? That shouldn't be difficult since I haven't actually set eyes on her in person in twenty-plus years."

Hatch took the papers out of Drew's hands. "She got a fucking restraining order? Are you kidding me? If anyone needs a restraining order, it's Andrew."

"Ms. Lawless convinced a judge that you're a threat to her. Honestly, with all the press surrounding this case, it's not terribly surprising. You can get one of your own," the special agent advised. "Look, I'm not sure what's going on. I've got a lot of data to get through."

"Some reporter loves you, man." Special Agent Garcia shook his head and gave them a whistle. "She's buried us in data about your mom. When we took on this case, we thought it would be high profile, but it's getting freaky now. That Gates chick is quite the conspiracy theorist."

Johnson gave his partner a slow look. "I don't think we need to talk about that in present company."

Garcia shrugged. "You're probably right, but I am going to ask him a few questions she's brought up."

"Shelby Gates?" Even the sound of her name kind of made his heart speed up. He hadn't realized she was actively feeding the FBI information.

"Yes, she's an investigative reporter," Johnson confirmed.

She was more than that. She was half his freaking soul. The better half. "I know her. She's quite intelligent."

"What's she found out?" Hatch asked. "Has she explained her theories about the three husbands Iris went through after she killed Ben?"

"We're checking into everything she's sent us, including the incredibly detailed floor plan she sent. She makes a good case for her version of the crimes. The problem is the police didn't do all the work they should have at the time. I know your father's death was ruled a suicide, but it's still sloppy work for a police force that's known for being careful."

So Shelby was making waves. "It was set up by my mother and her cohorts to look like a suicide. I still don't understand why she felt the need to kill my father's assistant when she could have inherited his stocks."

Special Agent Johnson raised his hand. "We actually have a working theory about that. I went looking into the old law firm that handled your father's business. A few weeks before his death, he had a new will drafted in the event of a legal separation. Your mother got none of the stock. He was clear about that. The stock was to be placed in a trust for the children, and he'd set up his personal lawyer as the trust manager. Iris was left money, but no stock and no voting rights. She claims she had no knowledge of the will that was changed. Because of state property laws, she could have contested that they weren't separated at the time and she was married to him when the stock gained its value."

Drew could play that out to its logical conclusion. "But the minute that will was brought out, questions would have been asked. The police would have known my father was thinking about a separation and they would have wondered why make a legal move like that when he was planning on taking his own life."

Hatch shook his head. "I didn't know anything about that. I'm surprised. Ben was making moves to try to protect you all. I wonder if his lawyer wasn't paid a bit to keep it all quiet after the fact."

Perhaps his father had suspected something was going on between Hatch and Iris. Otherwise, Drew was certain his father would have left the trust and voting rights in Hatch's hands. Was that why his mother had targeted Hatch in the first place? Had she realized she was losing her grip on his father and sought out the next best thing? It explained why she'd decided to fake her death and work with Patricia. It had been the only way she could maintain any semblance of control. She'd been able to easily blackmail her cohorts without the pesky problems of dealing with four children. She'd looked at her options and made her choice, and Francine Wells had taken her place.

Who would she sacrifice this time? What was her end game?

"Obviously, we're going to continue our investigation, but for now we do have to ask about the e-mails you've recently sent to your mother." Garcia seemed to get serious again. "We've got our cyber guys working on it, but they've already confirmed that the e-mails came from this house, from your personal network."

"E-mails?"

"Yes, that's what sparked the restraining order," Johnson explained. "Your mother received a number of e-mails detailing the numerous ways you want to hurt her. I suppose you're going to tell me they didn't actually come from you?"

"I haven't written anything to my mother." But he had a sinking feeling in his gut that he knew who had. "I would know how to hide my footprint if I was going to. I assure you I know how to send an e-mail you wouldn't be able to trace back to me. Not even your cyber unit."

Johnson grimaced. "They might have mentioned that to us. They were surprised that a man of your skill would make such a rookie mistake. I suppose you're not the only one who uses the network?"

"No, of course not. Everyone who lives in or visits this household uses it. I suspect my account was cloned and someone is using it to e-mail as me. Has the press gotten the story yet?" He didn't want to think about who it likely was. Who it had to be.

"The restraining order is only a few hours old, but you have to know that they'll find out about it soon," Johnson replied.

"It was that little fucker, Noah. He's working with her," Hatch spat.

Drew put a hand up, trying to silence Hatch. "Don't even start."

"Are you talking about Noah Walker? Because your mother has mentioned him several times. She's extremely worried that you're going to hurt him," Garcia explained. "But when I talked to Noah, he said he was fine."

"He's being used to set Drew up," Hatch insisted. "She's planning something."

Of course she was, but he needed to figure out how Noah played into it before they talked to the feds. "I'll look into it, Special Agents. I would more than welcome a member of your cyber unit to come here and look into the network personally."

"And hero-worship you? Those dweebs praise your name," Johnson said under his breath.

Yes, Drew was counting on it. If he could get a couple of them on his side, they would work harder to prove his mother was wrong. The cloned account would be easy enough to prove, but this would play out in the court of public opinion, and all they would read were harsh words coming from an awkward man, a man a lot of people didn't like. His enemies would use the bad press, and his mother was setting this whole thing up to play out with Noah working against him.

It all made him feel tired and old.

"I will cooperate in any way you need me to. I'll also ensure that I respect the restraining order. Do you need anything further from me? I need to get to my brother's reception." Where he would walk around like a ghost.

It would never end. His mother would play her games until one of them was dead and the other in jail.

Revenge, even if he managed it, would be such a hollow thing because he would be alone.

"What's going on?" Mia strode in wearing her designer dress, her heels clacking along the hardwood floors. "Is there a reason you're talking to my brother without a lawyer present?"

"It's fine," Drew tried to assure her. "Why are you here? I thought you would go straight to the reception."

"She wanted to go in with you so the photographers get us together," Case said, following his wife. "And she wanted to show off our stowaway. Big brother and Charlotte brought a friend. Hope you don't mind."

He minded. He didn't need more people around him. Big Tag and his wife walked in, giving the feds looks that told him they didn't trust anyone.

Who had they brought along? Charlotte's CIA-analyst sister and her upper-crust British husband? The chef brother and his lovely wife? Who would witness more of his humiliation?

"I definitely want to know why you're here and talking to Drew without a lawyer," a familiar voice said. "I also want to know why you haven't asked any questions about those files I sent you a week ago. Did you check out my investigations into the medical examiner's report? The ME was paid off. That is completely clear according to those bank records I sent you. It makes no sense that a fourteen-year-old kid with no resources would be able to figure out how to bribe the damn medical examiner. And why would he? Only one person could have wanted to cover up the fact that the second body wasn't Iris Lawless, and that was Iris Lawless."

Shelby strode in looking like the hottest amazon warrior ever to walk the earth. The Prada dress he'd purchased for her clung to every curve. The emerald color made her skin glow.

It no longer mattered that he was being investigated by the fucking FBI. All he cared about was getting close to her.

His instinct was to walk right over to her and haul her off, back to the bedroom, and not come out until he could breathe again.

And then he remembered that he wasn't going to put her through his hell. He hadn't thought she would show up tonight, but that had been stupid. She was invited. She was friends with Ellie and Riley. Carly would definitely want her at the party. Of course she'd come.

Did she have to look so luscious?

Special Agent Johnson took a step back. "I am going through all the data you sent."

Garcia didn't back off at all. If anything the fucker's smile turned up. "Ms. Gates, you're looking lovely tonight, and I'll be more than happy to discuss the case with you anytime you like. Why don't you come by the office? Say tomorrow around lunch?"

Drew started to step up, but Hatch put a hand on his shoulder. "Don't kill the feds."

But he so wanted to kill at least one of them. Garcia was staring at Shelby's chest. Not really her chest. Her breasts. Her gorgeous, soft breasts with those perfectly pink nipples that responded to his touch. What the hell had he been thinking? Why had he picked that fucking dress? It showed off way too much of her beautiful body.

"I expect to meet with you at your earliest convenience, Special Agent. I didn't do all that work simply for my health. I'm working on a point-by-point rebuttal of your interview with Iris Lawless," Shelby replied, her shoulders straight and eyes narrowed.

Garcia shook his head. "How did you get that?"

"I have my own sources," Shelby replied. "And they're incredibly good. I'll have no problem going to the press and making my case there if you don't want to give me a fair hearing."

"Call me tomorrow and we'll talk." Garcia turned to Drew. "See that you mind the restraining order. It won't do you or us any good if you try to confront her."

The feds turned and walked back toward the door.

"Restraining order?" Ian Taggart asked as the door closed behind the feds. "Can I see it?"

Shelby's pretty eyes had gone wide. "She got a restraining order on you? What the hell?"

Charlotte was reaching for the order. "It's a good play on her part. She's looking for sympathy and she's rapidly losing it. I don't think she understood how bad the backlash would be."

Taggart took the order out of her hand, his eyes looking over it. "We should request one of our own. I'll get the lawyer on it. We can find a friendly judge. She did. You haven't seen or talked to her, have you?"

"I have," Shelby said. "And I'll be happy to tell a judge she's crazy and will hurt Drew and any of his family if she possibly can. I felt threatened when she talked to me."

"Did she say anything to specifically threaten you?" Taggart asked.

"It was more the dude she'd brought with her that scared me and the fact that she's got a creepy vibe, but I'm more than willing to make up something. I'm a writer. I can come up with some great dialogue," Shelby offered.

Taggart put his hand up for a high-five. "See? That's what I'm talking about. Redheads are always the reasonable ones."

Shelby gamely slapped the big guy's hand. "Damn straight."

"You're not going to lie to the FBI." He wasn't getting her in more trouble than she already was in. "And I don't think you should be seen going into the party with me. I'll have someone bring you in one of the side doors so you avoid the photographers."

"No." Shelby went back to looking over the restraining order.

Drew stopped. "What does that mean?"

Hatch leaned in. "I think it means no."

Shelby took a step toward him. "It means no and it means that as I walk in, if anyone asks me questions about why I'm here, I intend to answer I'm here because I love my family and because Andrew Lawless, while clueless in the real world, is the greatest lover on the planet."

"No, he's not," Big Tag shot back. "I have the T-shirt. Does he have the T-shirt? Charlie told me there was only one made."

Mia was grinning at Shelby. "You're going to play it this way?"

"I am." Shelby kept her eyes steady.

"Thank God," Hatch said. "This is where I would usually go and have a celebratory drink. I hate being sober."

Mia started to say something about Hatch's sobriety, but Drew didn't have time for that. He reached out and pulled Shelby away from the crowd. "I thought we had a deal."

She didn't fight him or try to get away. No. She moved with him and when he stopped, she leaned over, her body almost touching his. "We did have a deal and I screwed that up. I let you down, and I need you to understand that it will not happen again."

Let him down? "Shelby, you did nothing of the sort. I've been perfectly fine with our arrangement, and I think we need to keep it going. I found out some new information tonight. It's about my father's will. I would love for you to look into it, but we'll have to talk about that on the phone."

"No, we won't. I'm having all my things delivered here. Remy's coming with them in a few hours. He thought it would be okay since I'm with Big Tag. He's totally cool with staying in Austin for a while.

I told him he could have the pool house since you should let Noah have his own room."

Noah. Would Noah be back after tonight's confrontation? Drew was going to be gentle about it, but he had to know if Noah was working with their mother. He had to know what their mom had on Noah. She would have something. If Noah was working with her, it was very likely because his mother was forcing him to.

Would he have thought that way before he met Shelby? God, she'd made him so fucking soft. She might end up being the death of him, but he was going to make damn sure he wasn't hers.

"You call Remy and tell him to cancel everything. You won't be allowed in this house again."

Fire flashed in her eyes. "No, Drew."

"You can't tell me no about this. I don't understand why you've suddenly decided to behave this way."

She stepped closer to him, her fingers tracing their way up his neck and making his dick immediately hard. "I missed you. I've missed you so damn much, Drew. Do you know what I do at night?"

"Shelby, this isn't going to work."

She ignored him completely. "I lie in bed and I think about you. I do it until I can't stand it a second longer, and then I touch myself. I let my hand find my pussy and I rub. I'm already wet because I've been thinking about you. I've been thinking about how good it feels when your cock is deep inside me, and that makes me warm and wet."

She was killing him. He wasn't sure what this play was, but he had to shut it down. "I haven't been masturbating because I've already taken another lover."

She stopped. "Have you?"

He groaned. It was right there. He could see it on her face. He could get her to back down and he just couldn't do it. He couldn't say the words that would make her hate him. "No. God, Shelby. No, I fucking haven't, but I should tell you I have."

"Drew, listen to me. There is nothing you can say that's going to make me walk away from you. If you don't allow me to hold your hand as we walk through those doors tonight, then I'll accept it and tell anyone who asks what my intentions are. I'm not writing the book. All I'm doing at this point is making sure Iris goes to prison for what she did. That's my goal. I'm going to write, but it's going to be fiction from now on because I'm tired of not writing happy endings. So I'm going to write fiction, and I don't actually have to make any money off of it because I'm marrying Mr. Moneybags."

"Marrying?"

Her chin came up. "I love you, Andrew Lawless. I'm willing to wait and give you time to deal with your large vat of personal problems, but in the end I'm going to marry you, and we're going to have a whole new generation of Lawless kids. And you should know that they're not going to be the only ones. Riley and Bran are changing their names back. I told them to, and I'm the alpha female of this group. I might have to throw down with your sister from time to time, but I'm taking charge."

She loved him? It made his hands tighten on her, his whole body lean in. She loved him? How the fuck could she possibly love him? He was an ass. He was utterly unworthy of her. "You're not in charge, Shelby."

She went up on her toes, her hands on his face and her lips hovering over his. "Watch me, Lawless. You're done here. You can control 4L all you like, but I'm the queen of this house. There will be no separation. We're in this together. I love you, and that means I stand beside you through everything. Good. Bad. Outrageously scandalous. It doesn't matter. We're together."

"We're not together." But his mouth was so close to hers. All he had to do was dip down slightly and their lips would mesh. He could kiss her for hours. He could sink himself into her, and for a while he would forget that the world existed.

"You can say that all you like." She was taunting him. "You can try to keep me out of my own home, but how long will you last? How long will you hold out when you understand that I'm out there longing for you? That I'll take you anytime, any way, because you're my man? I suppose you won't want me to keep an office at the 4L building?"

"You can't, baby. We talked about this."

She nodded. "I'll find an office space. I'll be fine. But I'm moving back in. Apartments aren't cheap here and you strapped me with a bodyguard so I need a two-bedroom. Luckily you have plenty."

"You'll go back to Dallas."

"No."

The *nos* were going to make him crazy. "You can't say no to me."

"Not about some things, but anything that keeps us apart, I can and I will say no. I was wrong to leave you, Drew. I made that mistake. You need to understand that I get it. You put everyone first. You make the sacrifices. But I'm not your sacrifice to make. You don't get to sacrifice me because I won't let you. I am yours, Andrew Lawless, and you should get with the program."

She moved slightly, and that was all he needed. Her lips brushed his and he couldn't stop. The minute he felt her arms go around him, he gave in.

One more kiss. One more minute. Just one more memory of her.

He kissed her hard and long, his body rubbing against hers. He could feel the press of her breasts against his chest, the slide of her tongue along his. His whole body was tuned to hers and, more than that, his soul seemed to find peace simply being near her.

He loved her so fucking much. She was his queen. She was his.

His to protect.

He kissed her for a second more and then gently pushed her away. "Shelby, I can't do this with you."

She took a step back. "All right. I'll find a place for me and Remy and an office space, but I'm not leaving Austin and I'm not lying. If anyone asks, I love you. I'm yours. When you decide you're ready, know I'm waiting." She smiled slightly. "I'll see you there tonight. Save me a dance."

He wasn't sure what had just happened. "I'm a horrible dancer."

"Then you're in luck because I'm quite good." She started to walk away, her luscious ass swaying. She stopped and her head swiveled back, her eyes on him. "And Drew? Don't flirt with other women."

Shit. She was hot on a normal basis, but when she was mean, she was a fucking volcano of sex appeal. Perfect. Sultry.

"I'll see you there, Drew."

"You should go back to Dallas. This won't work." He wasn't sure this was a Shelby he could handle at all. She might be too much woman for him.

A woman who wouldn't leave him despite his problems. A woman who could handle him. A woman who might be payment for all of his pain.

Not payment. Reward. A gift he'd never expected. One he would treasure and love and take care of forever. A woman he would honor because she was all the good things of the world rolled into one beautiful package. A woman he could build something with because she was the rock-solid foundation of the world he wanted to live in.

He needed her. Even watching her walk away hurt like hell. How could he live in the same city as her and not be close to her?

The power had shifted from him to her, and he wasn't sure that he didn't like it that way. Hadn't the power always been hers anyway? She was the prize and he the petitioner. Willing to do anything to protect and shelter and love her.

He'd said time and again that she made him crazy.

She made him better. She made him human. All his compassion and love flowed from her.

She turned and gave him a brilliant smile. "No going back. Only forward. There's no future without you. I won't leave you behind. Do you understand me? I heard what you said to Noah that night. You told him you would always save him. I'll always save you, Andrew Lawless. You are the be-all, end-all of my life, and I won't ever leave you. When you're ready, your future is here. I love you."

His vision did that weird, blurry thing as she turned away from him and joined his sister.

She loved him.

"You're going to let her walk away?" Hatch shook his head as Shelby joined Mia and the others.

"Apparently she's not going far. She's moving back in tonight. I would lock the house up, but I don't think it would work. She'd hire someone to break in and still be here waiting for me." She would be here. No matter what he did. No matter what he said or how he fucked up. No matter how awkward he could be or how lost he could get.

Shelby would be here to rescue him.

Was that what he'd lost all those years ago? Was that what had burned away in the fire? He'd lost his childhood, but now he figured out what that meant. Childhood was that time in a person's life when he believed someone would always save him. It was a time that marked a man, and he either believed he was worth saving or not. The two people who could have truly taught him he was worthy had died that night, his father murdered and his mother proving to be nothing but a lie.

His siblings had always been destined to leave him. Hatch's betrayal should have been the last nail in the coffin. He should understand that love and friendship weren't things meant for him.

She turned and there was a smile on her face that lit up his world. He should see things through the same dark glass he'd been looking through since that night, but he couldn't. She was here and she'd brought her light in.

He could choose. He could stalk back into the darkness. He could make her leave or, better yet, leave himself. He could go somewhere none of them could find him and start over. They were all together and all happy, and eventually Shelby would find some man who was actually worthy of her.

Or he could accept that *he* was worthy. He could accept that he wasn't perfect, but as long as he was there for her, as long as he tried, that was all she would expect.

He could forgive his father.

Dear God, he could forgive Hatch.

If he did that, maybe it would be easier to forgive himself for being human, for needing her, for being selfish enough to let her stay with him because he was stronger with her by his side.

She winked as she walked out, but he felt so fucking stuck. Stuck between the past and the future. Stuck between what he knew and what he so desperately wanted.

And it didn't matter because she would be here when he came home tonight. She would go to the party and offer him her hand if he was brave enough to take it.

His sister looked back at him, frowning fiercely as though he'd been the one threatening Shelby.

The door closed behind them as they left for the reception, and he was alone with Hatch again.

"You have to be able to see that woman knows what she wants. I understand everyone else has let you down, but you can't judge the world like that, son," Hatch pleaded. "You can't shut yourself off from all the good stuff in life because one bad thing happened."

"You did." He could see it so easily now. He'd thought Hatch's sojourn from the world had been about his guilt, but it had been pain. He'd loved and lost a woman. Perhaps she hadn't been worthy of that love, but it had destroyed Hatch all the same.

"I did. I buried myself away. I did it because the pain and grief and guilt were too much to bear, but I found something that worked so much better than alcohol. You. You saved me when you walked in that door, and I realized that I should have fought. I should have ignored the damn pain and been a man. I should have taken you all in because I loved your parents. I let my grief and guilt overwhelm my love, but I won't do it again, Drew. It's why I joined that damn sad-sack club and why, no matter what you do or say, I won't abandon you again. I'll stay sober because you might need me for something. Any one of you. I'll be what I should have been all those years before. I'll love you like my son, and I'll be a better father this time. And I'll never stop telling you that the best revenge you can have is to love that woman. It's to not let Iris win. It's to live your life and be happy, son. It's what she was never able to do."

Live his life. Live a life with Shelby. A life where he wasn't plotting and planning anything but the next way to please her. A life where he had a future. Where they had babies who would grow into obnoxious, nerdy kids he would be so fucking proud of. Kids who would play with their cousins and who would never spend a second thinking no one would save them.

It could all go to hell. He knew that. That one truth in the universe had been tattooed on his soul the night his father died.

What did any of it matter if he didn't try?

"I'm going to marry her."

A long sigh came from Hatch's chest. "I'm so glad to hear that. Whether or not you invite me to the wedding, know that I'm going to be so proud of you."

"I don't know how to deal with you." The thought of it twisted him up. There was still so much anger that sat in his gut.

Hatch put up his hands. "You give it time and know I'll be here for you. It doesn't have to be today. Doesn't have to be tomorrow. Just know that no matter what you decide, I'm here."

Was that all a father had to do? Be there?

He was saved from having to answer by a trill from his cell phone. A text came through from Noah.

Can you come out to the pool house? Need to talk to you. Please, Drew. It's important.

"I thought you said Noah went with Riley and Ellie?" Drew strode to the window.

"He did. He left an hour ago, but it looks like he came back. They took the Audi and it's sitting in the drive." Hatch was beside him. "You do know it was probably Noah who sent those e-mails."

Drew stared out at the pool house. There was a light on in the back. "I do. I also know what it means to be a scared, manipulated kid. My first instinct is to go out there and try to figure out how I can help him. When the fuck I did change? I should call the cops and have him kicked out, but I can't."

"He's your brother. You'll always walk in to save him."

"I think she wants to kill me." It was a sick feeling in his gut. And then he saw it. The curtains moved slightly, and he saw a masculine hand shifting the fabric, staring out. That wasn't Noah. A huge man was looking out the window, very likely the one Shelby had seen that day in the café. For the briefest of seconds, he caught a glimpse of his brother. Noah was on the sofa, his hands tied and a gun at his head.

A gun held by his mother.

The cell trilled again.

Please, Drew. Please.

"What the hell is going on?" Hatch asked.

His brother was about to be killed. Drew was right back in the moment. He'd stood on the stairs and felt the heat blast through him and knew he couldn't run. He'd called out for his father. For his mother. And then he'd glimpsed the bodies through the smoke and had known that he was alone.

He'd known that they were all his responsibility now. The door had been right there. He hadn't realized at the time that it would be blocked and barricaded. His first thought had been to run. He was a kid. He needed to get an adult. He could make it to the front door before the flames made it impossible. If he waited, there would be no way to get downstairs. They would be trapped upstairs, trapped with his siblings.

And even at fourteen, he'd known he would rather die than live knowing he'd left them.

He'd made his promises. It was time to keep the one to his youngest sibling.

"Call Taggart back. Tell him my mother's here and I'm walking into a trap. He can't have gotten far. He'll know what to do." Taggart would be armed to the teeth and he would have Case with him. If anyone could save him, it would be his brothers-in-law. "Then call the police. Keep Shelby from seeing anything she shouldn't."

Hatch's eyes went wide. "You can't go over there."

But he had to. If he didn't show up soon, his mother would follow through. She would cut her losses, and that loss would be Noah. He was certain she had a backup plan that involved his brother's corpse. "Keep them safe, Hatch. And I forgive you."

"Drew, he's been working against you," Hatch pleaded.

It didn't matter. "He's my brother. Tell Shelby I love her very much."

He walked out the door toward the pool house and the meeting he was fairly certain he'd been destined to have all of his life.

Chapter Nineteen

Shelby turned and looked out the back of the limo as it started down the drive. She stared at the house and wanted that door to open and Drew to call the car back. She watched the door, praying, until they made the turn and it was out of sight.

"I know you don't want to hear this, but I think he needs time," Mia said.

She would give it to him. She'd known simply walking back into his life didn't mean he would immediately give in. This was merely her opening move in what might be a long game. "What do I do if he locks me out of the house?"

Case snorted a little. "Remy can get in. Tell him there's a six-pack in the fridge with his name on it, and Remy will break right into that sucker for you."

"He's excellent at defeating security systems," Ian Taggart agreed. "One of his varied skills." Ian turned to look at Mia. "Was Crazy Eyes right? Are your brothers changing their names?"

Now she had crazy eyes?

Mia smiled as the car approached the gates. "Yes, she's correct. It's something we've all talked about. I'm going to change mine, too. Mia Lawless-Taggart. I think that makes me the most badass Taggart of all."

"When you've killed a man with a nail gun, we'll talk," Charlotte said, looking out the window. "I think it's a lovely idea. It will help Drew feel like a member of the family instead of simply being its defender. He won't feel so alone. And Shelby, that was very badass of you. He was practically panting. I'm surprised he's not chasing after the car right now."

"He'll play it cool." Taggart looked surprisingly comfortable in his tux. "But I suspect Shelby's going to find herself dragged into a broom closet at some point tonight. Don't be shocked if he can't help himself and then he gets pissed afterward. It's how guys handle shit like this. We lose control and take what we need and then get a little pissy about it, but that only means we need time to adjust our thinking."

Case shook his head. "It's how you handled it. I immediately apologized and begged my baby to come back."

Mia's jaw dropped. "Are you joking?"

Charlotte shook her head. "He learned this trick from his brother. They rewrite history. According to Ian, he welcomed me with open arms when I came home after five years away."

"That's totally how I remember it. I missed you, baby." Taggart winked his wife's way.

"Drew's going to be smarter than you both," Shelby said. Somehow deep down she knew it was going to be okay. "He's very logical. I can assure you he's sitting in that house thinking about what the odds are of him being able to hold out. He'll come to the proper conclusion that he can't and he'll give in."

She hoped.

She'd felt his longing. It had been right there in the way he held her, in how his lips had moved over hers. He had missed her. His eyes lit up the minute he saw her, and he hadn't managed to hold back his reaction.

If only he'd gotten in the car with her.

Damn the FBI agents. If they hadn't come around with that ridiculous restraining order, Drew might be sitting beside her. The coverage had started to die down. There hadn't even been reporters at the gates today. She was sure there would be plenty at the reception, but they'd stopped camping out at the gates, waiting for random shots of the elusive Drew Lawless.

She'd hoped since the coverage had died down that he would be a little more vulnerable, but the first thing she'd walked in on was the damn FBI giving him more bad news.

He'd relaxed for a moment. When he'd kissed her, his whole body had wrapped around her like he couldn't stand that there was any distance between them at all. In that moment, he wasn't thinking about how he could hurt her. He'd only been thinking of her.

He would come around. It was all about patience.

And research. She could move this process along by taking down Iris Lawless. She needed to prove that Iris had murdered a couple of husbands. She had some investigators working on it and the financials of the situation. The devil was in the details. In the legal forms and financial reports. She needed to see the bank statements and the wills. The transactions.

The wills.

She looked over at Mia. "Drew said something about your father's will. The feds found out something about it."

"I talked to Hatch while you were making out with big brother," Mia replied. "He said they found out Dad had changed his will a couple of weeks before he was murdered. Hatch is going to get a copy of it so we can go through it, but I think it proves Dad knew something was going on. The fact that he didn't name Hatch as our guardian meant he knew about that as well."

That explained a few things, but left other questions. Still, the idea of wills played around in her brain.

"I can verify that Hatch has done nothing in the last twenty years," Case said. "I ran a deep investigation on him the minute I got the clearance. Ian even used some of his contacts to make sure we were going deep enough."

"Hatch has been doing exactly what he says he has," Ian admitted. "From what I can tell, he very likely did get caught up in the assassination plan because Iris told him the money was for a divorce. He had an appointment with a lawyer set the week after Benedict was killed. Obviously he didn't keep it."

Mia sat back. "Hatch did something stupid a long time ago. Ever since Drew found him again, he's been family to us. I'm not happy he had the affair, but I can't wipe out everything he's done for us since then."

Hatch had acted more like a brother than a father, she supposed. The thought made a vision of her own brother cross her mind. Johnny. He'd been so protective and kind. Her brother had left her everything in his will. Somehow he'd been smart enough to actually have one. He'd left her all his research and everything he owned. He'd gone to a lawyer in LA. When she'd met with him, she'd thought he was skeevy and probably chased a lot of ambulances, but he'd made the transfer easy.

The limo rolled out onto the road.

Had Iris changed the plan when she'd figured out what that will would likely do to a potential investigation? Had she initially been planning to kill Francine? Or had she thought she would take the cash for herself? Had she changed the plan when she realized what the criminal clause in Benedict's contract could do for her?

Such a simple thing to change a name. One minute Iris had the world at her feet, and the next she didn't have any say because Benedict had changed one tiny document.

She heard Ian and Case start talking about something, but her mind was whirling.

The will might be important. She'd always thought she would get Iris in the tiny details. Most people looked at the big picture, but sometimes the real story was in the small print.

It was why she always requested the daily documents of a subject's life. Johnny had laughed at her once because she'd spent so much time going through a subject's day planner.

Sometimes a reporter had to get all the data and carefully sift through what seemed meaningless to find the truth. Little clues that seemed insignificant . . .

"Charlotte, you said you looked into all the contacts that were taken in the hack on 4L a couple of months back, right?"

She turned her focus back to Shelby. "I did. It was tedious and probably means nothing, but I thought it would be interesting to see if any of the hacked contacts had been . . . well, hacked."

"And had they?"

Charlotte nodded. "Oh, yes. A couple of them. I don't know that the incidents were related, though."

"Was Drew's lawyer one of them?"

Everyone seemed to sit up straighter, pay more attention.

"Our lawyer got hacked? 4L's?" Mia asked. "We have a legal department, but we also have outside counsel."

Drew had a ton of lawyers, but she was only interested in one. "I'm asking about his personal lawyer. Does Drew have a will?"

She would be shocked if he didn't. Drew was careful. The minute he'd had any kind of money at all, he would have sought to protect it.

But he was more than careful, and he'd had more than money to protect, but Iris was so good at exploiting the details. She was smart that way. She would use every single resource she could find.

Including her children.

Mia leaned forward as the sound of a cell phone trilling split the air. "He did. He left everything to me and Riley and Bran. To his siblings."

"Did he name you? For a while he was pretty freaky about the last name Lawless and anyone connecting the rest of you to him." An idea was playing in her head and it wasn't a good one.

Drew had asked Riley and Bran to legally change their names. Mia had taken her adoptive parents' last name. Drew had been the last Lawless. Would he have named them in a legal document? Or would he have been subtler?

Mia crossed her legs, sitting back. "He was obnoxious about that. I'm so glad we're doing an end run around him. I've already started the paperwork."

Ian Taggart was talking on his phone, but his brother leaned in. Case frowned as though an unsettling idea had taken root. "Did he name you in the will? By name?"

Mia went a bit pale. "No. He left his entire estate to his full-blooded siblings. We have to take a test to prove we're his siblings. Noah would pass it. According to that will, Noah would receive a full quarter of everything Drew owns if Drew dies. Oh, my God. She knows. She hacked his lawyer and she knows how his will is written."

Shelby's heart rate ticked up. "Now we know how she's going to come at him. He's going to need twenty-four-hour protection. I know he said he doesn't think he needs a bodyguard, but he's getting one."

Mia looked up at Case. "How fast can we get one out here? Or two or three?"

Ian put his phone down, and his big hand moved up to touch the button that connected him to the driver. "We need to turn around and go back to the house. Now. If you can't make a U-turn, stop and let me out. I'll run."

He was reaching down to his ankle, and when his hand came back up, there was a shiny gun in his hand.

Case immediately leaned over, mimicking his brother and pulling a gun from his own ankle holster. Apparently Taggarts didn't ruin the lines of their tuxedoes. "Trouble?"

"That was Hatch," Taggart said. "Iris has Noah in the pool house and Drew's on his way in. He said he couldn't talk him out of it. Noah's in trouble and Drew won't wait."

Shelby bit back a cry. Of course he wouldn't. Noah was his brother, and Drew would never allow him to come to harm if he could help it.

"But Noah's probably working with Iris," Case pointed out as the limo made a crazy turn. He had to hold on to the side with one hand to stay upright. "Who else could have fed her the info? I already talked to Drew about this."

"He knows," Mia said. "At least he suspects that Iris has something she's holding over Noah's head, but he thought shoving Noah out into the cold would do nothing but help Iris. He was trying to bring Noah fully over to our side, to turn him. I guess we waited too long."

"Or she moved the timing up for some reason," Charlotte pointed out. Like the two Taggart men, she had a gun in her hand.

"Hatch is calling the police, but it could take time if they don't have a car in the area," Ian said. "This is going to go down fast. She needs it to. We can't go in guns blazing. Case and I will go around the back and try to get in that way. Are there security cameras?"

Case looked down at his phone. "There are, but it looks like the whole system is down right now. I've got a feed to my phone. Someone shut it down. We need to reboot the system to bring the cameras back on line. It's the same one you have at your place, Ian."

Ian nodded. "Charlie, baby, I need you to see if you can get any of what's going on in there on film. Even if Lawless is already down, we might be able to catch Iris in the act."

"He won't be dead." Shelby's hands started to shake.

"Ian." Charlotte sent her husband a nasty look.

"I'm a worst-case scenario kind of guy, and the last thing Lawless would want is for his mother to get away with it." Ian pressed the button again. "Park out of view of the house."

The car came to a stop, and Shelby thought her heart was going to explode. This was really happening. Drew was caught in some web his mother had weaved and she meant to kill him. Ian and Case Taggart were his only hope, and they thought they needed evidence so Iris didn't get away with it.

Because they thought he might be dead.

God, he couldn't be dead.

Case looked at his wife as he opened the door of the limo. "You go around to the front and get inside the house. Take Shelby and get in the safe room on the second floor. If you see anything out of the ordinary, run. You are not going to engage."

"Case," Mia began.

He shook his head. "I can try to save your brother or I can protect you and our unborn child. Your choice."

"Go," Mia agreed. "I'll lock us in the safe room. But I'll get to the security cameras from there. I can reboot the system from the safe room."

Ian checked his gun. "Excellent. Charlie, see that they make it there."

Charlotte nodded. "Will do, baby. Be safe." She turned to Shelby, her eyes narrowing. "Don't even think about it."

But she was. She was totally thinking about running into the pool house and damn them all. She needed to see Drew. She needed to hold him and know he was alive. She needed to tell him again that she loved him. She loved him so much.

He couldn't be dying.

"Let's go and get the cameras turned back on. All you'll do is create chaos and make it harder for Ian and Case," Charlotte said as she started up the path. "Drew needs you to stay calm."

She followed Charlotte inside, and within moments they were in the safe room. Mia pulled up the cameras, activating the security systems. The monitors flickered on, and Shelby saw her worst nightmare coming true.

Drew took a deep breath and opened the door to the pool house. He entered, holding his hands up. "I see you've made yourself at home, Mother."

He was surprisingly calm. They hadn't immediately shot him the minute he walked through the door. That meant they had a plan, and plans took time to execute. What Iris didn't know was that the Taggarts had come to the house, and they would turn around and come back for him.

Right this second, having a couple of ex–Special Forces badasses in the family seemed like a good thing.

And then there was Hatch. Hatch would be calling the police. Hatch would do the smart thing and wait for them at the gate. He would take care of things.

He wished they hadn't fought. He wished he'd forgiven Hatch sooner. Yes, Hatch had done something bad, but now that Drew was here in this room, he wished he'd been more forgiving.

Did anyone ever wish they'd loved less? Did anyone come face-to-face with a gun and think *I wish I'd hated a little more*?

God, he wished he'd said the words to her. He hadn't even said the words to her.

I love you, Shelby.

"Nice of you to join us, son." His mother was dressed all in black, her long hair pulled back. She looked stark and predatory.

The big guy he'd seen in the window moved next to him. "Don't think about pulling a gun."

He held his hands up, his eyes looking to Noah. "No guns. Why is my brother tied up?"

"I'm sorry, Drew," he said, looking so much younger than his years. By all rights of age, he was an adult, but it was a frightened child who looked back at him. A kid desperate for someone to save him, someone he could trust.

Drew had been that kid, and no one had come for him. He couldn't leave Noah to the same fate.

Iris stepped up, putting a hand on Noah's shoulder. "Noah here has been a good boy. He's been helpful the last few days. I thought he was a liability in the beginning. You can't imagine my surprise when I realized Ben had the last laugh on me."

"Because he changed his will. You didn't find that out until afterward, did you?" The longer he kept her talking, the better.

Noah's hands were tied in front of him, his feet bound as well. He wouldn't be able to run, and there were at least two guns against them. How would Taggart handle things?

"Of course I knew. I had an excellent relationship with one of the secretaries at his firm. It wouldn't have stopped me from gaining the shares, but I immediately realized that the police would look to me when they found out he'd changed his will. That was when I realized I had to go as well," she admitted.

"Yes, if Father died or merely killed himself and that will had come out, the police would have taken at least a look at you. By dying yourself, you changed the story. You're quite good at handling the press." Drew had to force himself to remain still because the other man was maneuvering around, flanking him. Drew carefully began to turn.

Iris's hand came up, the gun leveled at him. "Don't you move an inch. I'll fire and this will be over quickly."

He stopped. Quick wasn't what he wanted, but he didn't like the big man with the gun behind him. "So you decided to become Francine Wells and insinuate yourself into Patricia Cain's life."

His mother shrugged one shoulder. "I was already sleeping with her. She was the one who convinced the others that Benedict had to go."

"Yes, Mommy liked to get around. Why Hatch?"

"They wouldn't do it unless I put up money, too," she explained. "We needed mutually assured destruction, but I didn't have fifty thousand. Your father would have noticed if fifty thousand had gone missing. I needed Hatch's cash, and it was an awfully good method of controlling him after for everyone else. The only problem that came up was this one. I certainly hadn't meant to get pregnant."

"I'm surprised you decided to keep Noah." Drew tried to watch the big guy out of the corner of his eye.

"I thought I might be able to use him against Hatch if the plan with Patricia fell apart. Babies look so much alike. At that point he would have believed what I told him. I ended up not needing to because Patty and I actually built something quite nice. It was good for a while, and Noah gave me access to some wealthy gentlemen as he got older. He served his purpose and now I get a bonus out of him."

Drew watched as a tear fell out of Noah's eye. His jaw clenched. *Shit.* Noah was going to need a damn therapist, too, after all of this. No one seemed to get out of his family without a shit-ton of damage.

"Did I serve mine, Mother?" It still hurt. It fucking hurt that she was his mother and she was so willing to sacrifice him. For what? Cash? Power?

Deep breath. The asshole his mother had brought along was behind him. He couldn't see the other man, but he knew the dude had a gun.

All this time and he'd been ready to put himself on the line. All this time and he'd been willing to sacrifice to get that revenge he'd always prayed for.

All he wanted right now was to see Shelby one last time. *Fuck.* That wasn't all he wanted. He wanted a life with her. He wanted forever with Shelby. She was his, and he couldn't die now that he'd finally figured out what it truly meant to live. It meant choosing to look past his own pain to something that might heal him. Someone. Shelby was his future, and he was suddenly desperate to have one.

But he had to be worthy of her, and that meant trying anything he could to save his brother.

"You were always a difficult child." Her eyes went somewhere behind him, as though she was trying to force her will on the man standing there.

Was he about to get shot in the back? "Well, I had bad DNA. What did you use against Noah to get him to turn?"

Keep talking. He had to keep her talking. He had to pray he wasn't about to get murdered. Just a little more time. He needed a little more.

"I'm sorry, Drew," Noah said, tears now running down his too-young face.

"Noah got involved with some unsavory characters. Some people I might have been involved with from time to time. They're quite loyal when you pay them well, and they were more than willing to help me explain the world to my youngest child. Sometimes things that seem coincidental are actually quite well planned. Noah believed he found Jase, but that wasn't the case. He did what I wanted him to do."

Ah, so the hacker was working with Mommy. Poor Noah. Drew remembered that moment when he'd figured out the world sucked, and yet it had been so much worse to find out how shitty his mother was.

"So you pulled out everything he'd done in a desperate attempt to survive and used it against him." He kept his eyes on Noah, trying to will him to see that he understood. He'd been desperate, too, once.

He was desperate now, but he couldn't be less than his loved ones thought he was. There was something powerful about knowing they loved him. His sister and brothers loved him. It was worth more than being needed.

Shelby loved him. She loved him so much she was willing to sacrifice her career for him. He was more important than her ambition, and that made him want to be worthy of her love. That meant not leaving Noah behind. He'd been a dipshit, but Noah was his brother. Noah was worth saving.

"I'm so sorry, Drew. I tried." Noah had gone a pasty white, as though he knew what was about to happen. "I didn't know it was her in the beginning, but she was working with Jase. I might have done more than write code for him. I'm so sorry I lied, but I wanted you to like me. Then she called and told me I would go to jail if I didn't write those e-mails. I knew you would figure it out, but I wanted more time here. I'm so sorry. I don't have anything to do with this plan. I told her I wouldn't do anything else."

So Noah had tried to pull away, had threatened to walk, and Iris had realized she'd lost power over her youngest. That explained the desperate play this evening. Noah was going to choose a side, and it hadn't been hers. Shelby had been right. He'd shown Noah what a family could be, and Noah was ready to jump ship. She was going to lose her spy and her only helper.

"It's okay, Noah." He looked up at his mother. "Why now? You might manage to kill me, which I suspect is your play. Obviously your friend behind me is going to shoot my brother, and you'll hope the police will think it was me. Then what? I turn the gun on myself? You have to know Hatch has already called the cops. He was in the house with me."

For the first time, his mother looked less than composed. She paled for a moment and then that steely will of hers returned. "A lie, Drew. And not a good one. Do you think my man wasn't watching? We saw Hatch leave and then the limo. We know you were alone."

Oh, wasn't that nice. Her "man" had seen the feds leaving and thought it was Hatch. That was excellent. He wasn't giving up the surprise advantage. Not now. "Well, I had to try. Still, I'm fascinated with this plan of yours. How exactly does Jase play into this?"

"Jase was my partner. A lovely young man with incredible skills. After I realized you had attained an enormous amount of wealth, I knew you would use it to come after Phillip, Steven, and Patricia. They were all so foolish. None of them believed you would figure out what they'd done. I knew then that I had to disappear. So I arranged a handy car accident after finding a vagrant woman who could take my place in the vehicle. I had some cash, but what I really needed was the documentation Stratton, Castalano, and Cain had on me. We knew we had to have proof of one another's crimes in order to keep everyone in line, but if they wouldn't believe that you were coming for us all, I had to take them out."

"So you found a hacker? Why did you need a hacker?"

"I never was any good with the technical stuff," she explained with a disdainful huff. "Jase procured new documents for me, and when the time came, he helped me pick them off one by one. Phillip was easy. He was already dying. He kept our letters in a storage unit. I understand he left something for his daughter as well, but I ensured you couldn't find the real proof."

He felt a hand on his shoulder and then the hard knock of metal against his spine. It was good. His enemy was close. He would want to try to get gunpowder residue on Drew, but he would have to move the gun to his side and shoot to do it. All of his hours of training with Case came back to him. They'd spent a good six months punching each other at the beginning of their relationship. Case had been working to win Mia back, and part of the way he'd done it was train-ing her brothers. Case had been patient, teaching him tactics and how to listen to his own natural instincts. He'd taught him how to use an enemy's body against him, where to hit, how to handle a hit.

How to wait for the perfect time.

"So Steven Castalano's heart attack and Patricia's overdose?"

His mother put a hand on Noah's hair, smoothing it back. God, the kid's therapy bills were going to make Bran's look like nothing. "All me and Jase. I arranged the meeting between Jase and Noah after he left the academy. I knew he still might be useful. I wanted to keep him close, and when I found out about your will, I knew what I had to do. I meant to allow this to play out a bit longer, but Jase has turned on me. I'll destroy him in the end, but for now he's got all the cards and he wants his money soon. I'm afraid I'm going to have to move up my timetable. I thought tonight would be perfect since the rest of the clan is off celebrating. The police know how worried I am about my son. Someone's been trying to hurt him."

His will. *Fuck.* He'd left everything to his siblings without actually using their names because he'd been desperate to keep their connections secret. They hadn't been. His mother had known. She'd probably known them all, been watching them all. "I suppose you think Noah's portion will come to you after you kill him."

"I'm not going to kill him, darling boy. Noah's not going to die. You're going to shoot him and then he'll save himself heroically. I already have a doctor on standby ready to report that being nearly murdered by his brother has left him in a medically induced coma. I can't actually have him die. Not yet. I won't let another will keep me from what I deserve. I'll hold a press conference from the hospital and talk about all the magnificent things we'll do with your fortune. All the people we'll help. As his mother, I'll be the one to manage his estate. Eventually, of course, he'll lose his fight. That was his choice. I was willing to have him by my side, but I can't trust him now." She nodded his way.

Not his way. She'd nodded to her partner.

Drew felt him move behind, one hand still on his shoulder, the other swinging up and aiming the gun at Noah. Drew planted his feet and pulled his elbow up and drove it back as hard as he could.

The shot roared through the air, and he could feel the heat from the muzzle of the gun roast his side, but he had to move, and now. Adrenaline pulsed through his system, heightening his senses. Somewhere in the background he heard a door crashing open. As he turned he saw blood bloom across Noah's chest.

He tamped down the fear and hauled himself around, his fist coming up. He braced himself for a fight, but the man's eyes went vacant, his body rigid for a moment before he fell to his knees.

That was when he realized Hatch was standing there with the Colt Drew kept in a gun safe in his hand.

"Don't you even try it, Iris," Hatch said. "Put the gun down. Do it now or I will shoot."

Noah slumped to the side, but Drew could see he was breathing. Drew had forced the shot to go wide when he'd thrown off his attacker, but his brother was going to need serious medical help.

"Let me take Noah and you can leave here, Iris," Drew said, trying to stay calm. "Go on and get out of here. Your plan is blown. Hatch never left and he's called the police. Your best bet is to run and do it now."

"She'll have to get through me," Hatch said. "I won't have her out there. I won't let her hurt my kids again."

"Your kids? These are Ben's children. He was a great man. You're a pathetic old drunk, Bill. And so easy to manipulate. Poor Hatch. Your hand's shaking and you always were slow. If I'm going down, I won't go alone. They're my children, and I decide when I'm done with them." Iris wasn't slow. She turned her gun toward Drew and fired.

Drew felt something slam against him. Someone. Hatch threw his body over Drew's, and they both hit the wall with a thud.

Drew reached for the dead man's gun. It was right there. Hatch felt like dead weight on top of him, but he had to move. His mother would be on them in a second, and she wouldn't hesitate.

"Poor Drew. You're just like your father. So very smart and yet incapable of doing what's truly needed." Her face loomed over him.

So much to say and yet it didn't matter. He realized that now. He'd wanted vengeance, plotted and planned and knew that when he had it, there would be such satisfaction in the experience.

There was none. Drew picked up the gun, hauled it around, and shot his mother neatly in the head.

There was a crashing sound in the distance and a low moan from the man who was still on top of him. Hatch. Hatch had taken a bullet for him. God, Hatch needed help. Noah needed help.

"Damn it," a deep voice said. "Case, we're going to need more than one bus. Drew, are you hit?"

"No."

Hatch was lying on top of him and suddenly he rolled off. Blood. There was so much blood. Hatch was bleeding. Drew got to his knees, staring down at his mentor. "Ian, you have to help Noah. He's been shot."

"He's got a bullet in his chest, but it didn't hit his lung. He's in pain but he'll live." Ian dropped to his knees, too. "I don't know about this one. We need to stop the bleeding."

Hatch's hand came up, weakly pushing at Taggart's. "No. Stop." He looked at Drew. "Love you, boy. Might not have been as good as your dad, but you were the best thing that ever happened to me. You tell the rest. You tell them I love them."

"Tell them yourself." Fuck, this couldn't be happening.

Hatch's lips turned up. "I did one good thing. She was wrong. You are mine. Might not be blood, but you're my boy." He coughed and bright blood bubbled up. "Best revenge I had. Loving you and Bran and Riley and Mia."

The world seemed to blur and he could feel something wet on his face.

"Don't go."

He could hear a siren in the distance. He gripped Hatch's hand and prayed.

Chapter Twenty

He hadn't looked at her all night. Shelby stared across the hospital waiting room and wondered if Iris Lawless wasn't going to have her revenge after all. The woman was dead and she was still coming between her and Drew.

Everyone was there. Case and Mia, the Taggarts, Ellie and Riley, and Bran and Carly. They'd taken over the waiting room, desperate for any news of Noah and Hatch.

They all sat together, surrounding each other, huddled for comfort.

All except one. Drew paced on the outer edge of the room. He'd paced for an hour, not talking to any of them.

After the cops had seen the video, they'd allowed Drew to go to the hospital. He still had plenty of questions to answer in the morning, but it was clear the police were treating him as the victim and not the criminal.

"This is what he does, Shelby." Riley looked over at his brother, a grim look on his face. "I hoped it would be different, but Drew shuts down when there's a tragedy. I'm worried he's going to push you away. You can't think it's anything but his way of protecting himself. He even does it with us. I don't know how bad it's going to get if Hatch dies. I don't know if we can bring him back from that."

Had this finally broken him? Had it finally done what years and years of turmoil and the fight to survive hadn't been able to do?

"I should go talk to him." She'd tried earlier, and he'd merely thanked her for being here and asked if he could get her anything. When she'd asked if they could talk alone, he'd declined.

She wasn't sure why she thought it would work a second time.

"I don't think that's a good idea," Riley said. "I think you should stay with us for a few days. Drew probably needs to be alone. I don't like the idea of him taking his pain out on you."

She looked over at him. He was so beautiful and so remote. So far from her. They were close, but there was so much more than physical distance between them.

"I don't like the idea of leaving him alone." She couldn't stand the thought of him going to bed tonight all by himself.

He wouldn't sleep at all. He would sit. He would drink. He would blame everything on himself.

They were through one hurdle. Noah was out of surgery. The bullet had lodged right beneath his shoulder blade. He would be in pain for a while, but his recovery would be fairly quick.

Drew had gone into the house knowing he could die, knowing he likely wouldn't come out.

"I want you to get used to the idea that he's going to push you away." Riley sat back, his eyes weary. "He can't help himself. I think he learned it at a young age."

She would sleep somewhere else tonight if he didn't want her around, but she wasn't leaving Austin. She wasn't leaving him.

She would have to try again. He'd been forced to kill his own mother. He'd had to watch as his father figure nearly died, still could. He didn't handle his emotions well.

She had to give him some space. "I'll let him be, but I want him to know I'm there for him."

Riley nodded. "All right, but know that if he's cruel, it's not really him. It's a reaction that has nothing to do with you."

"I can handle Drew." She prayed that was true.

Riley stood and Shelby followed his line of sight. A doctor was walking into the waiting room, his scrubs wrinkled.

They were the only family left in here. Shelby's heart pounded in her chest. She rushed across the room to Drew's side, but he was simply staring at the doctor. Drew's face was a stony mask as he waited for the doctor to speak.

"Mr. Lawless, it was close, but your friend is a stubborn guy. The bullet missed his heart, but we had to remove a part of his lung. He's got a long road ahead of him, but I think he's going to be fine."

A collective breath was released through the room, and the family started to hug each other.

Drew merely held a hand out and shook the doctor's hand. "Thank you. When can we see him?"

"He's in ICU the rest of the night. No visitors until tomorrow. Go home and get some rest," the doctor ordered. He turned and walked away.

"I've got a call in to hospital security about the press that's going to show up as soon as the story gets out." Case had taken off his jacket. He looked ready to settle in. "Ian and I will stay here and take care of things."

Drew nodded their way. "Thank you."

She'd expected him to argue. He could be so controlling. He would want to stay behind and send everyone else home.

He held a hand out to her. "Shelby, would you come with me? I'd like to talk to you in private."

The words were cold, unemotional. God, he was going to do it. He was going to get her alone and tell her he didn't want her, and she wasn't sure how she would handle that. Deep down she'd thought she could make him believe. They were meant to be together. After everything Drew had been through, he deserved some peace. She was the person who could give that to him, but what would she do if he wouldn't accept it?

How would she walk away from the love of her life?

"Shelby?" Drew was staring at her.

"Yes, of course."

"Then I'll drive us home." He glanced around, but no expression slid across his face. "Mia, do you need a ride? Charlotte, are you staying?"

Bran and Carly had ridden in with Ellie and Riley. Mia had come in a car with the Taggarts.

"Charlie's heading home," Ian said. "We delayed our flight, but if someone could drop her off, my brother is waiting for her at the airport in Dallas. She can't be away from Seth for too long." He kissed his wife. "Love you, baby. I'll settle things here and be home in the morning."

Riley held up a hand. "We'll take her. Good night. And think before you speak, brother."

Drew frowned. "What is that supposed to mean?"

But Riley was already walking away.

Mia and Carly hugged Charlotte, and then Shelby found herself walking out to the parking lot. Mia was chatting away, talking about how they would bring Noah home and what they could do to make up for the lost reception. Bran was saying something about how happy he was that his wedding hadn't been interrupted.

They were all so relieved. As though a huge weight had been taken off their collective shoulders.

All of them except Drew. Drew alone sat silent as he looked out the limo window.

Shelby had a sick feeling in the pit of her stomach that he was going to close the door on her.

She wanted to reach out, to hold his hand, but he seemed so far away. The last thing she wanted was to start this conversation in front of his family.

All too soon the car rolled to a stop. Drew got out first and turned, reaching to help her out. The feel of his hand in hers warmed her, but it was far too brief. When she was up on her feet, he switched his hold to her elbow and began escorting her inside.

Up ahead she could see the lights were on. There were still police milling around the pool house, and they would be there until morning. She was sure reporters would show up, too. How would Drew handle that?

Would she be here to help him with it?

She was getting emotional. She needed to stop and take a deep breath, but the horrors of the night were threatening to crash in on her. She'd looked down at that screen, and the first thing she saw was Iris holding a gun on Drew, and Noah slumped over. Mia had the presence of mind to start the tape, but Shelby had screamed, knowing Drew was one bullet away from joining his brother.

She'd lost it. She'd done what she'd promised Taggart she wouldn't do. She'd run to join him because there was no way she was allowing him to die alone.

Tears pooled in her eyes, but she wasn't going to shed them.

He led her through the door. Her bodyguard was there as promised. Remy Guidry was sitting in the living room, beer in hand, as though he'd been waiting for them to get home before finding his bed. The big gorgeous Cajun stood, giving her a wide smile.

"Hey there, *chère*. Heard you had a rough night. Let's see about getting you settled in," he said in that delicious accent of his.

Drew stared at him for a moment, and for the first time his blank expression disappeared. "You've been living with him? Taggart assigned this guy to watch over you? I ask him to find someone serious and he picks a fucking male model?"

Remy winked. "Now, that was strictly for fun. It was only a few covers. I assure you I've been taking good care of that girl."

Bran stepped in between them. "I'll make sure he gets back to

Dallas, as his assignment has come to an end. You two go on to bed. Carly and I will handle everything. Police, press, everything. You've done your job, brother. Rest."

Drew's jaw was tight as he started for the master suite. She followed him, her own tension making her move quickly, wanting to get this over with. Was he going to try to put her on that plane with Remy?

He strode through the door.

The minute she was inside, he closed it. She heard a click as he locked the door behind him.

She walked to the middle of the room and turned. She had to make him see reason. "Drew, I think we should . . ."

She stopped because he was moving toward her, his face flushed. He walked to her and dropped to his knees, his arms winding around her waist.

"Don't leave me." He whispered the words. "Please don't ever leave me."

She didn't try to stop the tears now. She let them flow. She held him tight and realized what had happened. He'd held it all in because he thought he had to be strong around his siblings. Because this softness, his fear and doubt and pain, they were hers. Because she was his safe place, the one person he would let go with.

She smoothed back his hair. "Never, Drew. Not ever. I love you. I was so scared. I thought I was going to lose you."

"I had to go. I made a promise to Noah." He lifted his head to look up at her. "It's over. I thought I would be thrilled. I thought I would be happy I was the one to take her out. I'm not. I just feel empty about it."

"Baby, she was your mother. It's okay to mourn her. You're not mourning the real Iris. You're mourning the boy she left behind. It's okay. I'll mourn with you. I'll get you through this."

She held on as Drew Lawless finally broke in the best of all ways. He cried and mourned and let her comfort him.

Sometime in the early morning hours, after they'd gotten naked and warm in bed, their arms wrapped around each other, Drew began to talk. He talked about his father, his mother, the life they'd had. He talked about how hard it had been to keep everything together. He held her close and talked.

Shelby listened, understanding she was hearing a story no one else ever would. She was hearing it because his story was going to be hers. Because his past was going to be laid to rest in honor of their future.

And when she finally slept, she knew she was home.

Drew watched the screen, a smile coming over his face as the twenty-eight-year-old douche bag was carted out of his Chicago home by the police. It was a pretty sight.

"Holy shit." Noah sat up in the chair he occupied beside Hatch's hospital bed. "Is that who I think it is?"

It had been eight days since that terrible night, and Hatch and Noah were both on the mend. Hatch was flirting with every nurse who came in and complaining bitterly about the food. Noah had been released a few days before, but never failed to come up to the hospital when Drew did. Noah seemed a little lost, hungry for family time, and Drew intended to give it to him.

They were all huddling together. It was what they did. It was how they survived, though now the huddle was a little bigger, a little brighter than it had been before.

Hatch smiled and nodded toward the TV. "That's your doing. Isn't it, Drew?"

A deep feeling of satisfaction went through him. "I had some help from Ian and Case. They were more than happy to tip off the FBI about Jase Calloway's side business. They don't like people selling black-market arms over the Internet. He's going down for years. And they found what he'd been blackmailing her with. Apparently he'd been smart enough to dupe the burn file. They found the confessions of everyone. The official cause of our father's and Francine's deaths has been changed to homicide."

He could rest. His father's name had been restored. They'd buried Iris only the day before. He knew he hadn't had to do it, but somehow he knew he would regret it if he didn't.

He'd learned something from his soon-to-be wife. It wasn't merely taking out his enemies that made him strong. Being better than them was the best revenge of all.

His mother couldn't break him. The system couldn't break him. He'd finally figured that out. He'd finally figured out that he was worth saving, too. And thank God his savior had come in such a delicious package.

Shelby walked into the room, a huge smile on her face. "Did you hear the news?"

His girl was always well informed. He nodded to the TV. "We're watching it."

"Are they going to come for me?" Noah asked.

Hatch snorted. "Hell no, son. Do you honestly believe your brother would allow that to happen?"

Noah sat back and relaxed a little. "No. Drew wouldn't let anything bad happen. But I think I might take a break from coding for a while. I think I'm going to study law in school. You can always use another lawyer, right?"

"Of course, he can," Shelby said as she crossed the space between them. "He gets into a lot of trouble."

"I don't anymore." He slid an arm around her, and his whole body seemed to relax at the contact. He always wanted to touch her. It was the little things that he really loved. Waking up with her. Teasing her. Being teased by her. He didn't mind at all when she called him her hot nerd. It was a good thing to be. "I'm going to be perfectly boring from now on. We've got the launch in a few weeks, and then we're all going to head out to the island. A family vacation before Noah has to hit the books and Mia's too pregnant to fly comfortably."

He would be surrounded by his family, enjoying the days. He wouldn't think about the past because he'd finally found his future.

"I will be more than happy to see the exit door to this hospital," Hatch complained.

His door opened again, and Riley and Ellie walked through.

"Is he complaining again?" Riley groused. "I managed to get him a ridiculously oversized suite. Do you have any idea how much this is costing us?"

"A good reason to take me home," Hatch shot back. "And get me a couple of nice nurses. I'll take a blonde and a redhead."

Ellie rolled her eyes. "I will pick out the nurses myself."

Shelby held up a hand. "Carly and I will help."

Drew took the seat next to Noah. Any minute now Bran would walk in with Carly, and Mia and Case would show up, and it would be complete chaos.

And that was just how he liked it.

He looked at Shelby. What she didn't know was she wasn't going to leave that island paradise as Shelby Gates. He was getting her out there and keeping her until she agreed to marry him. He'd planned the whole thing. A beach wedding and then a reception under the moonlight.

She didn't suspect a thing.

He was good at plotting. It came naturally, but he'd decided plotting was so much better when the goal was to make her smile.

The door opened again and happy chaos reigned.

He let it flow around him, perfectly happy because his family was finally whole.

About the Author

Lexi Blake is the *New York Times* bestselling author of the Lawless novels, including *Satisfaction* and *Ruthless*, as well as the Masters and Mercenaries series, including *Dominance Never Dies*, *Master No*, *You Only Love Twice*, and *A View to a Thrill*. She is also coauthor with Shayla Black of the Perfect Gentlemen series, including *Big Easy Temptation* and *Seduction in Session*, and the Masters of Ménage series, including *Their Virgin Mistress* and *Their Virgin Secretary*. She lives in North Texas with her family. Visit her online at lexiblake.net.